Fuzzy LOGIC

By Wolfgang Diehr

Pequod Press

FUZZY LOGIC
A Pequod Press Science Fiction Novel

Manufactured in the United States of America
First Printing 2022

V 10 9 8 7 6 5 4 3 2 1

ISBN: 978-0-937912-81-2

Pequod Press
P.O. Box 80
Boalsburg, PA 16827
www.PequodPress.com

DEDICATION

This book is dedicated to my grandson, Daniel Isaac Diehr.

H. Beam Piper Books and Continuations
Presented by **Pequod Press**

PARATIME

Down Styphon!

Gunpowder God

The Fireseed Wars

Siege of Tarr-Hostigos

The Hos-Blethan Affair

Kalvan Kingmaker

Great Kings' War

The Paratime Police Chronicles, Vol. II

The Paratime Police Chronicles, Vol. I

Paratime Trouble

Time Crime

TERRO-HUMAN FUTURE HISTORY

Fuzzy Logic

The Fuzzy Conundrum

Caveat Fuzzy

Fuzzy Ergo Sum

Space Viking's Throne

The Last Space Viking

Space Viking

The Way of the Sword-Worlds

The Merlin Gambit

Cosmic Computer

The Rise of the Terran Federation

ACKNOWLEDGEMENTS

Special thanks go out to the Pequod Press hard-working copyediting team, Victoria Alexander, Dwight Decker, Kathy Summy, Dennis Frank, Leila Smith, Mark Moeser and Douglas Cahill, who assisted with police procedure.

CHRONOLOGY

The Atomic Era is reckoned as beginning on the 2nd December 1942, Christian era, with the first self-sustaining nuclear reactor, put into operation by Enrico Fermi at the University of Chicago. Unlike earlier dating systems, it begins with a Year Zero, 12/2/'42 to 12/1/'43 CE. With allowances for December overlaps, 1943 CE is thus equal to Year Zero AE, and 1944 CE to 1 AE, and each century accordingly begins with the "double-zero" year, and ends with the ninety-nine year—H. Beam Piper.

28	First unmanned rocket, the *Kilroy*, lands on the moon.
30	The United Nations collapses.
31	Terran Federation formed.
31	The Thirty Days' War (World War III).
53	First human exploration of Mars; the *Cyrano* Expedition.
54 – 100	Further exploration of Mars, Venus, asteroids and moons of Jupiter.
92	Contragravity is developed.
95 – 105	First Federation begins to crack under strains of colonial claims and counter-claims of member states.
105	Venus secedes from the First Terran Federation.
106 – 109	World War IV (First Interplanetary War). Entire Northern Hemisphere devastated by nuclear bombardments.
110	First Terran Federation is re-centered in the Southern Hemisphere. Australia, New Zealand, South Africa, Brazil, Argentina and Uruguay agree to abolish nation states, creating a completely unified world. This marks the beginning of a new civilization. Lingua Terra begins taking shape.
127	Reformed Second Terran Federation establishes a single-world sovereignty when Britain becomes the last nation to join.

172	Keene-Gonzales-Dillingham Theory of Non-Einsteinian Relativity developed.
174	Venus secedes from the First Terran Federation.
183	The First Terran Federation is dissolved and the Second Terran Federation is established. New Federation imposes system-wide Pax.
183	Dillingham hyperdrive developed.
192	First expedition to Alpha Centauri.
200	Atomic Era dating adopted.
200 – 800	Period of exploration, colonization and expansion.
350	Marduk colonized.
399	Fenris Company chartered and Fenris settled.
409	Chartered Fenris Company goes bankrupt.
526	Native revolt on Uller against Chartered Uller Company.
629	Zarathustra is discovered and settled.
650	Poictesme is discovered by Genji Gartner and settled.
654	Fuzzy sapience is recognized and Zarathustra reclassified from Class III to Class IV world.

DRAMATIS PERSONAE

Clarence Anetrou—Attorney for Hugo Ingermann.

Gustavus Adolphus Brannhard—Chief Colonial Prosecutor and Pappy to two Fuzzies.

Frank Carr—Mallorysport Chief of Police.

Johannes Chang—Scientist working on the Zarathustran climate mystery.

Michael Duncan Clarke—Zarathustra Native Protection Force (ZNPF) officer stationed at the trading post near the *Jin-f'ke* lands.

Darla Cross—Actress and romantic interest to Dr. Hoenveld

Cinda Dawn—Intern working on the Zarathustran climate mystery.

Piet Dumont—Deputy Commissioner of Native Affairs, former Mallorysport Chief of Police.

Max Fane—Federation Marshal stationed on Zarathustra.

Ezekiel Farquar—Chief Assistant to Supervisor Sylvinski of the Bureau of Colonial Colonization of Class III Planets.

Gunnery Sergeant James Fitzpatrick—Space Marine Gunny.

Thor Folkvar—Tall, powerfully built chief of security for Morgan Holloway. Born on Magni, a heavy gravity world in the Federation.

Ned Foster—Assistant District Attorney under Gus Brannhard.

Enrico Garza—Businessman and financier of the expedition working on the Zarathustran climate mystery.

Victor Grego—CEO of the Charterless Zarathustra Company (CZC).

Captain Conrad Greibenfeld—Federation Space Navy intelligence officer.

Little Fuzzy—the first discovered Fuzzy, part of Jack Holloway's family.

Keezheekoni Helmut—Zarathustra Native Protection Force (ZNPF) officer stationed at the trading post near the *Jin-f'ke* lands.

Akira Hsu O'Barre Holloway—Morgan Holloway's wife

Jack Holloway—Commissioner of Native Affairs. Discovered the Fuzzies. Former Sunstone Prospector.

Morgan Holloway—Jack Holloway's son. Born on Freya and of half-Freyan ancestry. He has spent most of his adult life looking for Jack.

Patricia Holloway McLeod—Jack Holloway's older sister visiting on Zarathustra.

Dr. Jan Christiaan Hoenveld—Head of the CZC Science Division and arguably the premier scientist on Zarathustra.

Juan Jimenez—Division Head of Science Center Alpha.

Betty Kanazawa—Jack Holloway's love interest. Born on Terra, immigrated to Zarathustra to work at the CZC.

Ahmed Khadra—ZNPF officer.

George Lunt—Major in the ZNPF.

Claudette Pendarvis—Head of the Fuzzy Adoption Bureau and wife of Justice Pendarvis.

Chief Justice Frederic Pendarvis—Chief Colonial Judge on Zarathustra.

Tres Poe—Hired laborer for science expedition.

Bennett Rainsford—Colonial Governor of Zarathustra.

Douglas Rathbone—Member of a criminal organization devoted to enslaving Fuzzies.

Jason Roberts—Former police detective from Terra turned private investigator.

Ruth Ortheris Van Riebeek—Gerd's wife, former TFN espionage operative working at the CZC.

Captain Ralph Osbourne—Captain of the *F.S.N. Hikaru Hatori*, a Federation Navy Destroyer.

Gerd Van Riebeek—Division Head of Science Center Beta and former Deputy Commissioner of Native Affairs.

Gregoire Rutherford—Scientist working on the Zarathustran climate mystery.

Andre Sabahatu—Member of a criminal organization devoted to enslaving Fuzzies.

Captain Shade—Captain of the *Pequod*, a large space yacht. Works for Fuzzy slavers.

Clancy Slade—Restaurant and bar owner, local hero after killing Leo Thaxter.

Rheiner Sostreus—Genetically altered Freyan, throwback to pre-mutated condition.

Kim Trahn Sylvinski—Supervisor of the Bureau of Colonial Colonization of Class III Planets.

Johann Torseus—Genetically altered Freyan.

Starbuck "Buck" Trask—Federation Bureau of Criminal Investigation (FBCI) agent sent to Zarathustra from Terra.

Ray Trendell—Member of a criminal organization devoted to enslaving Fuzzies.

Joe Verganno—Computer programming specialist for the CZC.

Dmitri Watson—Scientist working on the Zarathustran climate mystery.

PROLOGUE

October 10, 658 A.E.

Supervisor Kim Trahn Sylvinski dropped the sheet of paper into the outbox and moved on to the next. Most work was done on the computer, which was a mixed blessing in itself, yet the accumulation of paper hardcopies continued to fill up file cabinets in government agencies everywhere. Sylvinski had five such cabinets in his private office. Unlike other, non-government agencies, most hardcopies had to be maintained indefinitely in case of catastrophic malfunction of the computer systems and the datastream.

Eventually, when the powers that be deemed it the appropriate time in some unforeseeable future era, the documents would be scanned into a computer, double-checked, edited, redacted and downloaded to one form of electronic storage media or another depending on where technology was at that year. If all of the stored hardcopies on Terra alone were shredded and recycled, it would supply enough fresh paper to fill the needs of the entire planet for ten years or more.

Sylvinski signed the next document and dropped it, too, into the outbox wishing it was actually a shredder. With a sigh he picked up the next document and started to sign it from muscle memory, then he halted himself. This was about the discovery of a new human race on a backwater planet some five hundred light-years from Terra. He remembered reading something about this new sapient species some time earlier in the datastream. Why was it crossing his desk now? He checked the date in the upper right hand corner. The document was over two years old.

"Farquar," Sylvinski barked into his intercom., "Get in here."

Chief's Assistant, Hickabbible Farquar appeared as if by magic in the open doorway. "You bellowed, sir?"

Sylvinski suppressed a smile. Only Farquar could get away with such mild disrespect. His weird sense of humor made a lethally boring job almost tolerable, and he was damned good at what he did—usually. "When did this document arrive?"

"Just came in on *The City of New Amarillo* from Zarathustra by way of, oh, every damned planet in the known universe. Somehow it got transferred from ship to ship by mistake and only recently found its way here. I did some checking and found that a representative from that planet came in one or two years ago, give or take a few months, with a mob of those hairy Zarathustrans to work out something or other with Terra-Baldur-Marduk Spacelines, or something to that effect. Last year the Federation Bureau of Criminal Investigation raided some casino or something where a mob of these aborigines were being forced to act as entertainers. All super-illegal and no doubt a lot of people got the death penalty because of it."

Some of Sylvinski's ire slipped away. The higher-ups couldn't get on his case for late paperwork he never had the opportunity to see. Still.... "I can understand the hardcopy getting mislaid, but we still should have received a digital transfer."

"At the time the document was sent out, Zarathustra colony had not yet installed the transmission tech," Farquar explained. "Until it became a Class IV planet it wasn't thought important enough to bother with. After the reclassification from Class III, the local military post expedited the transmission tech installation."

Sylvinski nodded. It made sense. "Well, nothing for that now. We have a problem. A team of investigators should have been out there straight away over a year ago. No telling what kind of mess has developed without our supervision. Slavery, like what happened on Loki, for Ghu's sake! This will require a very hands-on approach. Go home and pack. We are going to Zarathustra to sort out whatever jumble they managed to create. Great Ghu! It will take six months just to get there."

Farquar shrugged. "We will only experience three weeks of subjective time, Boss. Hyperspace distorts the passage of time. However, we won't be able to dabble much in each world's culture and entertainment.

We'll be too busy schlepping from ship to ship to get out there as fast as possible."

"Why is that?"

"Because ordinarily ships stop at each planet for a week before proceeding on," Farquar explained. "If we stay on any single ship on the way out we'll be adding several weeks to the journey. Fortunately, there is always an overlap of ships coming and going for data transfers. I'll get a copy of the schedule from the spaceport so we can plan our transfers from ship to ship."

"And you know this because…?"

"My brother is a ship's porter on some ritzy space yacht. Travels around a lot. We're twins but he looks about five years younger than I do."

Sylvinski found he was curious about this previously unmentioned sibling. "What is his name?"

"Ezekiel Farquar. He goes by Zeke."

So Hic was the only one with such an unusual name. Sylvinski set that aside. "Well, we still get full pay for the time in hyperspace. Too bad most of it will go to maintaining our homes while we are away. Fine. I want you to—"

"Requisition passage to Zarathustra, economy class, have James Beam temporarily promoted to fill your position while we are gone, arrange for home furnishings and personal items placed in secure storage…at Bureau expense, of course, as well as get written and recorded materials telling us anything and everything about Zarathustra up to six months ago, which will be the most recent information available here. I will have Personnel assign a personal assistant; Janice Goodfellow would be a good choice."

Sylvinski struggled a moment to place the name, then recalled a fairly tall and attractive woman with an unusual birthmark on her face. From what he had heard she was competent and efficient.

"We will also need a forensic accountant and computer man. I would suggest Franklin Farmer, as he is one of those computer geek protégées, and Dana Alexander from accounting services. I suspect we will also need a police detective with interplanetary jurisdiction in case things get sticky with whatever passes for a government on Zarathustra. I will ask around and see who we can get. We will also need somebody from Legal in case there are any ambiguities in the law, like the tax code. Clarence Burr has some off-world experience."

Sylvinski nodded. "And....?"

Farquar had to think for a moment. "Um...oh! Put in requests for two years advance pay to cover incidental expenses and our personal needs during the mission."

"With...?"

"Per diem, travel and hardship pay."

The Supervisor nodded with satisfaction. "One of these days you'll be able to take over my position. God help you!"

"Oh, that reminds me; we should take a Xenoanthropologist with us, as well," Farquar added. "I am sure we could get a volunteer from Sydney University. A good student, if not an actual professor. A post-grad, maybe."

"Very good thinking," Sylvinski said. "We need somebody who can measure the damage the locals have inflicted on the indigenous inhabitants. I'll get started on the authorizations for all of this while you round up the party."

Farquar headed out with his deceptive stride. He always looked as if he was taking his time, yet his pace was brisk.

Sylvinski sat at his desk and finished the paperwork. As he worked a small part of his mind considered the potential advantages of personally investigating the new government on Zarathustra. *No doubt the military stuck some flunky into the top spot as the new colonial governor. It would likely be somebody the military could push around if they felt the need.* Sylvinski saw the potential to swing a promotion for himself, if he handled things just right.

I

"I hate to see you leaving so soon," Jack Holloway said.

It seemed like everybody who was anybody connected to the Holloways was out in the clearing near the Fuzzy Reservation. Floating near the gathering was the *Adonitia*, Morgan's private hyperspace yacht, with portals open wide.

Morgan shrugged. "I hate to leave as well, Pa, but Akira insists that her parents should see the baby. And, since the *Adonitia* is headed to Terra anyway, it seems prudent to attend to everything all at once."

Jack understood. He was tempted to go with his son's family for a visit to Terra, maybe catch up on some old friends—if any were still alive and on planet. He could just dump all of his work on Piet Dumont and take off at a moment's notice. However, he wouldn't be able to take his other family with him: Little Fuzzy, Mama Fuzzy, Baby Fuzzy, Mike, Mitzi, Ko-Ko, Cinderella and Emily Dickinson. The background radiation of Terra would sterilize the lot of them.

The Charterless Zarathustra Company had gone through a lot of trouble identifying and coming up with a treatment for the Fuzzy birthrate problem. Considering it was the Fuzzies that cost the Company outright ownership of Zarathustra, it was more than magnanimous of Victor Grego to push his people to help them.

As much as he would like to get back out in space for a while, he wanted to be with his Fuzzy family even more. Not to mention Betty, who might not want to take a trip back to Terra even if he had decided to go with Morgan. Jack had a lot of thinking to do about where he and Betty were headed and they needed to be together for that.

"How long will you be on Terra?"

Morgan glanced over at Akira, who was chatting with Betty, while Heidi held John Morgan Holloway the Minor in her powerful arms. "Akira thinks three months. She wants to talk her parents into coming back with us. Her father is retired, last she heard, and her mother has no other family left on Terra, so bringing them here shouldn't uproot them from anything important and they'll be around to watch Little John grow up."

Jack smirked. "Will you have the in-laws living with you at the castle? That could get…interesting." The elder Holloway recalled the problems he had with Adonitia's brother. He hated to think that Morgan might run into something similar with Akira's family.

"Just until we find a piece of land they like, and build a new home for them. Close enough to visit, far enough for privacy." Morgan smiled ruefully. "For many years I had no family…at least none I knew of for certain, and now I may find myself with almost too much of it, if that is believable."

Jack laughed out loud. "I was number three of ten children, Morgan, and don't get me started on cousins! There were times when I thought there were too many of us when I was young. But, now and then, I find myself missing the rest of them. Especially Pat." Pain crossed his brow for a moment. "You will see to it she is buried on the hill under the tree on her old farm back home?"

"With a Thoran send-off, Pa. Thor Folkvar will officiate, unless the family back there objects, and the Thorans in my crew will be the pall-bearers. No silly contragravity casket for my Aunt! Um, with your permission, we'll have a Freyan wake."

Jack chuckled though there were tears in his eyes. "Like the one we had here? That would be the closest thing to an Irish send-off this side of Cuchulaiin. Pat would approve. Be sure all the family left on Terra can attend, especially Lori, her daughter, and Leila, my sister. Pat's boys may be off-planet, but look them up if you can."

"I shall." Morgan threw a bear hug around his father, which was returned. "We will also make a stopover on Freya on the way out. I'll need to look in on my holdings there and pick up a few things, plus register Little John as the heir to the Honirdity lands and titles. The crown won't like that since all lands without an heir revert to the kingdom were I to die without an issue. I also have to get the king to recognize Neu Freya as an off-world duchy or principality, which means paying tribute—or as you would put it, bribing the government. I expect we will be back in about a year, give or take a few months."

Jack did a double take. "One year? That would be a round trip to Terra and back without taking the time to step off the ship. How are you going to manage stopping at Freya and giving Akira time to convince her folks to come back?"

"Having my own yacht has its advantages," Morgan said. "I don't have to stop off at every, ah—*Podunk*?—planet between here and Terra. And my yacht has an upgraded hyperspace drive that will cut travel time a bit. While I am on Terra, I plan on looking into any new upgrades that may have come up since my last visit. Three months objective time out, three months back not counting the stopover at Freya. No way of knowing for certain how long we'll be on Terra. My new in-laws may prove reluctant to come back with us, while Akira is adamant about bringing them. Oh, I have the list of items you requested I bring back from there."

"Some real Terran coffee will be welcome, to be sure," Jack said. "You know you could make this trip pay for itself if you take a load of cargo to and from."

"Victor already beat you to it. A load of veldbeest meat, some locally produced alcohol, furs and leather," Morgan lowered his voice, "and more sunstones than you ever saw at one time. The largest shipment in the history of the colony. Five hundred million sols worth, in fact."

Jack's eyebrows went up and he whistled. "And you signed for all that? Are you taking extra security? There are space pirates out there, you know. And yachts are their favorite target."

Morgan laughed. "More security would just get in the way. Thor Folkvar and the Thorans are enough for anything that might come along. And the *Adonitia* is equipped with defensive ordnance. Besides, it is all labeled as XT3. Nobody in their right mind will touch that stuff…except for a Fuzzy."

Jack agreed, then a thought hit him. "Thor isn't taking his Fuzzy with him, is he?"

"And get arrested for violating the ban on taking Fuzzies off-world? No, Little Thor will go back to the Jin-f'ke until Big Thor gets back."

Jack nodded. "Good. I am surprised he was willing to go without his Fuzzy."

"Oh, he was reluctant enough, but his contract is pretty clear on his responsibilities."

Jack raised an eyebrow. "You want him to join you that badly? I would have thought you would give him a leave of absence or something."

"I definitely want him along with the shipment I am carrying, but I did offer to let him stay behind," Morgan explained. "Thor wouldn't have it. Magnians are real sticklers for adhering to agreements."

"Are you two going to talk all day or are we going to get this show on the road?" Akira demanded. She and Betty had walked over while the two Holloways were talking.

"Coming, my love. Heidi, let Little John say good-bye to his grandsire."

Heidi lumbered over and held out the infant for Jack to take. "*Vorsicht, mein Herr.* He ist a sqvuirmy vun. Und he ist already trying to valk."

"You're kidding. He is much too young for that. You should leave him here while you are gone," Jack said to Morgan and Akira knowing what the answer would be.

"And miss out on a year of his development? No way," Akira said. "Besides, I suspect you two would spoil him absolutely rotten."

"You better believe it," Jack said with a wolfish smile. "I missed out on that with Morgan. But, no, I wouldn't have you miss a minute of his growth. I missed everything Morgan lived through and wouldn't wish that on the both of you. Have lots of fun and don't be afraid to tell him how much you love him."

Everybody made their farewells, then Morgan's family and retinue boarded the yacht. Thor had to hustle as he had been making his own goodbyes to his Fuzzy. Little Thor stood off with Jack's mob. All the Fuzzies waved farewell as the yacht rose up. In seconds it was gone from sight.

II

Jack breathed a long sigh. Six months had gone by and he found he was still missing Morgan and his family. That was a big change from his early days on Zarathustra, as an elderly bachelor with no family on the planet. He hoped the trip was an easy one and Morgan didn't run into trouble with the royal family on Freya. No doubt the Freyans were still annoyed with him after the deal he worked out for the Magni-Freyan slaves he freed.

Jack's musings were interrupted by a high pitched squeal. He set aside the memories of his son's family and picked up the radio. It was Piet Dumont.

"What is it, Piet?"

"We got some potential trouble coming our way, Commissioner," Piet's voice replied. "Some mucky-mucks from Terra are over at Government House making all kinds of demands."

Jack snorted. That was Ben Rainsford's problem and he said as much.

"One of those demands is to inspect the Fuzzies' school and the Fuzzy Reservation. They seem to think our entire operation is in violation of some Federation code or regulation, or something stupid like that. Governor Rainsford is calling for you to shoot over to Alpha and help him deal with these mutts."

"Just me?"

"I got the impression that Mr. Grego and Marshal Fane will also be in attendance."

That makes sense, Jack thought. *Commodore Napier would probably also be called in,* he suspected. "All right. I'm on my way."

Why is it every time somebody makes planetfall they stir up a mess of trouble? Jack asked himself, as his aircar lifted and flew toward Alpha Continent.

* * *

John Carter inspected the vest one more time, then nodded in satisfaction: "Looks good. This should go off without a hitch."

The two men hunched over a table covered in odds and ends. The room itself was a shabby conference room in what used to be a hotel in Mortgageville before the whole area suffered economic collapse.

"I still don't understand why we can't use a robot or a drone," said the man next to him. "It seems…wrong to use a true believer like this."

Carter shook his head in exasperation. "Drones can't enter a building undetected, Tars. At least not one big enough for what we have in mind. And we aren't likely to get a volunteer who isn't a true believer, you know. Unless we work out the kinks in the—"

Tars looked unconvinced. "A robot then. Easy enough to program and they go pretty much everywhere."

Carter shook his head. "Again, no. This is a relatively new colony world and robots are at a premium. On Terra or Mars it might work. Even on Baldur or Odin. This planet has a very small population by comparison, and few people have the wherewithal to afford a robot courier. It would be noticed very quickly. Besides, on young planets like this the colonists don't like to compete with the 'bots for jobs and they have an unfortunate tendency to vandalize them. You may have noticed they have a shanty town outside of Mallorysport not far from here called Junktown. There are a lot of people living there who would cheerfully take a power hammer to any robot they came across, assuming they could afford to buy a power hammer. That could get rather messy under the circumstances."

Carter stuffed his pipe with something from Mars that wasn't quite tobacco and lit it. "This will require the hands-on approach. Fortunately, we have enough volunteers that it won't be a problem."

Tars snorted. "Martyrs to the cause. If this weren't so important, I would be disgusted by it all. No, wait, I'm still disgusted."

John Carter looked pointedly at Tars and said, "Just remember that it is important. Very important. Hopefully, we will get the, ah, other thing together and not have to use our own people in the future."

* * *

Bennett Rainsford, appointed and later elected governor of the planet Zarathustra, fought to control his temper. One of the two men before him was making demands. In itself, that wasn't a problem. Even what he was demanding wasn't particularly ire-worthy. The problem was the way he was demanding things. He spoke down to Rainsford as if he were a small idiot child.

"...and your tax code and records of any revenues received since you were installed as governor."

"There is no such thing as a tax code on this planet," Ben said. "This world does not tax its citizenry."

Kim Trahn Sylvinski's jaw dropped and eyes went wide. "What do you mean? How does this government support itself without taxation?"

"The Charterless Zarathustra Company takes care of that, for the most part," Victor Grego said. As soon as the words left his mouth he knew he had just made a serious mistake.

Sylvinski looked at Grego then turned back to Rainsford. "What? You mean this planet is in the pocket of a corporate entity? Outrageous!"

Leslie Coombes interjected. "No, it is not like that at all. The Company mines sunstones from the Fuzzy reservation, which is then placed in a trust for the benefit of the indigenous peoples. The government supports itself by taking a ten-percent administration fee. As for the planetary services, that was part of the lease agreement between the CZC and the new government."

"And we are still collecting fines and fees as well as renting out a substantial parcel of land to the Navy," Rainsford added.

Supervisor Sylvinski was about to object, then realized that he knew of no precedent prohibiting such an arrangement. He wished he had thought to bring Clarence Burr along for the initial meeting with the governor. He rallied by protesting he knew of no precedent in support of such a thing.

Gus Brannhard corrected him: "The colony of Niflheim is one hundred percent supported by the Chartered Niflheim Company. It has its own governor, appointed by the Federation, and a minimal legislature.

The only jobs available are those under the CNC and to keep things simple the governor and all other government officials and their staff are paid directly by the Company instead of taxing it out of them. With some military oversight, of course. As such, they do not have any kind of taxes, either. The CNC foots the bill for it all."

"And has been under multiple investigations for graft and influence peddling," Farquar, who had been silent until now, added.

Gus nodded. "True enough. But has anything come of those investigations, that I am as yet unaware? Every case I researched, ended with the investigators throwing up their hands in surrender."

Sylvinski was determined to win this particular argument. "Be that as it may, Niflheim is not colonized in the traditional sense. Everybody lives in space stations or on one of the moons. I think the situation here is completely different."

"Everybody on Fenris lives in a giant tin can," said a new voice. Jack stood in the doorway and continued, "The living conditions for humans between Fenris and Niflheim have a great deal in common. Yet, Fenris is run much like Thor or Baldur. Only the living conditions are changed. For that matter, Mars and Magni are also tin-can colonies."

Ben stifled a sigh of relief. He had been dealing with Sylvinski and company for the last four hours going around in circles. "Jack, meet Supervisor Kim Sylvinski and his deputy assistant, Mr. Hickabbible Farquar. Gentlemen, this is the Colonial Native Affairs Commissioner, Jack Holloway."

Jack smiled with genuine mirth. "Hickabbible? Your parents really hung one on you, didn't they?"

Farquar smiled. "Indeed they did. It is a family name, though. One in every generation has that honor. People generally call me Hic."

"Mr. Holloway, I understand you discovered the indigenous people of this planet," Sylvinski interrupted.

"In all fairness, Little Fuzzy discovered me. But yes, and I donated the majority of my northern properties to them for a reservation."

"How generous of you," Sylvinski said, "to gift their own lands back to them."

Jack started to feel his ire rise. He absently brushed a hand against his holster at his waist. The motion did not escape Sylvinski's notice.

"Is that a threat? Hic, make a note of this. And why is he armed in the Governor's office?"

Ben Rainsford spoke up in carefully modulated tones. "I am the Governor here and will decide who can or can't enter my presence armed. Jack's character is beyond reproach. He can come in with or without any weapon he feels the need to carry, up to and including planet busters. You two, however are strangers and will refrain from following Jack's example, that is, until I am satisfied you can be trusted."

The barb was not lost on Sylvinski and Farquar. The elder investigator was tempted to argue the point. Farquar quietly advised against antagonizing the most powerful man on the planet any further.

"Gentlemen, I suspect you are tired from your long journey from Terra and could do with a rest," Victor Grego said. He turned to Ben Rainsford. "Ben, do you have guest facilities here at Government House? If not, I can put them up at Company House."

Rainsford saw through what Grego was doing: offering to get the two pests away from him. "Thank you, Victor, but we have sufficient facilities to accommodate them. Besides," Ben turned to eye Sylvinski, "I suspect they will want to go through all of our files and records here. There's no point in adding a commute to their schedule."

Sylvinski had presence of mind to recall his staff. "I appreciate the lodgings, Governor. I have other members of my team with me. We can double up if necessary—"

"We have room to spare, gentlemen," Ben interrupted. "This is a young planet and everything was built with the expectation of more people coming. We can even arrange for your own floor to insure privacy and give you room to set up offices."

Sylvinski couldn't help being surprised. "That is very kind of you, Governor."

"I'll call Piet and ask him to forward all recent documentation here," Jack said. "No point in dragging our guests all the way out to the Fuzzy Reservation…"

"We will be visiting the reservation nonetheless, Mr. Holloway. The school and the Yellowsand mining operation especially. I believe you may have committed irreversible harm to their culture—"

"Without us," Jack said loudly, "their culture would be completely extinct within ten generations or so. Maybe you missed the memo on Fuzzy sterility and its cause, and how we are the only thing keeping the race alive."

In fact, Sylvinski had missed that detail. It wasn't common knowledge on Terra, yet. Still… "And yet, you couldn't treat their condition without destroying what culture they had?"

"No, we couldn't," Rainsford snapped. "Fuzzies are typically nomadic. We couldn't arrange for treatment on any kind of schedule, if they weren't close by and findable. And we can't perform genetic engineering to correct the problem without a competent representative of the race to understand what was being done and why, then give consent. A human adolescent could not agree to such a thing, legally, and neither can a Fuzzy who functions at that equivalent intellectual level."

Sylvinski was getting the message. Zarathustra might be a new colony but the governor was no bumpkin who could be impressed by an off-worlder with a briefcase. And his friends were equally competent, or so they appeared thus far. It was time for a change in tactics.

"Very good, gentlemen," Sylvinski said, with a more reasonable voice and a smile. "You seem to have things well in hand. I will still have to go through the steps, but I doubt I will find anything problematic. I hope the little show I just put on won't put anybody off. It was just a short-cut method to see if anybody was nervous. That usually means they have something to hide. You all passed nicely. Thank you."

He turned to Governor Rainsford. "If my assistant and I can be directed to our accommodations, the real work will start in the morning after we have had a chance to refresh ourselves and get organized."

Rainsford, slightly jarred by the switch of tactics, called up an intern to escort Sylvinski and Farquar to their quarters. Once gone, he turned to everybody in his office.

"What in the bloody Niflheim just happened?"

Grego choked down a snicker. Leslie Coombes explained. "He just Kellogged us."

"Kellogged?"

"Leonard Kellogg occasionally felt the need to get tough with somebody, even though he hated doing that sort of thing," Grego explained, "And when that didn't work he would back-track and take a more reasonable tone and say the tough act was just a feint. It worked fairly often, or so I've heard."

"He tried something like that with me, when he wanted to come out and look at my Fuzzies," Jack added. "He found out that I like to get tough for real."

Everybody recalled the beating Jack had administered to Kellogg, who was at least twenty years younger than the septuagenarian Jack, after the Goldilocks slaying.

Rainsford advised against Jack doing that to Sylvinski. "Even if he does appear to deserve it," Rainsford finished. "We will have to be on our best behavior while our *guests* are here."

"Ben, I am always on my best behavior," Jack said. "It just isn't always the best for people who get in my way."

* * *

Out on the terrace Ben's Fuzzies, Flora and Fauna, watched as the new Big Ones left Pappy Ben's office. They spoke to each other using their natural hypersonic voices.

"Not like the loud one," Flora said. "Make Pappy Ben angry."

Fauna nodded, a motion he learned from the Big Ones. "They want to make trouble for Pappy Ben. We help?"

"Not know how," Flora said sadly. "Not understand why new Big Ones make Pappy Ben angry."

Fauna thought for a moment. "Loud One say he go to Wonderful Place and look at Fuzzee. Pappy Jack not let anybody hurt Fuzzee."

Fauna agreed. There were still so many things the People did not understand about the Big Ones.

III

Emily Dickinson was finishing up her class on Big One Talk when Little Fuzzy came over. Like most of the teaching areas on the Rez, the class was held out of doors where the Fuzzies would be the most comfortable. Even after three years around Big Ones, they still were not comfortable being inside most buildings. Dr. Mallin once commented on this, suggesting that a cave-dwelling race would adapt to the claustrophobic confines of a building more easily than a nomadic race. Emily nodded in Little Fuzzy's direction and he quietly waited until she dismissed the class.

"I want all of you to practice the Big One words while you are out playing," Emily said. "Okay. Class is dismissed."

The young Fuzzies politely waited until they were away from the teaching area before yeeking and rough-housing among themselves. The younger Fuzzies, like Baby Fuzzy, were far more adept at learning Terra Lingua than the adults, much like Terro-humans.

Emily turned to her guest. "Little Fuzzy, it is pleasant to see you here. Is there something you needed to speak with me about?"

Emily Dickinson, unlike most other Fuzzies, had been adopted by an educated woman who had worked very hard to teach her proper speech. The success was nothing less than phenomenal. Then Emily and her "Mummy" were in an accident. The incident proved fatal to Emily's adoptive parent and caused an unusual head injury to the Fuzzy; she could no longer speak or understand the language of her people. Oddly, or miraculously, she could still speak and understand Terra Lingua.

At first she had difficulty interacting with the other Fuzzies. Her inability to speak with them in their own language had set her apart. Little Fuzzy, the *de facto* wise one at the school, worked to get Emily reintegrated into Fuzzy society. While she taught the younger Fuzzies proper diction, she was also relearning the language she had lost, mostly due to Little Fuzzy's help.

"We go hunting for lan'p'awn. You come with Little Fuzzy?"

"That sounds wonderful! I will get my chopper-digger and we can go."

Emily quickly collected her backpack and weapon and rejoined Little Fuzzy. After a short dog ride they dismounted and started looking for land prawns and goofers. Land prawns were getting scarce around the Rez. Goofers were still plentiful, though.

"Little Fuzzy, where did Pappy Jack go in such a hurry?"

Little Fuzzy shrugged. "Not know...um...I don't know. Pappy not...didn't have...um...time to say. Is good?"

Emily smiled. "You are getting much better, Little Fuzzy. It is good that you are setting an example for the others. We will have to ask Pappy Jack why he was in a hurry when he gets back. I hope it is nothing serious."

"Maybe nex' time Pappy Jack...will take us with...him in aircar."

Emily shuddered. She used to enjoy riding in the Big Ones machines with her Mummy, but since the accident the idea of going into anything such as a ground vehicle or aircar, frightened her terribly. She had huddled down in the back of the airbus with eyes closed and hands over her ears during the trip that brought her to the Fuzzy Reservation. Little Fuzzy insisted that she try to face the fear. Ruth van Riebeek spoke with her once a week and even Dr. Mallin came to the Rez once a month to help.

"I would rather not. However, Ruth says that I will have to if I want to function as a member of the staff. Not everything is readily reachable by dog mount."

Among Emily's duties was to act as an ambassador to wild Fuzzies who had not yet encountered the Big Ones. She had to work with Little Fuzzy in that capacity, as she still needed him to translate for her. Her education level was actually that of a Terro-human junior high school student. Her primary focus had been in language, but she also had some small understanding of social studies, anthropology, Federation history and arithmetic, including low level algebra. Physical Education and Home Economics were ignored, as the equivalent and more was taught at the Rez School. Not that ordinarily active Fuzzies, who were perfectly content to eat their food raw, needed it. Political Science proved to be beyond her comprehension; Emily, like most Fuzzies, just couldn't grasp the idea of many-many leaders telling everybody what to do. One was enough to a Fuzzy, and only as long as he or she was good at it. Electing new leaders after a set amount of time was a completely alien concept.

"Pappy Jack say there is new Fuzzy tribe over in sun's left hand area… um…east of here. Make talk…speak diff'rent from us and Jin-f'ke. Can go tomorrow to make friends?"

"'We can we go,' Little Fuzzy." Emily corrected.

"That what I said," Little Fuzzy said. Then he laughed at Emily's confusion. "I think we can go tomorrow and make friends," he said carefully.

"You are speaking better every day, Little Fuzzy," Emily said. "Soon I hope all of our people will speak as well."

Little Fuzzy laughed. "I tell you secret thing. Most of us here at the Wonderful Place know more Big One talk than we say. Pappy Jack and other Big Ones talk to each other and we listen, learn. But when they make talk to us they sound like we did when we first learn Terro Lingua." He stumbled a bit over the difficult word, "So we talk back same way."

Emily Dickinson stopped. "You mean I don't need to teach you?"

Little Fuzzy shook his head. "No. You help very much. We need somebody to help us speak and understand better. Big Ones think we are like children. Not take what we say serious. You know better. You can help much."

Emily thought it over. She was pleased that her people knew more than they let on, but still needed her help to learn even more—just as she needed them to relearn her native language.

"I am happy you told me this, Little Fuzzy. After we hunt could we practice the Fuzzy language?"

"Hokay! Ko-Ko an' Cinderella help."

* * *

Piet swore up a blue streak, then apologized to Jack on the viewscreen. Jack waved it off claiming he felt the same way.

"Everything will be put under an electron microscope, Piet," Jack said. "I get the feeling they have some sort of axe to grind and we're the grindstone."

"The only good bureaucrat is one-way off-world. Preferably orbiting a black hole with a decaying orbit," Piet said emphatically. "Nobody works harder to keep a job from being done right than one of those sons-of-Khooghras. They are going to throw several spanners in the works, you mark me."

Jack nodded in agreement. "I agree, but there is nothing to be done about it. Whether we like it or not, these bureaucrats represent the Terran Federation. We will just have to cooperate and hope Gus can maneuver us around any nitpicking issue they light on. I hate to ask this; do you think there is anything in our records that can come back to bite us?"

"In other words, is it possible I or somebody else has been cooking the books?" Piet responded. It was a fair question, even without considering Piet's somewhat checkered background. He didn't take offense. Jack had admitted to him that he had his own scrapes with the law in his youth.

"Commissioner, I can't imagine a more pristine set of records. So much so that these mutts might find it suspicious, because they are so clean. That addition on your house was bought and paid for by your Fuzzies out of their own pockets…or backpacks, really. The septic system you had installed was covered by the profits from the 'Fuzzy Flush' and the castle on the southern edge of your land grant was covered by your son. You were pretty well off before you became Commissioner of Native Affairs and your reputation for not liking people who don't work for their money is pretty much well known."

"Not to them," Jack corrected. "They will no doubt dredge up all the people I have killed for various reasons."

"All vindicated under veridication. You can relax. I'm more likely to be a target than you." Piet took in a long breath and let it out slowly. "After all, my closets have a few skeletons in them."

"Well you can be sure that nobody will be throwing anybody under the bus during this investigation." Jack pulled out his pipe, loaded and lit up. "Besides, you cleaned up nicely."

* * *

"...and I can't help but think that your community will be another target for these...people," Ben Rainsford finished.

He had to remember that as governor he couldn't say how he really felt about certain citizens lest it come back to bite him later. Even in a private communication with a man he liked and trusted. Johann Torseus nodded his understanding, a motion that to the unfamiliar looked as though his head was about to fall off his shoulders. Johann, Bürgermeister of the Principality of Neu Freya on Zeta Continent, was all too familiar with bureaucratic nonsense. In fact, it was his position to be the source of the occasional nonsense himself.

"Vhen do you t'ink dese pipple vill come to us? I must admit I am unsure vhat my aut'ority in dis situation ist. Should I send Rheiner to represent us?"

Ben's image on the viewscreen shook its head in the negative. "I checked with Jack on that. He said you should meet with these mu... individuals personally. In fact, they should come to you. We need to set the tone of the meeting and having you come to them might give them the idea that they have all the power."

Johann looked uncertain, or would to somebody familiar with his facial construction. "Governor, do you not t'ink dot dey could be...eh... put off by our appearance?"

Johann's people were all descended from Freyan criminals and the disenfranchised underclass that had been enslaved and sold to an off-planet concern for labor, very much against Federation law. Even worse, their children had been experimented on in utero to make them stronger for work in heavy gravity. As a result, some of the most beautiful humans in the Federation had been turned into near simian-like creatures.

"Johann, they should take you for who you are, not what you look like. Besides, I have met a number of Terro-humans that look a lot like your people."

Johann smiled and nodded. "Und it vhouldn't hurt t'ings if dey vere put off a bit in der process, mebbe? Put dem off der game, as *mein* Prince Morgan vhould say."

Ben chuckled. "I won't say the thought hadn't occurred to me. Mainly, though, you have to speak to these people from a position of strength. Right now you are the most powerful man on Zeta Continent, at least until Mor…Prince Morgan returns from Terra. Make sure that these mutts know it."

This time Johann chuckled. Governor Rainsford let his true feelings about the inspection team show. "Der vill be an appropriate reception committee vhen dey come, Herr Governor. I t'ink dey vill be impressed."

IV

"A monarchy on a Federation planet?"

Frank Farmer nodded. "They were sold a tract of land on Zeta Continent, well, the whole thing, actually. It went for..."—Farmer paused, then tapped a few keys—"fifty-million sols."

Supervisor Sylvinski's eyes went wide at the figure, then he recalled it was something on the order of one sol per acre. A pittance. Land on a new colony planet tended to be inexpensive, even free, but this seemed wrong to the commissioner.

"Any evidence that the Governor or anybody of importance walked off with a hefty bribe?" Sylvinski asked. "Or even some sort of special concession?"

Farmer shook his head. "Not so much as an expensive dinner, Supervisor. If a bribe happened, they went to a lot of trouble to hide it. There is a deal between the Charterless Zarathustra Company and the new miners on Zeta, but that is to be expected, I think. The settlers need to sell the ore somewhere and the CZC is the only game in town."

Sylvinski was dubious. "Where did the money from the sale go?"

"Into the CZC bank..."

"Aha!"

"...In a trust account to be used for the support of the government in case of some catastrophic event that the Yellowsand agreement wouldn't cover, at an interest rate of seven point seven five percent," Farmer finished. "That information is public knowledge. This Rainsford employs a great deal of transparency in his office."

"Damn!" Sylvinski said under his breath. Somebody entered the room and Sylvinski turned to see Dana Alexander. "Miss Alexander, have you found anything?"

Dana Alexander was short and fair skinned with long raven black hair. Heads often turned when she entered a room. "I went through a number of paper documents and found evidence of a series of bribes from the CZC to Governor..."

"Yes!"

"…Emmert."

Sylvinski blinked. "Emmert?"

"The previous governor," Farquar said. "He was bagged and tagged and sent to Terra to be tried on charges of misfeasance in office. A Mohammed O'Brien went with him."

If the former governor was charged with misfeasance in office, then he *had* to be taking bribes from the Charterless Zarathustra Company as they, like Farquar pointed out, were the only game in town. "Was the CZC implicated?"

"Yes and no. Rainsford must have planned on going after the CZC for that and a number of other crimes, but decided, or was convinced, not to," Farquar concluded.

"What makes you think that?"

"News articles and interviews with the Governor during his first week in office," Farmer explained. "He seemed very determined to lock up everybody involved with harming the natives. There are also reports in the datastream that speak of how the CZC solved the food shortage problem for the hairies," Farmer added.

"Fuzzies," Dana corrected. Farmer looked back at his screen, then nodded.

Sylvinski thought it over. A new government on a backwater world with no money and no other significant source of employment or revenue on the planet. Rainsford would have no choice but to keep the CZC up and running. The alternative would be a depression the likes of which not seen since the aftermath of World War III on Terra. The main office on Terra would see it that way, too.

"Ghu be damned, I am almost starting to like these people." The problem with that was that giving reports on nice people did nothing for advancing one's career. Sylvinski and company needed to bring back somebody's head on a platter.

"You would think nobody on this planet was out for themselves." Sylvinski thought for a moment. "Hic, didn't you say that we couldn't get a cop to come out with us because one is already here?"

Farquar nodded.

Sylvinski used jargon he picked up from an old flatty and said, "Then let's go shanghai this flatfoot and put him to work. Do we have a name for this guy?"

"Yes, sir. Captain Starbuck Trask."

"Starbuck? As in that Space Opera show or Moby Dick?"

Farquar shrugged. "No way of knowing until we ask him, Boss. I have the address where he keeps an office."

"Well, then, we should avoid the suspense." Sylvinski looked about and saw Janice Goodfellow sitting quietly at her makeshift desk. "Ms. Goodfellow, would you be kind enough to invite Mister—"

"Captain," Farquar corrected.

"...Captain Trask to join us? If he gives you any argument, show him the Notice of Authority papers."

Janice nodded. "Yes, sir. Should I take Clarence along?"

Sylvinski thought it over, then decided against it. Better to start things off on a cordial note, especially after what happened in the governor's office. "I may need to discuss something with him."

* * *

Captain Starbuck "Buck" Trask was wading through a stack of documents with the intent of finishing them up, then heading back to Terra. He liked Zarathustra and most of the people he had encountered on it, but he had duties to attend to back home. He almost wished he had a valid excuse to extend his stay. All the Fuzzy slavers appeared to be either dead, caught or on the run off-planet. If any remained on this world they were on their own and easy pickings for the locals. No reason for Trask to stick around.

He heard the buzzer that informed him somebody wanted to come into his office. Without bothering to check the video monitor, he tapped the button that automatically opened the door panel. Without a sound, the panel slid into the wall to reveal a young woman standing in the doorway.

Trask had expected Lt. Williams or one of his agents. The young woman was above average height, blondish and not unattractive, save for the sizeable birthmark that discolored much of her face.

"Can I help you, Ms…?"

"Make that "Miss." Miss Janice Goodfellow with the Terran Commission."

Confusion crossed Trask's face. "Terran Commission on what?"

Janice smiled. It was a nice smile. "Colonial and Alien Affairs. We are here to vet the situation and see if anything needs fixing."

Something always needs fixing, usually after a commission like this one louses things up, Trask thought. "What do you think might be awry, Miss Goodfellow?"

"Me? Oh, I don't have a dog in this fight, Captain. I am just an assistant to Supervisor Sylvinski. He will be making any determinations like that."

"I see." Trask tapped a button that closed the doorway. "Miss Goodfellow, this is a soundproofed office, so anything you might need to tell me in confidence will remain between us."

This time Janice looked confused, then realization took over. "Oh, Captain Trask, I am not here to file a report or anything like that."

"Then what…?"

Janice handed over the document she was given by Hic Farquar. "The Supervisor wants your assistance to investigate people in the Zarathustran government. We would have brought an agent with us but we were informed that you were already here."

Trask looked over the document and grunted. It looked authentic and pedantic enough to have come from the Terran Office. Trask ran the document through the copier, then handed the paper back. An electronic duplicate would be stored in the computer until he printed it out later for the hard files. "Miss Goodfellow, let me save the good Commissioner a lot of time and effort. I have already questioned several members of the local government, to include Ben Rainsford and Marshal Fane, under veridication, no less, and I can assure you a more straight and narrow crowd just doesn't exist anywhere. Your boss is wasting his time and the Federation's money digging for dirt on them."

Janice shrugged, "You may be right, Captain—"

"Buck will do, Miss Goodfellow."

"Buck, then," she replied, "only if you call me Janice. From Moby Dick?"

Trask nodded.

"You may be right, Buck, but the i's must be dotted and the t's crossed. Surely a man in your position can understand how things like this work...."

Trask admitted that he did, and that he also didn't like it. "Sylvinski... beg pardon, Supervisor Sylvinski, is likely to make a lot of trouble for people who don't deserve it. And it could come back to bite him on the sit-upon."

Janice shrugged. "I's and t's, Buck. I believe you know what you are talking about, but the Supervisor just can't take your word for it. And I suggest you keep any bias in this matter to yourself. He can make a lot of trouble for you, too, if he thinks you are tanking his investigation."

Trask smirked. "I never tank an investigation, Janice. I follow the evidence wherever it takes me. I have no choice but to assist your boss, and won't shirk my duty, even if he's on a wild goose chase. You can tell him, I am on the team. However, and I leave this up to you, whether you want to share this or not; I also never slant the facts. He shall have such evidence as exists. No more, no less."

Janice nodded. "I don't know what he hopes for. Still, even if he was willing to cross the line, I don't think any of the rest of us will."

Trask smiled. "Excellent. Now, since we will all be working together, I think we should get to know each other a bit. Are you opposed to having dinner with me while we fill each other in?"

Janice was a bit surprised at the offer. Most men were put off by her birthmark. Apparently Buck was of a better class of men. "Not at all. In fact, I would like to try some of the local cuisine."

"Really? Good. I know just the place. They do the best veldbeest in Mallorysport. Say tonight? 1900?"

"I would love to, provided you don't mind if I make it a working dinner."

Trask smiled wider. "Not at all. I may do the same."

V

The Psycho Sciences Center was bustling with people, both the large and virtually hairless variety and the small, extra hairy type. It was normal to have Terro-humans walking the halls, staffing committees, logging data and other routine work at the Center. Even the presence of a few Fuzzies was far from unusual, as they were often the main focus of study since their discovery.

The current state of affairs was far from normal. Fuzzies were everywhere: in chairs, on desks, climbing on couches and, most importantly, being examined by curious Big Ones. Dr. Mallin found himself more than a little harried as the Chartless Zarathustra Company Chief Fuzzyologist.

"Where is that intern I asked for?" Mallin roared at nobody in particular. It was a rare sight to see him lose his temper, let alone display any significant emotion beyond his normal tight little smiles. The last such outburst was during interrogation on the stand under veridication during the Fuzzy Trial.

"Out getting coffee," Ruth van Riebeek replied.

Normally, Ruth would be at the Beta Continent facility. These were not normal times. The recent repatriation of nearly a hundred Fuzzies from Terra and a few other colony planets had necessitated the need for psychological care and counseling for the diminutive Zarathustrans. Fuzzies, as a rule, were almost completely incapable of going insane. However, they had never been abducted and forced into slavery as entertainers before and didn't have the mental tools to come to terms with it.

"Ghu, I never understood the need for caffeinated beverages before all of this happened," Mallin griped. "And sugar! Lots of sugar for additional energy."

Ruth shook her head in amazement. Dr. Mallin was not acting like himself at all. Next, if things didn't settle down, he would start chain-smoking cigarettes. "You really shouldn't have your interns running for coffee. Especially that new girl from Heimdall. She is a junior psychologist and should be working with us, not running errands."

"I don't have time to do these things myself," Mallin snapped. He paused for a moment, taking a deep breath: "My apologies. I understand all too well the symptoms of stress. I will apply my training on myself and get back under control."

Ruth smiled. "It is healthy to blow off some steam now and then, Doctor."

Mallin nodded. "Yes, but not at the expense of others. I think a trip to the company gym may be in order."

Ruth tried to picture Dr. Mallin working with a gravity bar and just couldn't see it. Maybe the treadmill?

"Who wanted the black with extra sugar," a voice called out above the din. The soft Germanic accent proclaimed her to be a denizen of Heimdall. A woman in a lab smock with a tray full of coffee and tea weaved her way through the crowd toward a counter where she set the tray down. "Dr. Mallin, I believe this is for you."

Mallin took the triple sugar coffee and thanked the woman. After a long drink, he noticed that she had a new friend. "Have you adopted a Fuzzy, Doctor Tezza?"

"*Nein*. No, she seems to have adopted me. We were speaking in the corridor as I was returning with the coffee. She is one of the Fuzzies recently returned to Zarathustra."

"Ah." Mallin turned to the Fuzzy. "What name you?"

"My captors gave me no name, Dok'tor. My people call me Rockthrower."

Superior linguistic skills, Mallin noted. "You speak well, Rockthrower."

"The Masters demanded that we learn your language," Rockthrower explained. "So we could understand their commands better."

That made sense. Fuzzies trained to entertain Terro-humans would need to understand every order given to them precisely. Mallin knew of Emily Dickinson, the Fuzzy with a rare brain injury that erased her knowledge of her native tongue while allowing her to retain all she had learned from her Big One. Gerd van Riebeek was studying her at the Beta facility, or rather his subordinates in the psycho-sciences were.

"What did the Bad Big Ones make you do?" Mallin asked. Ruth was horrified that he would be so direct with such a question, then remembered that Mallin was likely the foremost authority on how to deal with the Fuzzies outside of Jack Holloway.

Rockthrower did not seem upset by the question. "Threw things into other things. Fris-bees through hoops, basketballs through other hoops, darts into small targets on walls. The Mas...Bad Big Ones said I was very acc-u-rate. Could be dart champion? Not good with bowling, though."

Fuzzy psychology was such that while they could be traumatized by a past event, like almost getting caught and eaten by a damnthing, they did not relive the event by talking about it the way many Terro-humans and Freyans could. It made it much easier to get to the root of a psychological disorder.

"Would you like to go play or hunt until we can talk further?"

Rockthrower look horrified. "No! Want to stay with Aunty Cindy! Please no make me go."

The sudden reversion of speech patterns suggested that separating the Fuzzy from Dr. Tezza could be damaging. "Dr. Tezza, normally, I would be against this kind of bonding between doctors and patients, as in our species it could result in unhealthy complications, but Fuzzy psychology is significantly different from our own. Would you object to Rockthrower staying with you, at least here in the center, while you work?"

"Not at all, Herr Doctor," Cindy Tezza said with a smile. "She is adorable. And I don't want to see her upset." She turned to Rockthrower. "Maybe you could help me with my duties?"

The Fuzzy brightened up and agreed.

"I think I have my own intern, now," she said with a smile.

"Very good, Dr. Tezza. But try to keep her out of mischief. Dr. van Riebeek, perhaps we should consider a Big Brother/Sister program?"

Ruth gave it about a millisecond's worth of thought. "I believe that would be an excellent idea, Doctor."

Dr. Tezza, with Rockthrower in tow, went on to perform her duties while Doctor Mallin turned to Ruth. "I have been meaning to ask; how is Little Gerd?"

"Still in quarantine but his antibody production is double from a month ago," Ruth said. "It is hard not being able to pick my boy up when I visit the hospital to see him. I think Shari misses her twin, too, though she isn't old enough to understand what's going on with her brother."

Mallin nodded. "I did some reading on Gerd's autoimmune deficiency disorder. I believe there is reason to be hopeful. We have come a long way since we cured, um, what was it called? Oh, right, AIDS, another autoimmune disease. I have every confidence that Little Gerd will be out rolling in the dirt like every other adolescent before you know it."

Instead of being cheered up, Ruth looked concerned. "I hope so, Doctor. This has been very hard on Gerd. As you know, fathers often see themselves in their sons and their accomplishments. He has been blaming himself for Little Gerd being sick."

Mallin nodded. "I understand. Perhaps I should set some time aside to speak with him."

"He would see through that in a second," Ruth warned. "He married a psycho-scientist, you know."

* * *

The intercom buzzed and Gus tapped the button to respond. "Yes?"

"A Supervisor Sylvinski to see you, sir."

Erica only called him "sir" when somebody of importance came around. Otherwise, per his insistence, she would call him "Gus." In this case the importance of "the somebody" was exaggerated, in his estimation. Gus considered letting the supervisor cool his heels in the outer office for a while, then thought better of it. The sooner he was dealt with the sooner he could be sent packing back to Terra.

Gus gave his desk a quick once-over to make sure that nothing was amiss, like a bourbon bottle out in the open, lit his cigar, then said, "Send him in, Miss Parker."

Sylvinski came in, surprisingly unaccompanied by his aid, Farquar. Equally surprising was that he had dressed casually instead of in the business attire he normally paraded around in. Zarathustra bush hat and khaki shirt with trousers tucked into black leather boots, all brand new. *Is he trying to put me off my game with his sense of fashion?*

The supervisor took in the Chief Colonial Prosecutor's office: the furs on the chairs and couch, the large caliber rifle on a rack above Gus's head and, most impressive, the damnthing head mounted on the far wall. Not at all what one would expect to see in a government office on Terra.

"Supervisor Sylvinski," Gus said as he stood and extended his hand. "To what do I owe this pleasure?"

Sylvinski accepted the bear-like paw, then took the seat in front of Gus's desk. "Thank you for seeing me, Mr. Brannhard. Interesting décor. Ah, I hope I haven't interrupted anything important."

"No. No, things are relatively quiet just now," Gus said. "Most of the major criminals are either dead or in prison and the new ones haven't risen to prominence yet. Right now it is just purse snatchers and veldbeest rustlers." Gus explained about the deaths of Leo Thaxter, Ivan Bowlby and Raul LaPorte plus the destruction and execution of the Fuzzy slavery ring. "Things are always fairly quiet for a few months after a public execution. Almost makes me wish we could execute somebody every other month. Too bad we can't shoot people just for being the kind of mutts who commit crimes."

Sylvinski smiled at the idea. Franklin Farmer had found the news articles about the mass execution that took place in Mallorysport. Over sixty men and women had been convicted of slavery and were shot in a very public manner. "Ah, yes, Governor Rainsford does have a way of making potential criminals think twice before embarking on such a career."

Gus smiled. "For the moment organized crime is almost completely kaput on Zarathustra. Amazingly, most of the slime balls wiped each other out. The low population works in our favor there. Sadly, it is just a matter of time before a new crime family rises to fill the vacuum."

Sylvinski agreed, then switched topics. "We need to talk about that new colony on Zeta Continent. Magni-Freyans, I believe they are called?"

Gus sighed. "I have been expecting this. Where is your attorney? Clifford Burr?"

"Clarence," Sylvinski corrected. "He is busy with research right now. I can manage without him for this."

Gus silently thought about pulling out his bottle and offering the supervisor a belt. It was a moment of whimsy and not seriously intended. It wouldn't do to have Sylvinski think he was a dipso. "Okay, let's get to the tilbra killing."

"Tilbra? Is that some sort of local fauna?"

Gus suppressed the urge to roll his eyes. "Quasi-rodent from Thor. We have a few down in Science Center. They are the Thoran equivalent to a mouse and fill the same niche in the environmental scheme. Now, what is the issue on which you wish to converse?"

If the barb was noticed by Sylvinski, he ignored it. "That little monarchy over on Zeta. Clarence was unable to verify its legitimacy."

"It is a colony of, shall we say, disenfranchised Freyans. They can't go back to Freya even though they are still technically Freyan citizens." *If he wants more information than that, he can get it from Johann.* Gus didn't feel he had the right to discuss the Magni-Freyans' past difficulties.

"Be that as it may, they are setting up their own little fiefdom," Sylvinski said. "It would set a bad precedent if it is allowed to continue."

"That precedent has already been set, Commissioner," Gus stated with confidence. "Fenris has a small colony of Ullerans there. The extreme climates don't bother them much given that Uller has similar extremes, though it is a good deal more seasonal. Multi-species colonies are hardly new."

Sylvinski waved that away. "Yes, Clarence found that little tidbit. The Ulleran colony is not a monarchy and the colonists adhere to Federation law. That is not the case for these, um…"

"Magni-Freyans."

"Yes, these Magni-Freyans," Sylvinski said. Then a light came on in his head. "Wait, why 'Magni-Freyans'?"

"They originated on Freya, then were taken to Magni for…work. They stayed there a few generations then found they had reason to leave for greener pastures."

"But the legality…."

Gus shook his head. "Actually, the Magni-Freyans adhere to Federation law as well. The only real difference is that of culture. The Federation has little to no control over that."

"The fact remains that it is a monarchist society on a Federation world."

"Freya is a Federation world and it has a monarchy," Gus pointed out.

"It was aa monarch when it was discovered, oh, three hundred years ago, I think," Sylvinski argued. "The Federation doesn't go around overthrowing existing governments when we colonize a Class IV planet."

Gus could think of three examples where the reverse was true. Unfortunately, it wouldn't help his case and only antagonize the commissioner if he pointed them out. Fortunately, he had another precedent he could cite.

"The Thoran colony on Imhotep," Gus said. "They are an autonomous colony, separate from the Chartered Imhotep Company and do maintain the same form of government as their home planet."

This was news to Sylvinski and he said so. "I will have to have Clarence look into that. I will still have to go over and inspect the...the Magni-Freyan colony regardless of what he finds."

"I expected no less," Gus said.

Supervisor Sylvinski said his goodbyes and left. Gus watched him go while his mind raced. *If Clarence Burr is any good at what he does, he'll soon punch a hole in my Imhotep comparison.*

VI

Hugh Lennon sat in his private yacht and fumed. The ship had just left hyperspace and was orbiting Zarathustra for the second time. The last time he visited this planet he ran afoul of one Jack Holloway. He considered himself to be a man who learned from his mistakes so while on Gimli, the closest inhabitable planet, he gathered as much information as he could on everybody of note on this world. Before making planetfall he would review that information again.

Instead of using a data pad, he had all the documentation transferred to hardcopy. He liked the tactile feel of the hemp paper and believed that there were details one could miss in the digital version that would be readily apparent on paper.

The first file was on Victor Grego, CEO of the Charterless Zarathustra Company. Up until the Pendarvis Decision, the CZC owned the planet outright. It was the discovery of the Fuzzies that destroyed that monopoly. Unsubstantiated rumor had it that Grego planned to have the Fuzzies exterminated before they could be proven sapient. That showed a lot of cold-blooded thinking, which Lennon could respect if not necessarily like. Yet Grego bounced back from it all by getting a lease on all of the unseated lands for the next millennium and became a champion of the Fuzzies at the same time. That showed a lot of flexibility in the face of disaster. Such a man would be very dangerous to antagonize…at least directly. Grego's only weaknesses were a daughter on Terra, reputed to be estranged, and the two Fuzzies that he adopted: Diamond and Sunstone.

Threatening a man's family was not to Lennon's taste. Besides, it was a dead end. Kidnap his Fuzzies to force his cooperation and he would look for any and every opportunity to destroy the kidnappers. And Grego had a planet's worth of resources to back him up.

Next on the stack was Ben Rainsford, Colonial Governor of Zarathustra. Rainsford was a naturalist by trade who was appointed, then later elected, to his position. No criminal record of any kind. Not even a parking ticket on Terra. No political ambitions until the appointment, either. That would make him difficult. Career politicians could be bought, bribed or even blackmailed. An appointee could be, maybe, if he didn't have a good staff to keep him straight.

Lennon didn't trust a government official that could be bought or bribed, which meant he didn't like government officials, period. There was always somebody out there with a bigger wallet. Blackmail, while effective, usually had a limited life span. The blackmailed could just decide "to Niflheim with it" and come clean just to get out from under the blackmailer's thumb. Whatever method Lennon chose to get his way would have to be legal.

That brought him to Gus Brannhard. Brannhard appeared as if by a bolt of lightning out of the ether: nothing on him before he opened a legal practice on several worlds, one after another. The obvious implication was that he was on the run from someone or something with a lot of juice. Whatever it was, the threat must have vanished because his image had been seen in the datastream all the way from Magni to Terra. A man on the run hides from that sort of notoriety. So, either he had significant cosmetic surgery, which was unlikely since people tended to make themselves more attractive rather than bear-like, or the threat he was running from was gone. The main point was that he was a brilliant litigator and would keep Rainsford out of trouble.

Next, he came to Holloway's file. Born in Melbourne, Australia, in a largely Americanized community. *They still use "Americanized" as a description?* Degrees in business administration and military history. Holloway left Terra forty-odd years ago to travel the galaxy. Involved in several incidents, arrested a few times, killed a hell of a lot of people in "self-defense" or while stopping a crime. Would vanish for a year or two, then reappear several star systems away. A lot of family including a son, recently discovered.

Lennon read on. This was the man who had pulled a pistol on him at the Fuzzy Adoption Center. While Lennon was prepared to admit he had acted badly on that occasion, he still didn't like having guns pointed at him. And being forced to leave like a beggar and run off-planet didn't sit well with him.

Still, Lennon wasn't the type to go looking for vengeance. It wasn't profitable and went against the Magnian way. He simply wanted a Fuzzy. It would have to be a strong one to adapt to Magnian gravity. A special enclosure was being constructed with gravity modification, but Lennon would prefer that the Fuzzy adapted, over time, to the new conditions. He wanted the Fuzzy to be able to roam around and not stay in the enclosure like a prisoner. And he had to get it legally. Magni had enough scandals since the Freyan slaves were discovered.

Lennon spit at the thought. Enslaving people was as ridiculous as it was abhorrent. Had the Magnian Cooperative been willing to spend a few more sols they could have had heavy-duty robots brought in instead of Freyan criminals and indigents to be experimented on. And they wouldn't have been made vulnerable to the buyout that John Morgan forced them into. The same John Morgan that turned out to be the son of Jack Holloway. Lennon had met the younger Holloway once during the buyout. A lot of character in the man. He even adapted to the gravity well enough that he didn't use the high-gee suit most off-worlders wore.

Lennon would have nothing to do with vengeance or slavery. He wanted a Fuzzy to come live with him, and it had to do so willingly, and legally. He knew his moral code would work against him there. It would be simple to send a shuttle down, grab a Fuzzy or two then space out before anybody could catch him. Or would it? The Fuzzy slavers that made such a ruckus were pretty much all caught and executed by now. No, the moral code, while inconvenient at times, kept him from doing things that got others arrested, killed, or run out of business. He would stick to it. Still….

Lennon noticed another folder he had neglected earlier. He picked it up and skimmed it, then reread it more carefully. A smile grew on his face as he did so.

* * *

Marshal Fane closed the jacket on the file he had been reading and looked across his desk at Police Chief Frank Carr. "Is this really a problem?"

Carr shrugged. "Terra seems to think so. Mostly these fanatics pass out flyers and try to raise money to terraform Mars to how it was about a million years ago. I guess technically that would be Martioforming. They have enough influence on Mars to push for adding ancient Martian to the required electives at the universities."

"'Required electives'," Marshal Fane snorted. "If it is required, it isn't elective."

Carr grinned. "You never attended college, I see. Well, a certain number of electives are needed to graduate with a degree of any note. But the students have a choice of what elective classes they take. For example, a foreign language is needed at most universities. Before there was a Federation those languages were usually French, German or Spanish. These days it is Thoran, Sheshan or Freyan. I imagine Fuzzy will find its way into the curriculum. Anyway, while a foreign language is required, the student chooses which one he takes."

The marshal had an evil thought. "Is Khooghra an option?"

Carr shook his head. "A language consisting of less than 100 words? I doubt it."

"Humph. We are getting off-topic," Marshal Fane said. He was a little chagrined that Carr realized he had never attended college. He had come up through the ranks straight out of secondary school. "According to the file, there have been cases of civil unrest on Mars and Terra. Nothing any farther out than that so far."

Carr looked confused. "Then why are we getting warnings from the Federation? We have five hundred light-years between us and all that."

"As a courtesy. Some of the leaders are traveling out to the more distant worlds. Presumably to drum up support for their cause."

Carr chuckled. "They would have to be pretty desperate to come all the way out here. The fare would cost more than they are likely to collect from any donors on this planet."

Fane nodded. "Agreed. Let's just hope that is all they are after."

"What else could it be?"

The Marshal's face became stern. "I don't know, and I hate finding things out the hard way."

* * *

Ned Foster rubbed his eyes then reached for his coffee, long cold. Even the super-insulating cups lost heat over enough time. He cursed himself for being too cheap to get polysteel tumblers with micro-collapsium lamination. Those things held heat or cold almost indefinitely, though they tended to be a bit heavy.

Ned glanced up at the clock and shook his head. It was well past quitting time. He would have to grab a bite in town on his way home. Maybe at Clancy's Soup Kitchen. Good food at unbeatable prices, although most people paid extra to cover the meals that Clancy provided for those in dire straits.

A light blinked on his desk console. Somebody was at the door. Ned rolled his eyes and thought: *always, just when I get ready to go*. He pressed a button and the door retracted into the wall to reveal Captain Trask.

"Captain, you were lucky to catch me still in. I was just about to leave."

Trask entered and extended a hand which Ned accepted. "Actually, I checked you out along with everybody else when I arrived on Zarathustra. You are well known for keeping late hours, Mr. Foster."

Ned was uncertain whether he should be flattered or annoyed that he was checked out by the captain of the local Federation Bureau of Criminal Investigation chapter. He settled on flattered, since he was considered important enough to be looked into.

"So, this isn't a social call?" Ned asked unnecessarily. He and Trask were not chatty enough to rate late visits in the office for anything other than work. "Are you looking for help or a confession?"

Trask chuckled. "That is a bit sticky. No doubt you are aware of the latest crop of troublemakers to arrive from off-world." It wasn't a question.

"Oh, hell, the Fuzzies in northern Beta have to know about those bush goblins by now." Ned indicated a seat for Trask and sat down behind his desk. "We were expecting them about two years ago. The expectation was that the Federation bureaucracy would come in, look around, see everything was running smoothly, rubber stamp the operation and go home."

Trask nodded. "Instead they, more precisely their boss, Sylvinski, seem determined to dig up all the dirt they can and throw the whole operation into chaos. Well, I have been drafted to assist them in this."

Ned showed no surprise. "Naturally, as the local FBCI chief, they would drag you in, especially since you are a newcomer and less likely to have been inducted into the good ol' boys club with Ben Rainsford, Gus Brannhard, Jack Holloway and Victor Grego."

"Exactly." Trask started to run a hand through his hair and realized he was still wearing his hat. He removed the headgear and absently set it on the desk. "Look, I already checked out everybody who matters months ago. Under veridication, in fact."

Ned smiled. "As you may recall, I was present for a couple of those interrogations. And Gus just loved that to Niflheim and back. He demanded to make it policy that no government official will ever be questioned under veridication again without a court order."

"And I don't blame him," Trask said. "In the Bureau we all get randomly veridicated at least twice a year. This is to keep us honest, of course, and I personally have never been caught short in an investigation, but it is still an uncomfortable invasion of privacy. Everybody has something, no matter how innocent, they don't want getting out." Trask took a deep breath and let it out slowly. "I am getting well off the track. I came here to get your assistance."

Ned's eyebrows shot up in surprise. "Mine? Doing what?"

Trask sighed. He didn't like what he had to do. "I want you to spy on the government."

"What?" Ned shook his head as if to clear the cobwebs. He didn't believe he heard what he just heard. "This has to be some sort of joke. You just said yourself that you investigated everybody who mattered under veridication...."

"In relation to Fuzzy trafficking. I didn't get into the nitty-gritty of how the government is run. I had no reason to at the time."

Ned Foster mentally counted to ten. Then another ten. "All right. You are in a corner and have to cooperate with these briefcase toting off-worlders. I get that. You have to clear everybody of everything. I get that, too. And Gus Brannhard isn't about to let anybody within a light-year of the veridicator purely on principle. What you might not get is that I won't spy on my boss and his friends. And, before you try, you have zero leverage against me to make me do otherwise."

Trask leaned forward and slowly said, "Are you sure?"

"Absolutely. I was raised on Yahweh in an Amish community. What we called sin you called business as usual. During Rumspringa, I found I had an interest and aptitude for law and left to attend university on Odin. I worked my way through mostly by building furniture, which I am very good at, and repairs on colonial style homes. I never cheated on a test, nor sold answers to other students. My extracurricular activities were all within the accepted norm, even while dating. And I am one hundred percent loyal to Gus Brannhard who gave me this opportunity even when my own practice wasn't doing well."

Trask nodded. "I knew all of that. That is why I want you to be my cat's paw here."

Ned leaned back in his chair. "And how, exactly, do you intend to get me to do that?"

Trask pulled a chip from a pocket. "This is my file on Gustavus Adolphus Brannhard. It is very detailed and very, very thorough. It includes how he stole millions of sols from a Terran crime boss, which led to his abduction last year. Now, nobody ever filed a complaint against him. The people he stole from prefer to handle these matters more directly. That does not make him immune from prosecution back on Terra. I could have a warrant for his arrest signed by Judge Pendarvis in an hour. He wouldn't like it, but with the Chief Justice, the law is the law. Period."

Trask set the chip on the desk. "You can keep this copy. I have several in a variety of very safe places, among which is a lockbox on Terra where I sent this information last year. Nobody will access it unless I end up dead or imprisoned. My boss will see to that. But, if I have to, I will arrest Brannhard."

Ned stared at the chip. Then he smiled. "Nice try. The statute of limitations would have run out on that case decades ago."

"Mr. Foster, you disappoint me," Trask stated in a flat monotone. "The statute starts from the day the crime is discovered. Since no formal charges were ever brought I can argue that the statute didn't apply until I uncovered the information myself."

Ned shrugged. "Even so, to my knowledge, everybody who could testify would be dead by now."

Trask shook his head. "There are still a few around, mostly in prison, and they would cheerfully testify against Gus for a reduction of their sentences. Then there are the computer tracks. Gus was good, but far from infallible I would wager. He would have left traces of his actions that could be recovered."

Ned sat silent.

"Now, I don't like any of this any better than you do. However, I have a job to do. And so do you, really. If nothing untoward is going on, you can't hurt anybody. But if there is, it is your duty as a Federation citizen and officer of the court to report it."

Ned picked up the chip. "If I do cooperate, what happens to all of this?"

Trask feigned confusion. "All of what? I have selective amnesia when necessary."

Ned grimaced. "Fine, you have your pigeon. Now get out. I'll call, if and when I have something to report."

Trask took no offense at being dismissed so rudely. He understood. He collected his hat and left without a word. As he took the lift to the parking structure he let out a long breath. He was surprised his bluff worked. He glanced at his wrist chronometer and realized he would need to hurry, if he didn't want to be late picking up Janice for dinner. A first impression was something you never got a second shot at.

VII

The collapsium-plated chamber hissed as atmosphere was vented out, creating a near perfect vacuum within. The internal conditions were intended to match that of the planet's exosphere. Gauges were checked, computers consulted and buttons pressed.

"Ready to inject the specimens into the chamber, Dr. Jimenez."

Juan Jimenez nodded and the technicians went to work. Next to Juan sat Cinda Dawn. Standing behind her was Rheiner Sostreus. Rheiner, though shorter than most of the men in the laboratory, was so incredibly massive that a normal chair or stool would collapse under his weight. Juan offered to have something brought in but Rheiner waved it off with a "*danke*."

A technician announced, "The specimens are in."

"Very good, Mr. Lugos," Juan said. He turned to another technician. "Anything yet?"

Mr. Chaney checked some gauges, then shook his head. "Guess we'll have to feed them." Juan nodded and more buttons were pushed. This time super-pulverized space debris from outside of the planet's atmosphere was gently added to the mix.

"What if this doesn't work?" Cinda asked nervously.

"Then we try other things," Juan said, as he watched the duraglass portal. "This is just a test to see how much energy a measured portion of the bacteria can produce. It will also tell us if we can keep them viable during transport to other planets."

Juan was about to say more when he noticed that some light was coming from the portal. Looking through it resembled the effect of moonlight on a foggy night. It was eerie and beautiful.

"Good. Good, now run the simulated cosmic rays. We need to feed both species of bacteria." Again, buttons were pressed and a hum similar to that of an X-ray machine could be heard. The light in the chamber brightened considerably. "Well, now we know that the, ah, photovores?

What do we call something that subsists on cosmic rays? We'll come back to that. The, um, cosmovores generate more light. We might not need the other variety—"

"They might work in a symbiotic relationship, Dr. Jimenez."

Juan turned and saw Dr. Hoenveld. He was late, which was unusual for the normally punctual scientist. "It is possible that the lithophagous bacteria, ah, jumpstart the, cosmovores, did you say? That may become the accepted term. I am unaware of any other species that subsists on cosmic rays."

If Dr. Hoenveld couldn't think of any other species, then they probably didn't exist or had yet to be discovered. Juan made a note on his data pad about the name, figuring he needed to protect his place in history. "Then, with Miss Dawn's permission, we should classify these as *cosmophagous bacterium cindadawnius*. And the cosmic matter eaters?"

"*Cindadawnius*?" Cinda processed the classification and decided not to argue.

"Oh, there are a variety of lithotrophs on almost every inhabitable planet," Hoenveld explained in his lecture-like tone. "I think something like *cosmolithotrophus bacterium cindadaw*—"

"*Rheinersostreus*." Cinda interrupted. "He was there when the discovery was made. He should get partial credit."

Rheiner shook his head. "You vere die vun making die discofery. You did all of die heffy livting."

Cinda brushed aside that ironic statement and stood firm. "Without you there wouldn't have been any discovery, or even an 'us' any more after we were captured by the slavers. Anybody have a problem with that?" Nobody objected.

"Cosmolithotrophus bacterium *rheinersostreus* it is," Juan declared. "There will be a lot of tests and experiments, of course. We can't just pick a planet and seed the sky with this stuff. We need to select a world with the right conditions—one that isn't already inhabited."

"It should be in a K0 star system, initially," Hoenveld said. "We should start with a planet as close to Zarathustran conditions as possible. Or rather the conditions Zarathustra had before the bacteria altered the climate. Distance from the primary, atmospheric conditions, even the presence of satellites could be a factor."

Cinda sighed. "Sounds like it'll be a long time before I can afford that new aircar I've been dreaming about."

"You will be compensated for the time, Miss Dawn," Juan said. "We will also be testing these little germs on nuclear radiation. Imagine these little things cleaning up the radiation left over from the wars. Assuming the fallout from the bombs doesn't give them indigestion."

Hoenveld sniffed disdainfully at the characterization. "I doubt they will be very effective in that sort of terraforming. The atmospheric pressure would likely kill them, unless we can introduce a useful mutation…."

"Vhat effect vill space traffic haff on der bacterium?"

Everybody looked at Rheiner.

"What do you mean, Herr Sostreus?" Juan asked.

"Effery day ve send shuttles und ozzer spacecraft t'rough die atmosphere into space und beck. Vould dis harm die bacteria up dere?"

Everybody was silent then everyone spoke at once.

"…disruption of habitat…"

"…breeding cycle altered…"

"…reproduction would be through mitosis, still…"

"…effect on planetary climate…"

"…wasn't there a study on the effect on the ozone layer? Maybe…"

Everybody was stopped short by a piercing whistle.

"Thank you, Rheiner," Juan said. "That's quite a set of lungs. Now, I want everybody to settle down. Rheiner brought up an excellent point. Hayes, run trials to see if the bacteria can survive near ground level without upsetting the ecological balance. Jones, come up with a way to test if our incursions through the upper atmosphere are affecting the… uh…cosmovores. Henson, get me the latest analysis on the ozone layers. I know, that doesn't have anything to do with the bacteria, but if our punching through it every Tuesday and Thursday is damaging it, I want to get ahead of it. Kiser, make sure our guests," Juan indicated the testing chamber, "remain comfortable. There will be a lot more tests over the next, oh, possibly years, and I don't want to send up another shuttle just to grab more specimens because we let these die. Everybody clear on what to do? Then get cracking! I expect nightly reports on your progress."

"Well, I guess I should send-off a message to Dmitri and let him know about all this," Cinda said. "Thank you for letting us sit in, Dr. Jimenez."

"Let you? This is your baby. Your friend Dmitri made sure to patent the discovery in your name almost instantly upon learning of it. You are lucky; a lot of men out there would have tried to take the credit for themselves."

"A lot of men wouldn't have had to deal with Rheiner, here," Cinda joked as she gestured a thumb in Rheiner's direction. "But Dmitri has been kind and helpful. I don't think he is even capable of stealing credit."

"Good to know. Maybe I should include him in future demonstrations."

Cinda shook her head. "He went out on *The City of New Chicago* last week to register the discovery on Terra. I get the credit for the, um, cosmovores discovery, but the study team gets their share as well. We will all get a place in the history books."

"One moment," Dr. Hoenveld spoke up. "As most of us know, there are no blood-subsisting species on this world. Blood has to be specially treated when stored to keep it viable. Has anyone considered the possibility that this bacterium might be responsible for this? If so, then we have to consider the ecological effects of introducing these organisms to another planet. We may not like mosquitoes, yet they play an important role in the food chain of Terra."

That brought everybody up short.

"All right, now we have more areas of study to investigate," Dr. Jimenez said. "Dr. Hoenveld, if you can make the time, please set up a study team for this issue."

* * *

Jack went over the reports, signed them, then set them in the outbox. The outbox, something new from the CZC; he automatically scanned the report, checked it for spelling and grammar, verified the signature, then made a digital recording of it. Jack hated it.

"I have some more documents to go over," Piet Dumont said as he walked in with a whiskey case full of files. On the side of the box was the logo for Old Atom Bomb Bourbon; it was the same box Jack had used when he first started out as the Commissioner of Native Affairs. The box had long outlasted its original contents. "Do we really need to go over every last thing from the last three years?"

"Yes, and maybe beyond that," Jack said tiredly. "Nobody is better at finding something, even if it doesn't exist, than a bunch of bureaucrats on a witch hunt. They'll go over every file right down to its subatomic makeup until they find something." Jack glanced at the file box. "Make sure there aren't any old files stashed in a drawer somewhere."

Piet thought for a moment, then said, "Maybe, I should tender my resignation. If they run a background check on me, things are sure to go badly."

Jack shut that right down. "Trust me, my past would look a lot worse. They'll say I have more bodies on me than Hitler. I skirted the law on more planets than I can name off the top of my head. And that duel between me and my son is sure to raise a few eyebrows. As a cop, and no offense intended, you just got lazy near the end of your career. I never found any evidence of you accepting bribes or tampering with evidence. And you were one hundred percent professional when we all went looking for my Fuzzies at the CZC. Like I said before; you cleaned up real good afterwards."

"You checked me out?" Piet grunted, then said, "Of course, you did. I would have done the same in your shoes."

"You might be in my shoes, if these Khooghras have their way." The viewscreen beeped. Jack tapped a button to see Betty Kanazawa staring back at him. "Betty! Did I forget a date?"

Betty laughed. "No, nothing so mortally tragic. I'm just letting you know that I am being temporarily reassigned. I am afraid it might affect our relationship."

Confusion crossed Jack's face. With a good aircar there was no place on the planet that wasn't much more than a few hours of travel. Where could she go that would impact their relationship? Xerxes? "How is that?"

"Mr. Grego believes that these off-worlders will be digging into all kinds of things and that you might need some help getting organized. So, for the foreseeable future, I will be working with you and Piet."

Piet hadn't meant to intrude on Jack's conversation, but in this case he just couldn't help it. "There is a Ghu! Betty, you have no idea what a godsend you will be. I'm sending Mr. Grego a case of Poictesme brandy."

Piet raced out of the room, presumably to box up some libations, before Jack or Betty could say anything to stop him.

"Where is he going so fast?"

Jack chuckled. "You know how people say, 'I'll do this or that,' but it is just an expression? Piet doesn't do that. I would imagine he is out making good on his statement."

Betty rolled her eyes. "Now where would he get a case of Poictesme brandy? Even Mr. Grego would have a hard time getting that."

"Well, I won't ask him. I'm afraid he would tell me and put his job at risk." Jack leaned forward closer to the screen. "Now, tell me, just how much work do you think we'll get done with me chasing you around the desk?"

Betty giggled. "Lots. I don't plan on running very fast."

* * *

The sign on the screen showed large white block letters on a bright red background: UNAUTHORIZED ACCESS. SECURITY CLEARANCE REQUIRED.

Frank Farmer grunted as he continued to tap away at his keyboard. Behind him, somebody spoke and he almost jumped out of his chair.

"Easy, Frank. I was just asking how it was going." Hickabbible Farquar leaned on Farmer's desk and looked at the screen. "I'm guessing, not well."

"I was doing fine up until I went after the CZC mainframe," Farmer said. "Damned thing has security protocols I have never seen before. The military's computers are children's notebooks compared to this. Hic, I don't know if I can crack it any time soon."

Hickabbible nodded absently. If Frank Farmer, Terra's foremost computer software designer—and unknown to society at large—a brilliant hacker, couldn't break through the CZC's encryptions, it probably just couldn't be done.

"I sure would like to meet the team that developed these security measures," Frank said.

"Be careful what you wish for," Hic cautioned. "Any luck with the other targets?"

Frank opened a file on another screen. "Lots of irregularities with the governor's bank and expense accounts."

"Really?"

"Don't get excited. These are from the previous governor. Ben Rainsford and Gus Brannhard set a new standard for integrity in office as far as I have been able to see. There was something odd about Brannhard's dealings with a Clancy Slade, though. Slade owned a house, but didn't really own the house, had a storage locker at the spaceport, but it wasn't really his, was essentially indigent, then became a wealthy philanthropist virtually overnight. Screwy, but I can't find anything specifically illegal."

"Do you think Mr. Slade did something on the down-low for Mr. Brannhard?"

Farmer shook his head. "If so, I can't imagine what. And where would Brannhard get that kind of cash?"

Hickabbible made a notation in his data pad. "I'll look into it. Show me a picture of this Clancy Slade." Farmer tapped a few keys and the image popped up. "Whoa! I don't think I would like to meet him in an alley, no matter how well lit."

Farmer leaned in toward the screen. "This is interesting."

"What's that?"

"According to this datastream article, Slade shot and killed one Leo Thaxter. And look at this." Farmer brought up another image on the screen.

"I don't get it. It's just another picture of Slade."

"No, it isn't. That is Leo Thaxter."

Hickabbible leaned closer to the screen. "Great Ghu, they could be twins! The Supervisor will want a look at this."

"Do you still want me to hack into the deputy governor's computer?

He came in after the last election so anything that happened before then he wouldn't have any connection with."

Farquar thought it over for a moment. "Might as well. Shake a tree hard enough and all sorts of things will fall out. Takagashi might have skeletons all his own buried in a closet somewhere. Let's see if we can find them."

VIII

The corridors of the Psycho Sciences Center bustled with the people coming and going at shift change. Cindy Tezza gathered her personal notes and equipment into her carry bag and prepared to go home. There was just one problem; Rockthrower wanted to come home with her.

"The doctors need to spend more time with you, Rockthrower," Cindy explained. "And my Wise One would not approve of my taking you home with me." In fact, Cindy did want to take the Fuzzy home, but doctor/patient relationships were discouraged and she was uncertain how that applied to human/Fuzzy relationships. "Tomorrow I will ask Dr. Mallin if it will be okay."

Rockthrower looked very sad, a look which could wrench the heart of even the most unfeeling human. "I understand, Cindy Tezza. I see you tomorrow?"

"*Jawohl.* I look forward to seeing you then. Okay?" The two made their 'good-nights,' then went in opposite directions. Cindy fought to keep tears out of her eyes. She reminded herself that it was just for one night, then she would speak with Dr. Mallin in the morning.

"Are you okay?"

Cindy turned to face the source of the question. It was Erena Taylor, one of the Company police. Erena was short, around five foot one, and slender. Cindy couldn't help wondering what so small a woman could do against a large man looking to cause trouble.

"I am fine, Erena. I just hated leaving Rockthrower for the night."

Erena nodded. "These Fuzzies can get to you pretty quick. If I didn't already have four children of my own to care for, I would get me a Fuzzy. But it wouldn't be fair, especially with the hours I keep. Which way are you going?"

Cindy pointed up. "To the rail stop on the roof."

"Oh, honey, don't you have an aircar, or even a ground roller, yet?"

Cindy shook her head in the negative. "Up until I started my internship all my money was for university. What little I had left after went to living expenses."

Erena knew what that was like. With four children and her husband between jobs, her whole family was living hand-to-mouth. "Wait, didn't you tell me that you were a datastream model for a while?"

"Yes, but my, ah, manager didn't handle the money well and we ran into tax trouble on Heimdall. By the time the dust settled there was very little money left. So, I took odd jobs to pay for university. That was one of the reasons I came to Zarathustra—no taxes. I can stretch the same salary twice as far."

Erena nodded emphatically. They came to the lift and waited. "I'll see you up to the roof. I can do my rounds on the way down."

"You guard the entire Center?" Given the size of the Psycho Sciences building she found it hard to believe one person could cover the entire area effectively.

Erena laughed. "Oh, Ghu, no! There are guards on every level. I am one of the floaters." She saw the confusion on Cindy's face. "That means I move all over the place. There are others doing the same thing. We look around in the areas the stationary guards can't see, and provide backup if somebody gets into a situation."

The lift doors opened and they both got in. Cindy pressed the button for the roof. "How did you get into security, Erena? I mean…um…"

"You mean how does somebody so small get into such a dangerous profession? You're not exactly a giant, either, you know. I think you only have an inch on me. Anyway, I have some skills. And in a firefight I make a very small target…not that it has ever come up. But, I have a useful little toy that makes a great equalizer, if I do run into something too big for me to handle." Erena patted the holster at her side. "CZC issued sono-stunner. It can drop a man faster than he can say: 'Wait, don't shoot!' Non-lethal to humans, although we can't use them around Fuzzies."

"Why not?"

Erena tapped her left ear. "Fuzzies have super-hearing and are susceptible to severe injury if a sono-stunner is used nearby. I heard of a case up in northern Beta where a Fuzzy died of a brain hemorrhage after being shot with a stunner. Mr. Grego has R&D working on a way to make the sound wave beam tighter so there isn't as much sonic spillage."

"My God! Would a loud stereo hurt them?"

"Hmm…I never thought to ask. Dr. van Riebeek probably knows. You should ask her."

"What do you do, if you have to shoot somebody when Fuzzies are nearby?"

Erena pulled a weapon from her belt that looked like a fat ink pen. "I have this. I need to be a lot closer, but it is very selective with who it affects."

Before Erena could explain what the device did, the doors opened and Cindy exited the lift. "We can talk more later. I can't miss my ride."

The rest of the way home, Cindy pondered the pitfalls and responsibilities of adopting a Fuzzy.

* * *

The Wiley, so named for its disturbing resemblance to an animated character from Old Terra, was intent on what was soon to become his lunch. The zarabunny, which only had a passing resemblance to its Terran counterpart, was equally intent on avoiding the dinner plans of its pursuer. Both were to be disappointed.

The bullet fired from the .22 knocked the zarabunny several feet to the side. The Wiley, frightened by the sudden noise and even more sudden disappearance of his repast, spun about and ran in the opposite direction.

"Got him in one," said the owner of the Baldurtech .22 small game rifle.

"Looks to me like he got away," the man with him replied. "Runs fast for such a goofy lookin' varmint.

"I'm talkin' 'bout the 'bunny. I ain't eatin' no Wiley. I hear they are as chewy as rubber and gamey as all Niflheim. Go get the 'bunny while I scout around for another."

"'K, Bo. We gonna need a whole lot more than the two 'bunnies we have so far."

"Bet'cha I get at least three more in an hour."

"Hope so. I don't wanna eat another tin of XT3."

Bo shuddered at the thought, then cursed under his breath.

An hour later the two men returned to their base camp to meet up with the rest of the party. They carried six zarabunnies and a nu-mu, a flightless bird roughly half the size of an emu. They were greeted by Weaver, the self-styled leader of the group.

The camp consisted of three tents, all made of fibroid weave, three ground vehicles and a collapsible shed. From the largest of the three tents could be heard faint noises.

"Not a bad haul," Weaver said. "This will make a nice change from the canned rations. Mai should do well with these."

"Not without some fresh vegetables and some spices," a female voice shouted out. "How much longer are we going to be out here?"

"Until it is safe to go back and grab a ship off-world," Weaver yelled back. "Everybody involved has already been arrested, shot or blown to Niflheim. Anybody lookin' for a bullet in the head can leave any time they like. Me, I like breathin' and movin' around outside of a cage." He grunted and shook his head. "If the long-range radios still worked we might have gotten a ride out of here before now."

The radios, part of the equipment issued by the *Pequod*, partially self-destructed when the *Pequod* was blown out of the sky by the Space Navy. That left only short-range radios good for twenty kilometers and the satellite network for news and entertainment.

"How do you feel about eatin' regular?" Mai shot back. "We done cleaned out most of the game and all of the tubers in this area. Bo, how far did you have to go before you were able to find any game?"

Weaver cut Bo off before he could speak. "Fine, you want to go back? What about the rest of you? Ready to risk it?"

"It has been, what, six or seven months since the *Pequod* was blown to atoms," said the man with Bo. "At least four months since the last arrest was made. And you know that each cell was ignorant of the rest, so they couldn't know about us from anybody getting veridicated. I think we are safe."

"I'm with Clem," Bo said. "In fact, we make ourselves more suspicious by camping out here. If a Zarathustra Native Protection Force vehicle flies over, what's our cover: 'We thought we would try a new place to look for sunstones?' I have a few sunstones to support the story, but—"

"Unless the cops have somebody on the force who knows better, our cover should hold," Clem added. "A lot of amateur geologists came here and found nothing. I say we pack it in and take our chances."

"I'm with Clem on that, too," Bo said. "We had to go a long way to get this little feast. We could have been spotted."

A new voice spoke up. "Odds are nobody will know us from Adam. Lots of prospectors come out, fail to make it and head back. I say we try to pass ourselves off as one of the prospectors, and then pack it in."

"What about the Fuzzies, Lars?" Weaver demanded. "Do we shoot them or let them go?" That brought everybody up short. "If this bunch makes it to the Fuzzy Rez, they'll talk plenty. People have been convicted of crimes and shot based on Fuzzy testimony. Or have you forgotten the men executed in a very public fashion after they were busted in that Mortgageville warehouse and the Beta camp?"

Everybody remembered the broadcast transmission: It went out to the entire planet on every form of broadcast media. Rumor had it that a short film of the executions and photos of the executed were going to be on display in the Fuzzy museum.

"This bunch has never been to the Rez," Bo said. "They don't even speak normal. Just all that yeeking. By the time anybody ran across them, we could be back on Terra headin' out to some new planet...."

"Let them go," Mai said. "I didn't know what you all were up to until I came out here. Now I am in just as deep as the rest of you, but I'll have nothing to do with killin' these poor people. Bad enough you kept them caged up for the last six months."

"I am with Mai," spoke up a large man with phenomenal muscle growth. "I don't kill anything unless I plan on eating it or it is trying to eat me."

"I dunno, Lars. They could talk—"

"To who?" Bo interrupted. "We're a thousand miles deep into the middle of nowhere. It would take a very long time before they got back any place where they could tell on us. By then, I hope to be at least a hundred light-years away. We have ground rollers. All Fuzzies have are their feet. They don't even run as fast as a full-sized man."

"As fast, no, but they can go a whole lot longer," Weaver spat. "And what about the Zarathustra Native Protection Force patrols?"

"They rarely come out this way and if they see a bunch of Fuzzies on the ground, so what? They see that all the time and keep to their own business."

"And, if they do get picked up, I would rather have the Fuzzies say how we let them go rather than have their bodies found later and more charges brought against us."

"Whether they find them live or dead, we still have a bullet coming. No discretion of the court," Weaver yelled. "And these Fuzzies can identify us."

"No," Bo said. "I draw the line at outright murder. I don't mind killin' somebody tryin' to kill me, like Lars said, but an unarmed man... or Fuzzy...well, I just won't go there."

Slavers with a moral code, Weaver thought. *What next, altruistic damnthings?*

"And what if the Fuzzies try to wave them down?" Weaver said. "You think a ZNPF patrol will ignore that?"

"Odds are if a Fuzzy sees more Big Ones, they'll scatter and hide," Lars countered. "After what we put those poor little people through I don't see them being real trusting of others like us."

Weaver could see he was outnumbered and gave in. "Fine. We break camp first thing in the morning. We leave the rest of the XT3, and whatever we don't eat tonight, with the Fuzzies and let them out of the cages after we break camp. No point in giving them a head start."

IX

Xenoanthropologist Kealani Ancheta reviewed all of the reports and documents made by Dr. Mallin, Gerd and Ruth van Riebeek, as well as the video records, starting with the home movies made by Jack Holloway. She shook her head in disbelief. How could anybody doubt the intelligence of these little people? The Fuzzy funeral alone was significant evidence. It showed that Fuzzies understood death. They used their chopper-diggers to dig the shallow grave instead of clawing it up like an animal, then carried the body, Goldilocks, to it, laid her down gently, then entombed her in the cairn with her effects.

Forget the talk and make fire rule, which while proof positive, the inability to do either proved nothing. A newborn Terro human couldn't do either of those things. It was the ability to learn how and teach others that was the true test of sapience. Not to mention the fact that Fuzzies fashioned tools. A Terran gorilla could pluck a reed from the ground and use it to dig insects from a tree hollow, but that was just using what nature provided. No industry on the part of the user was involved. A chimpanzee could even use a stick as a weapon. Again, just using what was already there.

Granted, a chimpanzee could also be taught to use a lighter to light a cigarette. But none of them have ever taught another chimp to do the same. Fuzzies could pick up a piece of wood or bone and make it into something new, something specialized for more than a single use or purpose. Of course, a Freyan kholf could make and use simple tools and they were still below the threshold of true sapience. Still....

She couldn't help thinking that the Charterless Zarathustra Company never had a chance at the Fuzzy trial.

Setting aside the portable viewscreen, Kealani reviewed a report on Khooghra intelligence. Khooghras did possess what could only be charitably called a language; less than a hundred word vocabulary and almost entirely in generalizations. Granted, they had mastered fire technology. They also practiced casual cannibalism.

Fuzzy intelligence was several orders of magnitude above the natives of Yggdrasil. Maybe even higher than that of the Lokians. The recorded language was nearly five hundred words and climbing. They had names for specific things, verbs, adverbs, nouns and a few pronouns. They didn't have fire until they learned it from the colonists, but they learned and then taught others which was the main point.

Even Terro-humans had to be taught how to start a camp fire; it was passing on that information that really proved sapience. In some ways Fuzzies could prove to be the most intelligent non-Terran humans in the known galaxy; save for the Freyans, who proved to be the mental equal of Terrans, once they were given access to more advanced technology. The Fuzzies simply needed a few generations of guidance to adapt to the more advanced culture of humanity.

That was another thing, Fuzzies cheerfully learned everything they were taught and retained it. What they didn't do was suffer culture shock. That put them one over the Sheshans. Give a Sheshan a better bow and they were thrilled with it. Show them a "stick" that made loud noises and killed at a distance and it was immediately proclaimed to be black magic, and then you had a fight coming on. A few tribes were nearly wiped out as a result. Sheshans had to be very gradually introduced to any advanced technology. Show a Fuzzy that same "stick" and they were hungry for more. Of course, Fuzzies hadn't developed any kind of religion that would slow them down.

The real question, according to her boss, Supervisor Sylvinski, was how much damage was done to the Fuzzy culture after meeting Jack Holloway. Kealani shook her head. From everything she had read, the Fuzzies virtually *had* no culture. Nomadic semi-familial clans, separating and joining other semi-familial clans. Low-level Paleolithic tools, no fire making technology...and worst of all, they had been on the verge of dying out.

The NFMp hormone was the problem. Not that their diminutive size didn't put them at risk from every predatory species they encountered. Birthrate is what made or broke most species. Had the Neanderthals of Terra enjoyed a two-percent increase in birthrate or a two percent reduction in infant mortality, they might have survived until this day. The Fuzzies had been way behind the eight ball with the NFMp hormone. Their only counter for it, prior to meeting Mr. Holloway, was by consuming a quasi-insectoid species, which first colonists named land prawns.

By an incredible coincidence, Holloway fed the native he dubbed, "Little Fuzzy," the one thing that would suppress the hormone. Even more surprising, the Fuzzy liked the stuff. If Kealani believed in Ghu, she would think He loved hirsute species and worked to keep this one around.

Without the help of Terro-humans, the Fuzzies would have become extinct in something like ten or twelve generations. Whatever damage to their minimal cultural achievements their encounter with humanity had brought about, it was overshadowed by keeping them alive. Of course, that was not what Mr. Sylvinski wanted to hear.

"I need to get out into the field," Kealani said aloud to herself. "I need to see Fuzzies in the wild; observe them and see how they live."

She started to make out a list of what she would need, then remembered that she already had a premade list. It was mostly the same from world to world. Field gear for slogging through the forests and veldts, canned rations, protein bars, water treatment tablets, rifle, bowie knife, backpack...in many ways it was similar to what the Fuzzies carried around, at least the ones on or near the Reservation.

On Thor they had aircars and all the little goodies brought in by the Federation, just like Freya and Uller. Sheshans were more resistant to the gifts of the Terrans, thinking most of it was black magic. Khooghras lacked the mental wherewithal to work even the simplest electronic device; a hammer was about the apex of technology that they could use in any meaningful way.

She would need a vehicle, preferably one with sound baffles to suppress the ultrasonic whine of the contragravity engine, like what the military used in covert operations. Would such a vehicle be available on Zarathustra? If not, she would have to set down beyond the range of the Fuzzies' hearing and try to observe them at a distance. A camouflage suit would be nice, but that was strictly military issue and unavailable on the open market. She would cheerfully get one from the black market, if she knew how and where to find it.

Kealani revised the list on her computer, printed it out (hardcopy was best for fieldwork) and shut it off. It would be necessary to get approval from Supervisor Sylvinski and authorization from the Native Affairs Commissioner. Sylvinski would be all for it, as he wanted any hook he could get to hang the local government on. Kealani didn't give a damn about what Sylvinski did or didn't want. Politics wasn't of any interest to her. She was a little excited about the possibility of meeting the famous Jack Holloway, though.

* * *

Not for the first time Gus Brannhard wondered how a society loaded with computers—big ones, little ones and everything in between—still managed to generate so much paper. So much so that entire regions of Terra had been deforested before the last Great War keeping up with the demand. Trees on Terra would be extinct by now if the Federation hadn't placed almost every species of tree on the protected list. Fortunately, hemp plants grew much faster and created a better quality of paper.

The buzz at the door shook Gus out of his reverie. He knew who must be on the other side or his secretary would have announced him on the intercom. He tapped a button and the door retracted into the wall.

"Come on in, Ned."

Assistant Colonial Prosecuting Attorney Ned Foster entered and the door closed behind him. Gus nodded at one of the chairs in front of his desk and Ned took a seat. "What can I do for you, Ned?"

Ned fidgeted for a moment. That in itself was unusual for the younger man. "Chief Prosecutor…"

"Gus. Just Gus."

Ned sighed. "I need you to fire me."

"What? That's fool's talk. You are the best APA I have. What the Niflheim! I doubt I could fire you if I wanted to. The Governor is very impressed with you. What is this about?"

"I am being forced to work against you." In a rush Ned explained his meeting with Trask the night before. "If I am fired, I can't be forced to spy on you and the Governor."

"It sounds to me like you are being forced out of loyalty to me." Gus reached into his desk and extracted a bottle and two glasses. He poured two fingers worth into one glass and the other almost to the top. He pushed the two fingers over to Ned. After they both downed half the contents of their glasses, Gus continued. "Trask is bluffing you. He couldn't possibly have anything usable against me."

"Then you didn't steal millions of sols from the mob?"

Gus chuckled. "Will you represent me if I did?"

Ned nodded.

"Good, you are now my lawyer and can't reveal anything I tell you. I took the mob for over a hundred million sols. Gave away all but ten percent of it to charities and the disadvantaged. I made a sizeable contribution to the land reclamation project, too. The ten million odd sols I kept I used to bounce from planet to planet and set up various law practices on those worlds. Some I sold when I left, others I just closed down before leaving. I invested most of it in the chartered companies of the more prosperous worlds."

"And you say Trask has nothing on you? Gus, you could be—"

"Arrested and charged for yadda-yadda-yadda. First of all, Trask can't charge me for a crime that the mob doesn't dare admit happened. No complaint, no charge. Period. The mob already took a shot at grabbing me up, and muffed it. The two who blew it were executed by a mob enforcer that we grabbed up before he could leave planet. I personally sent word back to the parties involved what had happened and what would happen to the next bunch that tried. Of course, we managed to get enough out of Smith, the assassin, to deal a nasty blow to their Terra-side operations.

"No, they will not try again. It will cost them way more than they are willing to risk. Trask cannot bring suit against me without a complainant, and the mob can't file a complaint without opening their books and letting the cops go through them. That opens them up to tax evasion and the questionable sources of their revenue. I am safe. If not, well, I've had a good run and hurt them worse than they can hurt me."

Ned looked relieved, then confused. "So can I just tell Trask to go jump off a bridge?"

"No," Gus said, then finished his drink. "Trask has no choice but to take orders from Sylvinski and his carpetbaggers. I'll bet he doesn't like doing it any more than you did. Now, do you think we have anything to hide?"

Ned thought about it for a moment. "Aside from what you just told me, no. Governor Rainsford is as clean as anybody I've ever seen. Jack Holloway has had his scrapes with the law, but nothing actionable, and he gets along well with the local cops. Victor Grego, however...."

Gus nodded. Everything said in Grego's office was recorded by the Navy. Those transcripts were now classified, but Sylvinski would have the pull to get them—if he thought of it. The most damning, of course, was his idea to have the Fuzzies trapped out before their sapience could be proven. Ben Rainsford had been particularly after Grego's hide for a while. Then the two men made nice, even became good friends. No telling what the Terran Commission could make of that: collusion, bribery, misfeasance in office, cover-ups....

"Where is that chip Trask gave you?"

Ned pulled it out of a pocket. It was in an anti-static sleeve. "Can you take that to Henry Stensen? I suspect it might have a little something extra that we won't like. Transfer the data to a non-networked computer first then wipe it, oh, about a hundred times. No point in letting Mr. Stensen get nosy."

Confusion again crossed Ned's face. "Mr. Stensen?"

Gus chuckled. "I forgot, you didn't get here until the rat killing was over with. Let me tell you about our Mr. Stensen...."

X

The viewscreens, mostly useless in hyperspace where there is nothing to see beyond an unending field of gray, showed a brilliant array of colors before transitioning to a view of a moon. As the moon grew larger on the screen, it shifted away to be replaced by a planet.

"Zarathustra, dead ahead, sir."

"Sound general quarters. Prepare for soft landing." Captain Zeudin pressed a button on his seat console. "Sir, we're preparing to make planet fall."

Morgan Holloway's voice replied from the console speaker. "Understood, Captain."

Captain Zeudin hesitated for a moment then spoke again. "Sir, is it your preference to land near the castle on Beta, or Mallorysport spaceport on Alpha?"

There was a pause, then Morgan spoke. "Best we go to Alpha first. I have to speak with Mr. Grego face to face. What I have to say can't be sent over an unsecured channel."

"Very good, sir." Zeudin suspected that would be his orders and disconnected the channel. "Helm, make for the spaceport. Normal speed. We don't want to draw too much attention."

Like most colonial spaceports, Mallorysport had originally been designed to accept full-sized cargo haulers, passenger starships and transports. As the city grew, and the population with it, more and more people used aircars to travel back and forth. As time passed, the air became just a little too busy for a full-sized ship to come down through it safely. There were always some aircar drivers who ignored the general warning to clear the skies, much like automobile drivers who would race a train to the crossing on old Terra before the last two Great Wars destroyed the railroad infrastructure.

Now, shuttles handled the flow of people and goods from space to the port. The only exceptions were the smaller space yachts favored by the ultra-rich. To date, only a dozen ships ever used the yacht bays: the occasional wealthy tourist, the ships seized by the CZC and the Navy from the Fuzzy slavers, and Morgan Holloway's yacht.

Possessing a customs waiver, Morgan wasted no time taking his personal aircar, stored at the port, straight to the Charterless Zarathustra Company Building. With him went two Thoran guards and a secured chest, significantly larger than a bread basket.

The trio was met on the 12th-level parking floor by Chief Steefer and Major Lansky. "Sir, if you will come with us, Mr. Grego is waiting, and very curious, to see you."

"Thank you, Chief," Morgan said. "The sooner the better."

* * *

Victor Grego waited patiently for his Chief Financial Officer to arrive at his office. The message he was sent only said that Morgan needed to see him straightaway. Grego assumed that Morgan was carrying a great deal of money and wanted it stored in the vault immediately. As such he had Chief Steefer arrange for an escort when Morgan arrived.

When Morgan walked in with two Thoran guards carrying a medium-sized chest, he concluded he'd wasted his security chief's time. While both Thorans resembled Terran mastiffs, one had a bare face while the other was extremely hirsute. Different clans?

"Morgan, I am surprised to see you back so soon," Grego said as he shook the younger man's hand. "Did you have some sort of trouble with your ship?"

Morgan looked grim. "Trouble, yes. With the ship, no. Victor, we have problems. Big Ones." Morgan gestured to the chest. He paused a moment then said something in a language that sounded a bit like Old Terran Norwegian. The Thorans set the chest down on Grego's desk, then stepped back. Morgan unlocked the chest with a magnetic key and threw open the lid.

Grego looked at the contents and became confused. "Sunstones. Looks like less than five percent of what you took to Terra. Were you unable to unload these?"

"Look closer,' Morgan said.

Grego looked closer. He couldn't see the problem. He was about to say so when Morgan took a small Geiger counter out of his pocket. It was a Stensentech miniaturized model.

"Watch this." Morgan held the Geiger counter next to the chest. It started clicking and the gauge went up. The radioactivity was slight, little more than that emitted by old glow-in-the-dark watches popular a few centuries earlier, but it was present where it shouldn't have been.

Grego was the first to admit that science was not his field. However, if there was one thing universally understood by a Terro-human, it was radiation. "Good God! Are these the ersatz stones created by Ingermann's gang?"

Morgan nodded. He knew Grego would catch on quickly. "I took my yacht first to Freya then went straight to Terra. When I got there I learned that counterfeit sunstones were flooding the market. In fact, Home Office was taking a beating in the stock market because of it. To reverse the downward spiral, I instituted an exchange program; people brought in the fakes and we exchanged them with the equivalent stone in size and perceived value. These are what came back."

"They were swapped out that fast?"

"Oh, yes. People who can afford a sunstone usually have the means to get around quickly. And to sweeten the deal we threw in a mini Geiger counter like this one so they couldn't be cheated again. Right now, or rather when I left, Home Office was commissioning a private police force to round up the sources of the fakes."

"But how did these get off-planet?" Grego said.

Morgan shrugged. "I have no idea."

Grego gave it some thought, and wondered if Ingermann's crew had worked out a back-alley deal, most likely with the Fuzzy slavers since they had the ships to haul the counterfeits off-world. "I'll bet they arrived on Terra the same time the enslaved Fuzzies did."

Another thought struck him: "Ingermann must not have known he was dealing with Fuzzy slavers, or it would have come out under veridication. Or, maybe, somebody completely unrelated stumbled on one of Ingermann's stashes and smuggled them off-world. We would have to interview a lot of ship personnel under veridication…no point. We don't know what ship and whether or not that smuggler is still employed...we may never find out how these rocks got off Zarathustra. We'll just have to be content with damage control."

Morgan nodded. "That was my takeaway as well. We cut into our profits with the exchange program. These,"—Morgan pointed at the chest—"were swapped out from the load I took to Terra."

Grego estimated the volume of the chest and the per karat value of the stones, had they been real, and whistled. "That looks like about twenty million sols worth."

"Twenty-six point five, give or take a few thousand. I have the actual count on my data pad. Chicken feed to the Company by itself, but the damage to our reputation—not to mention the fact that, there are probably more phony stones out there—and we have a king-sized problem on our hands."

Grego started to feel a little weak in the knees and took a seat in front of his desk. He thought for a moment, then decided on a course of action. "Chief Steefer, I want every available man under your command to take some Geiger counters and visit every shop and store, especially those run by the Company, and grab up any ersatz stones still on planet. If we don't have enough Geiger counters in stock, take a company card and buy up what you need from Henry Stensen. Before you go,"—Grego pointed to the chest of counterfeit sunstones—"put these in secure storage after doing a complete count. We'll hold these as evidence for Marshal Fane when he corrals these mutts. If he corrals them."

"I would issue portable veridicators, too," Morgan said. "While not as accurate as the full-sized model, we should be able to tell if the vendors were aware that they were selling counterfeits or not."

"Good thinking." Grego looked at Chief Steefer, who simply nodded.

Morgan turned to the Thorans. "Assist the Chief, please. I'll wait here."

Steefer nodded again and the Thorans followed him out carrying the chest.

"By the way, how *did* you get back from Terra so quickly? I didn't think you would be here for another six months."

"I bought a new top-of-the-line yacht. The *Adonitia* is still back on Terra with Akira and Little John. This newer model has the latest Abbott Lift and Drive engine that cuts travel time by twenty percent or better. And we crowded it all the way back." Morgan smiled. "Home Office gave me a *very* good deal on it, since they had an interest in my getting back here fast. Of course, increasing my holdings while stock prices were depressed helped."

Grego thought that it was unusually forward-thinking of Home Office. The sunstone market must be even more profitable than he realized. "What did you name her?"

Morgan became more somber. "*The Patricia*." Something on the stand near Grego's desk caught his eye. "Now where did you get a case of Poictesme brandy?" he asked.

* * *

Dr. Mallin set aside the report he was reading to regard the young woman who had just come into his office. "Doctor Tezza, I am pleased to see that you are prompt."

"Thank you, Dr. Mallin. You needed to see me?"

Mallin indicated the chair near his desk and Cindy Tezza took a seat. "I have been going over your transcripts and there is a glaring omission."

"Omission?"

"Field work, Miss Tezza," Mallin said imperiously, forgetting to address her as "doctor." "Xenopsychology is not like what was practiced on Terra so long ago. We are exploring new areas in cultures we are only beginning to understand. We must go out and study these people in their native habitats."

"You mean I need to go to the Fuzzy Reservation and study them at the school?"

"Well, yes, but that isn't really their native habitat." Mallin indicated his viewscreen behind him. The images displayed were that of the veldt and forest. "Areas such as these are where Fuzzies live. There are still thousands upon thousands of them out there that have never laid eyes on a Terro-human. Observing these people will give you the best insights into their culture and psychology."

Cindy shifted in her seat nervously. "Then shouldn't I go north and study the Jin-f'ke? The Terro-human presence there is limited to a trading post at the edge of their territory."

Clearly she keeps up on current events. Mallin shook his head. "Far too much damage has been done there already. The Jin-f'ke's entire culture has changed as a result of Terro-human intervention. They are, in most cases, hostile to our kind...and with some justification. Most of them have gathered into large communities, acting in concert for mutual protection from us. This is a radical shift from what the wandering nomads they were a few years ago. No, we must look at the Fuzzies who have not been subjected to negative contact, indeed, any contact at all, if we want a clear picture of their culture in its pristine state."

Cindy thought for a moment. "Fuzzies have no sense of religion or even history. They only know what they remember from personal experience and not much else."

"Mostly true. However, construction of tools and methods of survival are passed down from generation to generation," Mallin explained. "Not much of a history to us, but to the Fuzzies it is everything. Or it was until we got hold of them."

Cindy smiled. She had the kind of smile that would light up a room and its effect was not lost on Dr. Mallin. "The Reservation school has done a lot of damage in that regard. But without us they were doomed to extinction."

Mallin shook his head. "Some Fuzzies do not have the NFMp hormone that damages their reproductive systems."

"Yes, but if we all went away and left them to their own devices, would the non-NFMp Fuzzies amount to a large enough genetic base to keep the survivors viable?"

Mallin gave his tight little smile. "I see you have given the matter some thought. I think you will do well in the field. In fact, I learned of another young woman, an anthropologist, who has requested permission to do a field study on the Reservation. The Colonial Governor bounced the idea off of me to see if I thought it would be advisable. I advised him to check with Gerd van Riebeek since he is a Xenoanthropologist himself."

Confusion covered Cindy's face. "Isn't the governor an anthropologist, too?"

"He is, but he has been out of the field for some time and wanted to check with me as the Chief Fuzzyologist," Mallin's face contorted a bit when he said "Fuzzyologist." "I have been more involved in the study of Fuzzy psychology than anybody…with the possible exception of Jack Holloway, who is a layman." Mallin shifted in his seat. "But Gerd has been working with Fuzzies in northern Beta, so he should have been consulted."

Cindy could see where Dr. Mallin was headed. "I have the feeling you want me to go farther east on Beta Continent."

Mallin nodded. "Our presence in that area only amounts to flyovers by the Zarathustra Native Protection Force. It's quite possible the Fuzzies in that region might think the aircars are a strange bird or something. You and Miss Ancheta should be able to observe some relatively uncontaminated Fuzzies there. You should take along a security guard or two in case things get a bit sticky. Not for the Fuzzies, but there are a lot of things for which you should be wary."

"I thought the Fuzzy slaver problem was over," she said.

Mallin shrugged. "So far as we know."

"I could bring Erena Taylor," Cindy said. "I know her and I think she would do well."

Mallin shrugged. He was thinking of somebody much larger and more intimidating. "If you like. Just make sure she is up to the job."

Cindy thought about the financial difficulties Erena was having. "Does she get special pay for the assignment?"

Mallin recalled his own trip to Beta when Fuzzies were first discovered. The senior staff saw no bump in pay while the laborers were given hardship pay. He didn't become aware of that until he was temporarily promoted to replace Leonard Kellogg. "Yes, she will."

Cindy nodded. "Then I have no doubt she will be up for it."

XI

"So you left Akira and Johnny on Terra with her parents?"

Morgan's image on the comscreen looked as unhappy as a man could. "I am afraid so, Pa. I had to come back straight away but didn't think it fair to cut her time with her parents short. Thor Folkvar and two of my personal guards are with them and she can return any time she likes in the *Adonitia*. She might even be on her way already."

Jack leaned back in his chair and nodded. He, more than most, understood Morgan's predicament. "Well, with Thor Folkvar and two Thorans I can't imagine how she could get into any trouble. Especially on Terra. Now, what is Victor going to do about the sunstone situation? I don't need any secrets, mind you. Broad strokes will do."

Morgan looked away from the screen, then nodded and turned back to Jack. "First, and most obvious, we will have to talk with Lundgren, the, ah, Sinister Six's computer man, and Joe Quigley Junior and Senior over at Prison House. Brandon Murdock is dead, as is Hugo Ingermann. Doctors Darloss and Rankin are on work release on Beta under Gerd—"

"WHAT!" Jack almost grabbed the comscreen to shake it. "How are they not sitting on death row? Or better yet, dead already?"

Morgan backed away from the screen for a second when Jack blew up, then leaned back in. "Darloss and Rankin were not involved in the death of Sunfur and only learned of it afterwards. The Governor's severe laws-by-edict didn't cover accessory after the fact. That gave the defendants some wiggle room for a plea deal. I thought that you had been read in on that. Anyway, Gerd needed some qualified scientists on his staff and Victor worked out a deal with Ben."

And Ben Rainsford wouldn't say a word to me at the time because I was still recovering from the duel, Jack realized.

"I know you would have preferred to shoot them as a caution to anybody else trying to mess with the Fuzzies, but it really works to our advantage to have them alive and able to speak."

Jack nodded. *You can't question a corpse*, he thought. "What's to keep them from getting away?"

"Aside from miles and miles of nothing, but more miles and miles around the Beta Center? Well, every aircar has a tracking beacon; Victor had those installed right after the Fuzzy Trial to stop any more people from running off with Company equipment. They also have neck collars that will blow their heads off if they move too far from the Center. It is the same kind of collar used by the prison system for furloughed prisoners and work details. They won't even try to leave. And Gerd made sure their living quarters were just like the jail cells they were held in at Prison House."

Not exactly living the life of Riley, Jack thought. "Fine, let's get them into the chair and squeeze them dry. Bring in Captain Trask on that as this crosses planetary jurisdictions."

"Agreed. We will need to borrow the veridicator you got from the CZC during the Fuzzy Slaver crisis."

Jack had forgotten about that. On average, Fuzzies didn't need to be questioned and to the vast majority of them mendacity was an alien concept. And there hadn't been any Big Ones to question in several months. "Will Gerd come and get it or do I send it to him?"

Morgan shook his head. "I'll collect it with the yacht. This new one is still in need of a proper shakedown."

"Shakedown?" Jack said dubiously. "Five-hundred light-years through hyperspace didn't get it done?"

Morgan smiled and shook his head. "It also needs to go through some paces in a gravity well with atmosphere. I won't pretend to understand all of it. Captain Zeudin might be better equipped to explain."

"Maybe later. What can you share about those counterfeit sunstones? I have a fair amount of the real deal socked away for my retirement and would hate to see the bottom drop out of the market."

Morgan's face was replaced by Victor Grego's. "We think these are some of those rocks dug up and irradiated by Hugo Ingermann's crew. How they got off-planet is anybody's guess."

"Might have gone out with the slavers," Jack said.

Grego shrugged. "Maybe, but Ingermann was questioned under veridication before his execution and he knew nothing about that."

Jack thought for a second. "Maybe somebody in his gang was padding the paycheck with a little side action."

"Morgan and I came to the same conclusion," Grego said grimly. "And it is anybody's guess how many more of the fakes are out there."

Zarathustra was a big planet and even when you took a head count it came in at just over one point two million. And there was a Terra-Baldur-Marduk ship coming in every week. Add to that, the private yachts that had been coming and going like crazy over the last year, and it was very easy to see how some sunstones, real and *faux*, could slip away. Jack's first, last and only concern was how it would affect the Charterless Zarathustra Company, the planetary economy and, most importantly, the Fuzzies. Morgan could weather any negative effects on his investments if the CZC collapsed, as he had diversified his portfolio among many worlds. That could not be said of himself, Ben, Gerd or even Victor.

"I'll call Ben and see if he can't scare up some more Marines to cover the Rez and Yellowsand," Jack said. "There might be more of these Khooghras digging up fossils and irradiating them."

Victor Grego shrugged, although he couldn't imagine how anybody could have escaped detection after the dragnet they threw up across Zarathustra during the slaver crisis.

"I have been on the business end of a dragnet or two and know of a number of ways they could escape immediate detection," Jack said. "Curse me for a fool, for not considering them before now."

"No blame to you. We thought those vermin had been eradicated. Nobody considered that the stones might have left Zarathustra. Oh, and something else. There is an amber alert from Zeta. A fifteen-year old girl went missing along with an aircar. The tracker on the vehicle went dark somewhere over eastern Beta."

"Fifteen? She could be in a lot of danger if she is out there on her own. Uh…not to be indelicate, but most people on Zarathustra don't know what Johann's people look like. She could get shot by some fool thinking she was…I don't know what."

"Well, she is short and muscular, though not as much as Heidi. She is like Rheiner; very muscular but with the face of a natural Freyan woman."

A Freyan face, Jack thought, *nobody would shoot at anyone looking like that, at least not on purpose.* "I'll put the Zarathustra Native Protection Force on alert. Can you send me a photo image for us to work from?" Morgan tapped a few buttons and an image popped up on the left side of Jack's screen. "Good looking kid, even if she's built like she could bend a crowbar in half. Why the Amber Alert, though? Freyan women are considered marriage-ready adults at that age."

"On Freya, yes. Here on Zarathustra we adopted the Federation standard of eighteen. This was to keep things civil between the principality and the rest of the planet," Morgan explained. "We wouldn't want our young men taking liberties with underage girls when we start to integrate with the larger populace."

"When," not "if" they started integrating. "And everywhere but Zeta this would qualify as an Amber Alert anyway," Jack added. "Smart. We'll keep an eye out for her. Oh, what is her name?"

"Brünnhilde Autullis."

* * *

Hickabbible Farquar opened the door of his makeshift office to find a dwarf standing in the doorway with a fist raised. He stepped back a bit, then reassessed the man. He was short, perhaps five foot six inches, and so heavily muscled a Terran gorilla would look a weakling in comparison. He only needed a thick beard to complete the image of a dwarf from *Lord of the Rings*.

"Ah…may I help you, sir?" Farquar stammered out.

"Are you Supervisor Sylvinski?" rumbled the dwarf.

"No, I am his deputy assistant, Hic Farquar. May I inquire what business you might have with the Supervisor, Mr…?"

"Hugh Lennon of Magni Colony," Lennon said. "I understand your boss is trying to make things hot for the local government. Don't bother trying to deny it. Magni never had a bunch like yours come through, but I have been on enough planets to know the drill. I also know that the gang running things here is very tight and there won't be any Quislings to give you some ammunition."

He wants something and it'll be big, Farquar thought. "And you are here to give us…what?"

"A foot in the door."

Farquar was doubtful. He knew that Magnians' prided themselves on speaking plain and not resorting to hyperbole, though they could lie as well as anybody. "And which door, exactly, would that be?"

"The fiefdom over on Zeta Continent," Lennon said with a wide smile.

"I believe that is called a 'duchy' or 'principality,' Mr. Lennon."

"They can call it a sultanate for all it matters. It is illegal and I have the documentation to prove that."

Farquar hesitated. "If the Freyan colony is somehow illegal, and I am not saying that is the case, then the local government exceeded its authority by granting it separate dominion and government status. We will need to run it through our lawyer to determine that."

Lennon smiled. "You do that, Mr. Farquar. If you need any help I have some legal beagles ready to assist. But it won't take much."

"We will have to wait for Supervisor Sylvinski to return from Zeta Continent before we can move forward."

Lennon shrugged. It was an impressive display. "I have all the time in this world."

XII

"I forgot, you didn't get here until the rat killing was over with. Let me tell you about our Mr. Stensen...."

Trask turned off the recorder and chuckled. He had fully expected Ned Foster to go to Gus Brannhard and come clean. He chose not to listen in on whatever Gus was going to say about Henry Stensen. The bug he put in the data chip was illegal as all Niflheim, and he didn't want to compound the issue by getting information on an uninvolved third party. For all Trask knew Stensen could be a Federation spook. Whatever he may or may not be, Trask didn't want to know. You can't un-know something once you know it.

As for Foster, Trask had nothing but respect for the gentleman. He was prepared to fall on his sword to protect a man he respected. *Loyalty like that doesn't come around often.* Trask respected Gus, too, for that matter; he saw right through what Trask was doing and laughed it off. He was correct about the statute of limitations and the lack of a complainant. Even if he was wrong, the only real evidence Trask would have had was on the recording, and that was inadmissible as there was no warrant to use the bug.

Trask tapped the delete key and destroyed the recording. Foster might find the bug and he didn't want incriminating evidence on his own computer. Gus could easily get a search and seizure order after the bug was found if he wanted.

The file deleted, Trask started a program that would prevent any remnant of the data from being recovered. It was designed to defeat even Federation Bureau of Criminal Investigation recovery efforts. Nobody would ever find that file on his computer or anywhere else.

Trask's viewscreen beeped. He toggled a switch and the screen resolved to the image of Supervisor Sylvinski. He appeared to be sitting in an aircar of some type. The Supervisor did not look pleased.

"Captain Trask, have you anything to report?" Sylvinski said without preamble or pleasantries.

Trask shook his head. "Nothing you can use—"

"Let me be the judge of that," Sylvinski barked.

"Remember those old Two-D flatties where a spy says, 'I could tell you, but then I would have to kill you?' Well, if I told you, I would have to arrest both of us. Since I don't want to be placed in the awkward position of reading myself my rights, I am going to refrain from speaking about it."

"Look, if you don't cooperate—"

"You won't do a damned thing about it," Trask said in his most reasonable voice. "What I had was obtained under questionable legality, and wouldn't do you any good regardless. And if you tried to bring me up on charges for withholding my data, I would have to disclose the nature and source of that information, and who ordered me to get it."

The past tense was not lost on the commissioner. "Had?"

Trask smiled. "I destroyed it as thoroughly as if I dumped it into a mass-energy converter."

Sylvinski snorted. "You could have just told me you didn't have anything, yet."

Trask nodded. "I could have. I don't like lying. And this way you know where we stand with each other. Let me be clear: I don't like this assignment. It smacks of abuse of power and has me going after people I know to be honest men. That said, I checked and you are within your authority. Barely. But I will not, under any circumstances, skirt the law on yours or anybody else's behalf. If I find something you can use, like it or not, I will turn it over to you as long as it is within the letter of the law."

Sylvinski's face contorted in a manner that Trask couldn't read. Finally, he said, "Very well. I want evidence that will stand up in court, if that is where this ends up going. I have people I must answer to as well, Captain, so every i must be dotted and every tee crossed. Contact me when, and if, you get anything relevant."

"Is everybody in your group that obsessed with i's and tee's? Whatever. I will be in touch, sir." *And I pray to Ghu I don't find a damn thing.*

* * *

Jack Holloway sat behind his desk looking at the four women, and one Fuzzy, standing before him. The first one he knew *intimately*. Betty Kanazawa was fresh off the transport and ready to get to work. The rest were new to him.

One was of obvious African descent, short, thin and attractive. The one in the middle had a slight Germanic accent but was definitely not one of Morgan's friends from Zeta. Something was familiar about her though Jack couldn't place it at that moment. Well, pretty girls always caught his attention so he might have just seen her in passing and it made an impression. Jack quickly recognized the accent as coming from Heimdall, a planet he had visited many years earlier. The third woman, also attractive, had some obvious Asian ancestry. Possibly Filipino? Looking at her, Jack got the sense that she could handle herself in a bad situation.

The Fuzzy, Jack had met before when she was returned to Zarathustra after being rescued from slavers on Terra. "Hello, Rockthrower. Are these your friends?"

"Aunty Cindy and Aunty Erena friends, from Psy-cho Science place," Rockthrower explained. "Not know Aunty Kealani until today."

"Commissioner Holloway," Kealani spoke up, "it is an honor to meet you."

Jack sat a little straighter. "An honor?"

"Yes, sir! You single-handedly discovered the tenth human race. In Xenoanthropology circles you are something of a hero. The news articles about your discovery along with the transcripts from the Fuzzy Trial are now required reading."

Jack refrained from rolling his eyes…barely. The indigenes never got credit for discovering the new sapient species that landed on their planet. "Well, Miss…" He glanced at the application before him, "…Ancheta, most of the credit should go to Little Fuzzy. In all fairness, he discovered me. Now, according to your application, you want permission to go out to eastern Beta in the hopes of observing Fuzzies in the wild? What is wrong with the bunch we have here?"

"Well, ideally, it would be best to see them where Terro-humans haven't interfered with their culture." Kealani tactfully omitted the word "contaminated."

"Hmm. You wouldn't be the first. We had a few xenoanthropologists come out last year," Jack said. "One was killed by a damnthing and another was severely injured by tunnel worms." Jack looked Kealani over to size her up. "That bowie knife there. You know how to use it?"

In answer Kealani stepped back away from the desk and took out the blade then went through a series of moves with it. Her motions were fast, almost a blur, but to Jack's experienced eye she was precise in her actions: no wasted movements, no fancy flourishes; just serious and lethal form. He spotted influences of Filipino Kali in her weaponless hand and arm motions as well as Pensak Silat. Her leg motions were pure Muay; Thai kickboxing style. Jack could easily imagine an opponent being stabbed, punched or kicked into submission.

There was something especially familiar about the woman's overall movements. Jack was certain he had seen them before. "How many martial forms are you trained in?"

Kealani sheathed the blade and returned to her place next to Cindy. "I am adept at Kerambit, though I picked up a few things from other disciplines. My father and uncles are all martial artists in various schools. I am also good with pistol and carbine." She patted her holstered side arm. "I am trained with my Glock 19 and AR-15."

Jack recalled that Glock was one of the companies that survived all the way back from First Century Atomic, though it had changed hands many times and finally relocated to Baldur some two hundred years ago. "Well, I won't have to worry too much about you out there. Just keep in mind that there are critters on this planet that would use that blade for a toothpick." Jack turned to Cindy Tezza. "How about you?"

"I do not know any martial arts aside from some Krav Magraw, Herr Commissioner, but I can handle a rifle. I used to go hunting with *meinem Grossvater*." Cindy was a bit nervous and her Heimdallian accent became stronger. "I was raised on a farm where I fed and cared for the animals and hunted the metabunnies that would get into the crops."

Jack recalled that metabunnies, another example of colonial naming conventions, were herbivores that looked slightly less like Terran rabbits than a zarabunny. They ran up to sixty pounds and could deliver a nasty bite when threatened. They also ran like all Niflheim was after them when frightened. It took a steady hand and more than a little nerve to bring them down. Fortunately, they were good eating.

"Miss—excuse me, Doctor Tezza, are you out here for much the same thing as Miss Ancheta? Will you two be working together?"

"*Nein*. I will be working to observe the Fuzzies' intellectual and emotional reactions to the stimulus of their environment," Cindy protested.

"It was not a question or even a suggestion," Jack interrupted. "I want you and Miss Ancheta working side by side if not exactly together. I don't want to get all sexist, but a woman alone is damnthing fodder. Even with Miss…"—Jack rechecked the documents before him—"excuse me, Mrs. Taylor along for security."

"I suppose you will insist on some big strong man to help us poor clueless women?" Erena said.

Jack chuckled. "Not at all. My sister Pat was all woman and worth three times her weight in damnthings. I don't underestimate anybody based on their gender. No, it is your inexperience with the local flora and fauna out there. And don't underestimate Fuzzies. The mob up north took out a number of slavers very handily. I will require you to take along some help, but it will be a Fuzzy or two. I'll ask for some volunteers. If you are lucky, Maid Marian will want to go. A better archer I have never seen on any planet."

Erena was shocked. "A Fuzzy? But they, um, they're—"

"Small? Compared to a Terran, yes. But they have been surviving out in the wild for umpteen-thousand years, with no help from us. A furry of Fuzzies on dog mounts took down a damnthing last year with spears and arrows." A thought struck Jack. "You will also be taking along a few Curtyses. They will protect you from the smaller threats and even harry a damnthing should it be necessary. Can any of you use a high-powered rifle?"

Erena and Kealani admitted that they could.

"Good. You will need to sign some out before you go into the field. The Zarathustra Native Protection Force armory will have something suitable, I am sure. If not, then go down to Betatown and see Ray Pulver, our local gunsmith and best bore man on Zarathustra. I met him in passing on Mars when I first left Terra, oh, over forty years ago, and he was highly recommended then." Jack indicated the .22 Erena had on her shoulder. "That peashooter will be good for anything small, like a goofer or even a young bush goblin, but it would only get a damnthing's attention, which you *really* do not want."

Jack glanced out the window and spotted a land vehicle. "That ground roller of yours. Does it have silent mode?"

None of the women knew. It had been sent ahead by Dr. Mallin for Cindy and Erena's use in the field. The women had expected an aircar, not a ground-bound rover. "Let's hope it does. That will draw less unwanted attention from the more dangerous animals, and the Fuzzies are less likely to hear it coming from as far away as an aircar.

"Doctor Tezza," Jack tapped the documentation on his desk, "Dr. Mallin spoke highly of your work at Science Center. Miss Ancheta, I know nothing about you though you seem like a solid person to have along on a safari. Mrs. Taylor, I know that Chief Steefer doesn't allow slackers to stay on the payroll. Here are your permits." Jack turned and raised his voice out the window, "Little Fuzzy, do we have anybody who wants to go on a safari?"

Betty, who had stayed silent during the back and forth, turned to the trio and said, "Better listen to him, girls. This man knows more about the flora and fauna on this continent than anybody. Ignore his advice and Beta will eat you alive."

XIII

Supervisor Sylvinski regarded the massive individual standing before him from across his desk. Farquar had escorted the man into the temporary office saying he had something very important to say, the second after he terminated the link to Captain Trask's office. The man before him was short, maybe five and a half feet tall, and well beyond muscular. The chair, on which the visitor sat, strained under his weight.

"Mr. Lennon, I understand you have something you wish to talk about?"

"I see you are back from Zeta. So soon?"

"This was just a flyover to get the lay of the land," Sylvinski explained. "Now, how may I help you?"

Lennon smiled. "I understand that you are trying to bring this government down."

Sylvinski shook his head. "No. Only if it proves to be corrupt or incompetent. So far there is precisely zip to support such charges."

"Of course," Lennon added, "finding something juicy and damning would help to give your career a boost. Let me help. That little fiefdom on Zeta is illegal."

Sylvinski leaned forward on his desk. "How so? They bought the land; or rather it was bought for them, and they have done nothing but erect several little towns and started mining operations."

Lennon looked up at the ceiling as if there were something interesting there. "According to Federation law these people do not have the authority to set up their own little kingdom on a Federation world. Immigrate, yes. Establish a monarchy, no."

Sylvinski thought it over. *If Governor Rainsford authorized an illegal colony, he would be guilty of something.* He wasn't sure of what; that is why he brought along Clarence Burr, the lawyer. He didn't let his hopes rise, though, as Gus Brannhard's Thoran-Imhotep precedent was still on his mind.

Sylvinski shifted in his chair. "Interesting. But I suspect you want something out of this. Mining rights to Zeta, maybe?"

Lennon shook his head. "I have all the mining concerns I can handle now, and have no interest in taking anything away from that colony. No, I just want to take a couple Fuzzies with me to Magni."

Magni? That explained the phenomenal musculature on Lennon. "I am not certain that Fuzzies would be able to survive in the gravity of your world. Then there is the matter of the environment. Magni is a tin-can planet like Mars or Fenris, isn't it?"

"Humph. I dislike the term 'tin can' for our settlement, but you are essentially correct. Magni is believed to have been a rogue planet captured by the primary's gravity well. This is fortunate, actually, as blue giants tend to have a very short lifespan and a planet would not have time to cook properly otherwise."

Sylvinski glanced at Farquar and nodded.

Farquar said, "Blue giants have an estimated stable existence of roughly two million years; give or take a few millennia, before it uses up all of its fuel and degenerates into a black hole or white dwarf or some other form of degenerate matter. It takes a planet around a billion years just to cool off enough to have a solid surface."

"Thank you, Hic," *How does he always have the answers?* Sylvinski returned his attention to the Magnian before him.

Lennon nodded. "Magni is the only planet orbiting the sun, there. That would not be possible unless an astral body entered the system and achieved a stable orbit. Still, there is no atmosphere to speak of, nor native life of any kind."

Sylvinski digested the factoids before speaking. "Then there is nothing I can do to help you, Mr. Lennon. The planet you just described, in addition to tremendous gravity, would be a living death for these Fuzzies. I am no scientist but it doesn't take a genius to see that taking a native from a near paradise, at least compared to Terra, and putting them into an environment consisting of metal walls and canned air would be cruel at best."

Lennon shook his head. "I have no intention of subjecting my

Fuzzies to any such thing. My resources are great and I can afford to create a habitat that would be very pleasant for them. Even as we speak a biodome is being erected that is ten miles in diameter. It will be completely collapsium covered and the outer shell will be equipped with solar panels for power—"

"Ten miles?" *The cost of such a thing would be incalculable!* "Why solar panels? Atomic power is far more efficient and cheaper to use, contrary to what the environmentalists would have us believe."

Lennon smiled. "I know that Fuzzies are extremely sensitive to radiation. They would be sterilized or worse, if subjected to even small doses. Even atomic piles surrounded by collapsium could leak, since we can't hermetically seal the plutonium and still use it for power. And, as we have already discussed, Magni orbits a B2 blue giant. A B2 will kick out enough solar energy to power the dome no matter how large a demand it requires. And it will require a lot, as I plan on equipping it with contragravity. The Fuzzies will be frolicking in a forest that I will install under gravity set to be just like Zarathustra. For them, gravity will be normal, the environment will be pleasant and all of their needs will be attended to. I will even bring in some of the native flora and fauna from Zarathustra."

Sylvinski leaned back in his seat. "And when will construction of this, ah, biodome be completed?"

"It should be ready by the time I leave this planet. But, just to be sure not to inconvenience the Fuzzies, one of my ships will come here to tell me when it is done. I won't fall victim to the old 'two week' estimate."

Lennon fought, successfully, to keep a smile off of his face. He could almost see the wheels turning behind Supervisor Sylvinski's eyes. Could he bring down Rainsford for having an illegal monarchy on planet? Would it nail down the promotion he had been after? Could it also get his hooks in Victor Grego? The wheels turned and turned. They would turn to the Fuzzies, next. Could he legally send Fuzzies out to live on a distant planet if Rainsford was impeached or arrested? Would he be able to get it past the Native Affairs Commissioner? And what about the military base on Xerxes? Would the Navy allow him to take Fuzzies off-world regardless of what was happening to the government?

Sylvinski sighed. “Rainsford is not a professional politician. His claims of ignorance would be readily accepted. Brannhard should know better, but even if we did go after him, Rainsford could simply issue a pardon and he would skip away scot-free. I doubt it would take long to get the colony properly legitimized, anyway.”

Lennon nodded. “Oh, I am quite certain of that.”

Confusion crossed Sylvinski’s face. “Then why suggest it?”

Lennon leaned forward and spoke softly. “Smoke and mirrors. I really don’t want to see the new colonists inconvenienced, although, I imagine, you will have to go there and root around for a bit anyway. But,” Lennon held up a finger,” while you have Rainsford’s crowd working to defend the colony on Zeta, you can go after somebody else in his government. And this is a very important individual.”

“Oh? And who would that be?”

Reaching into his briefcase, Lennon extracted a file that bore the name “Juan Takagashi” on it.

* * *

Carthoris Carter felt happy and proud. He had been selected out of several volunteers to go on this sacred mission. Like most of his brethren, he was a Son of Mars sent out to spread The Word about the truth of the human race. “We Are All Martians” was their mantra. To restore Mars to its original vitality and beauty was their duty.

Not every believer in the Martian Origin Theory was born on Mars. Supporters numbered in the millions all across the Federation and sent such money as they could for the cause. It was unfortunate that even with the millions upon millions of sols donated by fellow devotees it was far from sufficient to Martioform the mother world to its former glory. The expense of towing asteroids made of dirty ice to restore the oceans of Mars ran into the billions and more. Even though the Federation was doing that anyway to keep Mars colony supplied with water, it was too little to restore an ocean and, even if it did, the cost was a drop in the bucket compared to the other projects that would have to be started: restoring the circulation of the magma at the planet’s core, thus rebuilding the magnetic shield, recreating the atmosphere as well as the atmospheric pressure, making the soil arable for new crops to be planted, as well as use genetic manipulation of the lower orders of Terran animals and plants to recreate the flora and fauna of ancient Mars.

Carthoris privately admitted that the genetic engineering idea was, perhaps, a step too far. There were even a few fanatical sects that wanted to create the odd creatures from Edgar Rice Burroughs' and Ray Bradbury's imaginations. Fortunately, wiser and saner minds were in control. It was far better to just select Terran plants and animals that were as close to the original Martian species as possible, and then seed the planet with them.

All that was necessary were some sympathetic scientists and several kings' ransoms to achieve it all. Sadly, the Federation was unsympathetic to the cause. They needed to be swayed to release the funds to make a revitalized Mars a reality. That is where Carthoris came in.

Most of the buildings around him were made of polysteel and collapsium. A few were constructed from Duraglass, a material that was absolutely transparent yet stronger than even polysteel. The Charterless Zarathustra Company Bank and Trust was one of them.

The CZC bank stood directly in front of Carthoris as he approached. He stopped for a moment and inspected his reflection. On Victor Grego's orders the Duraglass on the bank was given a special lamination that acted as a two-way mirror. The people inside could see out as if there were no barrier between them and the outside. Outside, the Duraglass acted as one giant mirror, obscuring the secrets within.

The man in the reflection was up on the latest clothing style; a khaki suit with blue pocket flaps, old-style Australian bush hat, and high black boots with pants legs tucked in the top. The only unusual things were the long coat popular in the American West back in the First Century and the black vest popular with men who spent a great deal of time out in the open country. Carthoris selected the coat to distract attention away from the vest.

Just as Carthoris reached for the door button a voice from behind surprised him. It was a wrinkled elderly man in an old faded space ship uniform, non-military, asking for spare change. Carthoris was about to wave the man off when a thought struck him.

"Sure thing, Pops. Here." Carthoris pulled out his wallet and gave it to the man. "In fact, you can have this watch and my hat, too."

The man stood as if stunned, then slowly accepted the proffered items. "Are…are you sure about this, Mister? I mean, that is a very nice hat, and your identification papers are still in this wallet. I didn't mean to clean you out."

Carthoris laughed. It was an honest, full-throated laugh. "Pops, I don't need that stuff. Not sure, if I ever really did. But it looks like you could use it. Here,"—keys came out of a pocket and made an arc through the air until they were deftly caught by the beggar—"there are three months left on the lease and it is all paid up. Use my apartment in good health. The address is on my ID. I won't need it anymore, either."

"Are you going off-world?"

After a second of thought, Carthoris nodded. "Yep, I guess I am. Help yourself to anything you find in my place. I'll be traveling light and won't be by to collect anything." Carthoris started to check the time, then remembered that he didn't have his watch anymore. *It doesn't matter*, he thought. "It was nice meeting you, Pops. Say, what is your name?"

"I don't always remember it," the man admitted. "Folks around here just call me Parsec Paul."

Carthoris extended his hand and Paul took it. "You have a good day, Mr. Parsec. Oh, and you might want to go over there a ways. You might see something really interesting if you keep watching the glass." Carthoris turned and started for the bank entrance. On the way he pulled off his long coat and tossed it in Parsec Paul's direction with a declaration stating that he wouldn't need it, either.

Parsec collected the coat then retreated across the breezeway. He sat down on a bench and put on his new-to-him hat. He watched the front of the bank for a while until the fog that often overtook his mind started to roll in.

Parsec had just stood up to leave when he noticed a bright flash and something that sounded like a muffled thunderclap issue from the bank. Less than a minute later a police klaxon sounded and several patrol vehicles and an emergency crew arrived.

Through the fog in his mind emerged the realization that the nice man who had given him so much had to be dead. It would take a few hours before Parsec Paul would put it all together and realize that the young man had caused the explosion. He was fortunate that it all slipped away again before he went to sleep on the nice young man's bed.

XIV

"Suicide bomber, Governor."

Ben Rainsford felt weak in his legs. It was fortunate that he was already sitting down. "Why? Who would do such a thing…?"

"A Martianist," Marshal Fane explained. "Vest bomb. Took out about twenty people as far as we can tell right now. The bank tellers were all behind Duraglass partitions but some of the blast went through the slots and speaker mics. Relatively minor injuries for them. Instant cremation for everybody else."

Marshal Fane was about to say more, then noticed that Rainsford looked pale and might even be on the verge of losing his lunch. *Dammit,* he thought, *the Governor isn't used to things like this. Nobody should be.*

"Can…can we be sure it was a Martianist extremist?"

"Security camera recorded the whole thing. The guy came in, looked around for a moment and seemed to hesitate until one of those Company cops decided he was acting suspicious. When the cop went over to the man to see if he was okay, the mutt screamed 'Restore Mars!' Then it went…well, hell, you already know how it went."

Rainsford shook his head. "How does something like this happen in this day and age? The last terrorist attack was, what, over thirty years ago? Just before the Isis Insurrection, I believe. Those idiots wanted to set up a government run by Muslim extremists, for Ghu's sake. What do these Martianists want? And how does attacking an out of the way colony world like Zarathustra get it for them?"

"Mostly, Martianists want to restore Mars to its original state before it lost its magnetic shield and the water and atmosphere leaked out into space." Marshal Fane thought for a moment. "Getting us mad at them won't get them what they want. This planet isn't important enough to make the Feds take a lot of notice."

"Stockholders on Terra will take lots of notice," Rainsford said. "This could be an attempt at a blackmail scheme. For that matter, how do we know that we are the only target? This could have been in the works for years before they all came out to play. This same scenario could be playing out on dozens, even hundreds of other planets right now. Terra, Gimli, Thor, even Mars...."

"Not Mars," The Marshal said. "Mars is like Mecca to these fanatics. No violence on their part would be tolerated by the mainstream believers. But you may be right about the other planets. I think worlds like Fenris and Magni are safe. Blowing things up from inside a tin-can colony could get beyond messy, and that would mobilize the Federation to hunt the entire movement down."

"Well, whatever is going on out there we might not know for another six months or more." Rainsford stood up and walked to his terrace. Marshal Fane followed. "We need to go on full alert, Max. But quietly. We don't want to start a panic. Has the video gotten out?"

"No, I seized it the second I learned of it. Grego's people were very cooperative to that end. That doesn't stop word of mouth, though. Or those damned streamers. If one of those mutts was sniffing around the bank when all Niflheim broke loose, we won't be able to contain it."

Rainsford had a thought. "I would bet these Martianist extremists would have had a man outside to record the incident. There are specialized cameras that can see past the mirrored glass. But, if so, why haven't they released a recording, yet?'

The same thought had occurred to Marshal Fane as well. "They might be waiting for us to give a false story to the press then release their own version. It would make us complicit in a cover-up."

"And cost us the trust of the people," Rainsford finished. "That's a trap we will not fall into. Give a statement to the media saying: no details will be forthcoming until we have made a thorough investigation of the incident. Tell them, we don't want to comment on an ongoing case, not at this time. No cover-up, but no information, either."

Ben is getting good at this sort of thing, Marshal Fane thought. "The extremists will give their own statement sooner or later."

"Unless we find a way to catch them quick, that can't be helped. Great Ghu, I wonder what Victor Grego is going through right now?"

* * *

"How in the hell could something like this happen!" Grego shouted.

Everybody shifted uncomfortably in their seats but nobody spoke. It was most unusual to see Victor Grego lose his temper in a board meeting. Even more unusual to have all the department heads in the same room as the board members. On comscreens were the heads of Beta and Gamma Science Centers.

"God damn it to Nifflheim! All right, we can't undo it, so we need to get on damage control. Chief Steefer, you have a military background. What do you suggest we do?"

The Chief thought for a moment. "A military background isn't what you need, Boss. It's a security expert. Fortunately, with me you get both. First, set up detectors and processing stations at the entrances of every high profile target. They can't spot thermite or Cataclysmite on a person, but the triggering mechanisms will show up well enough."

"You mean to have people empty their pockets, then walk through a detector like at a spaceport?" Evan Amuratsu, born and raised on Imhotep and always sweating in the relatively warm temperatures of Zarathustra, shook his head. "The citizens will object to the bother."

"They would object a whole lot more to getting blown up," Morgan Holloway countered. "People want more than almost anything to stay safe." Morgan turned to Grego. "We should get some trained dogs to sniff out explosives in these areas, also."

Chief Steefer seconded the idea. "We do have some bomb-sniffing dogs down in the kennel and the police force keeps the same on general principle."

"We do?" Thomas Benson, late of Marduk, said. "I agree we need them, but there hasn't been anything like this in decades. Why do we have these dogs?"

"Because it is better to have something and not need it, than to need something and not have it," Grego said. "Almost anything we need on this planet we can make ourselves pretty damned quick. But nothing replaces a trained dog in many areas, and they can't be trained overnight."

"And these dogs belong to the CZC Fuzzies," Chief Steefer added. "As such, most of the expense of keeping them is covered by the Yellowsand mining royalties."

"Okay, what else can we do?" Grego said. "Do we have any lightweight explosive resistant armor we can issue our security forces?"

Juan Jimenez spoke up. "We do have fibroid vests with polymer inserts that are bullet-resistant, but the material is too bulky to make an entire suit out of. The vests, boots and helmets are as good as we can do without hampering the wearer too much."

"Duraglass mazes," Morgan said. Everybody looked at him. "Surely you all went to a funhouse as a child. Even Freya has those. Well, we make a maze like that for everybody to go through when entering a building. Nothing elaborate, just something to put a lot of Duraglass between people while they conduct their business. That way, if a bomb does somehow slip through, the damage would be minimal."

The PR man, Forsythe Andrews, also chimed in. "We can cover their use by having holo images projected in the glass with advertisements and PSAs. The people will assume it is a new marketing ploy."

Trust a public relations executive to make sunstones out of veldbeest droppings, Grego thought. "All right, then. It sounds like we have a plan. Chief Steefer, we will reassign any security people needed by the constabulary. This is something new on this planet and the local law-enforcement officers might need backup. Make sure they get it."

"We should try to find an expert on these Martianists," Conrad Cross, formerly of Odin, said. "Somebody who might understand these *scheisskopfs'* thinking and motivations. Do we have anybody like that?"

From the comscreen dedicated to the Beta Science Center, laughter issued forth. "Indeed we do, gentlemen, and she is currently working at the Alpha Science Center in the psycho-sciences department."

Grego raised an eyebrow. "Who would that be, Gerd?"

Gerd van Riebeek smiled wide. "That would be my lovely wife, Ruth."

* * *

Ray Pulver inspected the rifle bore, then nodded in satisfaction. He loaded two cartridges before handing the rifle to Cindy Tezza. "Now watch it, Sweetheart. It has quite a kick and will try to take your bloody shoulder off, even if you are used to it. Have you ever used a rifle of this size before?"

Cindy shook her head. "No. A .22 is the most I ever needed to use back on Heimdall. I would hunt small game on the farm with *meinem Grossvater*." While Cindy listened intently, something had stirred in the back of her mind. Being called "Sweetheart" by a stranger seemed odd, but instantly sparked deep down memories.

"Hmm…maybe an old-style military recoilless would be better for you. Not as much power, but it will drop anything short of a damnthing. I may still have some old M16L07s lying around. Not the latest in military small arms, but very accurate."

"Yes, that sounds good." Cindy had no idea what an M16L07 was but she grasped the concept of "recoilless" well enough.

"And what about you Angels?" Ray asked the other two women.

Kealani nodded. "The largest I ever used was a 12.7 express rifle. Knocked me on the butt the first few times, but I learned how to handle it."

Ray was a bit surprised. "Jack Holloway uses that model. He took down a damnthing on his property with it. Little thing like you must be tough as nails to handle all that firepower. How is your accuracy?"

Kealani grimaced. "Not great. I do much better with my reconstructed Remington AR-15."

"Hmm…I think you would do better with an M16, also. The M16 doesn't have the power of the 12.7 or even .30-06, but you can use the full auto if something really nasty, like a damnthing, comes at you. It might not kill it, but it will definitely think twice about coming after you. And you, Miss?"

Erena smiled. "Missus. I trained under Chief Steefer. He expected everybody to be able to handle a wide range of weapons. I won't say I can use the 12.7 like Commissioner Holloway, but a .30-06 is doable."

Ray nodded. "Good. Once I check you out on the weapons, you can buy or rent as you like. Since you ladies are together you get the special discount I reserved for Miss Tezza, if I ever met her."

"Discount?" Cindy was surprised. She had never met Ray Pulver before this moment. Then it struck her, "Sweetheart," "Angel": the penny dropped. "You followed my modeling work!"

Ray nodded. "I followed your career, then found you by chance some years after you retired on one of those ancient social sites, when chat rooms were in fashion. I have almost everything you ever did. I am also part of a discussion group centered on your work. You have a sizeable following here on Zarathustra."

Cindy was stunned. The memories of a fantasy relationship with a fan from off-planet seemed so long ago. There was always a few months' turnaround time for the messages to go back and forth, suggesting he was well away from her world. It never occurred to her that her modeling work had made it this far out from Heimdall. "Really? Do you have any favorites?"

Ray Pulver blushed slightly. "There were two sets where you wore this pink and white dress. White ruffled sleeves and a sort of old style bodice. Not sure what it is called. I was very fond of your work in those sets…in and out of the dress."

"Oh! The polka dress. I had to leave that on Heimdall. But, please, don't let anybody know that I am here," Cindy asked. "I am working in a new career area and I don't want to jeopardize it. Not everybody is as open-minded as we are."

"My wife, Denise, will be sad she missed you as I have told her about you. Well, not everything. I am just excited to meet my dream girl in the flesh after all this time," Ray smiled and winked. "Your secret is safe with me, and even more now."

Ray turned back to the other two women. "So, shall we see how you all do on the range out back?"

"What is this?"

Ray Pulver looked down and spotted the Fuzzies. One was pointing at the weapons rack. "That there is a boomerang from Terra. You throw it and it comes back to you."

Rockthrower looked doubtful. In her experience Big Ones would tell her not-so things when she was on Terra. Trust did not come easy to her. "Why come back?"

Ray didn't bother going into the physics. "If you throw and miss, it comes back and you can try again."

Rockthrower was amazed at the concept. "Show me, pliz?"

"Ok, Cobber, but it's been a long time since I have thrown one of those around. Come out the back and let's have a crack at it. And your friend can practice with her bow, too. I have some nice hollow aluminum shafts with Teflon heads she can try out."

Rockthrower could barely contain her excitement as they moved to the range.

* * *

The sun was high in the sky when camp was finally broken. Tents were pulled down, trash burned and buried and, most importantly to the campers, any and all equipment used for capturing Fuzzies destroyed. Communication devices used to contact the Fuzzy Slaver network were also destroyed even though they no longer functioned. Documents with instructions were shredded and burned, clothing that might be considered suspicious also destroyed. Even sono-stunners, anesthezine gas, save for a single canister, and maps depicting Fuzzy migration patterns were eliminated.

"We still need to do something with the cages," Bo said as he looked over the campsite. "What do we do with the Fuzzies?"

Weaver gestured to the sole remaining canister of gas. "We gas the Fuzzies, then take them out of the cages and flatten them. Go over them with the ground roller until they are nice and tight, then toss them into the river. That should confuse the detectors if the ZNPF bring any out."

A scream came from behind Weaver. He turned to see Mai. She had a look of absolute horror on her face. "You are going to kill all those Fuzzies like—"

"What? No! The cages and the gas canisters. We want to compress the metal into an unrecognizable shape and toss it. We can't burn it and we don't have an M/E converter to throw it into. The Fuzzies will just take a little nap and wake up well away from the camp site. This gives us a good head start. I still think we would be better off to kill them all, but

I won't buck the rest of you on this. I'll even go so far as to leave them a good distance from any Wiley tracks and return their weapons. That reminds me; anybody with a souvenir, like a chopper-digger or *coup-de-poing* axe taken from the Fuzzies better leave them behind. Anything that could possibly be connected to the little furballs could give us away.

"After all the whoop-de-do half a year ago, it won't take much for anybody to be grabbed up and questioned. So if you got any keepsakes from this little adventure, leave them with the Fuzzies." Weaver turned to Mai. "If you are going to listen in on somebody else's conversation, make sure you get the whole story before breaking into hysterics."

Mai was too relieved to respond.

"Bo. You got those sunstones?"

Bo pulled out a small bag from a pocket. "Right here, Weave. Picked them up from a fence back in Mallorysport. Want a look?"

"Just keep them safe. We may need to use them to justify our being out here. Now let's get it done, people! Oh, and take the XT3 out of the tins and flatten them, too. Nothing metal stays behind with the Fuzzies."

* * *

"The police are still investigating the blast at the bank this morning. The bomber, identified by the FBCI as Carthoris Carter through an as yet undisclosed source, did not leave any indication of his plans at his apartment. Currently, the police have no comment about the possibility that Carter might have had a connection to the growing Martianist movement. And now, with sports, we have Richard Simon."

"Thanks, Candice. It was a grueling match between the Alpha Zarawolves and the Beta Damnthings..."

Jack turned off the viewscreen and lit up his pipe. From the kitchen he heard Betty say something that he didn't quite catch.

"I said I wish you hadn't turned off the news. I have a bet on the Zarawolves."

Jack snorted out puffs of smoke from his nostrils. "We can get the scores from the datastream," he said absently. His mind was elsewhere. Ever since Terro-humans and Fuzzies came together, Fuzzies had been kidnapped and forced to rob the CZC gem vault, trapped and sold as slaves, then forced to learn how to lie just to convict Thaxter and company. Now there were idiots blowing themselves up and killing innocent people. It was blind luck that no Fuzzies were in the bank. Not that Jack was oblivious to the loss of human life in the terrorist attack, but Fuzzies shouldn't have to pay for Terran stupidity.

"You are thinking about that bombing in Mallorysport, aren't you," Betty asked.

Jack nodded. "Are you a mind reader now?"

"Pffft! That was just on the news when you turned off the 'screen. It doesn't take Carnac the Magnificent to make that connection."

Jack nodded again. "No, I suppose it doesn't. Terrans doing horrible things to other Terrans doesn't bother me as much as the thought of the fallout on Fuzzies. Our species has been doing atrocious things to each other since one cave man clubbed another. That is the human condition. But how do we keep the Fuzzies safe from idiots like that bomber?"

Betty thought for a second. "What is Victor Grego doing about it?"

"Ben says he is adding trained dogs to the security force. The kind that can sniff out explosives."

"Hmm…it would take a long time to train our dogs over here. Assuming that they are capable. Not every dog will understand what is required. Say, isn't a Fuzzy's sense of smell almost as keen as a dogs?"

Jack thought it over. Taste and smell were closely linked in *homo sapiens terra.* Fuzzies had the keenest sense of taste of any known sapient species. That should mean their sense of smell should be highly developed as well. Assuming that they were wired enough like the Big Ones. Fuzzies working outside and inside of buildings as bomb detectors. Something would have to be set up to protect the Fuzzies in the event another bomb went off near them. A Duraglass partition near their post might work. Jack explained his theory to Betty.

"I'll call Mr. Grego's secretary and ask her to relay that idea," Betty said. "I think they will have to run tests to see if you are right."

Jack grunted, still deep in thought. An idea struck him: "If the Fuzzies can sniff out explosives, it might be better to have them walk the streets sniffing people and buildings. Cataclysmite smells like all-Niflheim to a human if you get close enough, and a Fuzzy can communicate better than any dog."

"Oh, that sounds like a great idea," Betty said as she came out of the kitchen. "I'll bet the Fuzzies would love helping out us nose-blind Big Ones." She took a seat on the sofa. "Now, what about that dishwasher you said you were going to have installed?"

XV

Ruth van Riebeek exited the lift and went to Myra Fallada's desk. Before she had a chance to announce herself, Myra told her to go right in. "Mr. Grego is expecting you."

Well he should, since he is the one who called me up here, Ruth thought. "Thank you."

Ruth went through the doorway and froze. She took in the office with the contragravity representation of Zarathustra orbited by Darius and Xerxes, not to scale, of course. She had never been in Victor Grego's personal office before, not even when she was an agent for the Navy spying on the Chartered Zarathustra Company. Even though Grego rehired her, she was always a bit nervous around him. Spies, on average, don't make nice with the target of their vocation after being outed.

"Ruth, please come have a seat."

Ruth turned and saw Grego seated at his desk with Dr. Mallin and Marshal Fane. She had no idea what she had been called up for and that added to her agitation. She took the proffered chair between Mallin and the marshal and tried to steady her nerves.

"How are the children doing?" Grego asked.

"Doing well, sir. Gerd, Junior is finally out of quarantine."

"The artificial antibodies are working?" Dr. Mallin asked.

"Yes, Doctor. After all this time, we were finally able to take him home from the hospital," Ruth explained. "May I ask what this is all about?"

Confusion crossed Grego's face, then understanding. "My apologies, I should have realized how this must look with your immediate supervisor and the Marshal here. You are not being called on the carpet, Ruth. We want to pick your brain a bit."

"Pick my brain?" Ruth glanced at the senior psycho-scientist. "What could I possibly know that Dr. Mallin doesn't know better?"

Mallin shook his head. "I imagine there are any number of things you would know better than I, Dr. van Riebeek, given the differences in our life experiences. In this instance we would like to hear your thoughts on the Martianist movement."

"What?" Ruth recalled Gerd that once called her a closet Martianist. Naturally, his sense of humor had kept him from explaining to her what Mr. Grego wanted to see her about. A little late payback, for not telling him she was spying on the company, way back when they first became involved. "What would you like to know?"

Grego explained what they knew about the bank bombing and Marshal Fane added what they suspected. "I invited the Marshal to listen in, as whatever information you might have, may be useful to him as well."

Ruth shook her head. "I don't know if I will be of much help. I was never a member of the Martianist movement; just a curious observer."

"Your background in the psycho-sciences makes you a trained observer," Dr. Mallin said. "Not to mention your other vocation with the Navy. Please share those observations."

Ruth gathered her thoughts, then started began: "As you surmised, these are not the mainstream members of the Martianist movement, who are peaceful on the whole. This would have to be an extremist faction, which would make them much more dangerous. I never interacted with any of the extremists, as far as I know, but their motivations would seem fairly obvious. They want to restore Mars to its original viability as a Class IV planet—"

"Don't you mean, Class III? It was uninhabited, after all," Marshal Fane interrupted, "until the Federation established its first colony."

"Not according to them. Remember: 'We Are All Martians' is their credo. We haven't colonized Mars; we just went home, as they see it. And they believe Freyans are a lost Martian colony, closer to the true Martians, than us Terrans."

"Closer how?" Grego asked. "Freya is something like three hundred light-years from Mars."

"Unlike Terra, Freya didn't have any indigenous monkey boys to interbreed with, as Gerd would say," Ruth explained. "The Martianists think the old Martians developed something like the hyperdrive to get to

Freya, then some sort of accident caused them to lose all physical evidence of their origin. Oral tradition would only keep the memory alive for so long before it became a myth or legend, and then was lost altogether. I suspect that if Martians did colonize Freya, the original colonists became the basis of their religion."

"DNA analysis proved centuries ago that some of our genetic makeup came from the Neanderthals," Dr. Mallin explained. "As such, we would not be considered pure Martian stock like the Freyans."

Ruth paused as she considered possibilities. "Freyans are revered by the Martianists, as a result. But Zarathustra is an out-of-the-way backwater planet with a miniscule population. Even with the sunstone revenues these extremists couldn't extort enough money from us to forward their mission to restore Mars by even a fraction of a percent. There has to be something else they want."

"Maybe somebody of importance to them is in Prison House," Marshal Fane suggested. "This could become something like 'release Jor-El or more will die.'"

Grego chuckled. "Wrong planet. But you might be on to something. Ruth?"

Ruth shook her head. "No, the bomber said 'Restore Mars,' not 'Free Jor-El' or whomever. They are not after a person."

"Okay," Marshal Fane said thoughtfully. "It isn't attention, as we are too far from, well, everywhere to get any notice. It isn't money since, for their needs, we wouldn't be able to pony up enough to do any good. It isn't a person of interest to them. So what's left?"

"Some *thing*," Mallin said. "Now we just need to figure out what that thing is."

"No we don't," Grego said, with some disgust. "They'll tell us. Right before or after the next suicide bomber strikes."

* * *

The veldt dominated the horizon with just a tree here and there to break up the monotony. The vehicle rested firmly on the ground with the contragravity off and the hatch wide open. Standing a few meters away was the young woman who had been forced to make the landing. She yelled something at the aircar in a language few people on Zarathustra would be able to understand. When she had exhausted her limited knowledge of Freyan and German invectives, she settled down and sat on the edge of the open hatchway.

"It's my own fault," Brünnhilde groused. "Father said the aircar needed maintenance but like a fool I took it anyway. He should have told me the power cell was nearly exhausted!"

Brünnhilde didn't understand why the radio didn't work. She assumed that it was supposed to be powered by the now dead power cell instead of having a separate power supply. Power cells lasted oomphty-thousand hours, normally, and rarely ran out of power so the designers probably didn't think it necessary to add a second battery for emergencies. Most of the aircars and other equipment were all second-hand in Neu Freya. The power cell for the aircar could be twenty years old, for all she knew.

Even more annoying was the fact that there was plenty of solid fuel. The problem was that without contragravity, she couldn't get off the ground to use any of it. Aircars were not the least bit aerodynamic, since the contragravity provided all of the lift.

Brünnhilde considered sitting still and waiting for somebody to find her. That lasted for one night. When she got hungry, she found only Terran Federation Armed Forces Emergency Ration, Extraterrestrial Type Three and some protein bars. She had never tried XT3 before though she was well aware of its reputation. Her people's metabolisms being what they were, she knew she couldn't go long without food.

Grimacing, Brünnhilde extracted a tin from the stored rations and opened it. She sniffed it and decided it smelled mostly like a pound cake, not much different from the occasional treat she had on Magni. Pulling a pinch worth out of the tin, she tasted it.

"Gods above and below, this is worse than I thought!" she exclaimed. Brünnhilde considered tossing the remainder away. Two things stopped her. First, it was against the Freyan way to leave debris on the ground. She heard horror stories of how Terra was polluted beyond measure before the last two Great Wars. The second was that she had to eat something and didn't see any other options at the moment. XT3 was offensive to the pallet, to be sure, but nutritionally sound and would keep even a genetically engineered Freyan going for a good long time.

"Be it so unpleasant, that which must be done 'tis best done quickly," Brünnhilde paraphrased the line from some Terran play she'd seen. Throwing the contents of the tin down as quickly as she could, she finished it all, then drank a quart of water, hoping to kill the aftertaste. "By the Gods, I would rather eat an animal raw than any more of this stuff!" She debated having one of the protein bars, then decided against it. No telling how long it would take to be rescued and she knew very little about what was safe to eat on Beta Continent.

After thinking it over, Brünnhilde decided that waiting for help was not the best plan, since nobody knew where she had taken the aircar. So, she gathered up all the supplies she could. Fortunately, she had had the foresight to bring along a backpack with a medical kit before running off with the aircar.

She had hoped to do some hiking near the Rez and maybe see some Fuzzies. As yet, no Fuzzies had been brought to Zeta Continent. Brünnhilde knew that Fuzzies were sapient beings that humans were allowed to adopt. It didn't seem fair that none of her people had any as yet. Her father, Gunther, insisted that they were not ready for the added responsibility. The colony was still young and there was much to do before they could be responsible for the well-being of other sapient beings.

Brünnhilde accepted her father's explanation. It wasn't that long ago that her family had labored in the mines. Even children, as young as seven winters, had toiled in the Magni earth. New mining concerns were being opened up on Zeta Continent to make the colony self-sufficient. However, there were other positions that needed to be filled that her people had little to no experience in.

The Magnian slavers had not made any effort to teach their slaves anything more than what was necessary to work the mines, a few support positions and communicate with the masters. Language and how to use mining equipment was nearly the sum total the slavers had permitted them to learn. Fortunately, much had been handed down by word of mouth, through their mother tongue, Sosti, arithmetic, Freyan history and even some limited science.

Running a new colony required a great deal more knowledge. When John Morgan wrested their freedom from the slavers, he immediately set up learning centers with teaching machines. By the time he could arrange for the Magni-Freyans to be transported to Zarathustra, most of the freed men and women could hold their own in a middle school environment.

Now, with the new colony, most people were learning new jobs from the beginning with the help of the Charterless Zarathustra Company, as part of the mining agreement with Victor Grego. Sadly, as Gunther explained, an entire colony of people being trained from scratch didn't have the time or ability to work with the Fuzzies.

Well, if the Fuzzies couldn't come to Brünnhilde, then Brünnhilde would just have to go to the Fuzzies. Taking her father's aircar, one of the few in Neu Freya, she took to the sky and headed west to Beta Continent, which led to her current circumstance.

Brünnhilde filled the backpack with as much as it could carry: XT3, protein bars, water, extra clothing and anything else she could scavenge from the downed aircar. The .500 Magnum and two boxes of ammunition from the glove box she tucked into her belt and backpack. When done, the pack weighed over seventy kilos. For Brünnhilde the weight was easily dismissed. Checking her compass, she chose west and proceeded.

In the distance, she spotted a large animal that looked like the damnthings she had learned about in school since making planetfall. It was a large animal, about the size of a Terran rhinoceros, which had a single horn on its forehead and one on either side of the lower jaw. Even her people found it prudent to give such creatures a wide berth. The damnthing was grazing on the willow-grass and hadn't seen her. She slowly ducked down so as not to draw its attention through sudden movement.

Carefully, she made her way through the high grass until she found a shallow ravine. Brünnhilde jumped down then started running as fast as the uneven terrain would allow. She vowed to fashion a weapon of some sort as soon as she was safe, after cursing herself for a fool for not bringing her father's rifle.

She doubted even the .500 Magnum in her belt could stop a damnthing. A sturdy spear might be better, she thought. While she enjoyed the phenomenal strength and vigor all of the engineered Magni-Freyans possessed, she had no illusions that she could face something like a damnthing or zarawolf without some serious weaponry.

* * *

The aircar slowed as it approached Beta Continent. While there were no ordinances requiring air traffic to slow to subsonic speeds, it was considered rude to create sonic booms over inhabited areas. With the discovery of the Fuzzies, virtually the entire northern region was considered an unofficial "speed zone."

Cinda looked out over the landscape below her. The last time she came to Beta Continent was for the big party at the castle. In fact, that was her only time. Most of her time on Zarathustra was on Alpha and Zeta continents.

"How long has…um…Broomhilda? How long has she been missing?"

Rheiner shrugged. "Brünnhilde. I don't know for certain. Die alert came out around tvelfe hours ago."

"Great Ghu, I hope some prospector or hunter doesn't find her first," Cinda said. "Most people on Zarathustra have never seen one of your people and might mistake her for…um, something—"

Rheiner chuckled. "Ve know dot most of *mein* people look strange to ot'ers. Brünnhilde ist in no danger by dot. She ist like me, a t'rowback, to vhat *mein* people looked like before die experiments. Her face vould be considered qvite beautiful dough she ist still fery muscular."

"Oh! Is this one of your daughters?"

Rheiner laughed out loud. Cinda knew that Rheiner was required to father as many children by as many Freyan women as possible. As a throwback himself, the Freyans hoped his contribution would help the following generations to reclaim their original beauty. "I am only zwanzig…um, tventy vinters. Brünnhilde ist fifteen. I vas not so precocious at six as to be her sire. I am only die first, ah, t'rowbeck. Not die only. Brünnhilde ist die next eldest und first of die females. Die eldest of my offspring ist four vinters. So far all of *mein* kinder are also t'rowbecks."

"I see. Since you and she are both throwbacks, as you say, will you be expected to marry her, to help generate more?"

Rheiner shook his head. "*Nein*. Ve marry who ve vish. She may efen leave Neu Freya und go out into die galaxy und find a mate among natural Freyans or efen Terrans. Ve do not dictate who marries who."

"But you are required to, um, impregnate multiple women...."

"Perheps required ist too strong a term. Reqvested ist better." Rheiner thought a moment then smiled and added, "Any young man ist easily directed into such t'ings, I t'ink."

Cinda laughed. Rheiner was certainly correct on that score. "You don't seem too worried about Brünnhilde."

"Ach. *Ja und nein*. She ist young *und* ignorant of dis vorld but still she ist a Magni-Freyan. Very few t'ings can harm us, if ve are careful." Cinda recalled the multiple gunshot wounds Rheiner shrugged off when they were captured by the Fuzzy slavers. He didn't exactly enjoy being shot and the bullets didn't bounce off his tough skin, but he wasn't slowed down in the least.

"*Und* she ist a bright vun, if not mature enough to make goot decisions, yet. I t'ink ve vill find her alife *und* vell. Maybe a bit hungry *und* homesick. Still, dere are a few t'ings in de vild dat I vhould not vant to meet, so I don't vant her to be lost too long."

"*Want* her lost?"

"*Ja*. On Freya it ist normal for a boy to go off into der vilderness vhen he ist t'irteen vinters. It ist a rite of passage. My people haff not done dis vhile ve vere slafes, obfiously, but die old vays are coming beck und ve are not limiting dis by chender. A small veak *Fräulein* from Neu Freya ist more den a match for effen der mightiest men on old Freya. Brünnhilde ist chust doing it a little more recklessly den I like."

Cinda had another question but was unsure how to phrase it so as not to give offense. "Are there many Freyans, um, like you...?"

"Some. I vas die first to look, ah, more normal. Dere are t'ree more males und two females, including Brünnhilde. Dis ist not counting die kinder dat I haff sired. Six boys und t'ree girls. All are like me und Brünnhilde."

"All of them?" Cinda thought a bit about it. The gene clusters that accounted for Rheiner's appearance had to be a dominant trait. For all of his offspring to have the same traits might mean that the gene tampering that created his people might have been flawed and was weak by comparison. She set that aside. She was a geologist, not a genealogist. "Are these women married? The ones you, um, work with?"

Rheiner nodded. "*Ja*. It vould be unfair for die *Frauen* to raise die *Kinder* alone. Dere ist some assistance from der *neu* government, of course."

"And the husbands do not object?" Cinda had some difficulty imagining that a man would cheerfully allow his wife to be impregnated by another man.

Rheiner shrugged, which was an impressive display with his musculature. "On Freya *dere* ist a tradition vere vhen a man cannot sire *Kinder*, he chooses anot'er man to perform die task. The surrogate *fa'ter ist* invited to *das Heim* home for a veek or so vhile *der Mann* goes out hunting, or some odder pretext. Vhen he returns die couple vait for a mont' to see if die *Frauen* ist vit' child. If not, die process is repeated, sometimes vit' die same, ah, donor, sometimes a *neu* surrogate ist chosen."

Cinda recalled that one of her university professors was from Kenya where they had a similar tradition. "And you are the surrogate of choice, then?"

"Ach! Mine ist a unique role. Since ve are trying to reclaim our original appearance. Many choose not to participate. It ist a matter of choice." Rheiner glanced at the chronometer on the instrument panel. "Ve haff been at dis for six hours. I vill set down so ve can eat lunch, den ve can try again."

Cinda glanced back at her two sleeping Fuzzies. "Sarah and James should enjoy a quick romp out on the ground. No doubt the dogs could use a break as well. I hope Brünnhilde doesn't run into any trouble."

"Ha! I hope trouble doesn't run into Brünnhilde."

XVI

Governor Rainsford, Chief Prosecutor Brannhard and Assistant Prosecuting Attorney Ned Foster faced Supervisor Sylvinski, Deputy Commissioner Farquar and Clarence Burr, Esq. from across the conference table. On the table was a voice recorder in place of a stenographer.

"You requested this meeting," Rainsford said, "so why don't you start?"

Sylvinski nodded and opened a file. "I understand the new colony on Zeta Continent operates under a monarchist style of government."

Gus made a so-so motion with his right hand. "Loosely. They are basing their system of government on that of Freya. As such they consider their realm a principality, though they will call it a duchy until the ruling sovereign on Freya recognizes it. However, things are run primarily by a Bürgermeister, who acts as sort of mayor."

Burr spoke up, "Is this person elected by popular vote?"

"More like general consensus. Herr Torseus is John Morgan Holloway the Lesser's right hand man. The Freyans regard Mr. Holloway as a liberator and prince of the realm. Traditionally, the prince of a realm designates a Bürgermeister to handle the day-to-day business of running things, and then acts as prince regent when the prince is away tending to other matters."

Sylvinski looked confused. "The Native Affairs Commissioner?"

"No," Rainsford said. "His son, who is half Freyan by birth. Commissioner Holloway is designated as 'the Greater.' It's a Freyan naming convention."

Nepotism in government, Sylvinski wondered. Frowned on but not technically illegal. "Then it is a monarchy. As such its presence on a Federation colony world is illegal."

Gus snorted. "I thought we already settled this. The Thoran colony?"

"Is recognized as a legitimate governing body by the Thoran ruling class," Burr said. "Does the colony on Zeta possess the same level of recognition from the Freyan king?"

While Gus searched his memory for a precedent that rendered such recognition unnecessary, unsuccessfully, Ned Foster spoke up. "They have six months real time to attain such recognition from Freya."

Bless you, boy, Gus thought.

"Real time?" Sylvinski whispered to Farquar.

"Six months plus travel time to and from the planet they need the recognition from," Farquar responded. "With travel times varying from world to world this was a necessary stipulation in virtually all contracts between planets."

How does he always know these things? "And how long has it been thus far?"

"Excluding the travel time, we have a month or so to go," Rainsford stated.

"And this lesser Holloway is attending to this?" Burr asked.

"It is my understanding that Mr. Holloway is visiting Freya," Gus said. "What his exact business there is you will have to find out from him when he returns."

"And when is this, exactly?" Sylvinski asked.

"We would have to ask Jack…that is, Commissioner Holloway about that," Gus replied. "My understanding is that it could take a year or more to make the round trip as he is also visiting Terra en route."

Sylvinski affected a somber mien. "That would put him several months out of the grace period."

"The contract is considered valid at the time it is signed by the proper authorities. We will have to wait until Morgan Holloway returns to see if it is within the grace period," Ned Foster countered.

Sylvinski glanced at Burr, who nodded. "Very well. In the meantime I will need to visit this Neu Freya to see if any other infractions have occurred."

Rainsford frowned. "That could be a problem, Supervisor. The Freyans are somewhat insular and discourage visitors."

"It would be a much larger problem for them, if I am barred from access to their little colony," Sylvinski said. The threat was implied not just in the words but his tone of voice as well.

"Governor," Gus said, "I am sure I can smooth things over with Bürgermeister Torseus. Besides, I would love to escort our guests there." *And watch the expressions on their faces when they meet the residents.*

* * *

Junktown, the last stop for many of the disenfranchised citizens of Zarathustra, was still largely made up of clapboard shanties and hovels. The combined efforts of the Charterless Zarathustra Company, along with the humanitarian works of Clancy Slade, had succeeded in raising some low-cost housing and single occupant pods.

Rubbing elbows with Junktown was Mortgageville. It was the collapse of Mortgageville that led directly to the formation of Junktown. Almost entirely vacant, Mortgageville consisted of closed businesses, abandoned warehouses and even a few small hotels, also closed.

In the conference room of the Bactria, a small closed inn on the border between Mortgageville and Junktown, sat several men and women around a long table. Each person had a name plate in front of them. To the casual observer the names appeared to be fanciful aliases. They were not.

"Carthoris Carter was successful in his mission," said the man with the nameplate that declared him to be Tars Tarkis. "The opening salvo has been launched. We will need to be more careful, now. From now on, use the mundane aliases that will allow us to blend in with the local populace."

"I have written up our manifesto," Ulysses Paxton said. "I can have it transmitted from a blind terminal at one of the cafés to any news outlet we choose."

"We may have to have a few more demonstrations before we are considered a real threat," Dejah Thoris added.

Tars Tarkis nodded. "Not to worry; we have several more volunteers available on this planet. A few are actually chomping at the bit to become a martyr to the cause."

"I only hope they haven't relocated the artifact to some other world," Ras Thavis groused. "It could be a hundred light-years from here by now."

"I doubt it," Tars Tarkis countered. "Anything as large as the artifact would require a *Leviathan* class transport ship to get it away from Zarathustra. The CZC does not have anything like that on or near this world. In fact, up until recently they didn't have any interstellar capability at all. And the hyperspace yacht they acquired is far too small for the job. That means they will have to send for a transport. The nearest world to have anything like that is Yggdrasil."

"Yggdrasil?" Tan Hadron said with surprise. "What would the Chartered Yggdrasil Company need with a *Leviathan*-class transport?"

Ras Thavis snorted. "To take guano back to Terra for the soil reclamation project in the northern hemisphere. I think some of it is also diverted to Australia in an attempt to make the outer areas of the Outback arable."

"Just so," Tars Tarkis nodded. "And as such the Navy couldn't just walk in and commandeer one. I suspect they would have to request one from Terra, six months travel time for the request, incalculable days or weeks before the government approves the request since the Navy doesn't keep such ships, as far as I know, then six months return time."

"Three months return time," Vor Daj corrected. "The transport is unlikely to stop at every planet between here and Terra, so it would be a lot faster on the return trip."

"I had not considered that but you are correct," Tars Tarkis said. "The artifact is nearby though I wouldn't count on it staying much longer. The transport could arrive any week now."

"We will have to accelerate our plans," Dejah Thoris said. "We need to select our next targets carefully."

"Why don't we just abduct the Governor and hold him for ransom?"

Everybody turned to look at Gahan Gathol who had been silent up to that moment.

"The Governor is too well protected," Ras Thavis said, shaking his head. "His office is in the same building as the constabulary, and after the bombing everybody will be on high alert."

"There is another, possibly even better target," Ulysses Paxton said. "And I doubt he has any idea that he even needs protection."

* * *

Mallorysport Spaceport had two settings: nearly empty and packed to overflowing. It was easy to anticipate which it would be by the hyperspace ship schedule. When a ship was in, things got crazy. No ship, no crazy.

The City of Neu Stuttgart was currently in geosynchronous orbit, hence the insanity that surrounded the blond man as he worked his way through the crowds. He had no luggage save for a backpack of Freyan design. His boots and metal bracers also spoke of a Freyan origin.

He passed the information booth and the travel advisory board and went straight out to the line of taxis. After scanning the line of available cabbies he waited until several had left then went to the next in line.

"Where to, Bubba?"

"An inexpensive hostel, if you please."

The cabbie studied his new fare's face for a moment. "Have I picked you up before? Your face is familiar, but I can't quite place it."

"In your line of work I would imagine you have seen thousands of faces," the fare said. "Surely they would start to blend together after a while."

The cabbie nodded. "That they do, but some tend to stick out and stay with me. A few weeks ago I picked up a guy with a face like none I had ever seen before. Built like a tank, he was. Really nice fellow. Well, if I have seen you before it will come to me eventually. After a cheap room, eh? Squeamish about being around the underclass?"

The fare shook his head.

"Okay. There is a place not far from Junktown. It can be a little rough if you aren't careful. Maybe you would be able to swing slightly better digs?"

Again, no.

"Okay, it's your nickel."

"My what?"

The cabbie guffawed. "Nickel. Old unit of currency on Terra worth around five centisols, give or take. You must be from Freya." The fare nodded. "From what I have heard about your people you can mix it up pretty good when you have to. All the same, I hope you have a dependable sidearm."

"I do, and your caution is well taken. *Kr'enta*! I forgot to exchange my currency. Can you except Freyan *gilkas*?"

"I can, but you would get a better rate in the station or at a bank," the cabbie said. "Let me see what you have." The fare pulled several coins from a pocket. "Great Ghu! Those are gold! You will definitely want to take those to the bank. Better rate than I or the station can give you. I think you can afford better accommodations than you thought, too."

"No. After the bank take me to this Junk Town, coachman."

"Coachman! You really are from Freya. Call me Al, Bubba."

"Certainly, Al. And my name is not Bubba. Merlin is close enough."

XVII

Captain Buck Trask looked at the indigent man across from him with a growing sense of impatience. *It isn't his fault that he can't keep things straight,* he reminded himself. *It was something on a level with a small miracle that the man had come forward at all.*

"Sir, can you think of anything else the man said or did?"

Parsec Paul, cleaned up and wearing the clothing he found in Carthoris Carter's apartment, fought to recall anything else and failed. Even under the best of circumstances his memory was dodgy. If not for the fact he saw the news broadcast about the explosion, he might never have made the connection between the incident and the nice young man who gave him so much.

Lt. Williams operated the veridicator while Trask asked the questions. "So, you approached him for some spare change and he just gave you everything he had?"

"Yes, sir. He just gave me his wallet and coat and keys, and said he wouldn't need them anymore. I gave the cops the wallet. They didn't want the money, too, did they? I still have most of it...."

The light over his head stayed an unwavering blue.

Trask shook his head. Parsec Paul had answered every question put to him with Ghu's own truth and the veridicator bore him out; that is, when his mind was clear enough to form a cogent memory. He simply didn't know anything else of value.

"Thank you, Mister...um...Parsec?"

"No mister needed, young fella. I seem to remember being a captain on a hypership but I can't be sure anymore, so just Parsec Paul will do," he said. The globe still stayed blue. "Say, will I be able to go back to the apartment the man gave me? It's so much better than my place over in Junktown."

"I am afraid not, mi—Parsec Paul. We will have to let the forensic techs go through it and that might take a while." Trask reflected that on Terra, where all of the latest tech was available, the apartment could be processed in a day or two. This wasn't Terra and the equipment was at least a few years behind what he was accustomed to. "We will arrange for other accommodations. After everything is processed and, if Mr. Carter has no family on planet, the contents of the apartment will be yours since you say he gave it all to you and the veridicator backs you up. Jason Roberts is coming to pick you up. We will give him the voucher for your temporary lodgings and another for lunch, since you have been kept here through the dinner hour."

Parsec Paul brightened up. "Two meals in the same day, and I didn't have to go to the Soup Kitchen to get it."

"Two?"

"Mr…um, Carter? He left a full fridge and pantry. I like the Soup Kitchen, but hate getting handouts too often."

The intercom buzzed. "Captain, there is a Jason Roberts here to collect Mr. Paul."

Trask acknowledged the call and Lt. Williams unhooked Parsec Paul from the veridicator. "Looks like your ride is here. Lt. Williams will see you out. Oh, and we will expedite going through the groceries and send them to you." *Poor bastard looks like he needs them.*

"Lt. Williams, swap out Parsec Paul's money with its equivalent from petty cash. Forensics will want a go at it."

After Parsec Paul was shown out, Trask returned to his office and turned over what little he had in his mind. Martianists on a backwater world some five hundred light-years from Mars—what the hell were they doing here? That it was Martianist extremists was not in doubt. Even without the pre-death exclamation of "Restore Mars," it was fairly obvious. The wallet Parsec Paul turned in contained all of Carthoris Carter's papers: aircar license issued on Mars, travel permit, also from Mars, a list of addresses with one, the CZC bank, circled, a picture of what might have been the dead man's wife or girlfriend and, according to Paul, some six-hundred odd sols, now gone.

Trask's mind circled around something Parsec Paul had mentioned. Three month lease on the apartment, paid in advance, and a solid wad of cash for walking-around money. Carthoris Carter didn't come to

Zarathustra just to go all blowie-uppie; he had expected to stay a while. What, or who, changed his mind?

The name was enough to mark the terrorist as a denizen of Mars. In the old Edgar Rice Burroughs novels, Carthoris was the son of John Carter and Dejah Thoris. The Mars Colony residents tended to go overboard in identifying with the fanciful fiction about the planet. The fad to name children after the characters went in something like thirty-year cycles. *If they ever find an Old Martian phonebook with real Martian names in it, there will be a lot of renaming going on.*

But why export their lunacy to Zarathustra? Even extremist terrorists had to have some sort of justification, at least to themselves, for committing mass murder. Trask went down a mental list of possibilities and dismissed them in turn until he came to the last; there was something on Zarathustra the Martianists wanted. Something no other planet had. But what? He would have to speak with Marshal Fane and maybe Victor Grego to find out. Then it hit him. *Wasn't there some sort of whoop-de-doo over a rocket ship of some sort before I came to Zarathustra?*

Glancing at the list again, Trask made a note to follow up on the other addresses and would advise Marshal Fane to assign some officers to watch them. He glanced at the wall chronometer and grimaced. He would have to break his date with Janice Goodfellow. Too bad for the Martianists if he caught them. He didn't appreciate having his dinner plans thwarted.

Trask typed out a combination on the comscreen keyboard. A woman appeared on the screen. "Marshal Fane's office. May I help you?"

* * *

"Gotta be Martianist extremists," Jason Roberts said.

From the cockpit Mike Hammer asked, "What Martianist, Boss?"

Jason smiled. Every other Fuzzy on the planet called their Big Ones "pappy" or "Mummy." Mike Hammer recently switched to "Boss." *Now which Mickey Spillane book did he pick that up from?* "Martianists are people that believe all Big Ones came from Mars, Mike."

"Mars is a planet like Zarathustra or Terra, but not as nice," Parsec

Paul added. "I think I was there at one time. All sand and rock and tin-can colonies."

That prompted a discussion on tin-can colonies, what they were, and other planets that had them between Mike Hammer and Parsec Paul. Next Parsec Paul had to explain that Mars wasn't like the one in the no-so stories Mike had read. It took a moment for Jason to drag them back to the original topic.

"Why do you think it was Martianists, Mr. Roberts?"

"You said the name on the papers in the wallet was Carthoris Carter," Jason explained with long-practiced patience. On Mars they are lousy with silly names like that. The Martianist movement was born on Mars some, oh, forty or fifty years ago. Sometimes new members from other planets like Baldur or Odin will take on new names when they join. It is like a secret handshake to these wackos."

"These Martianists go around blowing things up a lot?" Parsec Paul asked.

"Well, no, but I can think of one thing on this planet, or used to be, anyway, that they would want really badly." Parsec Paul just stared blankly. Jason continued. "That so-called Fuzzy rocket they found in northern Beta. The CZC scientists proved that it couldn't possibly be a craft that carried Fuzzies here a zillion years ago. So, if it wasn't made by us humans, or Fuzzies, or any of the other eight known sapient species, what is left?"

"Martians," Parsec Paul and Mike Hammer said in unison. "But the Martians died out thousands of years ago," Paul added.

"Exactly!" More blank stares. "Look, the Martians had to know that Mars was a dying world and they needed to go somewhere else. The Martianists believe that *homo s. terra* originated on Mars. They also claim that Freyans represent another lost colony and even believe that they would be of purer Martian stock than Terrans. In other words, they think that our ancestors mated with some of the Terran ape-men along the way, diluting the Martian blood. That is why Freyan women are so much more attractive to us; no Neanderthal DNA in the mix."

"So you think Mr. Carthoris blew up the bank to force the

government to give them the rocket?" Parsec Paul was getting clearer on the subject.

Jason was glad to see Parsec Paul was having one of his more lucid moments. "Yup. I would bet sunstones to seashells that they will be sending a manifesto to the news agencies real soon, if they haven't already done so."

"Why make people dead in bank?" Mike Hammer asked. "Why not just ask nice for rocket? Big Ones give Fuzzies nice things all the time."

"Mike, you have read all of the Sherlock Holmes and the Mickey Spillane books. Haven't you learned that Big Ones do foolish things for even more foolish reasons?"

Mike Hammer nodded. "Sometimes Fuzzies have fights, too. Not just Big Ones do foolish things."

"No single species has the market cornered on foolish behavior," Jason said. "Not even Khooghras."

"So what are you going to do, Mr. Roberts? Go after these Martianists yourself?"

Jason shook his head. "No, I am going to speak with Marshal Fane and see if he would like some help on this. Pro bono. Of course, if we crack this case and there is a reward, well…."

* * *

The yacht, on loan from the CZC as Ben Rainsford refused to spend government money on a private yacht, settled on the landing pad near a building that declared it to be the Rathaus in large illuminated letters.

Supervisor Kim Trahn Sylvinski stepped out and eyed the building. "What is a Rathaus? An extermination company?"

"I wouldn't repeat that question in front of the locals," Gus Brannhard cautioned. "It is old German for a government house, more or less."

"A bit on the nose, eh?" Sylvinski chuckled. "Why German instead of plain Terra Lingua? Or Freyan, for that matter?"

"The Freyan language is called Sosti." Gus gave the commissioner a quick brief on the history of the Freyans from Magni, omitting the part about genetic engineering. He wasn't about to miss Sylvinski's reaction when he met Johann and his people. "You will have to ask Johann about that. I imagine they chose to use German as a nod to their past; many of the Magnians came from Heimdall, and because Sosti would be impossible for most Terrans to work with for anything too technical. Besides, after generations of using German they are more comfortable with it than their native tongue or Terra Lingua.

"Ah, here comes Bürgermeister Torseus, now."

Sylvinski turned to face the approaching party and nearly jumped. What he knew of Freyans did not match the near simian-looking people before him. To his credit, he kept his face somber and extended his hand when Johann extended his. He even retained his composure, when the Freyan grasped his forearm and responded in kind.

"*Herr* Commissar, I am Johann Torseus, Bürgermeister of Neu Freya. Velcome."

"I am honored that you came to meet me in person, Herr Bürgermeister." Sylvinski recalled that 'Herr' was the German form of mister from old flatty movies.

"I imachine you are tired from your churney und ve haff prepared rooms for you und *Herr* Brannhard und their staff. Ve haff also prepared a banquet for vhen you are refreshed."

"Thank you, *Herr* Bürgermeister." Sylvinski signaled the yacht and his staff, consisting of Dana Alexander and Janice Goodfellow, stepped out of the yacht and gathered behind Gus and Sylvinski.

Johann looked visibly startled when he saw Janice, as did his retinue. One young man even pointed at her and whispered. Janice had been the subject of stares and whispered comments all her life, but it didn't mean she enjoyed it.

Gus, fearing an incident, stepped forward and spoke softly to Johann. "What's going on?"

Johann fought to turn his eyes away from Janice. "Dein freund has die Mark of die Gods!"

"What?"

"I vill explain later." Johann turned to Janice. "*Fräulein*, please forgive mein people. No disrespect ist intended. Qvite die opposite. Come into der Rathaus. You vill be treated as an honored guest."

Janice Goodfellow didn't understand what was going on. Nonetheless, she accepted Johann's proffered hand and tried to ignore the growing crowd of Freyans that were looking at her. *Now I know how Fay Wray must have felt.*

Sylvinski was about to demand what was going on when he felt a sizeable hand on his shoulder. For a moment he thought it belonged to one of the Freyans until he turned to see that it was attached to Gus, who was shaking his head.

"We don't know what is going on and it would be wise to find out before starting anything. Remember, different cultures, different rules."

Sylvinski nodded. For all he knew Janice Goodfellow looked like one of the Freyan deities, though he doubted it. People tended to make their gods more beautiful than themselves and with everything he'd heard about the women of Freya that set the bar very high. No Terran woman could possibly attain that level of beauty, at least not without significant cosmetic enhancements and maybe not even then. Sylvinski shrugged it off. He had time and could be patient. Besides, his visit to Neu Freya was all a distraction from his real target, anyway.

XVIII

"Gods and monsters! I knew I had seen those moves before."

Betty closed the file cabinet and turned to the source of the exclamation. "And what moves would that be?"

"That Miss Ancheta who was in here before," Jack replied. "I got curious and asked Frank Carr to send me whatever he had on that trio who came in earlier. Erena Taylor works for the CZC so I didn't need to know much about her. Very little gets past Chief Steefer. Married, four children, husband between jobs but he isn't a slacker.

"Miss Tezza, as it turns out, was a datastream model."

"Oh, really?" Betty said slyly. "Any samples of her work, there?"

Jack nodded and opened a file on his computer for Betty to see. Most of the work was tame by current standards. Betty eyed them critically.

"Making Hasenpfeffer in the nude could be dangerous," Betty said. "She could have been spattered with cooking oil. Oh! In that photo there she has a bandage on her breast. Told you it was dangerous. Overall she looks like a real girl-next-door type." She scanned several images. Many of the images showed Cindy working out on a farm, riding an older style ATV, and cooking, all in unlikely states of dress. "Cooks, cleans, tends farm animals and even works the farm machinery. Not hard on the eyes in the least. I can see the appeal to men. So what is she doing hundreds of light-years away from Heimdall stomping around in the field? She looked to me like she could still model."

"Psychological studies of Fuzzies in the wild, remember?" Jack explained. "She retired from modeling and switched to psychology."

"Huh. And Miss Ancheta?"

Jack turned in his chair. "That is a whole 'nother story. Did I ever tell you about my younger days when I first left Terra?"

Betty searched her memory. "Oh, yeah. You and, um, Trapper Johnson?"

"Tagger Johnson," Jack corrected.

"Right! You and he bounced around from planet to planet for some years while you were learning the ropes."

Jack nodded. "On one of the planets he took me to…I don't recall which one at the moment…Oh, wait, yes I do; Bathala…he hooked me up with some young men who were martial arts masters. One of them, Phil Matedne, Jr., could hunt damnthings with a stick! Not much bigger than Miss Ancheta, but he could hand out a beating with the best of them. His brothers were nothing to sneeze at, either.

"As you know, I was a Golden Gloves boxer back in college and had a green belt in karate at that time. Well, I sparred a bit with Phil and couldn't lay a finger on him. The whole time he slapped me around like a cat playing with a mouse. I wasn't going to be on-planet long enough to do more than learn blade and stick, but I learned more in those five weeks than I ever had before or since. Phil taught me how to use the blade and his younger brother…mmm…Ken! His brother Ken taught me how to use a stick. He was a master at Escrima. I rarely get to use those skills any more but I still practice in my spare time."

Betty looked at the computer screen but couldn't find what got Jack so excited. "I don't see the connection."

"Kealani Ancheta is really Kealani Matedne," Jack burst out. "She is Phil's daughter…and prize student if I am any judge."

"Really? Huh. Small universe. Why the *nom de voyage*?"

Jack scrolled down the screen. "Here it is; Kealani made a name for herself in martial arts competitions and worked as a stunt woman. She may have even worked with Darla Cross before she moved here. I would think the name change was to stay under the radar while she is working on her post-grad degree in anthropology. I can understand that. People hear that you are some sort of big fighter and some Khooghra wants to test you to see if your reputation holds up or maybe for the bragging rights if they get the better of you. I went through enough of that on Terra. Miss Ancheta would rather not have the distraction from her studies, I imagine."

Betty was about to ask another question when the comscreen beeped. It was Gus Brannhard. Jack shook his hands and Gus did the same on screen.

"Gus, I heard you were playing tour guide to those…uh," Jack was about to say "Khooghras" then thought better of it. He didn't know who else might be listening. "…visitors from Terra."

"I am. In fact I am over in Neu Freya now," Gus said, lowering his voice. "Jack, you were on Freya a lot longer than I was, so maybe you can explain something to me." Gus went on about the strange reception they received and the Freyans' reaction to Janice Goodfellow. "Supervisor Sylvinski is in a snit because everybody is acting like Miss Goodfellow is in charge. Not just of the delegation but Johann's people, too. You would think she was Venus stepping off the half-shell, the way these Magni-Freyans are carrying on."

Jack thought it over and nothing jumped out at him. "Is this Miss Goodfellow attractive?"

Gus shrugged. "Sure, as Terrans go. Tall, slender, everything where it belongs in the right proportions, but next to a Freyan woman I would have to say she is nothing exceptional."

Betty rolled her eyes. "None of us are, by that standard."

"You hold your own real well, Betty. Gus, is there anything unusual about her?" Jack asked. "Her perfume or hair style? Anything?"

"Johann said she has the Mark of the Gods, if that tells you anything."

"Mark of the…does she have a birthmark that they can see?"

"Yes. It covers about half her face. I thought it impolitic to inquire why she never had it removed. Why? Is that significant?"

Jack threw his head back and laughed. "You better believe it! You should have led with that. Part of what makes Freyan women seem so attractive to us Terrans is that they don't have a single blemish, save for those caused by injury, on their skin. They don't even get freckles. I heard it might have something to do with their planet orbiting a K0 star. Anyway, birthmarks are so rare as to be almost unheard of on Freya. When somebody, male or female, has one it is believed that they are favored by the gods. They are often encouraged to join the clergy, if you can believe that. But these marks are typically very small and easily concealed. With a large birthmark in a prominent location the Freyans would think that the gods *really* favor her."

"Birthmarks happen fairly often in Terros," Betty said. "I had one, in fact. Wouldn't they be considered a big deal on Freya, too?"

Jack arched an eyebrow. "And where would this birthmark be? I think I would have noticed."

Betty actually blushed. "Oh, I had it erased when I was still in my teens."

Jack nodded. "And there you have it. Terrans tend to be a bit vain and have perceived imperfections removed. Miss Goodfellow may have a better sense of self-worth so she never bothered." Jack felt Betty's eyes burning holes in the back of his head and realized the comment about "self-worth" may have been misconstrued. *I'm going to pay for that one later.*

Gus sounded like he had his doubts. "But to get this kind of treatment?"

"Didn't you take an anthropology course in college, Gus?" He hadn't. "Well, to some Native American tribes people with birth defects were considered sacred. For that matter, so were men who chose to dress and act like women."

"Well, with that kind of thinking, wouldn't the genetically engineered Freyans be treated like kings on their home world?" Gus asked.

Jack shook his head. "Freyans understand genetic manipulation, thanks to our influence on their culture. Worse yet, the Crown and noble class, having some responsibility for Johann's people's plight, would make things very difficult if they dropped in to say "Hi, look at what the king and his nobles did to us." Rheiner would likely be considered a real catch with his Freyan throwback features and inhuman strength, but Heidi could be stoned in the street."

Gus couldn't recall ever seeing a public stoning during his brief stay on Freya. Still, Jack's account would be a trustworthy one. "Okay, so what should Miss Goodfellow expect, and what will be expected of her?"

"She'll be treated like a queen during her visit to Neu Freya. Any man there would cheerfully take a bullet for her, even if they weren't so damned bullet resistant. She may be asked to bless some pregnant women or render a judgment on some dispute or other. I am sure Johann will be able to guide her through the ordeal. Give her a briefing and make sure she doesn't let it all go to her head. Freyans are nobody's fools and if she starts acting like a prima donna things could get ugly. And under no circumstance let her accept a bracelet from anybody! That is as good as a betrothal there."

"A bracelet? Oh, yes, I recall. Morgan and Akira traded bracelets at the wedding ceremony." Gus glanced away from the screen. "There she is now, with Johann. Some young man, at least I think he is young, is going over...Oh, Ghu!" Gus left the viewscreen on as he raced away.

"What just happened," Betty wondered.

"I'll bet Gus just spotted a potential suitor and ran to block the betrothal," Jack chuckled. "I would pay a lot of sols to see *that* confrontation."

"Hmm. Back to Miss Tezza, what did you think of the photos?"

Jack grew wary. "What's the right answer, here?"

"Relax, killer," Betty laughed. "I won't shoot you for thinking another woman is pretty. I was just wondering how you would like to see some of the stuff I posed for when I was younger."

It took several minutes before Jack was able to answer that.

XIX

The hotel was as low-rent as promised. The rooms were small, the walls in need of paint and even some soundproofing. Still, it was clean and in otherwise good repair. The previous planetary administrator, Colonial Governor Nick Emmert, had a serious jones about disease prevention and instituted a number of regulations in all eateries and hostels to reduce the possibility of a pandemic. His successor, Bennett Rainsford, saw no reason to change those regulations so even the lowest boarding house was subject to inspection and fines if the level of cleanliness required by law was not met.

Coming from Freya, Merlin appreciated the grime-free environment although he thought they took it a bit too far. No matter. He had other concerns. He looked at his wrist chronometer and decided it was time to go out. Then he checked his gun, made sure he had extra rounds, covered his bright blond hair with a range hat and left his room.

In the hallway he passed some men of questionable hygiene, something even the previous governor's edicts on cleanliness could do nothing about, and likely even more questionable morals. That was to be expected this close to Junktown. In fact, Merlin had counted on it. Across from the hotel Merlin spotted what he presumed to be a dive bar. The name spelled out Babylon Inn if one looked carefully at the lit and unlit portions of the neon sign. Little money had been invested in the maintenance of the establishment. Merlin went in.

The interior was even more seedy and ill-kept than the exterior. The only nods to cleanliness were the glasses and bar. The local ordinances were taken seriously in that respect. The floor was swept enough to clear large debris and little else. *Some inspector is being paid off*, Merlin surmised.

Merlin took a seat at the bar and waited to be noticed. A number of women in very revealing attire looked him over while the bartender seemed to ignore his presence. After the barkeep walked by three times and was in the process of going for a fourth, Merlin reached over and grabbed the man by his shirt, then pulled him halfway over the bar.

"Walk past me again, without taking my order, and it will not end well for you," Merlin said in carefully modulated tones. "Now, I will have Freyan ale, if this dung heap can manage it." He pushed the barman back and waited.

The barman reached under the bar and brought up a polysteel baseball bat. Non-regulation for actual game play, but a standard item in many a dive bar. He was stopped short by the very large caliber pistol aimed in his direction by Merlin.

"It will be a far more pleasant evening for both of us if you simply get me my drink."

The barman grunted and returned his bat to its resting place under the bar. "This 'dung heap' doesn't carry fancy stuff like that. We have pilsner, stout, dark and amber beers. If you want something stronger you'll have to go with hard liquor, or go someplace else."

"Then I will have a stout and a dark mixed half and half in a tall pitcher. And the gentleman trying to sneak up on me from behind with that Bowie knife would be well-advised to return to his table."

In the mirror behind the bar Merlin could see the look of surprise on the man behind him. After a brief internal debate, the man returned to his table and sheathed his blade. Merlin likewise holstered his gun, though he left the strap off.

The barman returned with the pitcher. "When you walked in, I thought you were just some pretty boy slumming it. Now I can see you didn't just fall off the melon lorry. Where're you from, if you don't mind my asking."

"Originally Freya," Merlin said. He poured some beer into a glass and tried it. The barman could see that it wasn't to his taste. "After that, lots of different places. I heard about the land boom on Zarathustra and thought I might make a go of it here. Instead, the local chartered company swung some deal to keep damn near the entire planet. I wonder how much kickback the Governor got out of that deal."

The barman shook his head. "I wouldn't throw talk like that around too much. That deal the Governor Rainsford struck with the CZC is keeping this planet tax-free. And Rainsford doesn't have his nose buried up to the neck in the CZC's arse, like the last governor did. He is a bit too law and order for most of us in this part of town, but he doesn't regulate gun carry or alcohol like they do on a lot of planets. That makes him aces with most of the voters. And the only guy who had a snowball's chance on Niflheim of beating him in an election is now his deputy. We don't have term limits on this planet, yet, so I would cover any bet that he'll be in office until he either gets bored with it or drops dead. My money is on 'bored' as you won't find a man on Zarathustra who would be willing to shoot him."

Merlin appeared to be digesting that factoid. "Too law and order, eh? How is a man supposed to make a sol on a world like this? No land, limited job market…."

"Oh, there is always an opportunity if you know where to look," the barman said. "But you would have to be vetted, first."

"Vetted?"

"Yup." The barkeep pulled up a device from under the counter. "This is an older model portable polyencephalographic veridicator. I picked it up at the pawn shop a few years back. I don't even want to guess where it came from. If you are willing, I can just hook you up, ask a few pointed questions and then we can go from there."

Merlin's eyes narrowed. "What kind of questions?"

"Oh, the usual. Are you now or have you ever been a cop? Are you a bounty hunter? Are you lookin' for some guy who put your sister in a family way? That sort of thing."

Merlin weighed his options then agreed. "I won't answer anything personal. My business is just that—my business."

The barman nodded then pulled two electrodes from the device, wiped them with rubbing alcohol then placed them on Merlin's temples. Several of the bar's patrons watched. Most had seen this before. Places like this tried to ferret out undercover cops fast. "Okay. We'll start with something simple. Is your name really Merlin?"

"No." Blue.

"Good. Most of us don't use our given names either. Now tell me a lie for the baseline."

"My name is Darla Cross." Red.

"Movie buff, eh? Okay, now for the meat and potatoes. Are you a policeman?"

"No." Blue.

"Have you ever been a policeman?"

"No." Blue.

"Are you a bounty hunter?"

"No." Blue.

"Are you from Freya?"

"Yes." Blue.

"Have you ever committed a crime?"

"That depends on who you ask." The globe went from blue to indigo then back to blue.

The barman thought it over for a moment, then shrugged. "I know what constitutes a crime varies from world to world. Let's try this; have you ever shot anybody?"

"Yes." Blue.

"Killed anybody?"

"Yes." Blue.

The barman recalled the cannon pointed at him earlier. "Okay, this one is for all the chips. Are you after anybody in this bar?"

"Not as far as I know." Blue.

"Good enough for me." The barman unhooked the electrodes then stowed the veridicator. "Oh, I should have asked if you are a private detective."

"Well, you can hook me up again, but the answer is no."

"Nah. No need. Most dicks are former cops. We already cleared you of that. Besides, last I checked, there was only one active peeper in Mallorysport worth a damn, and he has at least ten years on you and works with a Fuzzy."

Merlin acted surprised. "A Fuzzy detective? Sounds like something out of a comic book."

The barman laughed. "It does, doesn't it? So, you are new to this world and looking for opportunities. What catches your fancy?"

"I guess there is no point dancing around it," Merlin said. "Looking to get a line on some sunstones. I have an off-world buyer willing to deal in bulk at twice the rate the CZC is paying."

The barman weighed it in his mind. The CZC paid four hundred and fifty sols a karat for quality gems. On Terra those same gems went for twelve hundred sols or better a karat. Somebody paying nine hundred sols per only cleared around three hundred sols in profit, assuming he didn't have to deal with a lot of middlemen in his distribution network.

"Twice? Seems like he isn't going to clear much."

"On Terra, no," Merlin explained. "But sunstones bring in much higher prices the farther you get from Terra. And Zarathustra, I would imagine. On Imhotep they go for fifteen hundred sols per karat. On, um, Hiawatha even more. Transportation fees get outrageous the further from Terra you go. That's why my buyer wants it in bulk. More than that I won't say."

The barman nodded in understanding. Tell the wrong person too much about your operation and you could get cut out of it pretty quick. "Do the stones have to be legitimate?"

That brought Merlin up short. "Huh? What do you mean?"

"Somebody found a way to fake up some sunstones a while back and started spreading them around. Good stuff, not like the hollowed out pebbles with an LED inside. As far as I know, they were completely indistinguishable from the real thing." Merlin took another drink then asked how the counterfeiters were caught. "What makes you think they were caught?"

"Easy. Because you just told me about them. For word to get around, they had to be found out at some point."

The barman nodded. "True enough. The details are a bit sketchy on that. As I understand it, the CZC found a way to test the stones and weed out the fakes. Affie would know more about that than I would, but I haven't seen her in here for a while. Word is she got pinched with a bag full of fakes. Somehow she beat the rap, but she hasn't been in here since then. I also heard she had a big strike so she might be hanging out in a better class of joint than this."

Merlin appeared very interested. "Affie? Is that a first or last?"

The barman shrugged. "Don't know. That's all we ever called her here."

* * *

Juan Takagashi read the report before him, made a few notes, then signed off and set it in the outbox. He still had several more such documents to sift through before the end of the day.

The next paper was the final authorization to commence construction of the annex to the naval base west of Mallorysport. The Navy was paying rent on a sizeable tract of land and this allowed them to expand. The CZC sold the land back to the government, allowing Ben Rainsford to rent it out. The extra income from the Navy would be cached in a special account where it would just sit and gain interest. This was a fallback in case the market on the sunstones ever collapsed. No amount of money would support the government and planetary services indefinitely, but it would give the colony time to switch over to a taxation system without any interruption of services.

Juan smiled and signed the document. Not long ago Ben would have tackled the pile of paperwork himself while Deputy Colonial Governor Juan Takagashi just sat in his office twiddling his thumbs. Now there was a more equitable division of labor and Ben freed up some of his time and reduced his stress.

The intercom beeped. "Yes?"

"A Deputy Commissioner Farquar, Mr. Burr, and Captain Trask to see you, sir."

Juan didn't recall having any meetings or appointments scheduled. He checked his calendar and found nothing for the rest of the day. "Send them in, Sue."

The three men entered. Captain Trask he had met before during the Fuzzy slaving investigation. Deputy Commissioner Farquar he knew of only from what Ben had told him. Burr he knew nothing about.

Juan stood and extended his hand. "Gentlemen, how may I help you?"

Trask spoke up first. "I am afraid these men are here as part of the probe in local politics and your name came up in connection to some legal issues back on Odin."

Juan let the hand drop. "Legal issues? I don't understand."

Clarence Burr took out a data pad. "You served under Colonial Governor Ross Martin on Odin from 642 to 647 AE. In October of 646 AE Governor Martin was investigated for accepting bribes, kickbacks and giving government contracts to his cronies under very favorable, to them, conditions. He was impeached in February of 647 AE, removed from office then tried and found guilty resulting in a twenty-five to life sentence to be served on Hugin, the penal colony moon orbiting Odin."

"Yes," Juan said. "I testified at the time that I had no direct knowledge of Martin's actions during his tenure as governor. Under veridication."

"We are aware of that," Farquar said. "You were cleared of all of Martin's crimes. When the new governor took office, he completely re-staffed the entire Cabinet to remove any taint of Martin's influence."

"Yes, and we were given a decent separation package to allow us time to find new positions elsewhere. 'On another planet,' was his suggestion." Juan shrugged. "Governor Swan understood that while we were all cleared of wrongdoing, we would be haunted by our connection to Martin and our best bet for a fresh start was off-world."

"Understood," Burr said. "You left Odin in April of 647 AE and made your way to Thor, where you opened a legal practice in August of 647 AE. Unlike your previous practice on Odin, this one failed to thrive. In 649 AE you closed the practice and moved to Zarathustra. Here, you opened yet another legal practice in June of 650 AE. You were doing well until you ran for Colonial Governor against Bennett Rainsford, who defeated you by a surprisingly narrow margin. After the election you were offered the position of Deputy Colonial Governor."

Juan Takagashi looked at the ceiling then back down at Farquar. "Is there anything else about my life you feel the need to tell me? I already know all of this. I lived it."

Trask spoke up. "A few months after your departure from Odin, there was a general audit of the treasury and a substantial amount of money appeared to have vanished. Everybody who ever had access to the accounts were rounded up and veridicated without success. A bench warrant was issued for those that had already left planet. All but three have since been found and questioned on whatever planet they settled on. That just leaves you, Olaf McKenzie and Floyd Vogel."

Juan thought about the two other men. Both seemed like upright types who wouldn't have anything to do with something like robbery or embezzlement.

"Then you are here to…?"

"Question you under veridication about your possible involvement in the theft of treasury funds from Odin," Farquar explained. "Your planet-hopping made you difficult to track down, especially to this backwater world. So, will you cooperate and submit to veridication?"

"Certainly," Juan said. "Just hand me your warrant issued by Chief Justice Pendarvis and we will settle this matter."

Farquar and Burr glanced at each other and grimaced.

Trask gave the impression that he was striving hard to suppress a smile.

"Gentlemen, surely you know it would set a bad precedent for a high government official to submit to veridication without a warrant," Juan stated, "especially without counsel present. Chief Colonial Prosecutor Brannhard is currently away dealing with your esteemed boss over on Zeta. I do not believe the timing of this little meeting is a coincidence. When you obtain the warrant, I will call for Brannhard to come and sit in. I will not take the seat unless and until you do."

"So are you saying you do not want us to rule you out as a suspect," Burr asked.

Juan shook his head as if in disbelief. "Really? Mind games? Do you think for a moment I will ignore my rights just to get you off my back? Gentlemen, as you well know from your background check on me," Juan pointed at the data pad, "I am a more than competent lawyer. Save the psychology for some mutt who is stupid enough to fall for it. Now, I have some work I need to get back to. Oh, and before you try to get me removed from my position, let me point out that Zarathustra is still a young colony and the law here hasn't evolved to the point where a government official can be removed from office for *suspicion* of wrongdoing. You will have to come up with something tangible and actionable. Now, good day."

Farquar and Burr left with dark expressions. Trask flashed a quick smile at Juan before following the two men out.

Outside of Government House, Burr sighed. "I underestimated him. I'll bet he was a crackerjack lawyer before he took that government job. The failure of his practice on Thor made me think otherwise."

"Thorans tend to deal with criminals rather quickly, Terran or homegrown," Trask said. "I read several reports about some grifter or thief being dealt with in a rather severe manner by the locals. And colonial law has it that native law supersedes Federation laws on the home planets of alien races. Not much left to defend when the Thorans get through with a perp."

Burr could see Trask's point. "Well, we'll just have to get that warrant from the Chief Justice."

"Good luck with that," Trask said.

"Do you have reason to believe he won't cooperate?" Farquar inquired.

"Only the fact that we don't have any legal documentation that would compel such cooperation. That file you got may be all well and factual, but without the official bench warrant you don't have a legal leg to stand on. Chief Justice Pendarvis is a real stickler for the letter of the law. Oh, and not for nothing, he can't be intimidated, either. That was why he presided over the Fuzzy Trial."

"The warrant may be on file at the police station," Burr suggested. "Do you have any idea how many millions of files are transmitted from each hypership when they come in? They could have it and not know it."

Trask thought about that. Marshal Fane was very good at his job but he didn't have time to review every single scrap of info that came in. Even on Terra they didn't sift through every single file. They would wait until somebody committed a crime, then do a Boolean search to get everything known on the perpetrator. Files marked urgent would be looked at right away. Something as minor as a bench warrant might take months, even years to get noticed.

"Let's go talk to Marshal Fane and see if he is feeling helpful," Trask said. He turned to Burr. "I strongly advise you to let me do the talking. Max Fane is under no onus to help us if he doesn't feel like it. If we annoy him, it will not go well."

"Wait, you are the senior man at the FBCI here on Zarathustra," Farquar said. "Don't you have access to all the same files?"

"On Terra, yes. All that and more. Here on Zarathustra where we have a minimal presence, not so much." Trask shrugged. "When this planet gets a larger share of warm bodies, that will change. For now we have to rattle a tin cup at the local law enforcement officers for anything we need. The Marshal has been very cooperative thus far and, if we don't annoy him by getting in his way or trying to push him around, he'll likely stay that way." Trask stared at Burr. "I can't stress enough the value of letting me keep it that way."

"I'm getting the feeling, you hope this will all come to nothing," Burr said accusingly.

Trask shrugged. "I checked everybody out personally, when I first hit this planet. The deputy governor was never veridicated, but I read character pretty well and didn't get the sense of any red flags with this man. Regardless, if he committed a crime I'll do everything in my power to see that he is called to account."

Burr nodded then was surprised by something. He watched as a Fuzzy with a dog moved away. "Did that Fuzzy just sniff us?"

XX

The Alibi Inn was, perhaps, the seediest bar in Mallorysport. It was well known for its questionable clientele and equally questionable business ethics. The owner of the bar was never around and the bartender worked harder at keeping ignorant of the affairs of the patrons than he did pouring drinks.

Sitting at the end of the bar was a new face. New faces stood out like a land-prawn at a goofer convention. As such, nobody wanted to get close to the newcomer for fear he might be some sort of undercover cop. The man seemed not to notice the standoffish way the others acted in his presence.

Noticing that his glass was empty, the bartender wandered over to the man. "Refill?"

"Of whiskey, no," the man said. "Now that I know you don't water the drinks like some places I have been to, I'll try a Three Planets."

The bartender's eyes widened a bit. A Three Planets was not for the weak of constitution nor the light of wallet. An undercover cop would never order such a drink; it would almost certainly impair his ability to function. And an off-duty cop wouldn't want to spend that kind of money.

"Coming right up, sir." The bartender went to the auto-mixer and typed in the combination. Few humans could mix the drink manually and have it come out just right due to the very specific proportions of the concoction. He returned with the drink and watched the man throw it back in a single pull. "Ghu on a goat, man! I didn't think anybody this side of Gus Brannhard could drink like that."

"Gus who?"

"The Colonial Chief Prosecutor. Before he got jumped up, he was a defense attorney and used to come here to meet with some of his clients. The man drank bourbon like it was iced tea!"

The man nodded. "Sounds like somebody I could get on with… before his promotion. Hit me again."

While the bartender refilled the glass a woman from the other end of the bar came over and sat down next to him. "Buy a girl a drink?"

The man looked her over. "A girl, no. A woman, certainly. Bartender, another of whatever the lady is having."

"So, what's your name, killer? I am Affanita."

"You can call me Merlin."

"Merlin? Like the King Arthur magician?"

"Actually, it is more of an approximation of my, um, 'handle.' My true name is unpronounceable to most Terro-humans."

"Terro—" Affanita took in the bright blond hair, light skin and male model good looks. "You must be from Freya."

"Guilty as charged," Merlin said. "Before you ask, no, I wasn't exiled. I grew up near a Terran military installation on Freya and heard the Marines talk about all of the exotic planets they had been to and decided I would go out and see some for myself."

The bartender set the drinks down, then retreated. He heard just enough to get an idea that the man wasn't some sort of cop.

Affanita picked up her drink and took a sip. "How has it been going for you so far? Been anyplace interesting?"

"Odin, Thor, Yggdrasil, Magni, Gimli, a few others."

"Magni?" Affanita searched her memory then recalled that Magni was a heavy-gravity world. "You must be pretty stout to handle that kind of world."

Merlin shrugged.

"So what brings you to Zarathustra, big guy?"

"It was the last stop on the space line before the turnaround. I heard about the Fuzzies and decided to take a look. I also heard about the sunstones and considered doing a little prospecting. I'll need to find some work to get a stake, though."

He needs money for a stake and he drinks something as pricy as a Three Planets? Affanita frowned and shook her head. "Sunstone prospecting is a bad idea in the current climate, if you are new to it. There was a ring passing ersatz stones about a year ago, then a big blow up with Fuzzy slavers about six months ago. Right now, being out on Beta is hazardous to your health. The Fuzzies on the Rez are suspicious of new faces, the northern Fuzzies would chop you up as soon as look at you, and the ZNPF—"

"ZNPF, what's that?" he asked.

"The Zarathustra Native Patrol Force, they keep watch on the Fuzzies, so nobody messes with them. Old Man Holloway, who runs it, has skin thicker than a damnthing hide. The ZNPF is still swarming the continent with triple the Marine support. At best, you'll be picked up and veridicated to within an inch of your life. At worst, they'll never find your body."

Merlin feigned ignorance. "Fake sunstones? How do they do that?"

Affanita shook her head. "I don't know and I don't want to. Anybody caught with a fake sunstone better have a real good explanation why they have it. Everybody who was involved in the counterfeiting ring is either dead or in prison. I have better plans for my retirement."

It appeared that Merlin's interest was piqued. "Really? How were they caught?"

"Don't you get the datastream? The *faux* stones have a radioactive signature. Harmless to us, but Fuzzies are super-sensitive to radiation, so if anybody were to give one a fake sunstone they could be charged with reckless endangerment. That would earn you a bullet in the head. Look, I am a sunstone prospector, and somebody tried to pass those rocks off on me. I got busted so fast it made my head spin. Mr. Grego himself had words with me about it. Lucky for me he isn't the ogre people make him out to be."

"Really? It seems to me that somebody taking the fakes off-world could make a good amount of money, provided he didn't plan on staying on whatever planet he sold them on."

Affanita shook her head. "Don't you believe it! By now the word has been sent out to every established colony in the Federation. And the ones that are just getting started, and not on the regular space-line routes, will still be struggling and won't have any money or interest in non-essentials like jewelry. Only a complete idiot would still try to make a go of counterfeit sunstones."

Merlin looked interested. "So, any fake sunstones would have had to have gone out, what, a year ago?"

"At least." Affanita nodded then threw back her drink. Merlin signaled for a refill. "I heard about this guy who claimed to have found a whole chest of stones at an old B.I.N. warehouse. I guess that would be an H.I.N. warehouse now."

Merlin became more engrossed. "Really? Were they real or counterfeit?"

"Beats me." Affanita emptied her glass and the bartender quickly refilled it. "It was one of those 'my friend's cousin's son's roommate's father's mistress said' kind of things. Don't know if they were real or not, and the story has it that the guy smuggled them all off-world…and maybe himself, as well."

Merlin threw back the rest of his drink and shook his head at the bartender when the man reached for the glass. "Humph. Well, selling counterfeit anything isn't an honorable thing to do."

Affanita gulped and coughed. "Whoo, boy. You really are from Freya. Most Terros,"—she pronounced it 'TEAR-ohz'—"don't sweat the honor of things. They just try to get in as much money as they can without getting caught. Some are more honest than others, but that is about as good as it gets." Another long drink. "I would say that Mr. Grego is a straight-shooter. He had the chance to throw me in the slammer just to make an example of me, but instead let me help him bring down the counterfeit outfit and even let me keep the real stones." Affanita stopped, looked down at her glass and frowned. "Too many of these make me a bit too chatty. I never told anybody about that before."

"Is there some sort of prospector's code to keep you from sharing this?"

"Nah. There are a number of unwritten rules, like no claim-jumping and mutual protection, but counterfeiters could ruin the sunstone market which would hurt all of us. If anything, we would all band together and lynch the bastard if we caught him first." Affanita finished her drink and something caught her eye. "That's an interesting chronometer on your wrist. Bright blue light on it. Is that to help you find it in the dark?"

Merlin smiled. "Yes, it does help me find my way through the darkness."

* * *

Betatown boasted all of a dozen buildings. Three of these buildings were drinking establishments; the largest of these drinking establishments, a bar and grill, also boasted boarding accommodations. The Xerxes Inn typically catered to sunstone prospectors, ranchers and farmers from the few private land owners that received a grant from the Charterless Zarathustra Company where they grew or produced the things the CZC couldn't be bothered with, the occasional criminal element, such as veldbeest rustlers or claim jumpers, and the odd tourist types such as Cindy Tezza, Kealani Ancheta and Erena Taylor.

Kealani, who did the most traveling for her field of study, took the lead and selected a table. Cindy and Erena followed and took a seat. Kealani took in the few other patrons before sitting down.

"We should definitely stay together while we are here," Kealani said. "Small towns on the edge of nowhere like these tend to attract an unsavory element."

Cindy noticed that there were no other women around. She thought for a moment that her very short shorts might attract unwanted attention. "I think we are a bit conspicuous. I am starting to think my choice of clothing was not wise."

Erena shook her head. "We could be wearing fibroid sacks and would still stick out. Five will get you ten somebody in this town will try to proposition at least one of us. Even odds on which one."

Kealani turned her attention to the menu. It was laminated paper instead of a holographic projection. "They have wild veldbeest, domesticated veldbeest, something called a **Frikadelle**, banjo bird, whatever that is…?"

"I'll have the **Frikadelle** with *pommes frites*," Cindy said. "I hope they have middle sharp mustard."

Erena looked at the menu "What is a *Frikadelle*?"

"On Heimdall and Terra it can be ground beef, ground pork or a combination of the two formed into a small meatloaf," Cindy explained.

"There are some spices, onion and egg in it. I don't know what meats it would be made from here."

"Likely veldbeest or riverpig," Kealani opined. She had been researching the local flora and fauna as part of her preparations for the field study. "Veldbeest tastes a bit like bison. I haven't tried the riverpig, yet."

"We use both, actually." The women turned to the new voice. It was a middle-aged man with short graying hair. "If you are familiar with the original German recipe it will seem a bit different from what I serve." The man looked at Cindy. "Is that a slight Heimdallian accent I hear?"

"*Jawohl, mein Herr,*" Cindy said. "Have you been to Heimdall?"

"No. I came here from Imhotep. Got tired of always being cold. We do get a lot of immigrants from other planets. I make it a game of trying to guess where people come from by how they dress and speak. Now this one," he indicated Erena, "sounds pure Aussie from one of the Americanized settlements back on Terra. And this one, well, you are a new one on me."

"I think I'll give you a chance to guess before we leave," Kealani said. "I'll try the *Frikadellen*, too. The rice on your menu; is it Terran introduced or something local?"

"Local, but there is so little difference most people can't tell from the taste."

"I'll have that, then. And some fried poolball fruit."

"Very good. And you, little lady?"

Erena shrugged. "I guess I'll have the *Frikadellen* as well. With fries."

"Rockthrower, Maid Marian, what would you like?" Cindy asked the Fuzzies. Both said XT3. "That should do it."

The man nodded. "Okay, be about ten minutes. If you need anything else, yell for Mac. Oh, drinks?" Cindy had a beer, Kealani some wine and Erena, who was technically on duty, accepted a cola and the Fuzzies just had water. "I'll be back in two shakes of a goofer's tail." He paused and said in a low voice, "Mind the other patrons, ladies. Women are few and far between out here and not everybody is polite when they meet one. Especially with three attractive young ladies like yourselves."

Erena patted her holster. "I think we will be okay. Thanks for the heads-up."

Mac nodded and went to get the orders filled. Cindy went to the ladies' room along with Erena. Kealani stayed at the table and waited for the food to come. Behind her she heard the door open.

"Mac, three beers."

Mac came out of the kitchen to find three men in dirty clothes and boots. "I told you three to get out and stay out the last time you were here."

The man closest to the bar pulled a small bag from a pocket and spilled out a few small stones. They started to glow in his hand. "We can pay for the damages from last time and a little extra for the trouble."

Mac accepted two of the stones and looked them over. They glowed brightly in blue and gold hues. Mac pulled a small scale out from under the counter and weighed each sunstone. "The blue one will cover the damages, but if you want anything else I can't make change for the gold one."

"Keep the change. We said we would give you a little something extra for the trouble. Think of it as getting ahead of our next bill, if you like."

"Your next bill better not include more damages, Cutter," Mac warned. "Next time I won't just bounce your asses; I'll shoot 'em. Ah, Niflheim! Your friends are already starting trouble."

Cutter looked back and saw his comrades trying to chat up the young woman at a table. She clearly did not enjoy the attention. One tried to grab Kealani in a very inappropriate location and all Niflheim broke loose.

From her sitting position, Kealani shot an elbow into the offender's crotch, doubling him over. Next, standing so fast the chair she was sitting in toppled over, she took a martial stance. The second man, trying to grab her from behind, found only empty air as Kealani kneeled down and did a sweeping kick that bowled the man off his feet. Without pausing to inspect her work, she spun around back to the first man, who was still doubled over, sending a knee into his conveniently placed jaw. This she followed up with a thrust palm into the nose. The other man struggled to get back on his feet and managed to get to his knees when Kealani drew her blade and thrust it at the man's throat, stopping a hair's breadth from cutting it.

"Hey!" Cutter yelled as he went for his gun. He stopped at the sight of a gun barrel pointed directly at his face.

"I believe the odds are about even as it is," Erena said as she cocked the hammer. "Wouldn't you agree?"

"Um," Cutter said brightly. "Yes, ma'am. Looks fair to me."

Mac, who had pulled a polysteel baseball bat from under the bar, chuckled as he reached over and pulled the gun out of Cutter's holster. "Miss? I think you can put that knife away, now. I would bet sand to sunstones these boys have learned their lesson. Right, boys?"

"Yessir!" exclaimed the two men.

The one with the blade at his throat looked pale, as if all the blood in his body settled in his feet. "Uh, miss, I would like to pay for your dinner, provided I am alive to do so."

Kealani looked disgusted and amused at the same time. "Thanks, but I will pass." She retracted the blade then sent a swift elbow into the man's jaw. "I didn't like the way he asked."

"*Mein Gott! Was ist los?*" Cindy, surprised at the scene before her, slipped back into German. Next to her, Maid Marian and Rockthrower readied an arrow and boomerang, respectively.

Mac had no idea what Cindy had said, but could get the gist. "No worries, miss. These boys were just leaving. Right?" They all agreed. Before they left, Mac confiscated their pistols and rifles. "You'll get these back tomorrow, after these ladies are well on their way. Ah, the orders are ready. Ladies, these fine young gentlemen are paying for your meals and accommodations," he added as he tossed the yellow sunstone in the air and caught it. "This comes under 'damages.'"

XXI

"...and that is why you can't go back to Freya?"

Supervisor Sylvinski shook his head as if to clear it. Johann explained why his people looked as they did and why they were not welcome on what should have been their home world.

"Why should the current ruling party care about what the king did, what, how many years ago?"

"Four hundred und fifty-t'ree," Johann supplied.

"Four hundred and...?"

"That is in Freyan years, Commissioner," Gus explained. "Freya orbits a K0 star like Zarathustra, but they are about half the distance from their primary. It is closer to two hundred and fifty Terran years."

Sylvinski harrumphed. "Still, everybody involved, at least initially, would be dead now. Wouldn't they?"

Johann nodded. It looked like his head was about to roll off of his shoulders. "Ja, but der line of succession ist a hereditary vun. Usually. So die current king ist der great-great-grandson of der king who sold mein ancestors into slafery. Dot vould be embarrassing to die crown. Especially after die experiments dot resulted in our current appearance." He shook his head sadly. "A few of our young could return, but only die vuns vit' handsome or beautiful faces. Very muscular men vould be velcome as dey can do very hard vork. Die *Fräuleins*, not so much. Dey are too powerfully built to be readily accepted in Freyan society."

"The deal Morgan made with the Freyan king and the Chartered Magni Cooperative resulted in a substantial payment to Johann's people," Gus added. "That is where they got the money to purchase Zeta Continent."

Gus went into the details of the deal Morgan Holloway had brokered with the Chartered Magni Cooperative. The Federation stepped in and interrogated everybody involved under veridication. Those that genuinely had no idea that the miners were slaves were given probation and negotiated the deal with Morgan. The ones that knew what was going on were sent back to Terra to be put on trial. "Last I heard, almost all were found guilty and sentenced to death. I imagine they are now just so much ambient energy in an M/E converter."

"Nein, Herr Brannhard," Johann said. "Dey are currently in detention on Gimli."

Gus was surprised at that. "What? Why?"

"Prince Morgan explained to me dot vhen Terros commit truly vile crimes against non-Terrans dey are tried und convicted, den sent to die vorld vhere dey committed dose crimes for punishment."

Gus nodded. "This is true, usually." He related the example of the Lokians. "But this is something of a special case, I would think. The Federation can't send the slavers to Freya for punishment as nobody remaining there had any part in the situation. None still living, anyway. The crown would be embarrassed and refuse to allow it, I would bet. And they couldn't do it on Magni, at least not now, since your people aren't there anymore."

Johann nodded. "Ja, but Prince Morgan negotiated a deal for die slafers to be punished on vhateffer *neu* vorld ve settled on. Dot vould be here."

"What?" Gus chewed on that for a moment. "Hmm. I don't have any objections to it, but why am I learning about this just now? Does Ben know?"

"Dot I don't know," Johann admitted. "Prince Morgan may haff t'ought dot dein gofernor might not allow die colony here if he knew about dot."

Sylvinski laughed. "I saw the footage of the sixty-odd executions of the Fuzzy slavers. I think Gov. Rainsford world not only approve, he'd televise it."

Gus grimaced but had to agree. "So, when can we expect this shipment of doomed souls?"

"As soon as Prince Morgan gets die approval from die Crown on Freya dot dis ist a legitimate princedom," Johann said. "Ve vill haff die aut'ority to execute or effen pardon any ve choose, I t'ink. Not dot I t'ink dere vould be any pardons, mind you. Ah, only dose of us in die goferment know of dis. Mein pipple are mostly unavare dot ve vill be able to take personal vengeance on die Masters."

Gus recalled some of the methods of execution in use on Freya and shuddered. He wondered if Johann would commission a catapult to be built so that the prisoners could be launched into a mountain side. The thought did bad things to his otherwise strong stomach.

"Very interesting. I'll make note of it. I don't expect it will be an issue as the Federation was already involved in this." Sylvinski agreed, then switched back to the prior topics. "Now, what about your living expenses? Did all of the money go to the land purchase and travel?"

Johann laughed. "Nein, nein. Ve vere also giffen beck vages. Fife chenerations vort'. Und ve vere exempt from die usual taxes. On Terra ve vould all be considered modestly vealt'y."

Now Sylvinski was confused. Here were a people who could easily afford to live, if not in the lap of luxury, at least very comfortably in leisure. Yet here they were on a backwater world building a colony and taking over the mining interests formerly owned by the CZC.

"Ve vere born *und* bred to hard labor, Herr Commissar. My people do not do vell in idleness. Den dere ist die fect dot ve can't mofe to a planet vit' high background radioactiffity. Ve vere engineered to vork in a high-radiation enfironment. Staying in such an enfironment might force us to stay as ve are now. Or at least slow die regression to our ancestral forms. In a low-radiation enfironment ve haff a better chence of regaining our heritage. Rheiner ist an example of dis. Ve vant our Kinder to look as our ancestors did. So, ve come to a low radiation vorld und set up a colony avay from odders dot vould stare und point and make a new home for ourselves. Dot means building villages, *neu* housing, schools, hospitals…much of our personal vealt' vent into dot. But ve hope to be self-sufficient in *zehn jahre*…ehh…ten years.

"Wait." It took a few minutes for Sylvinski to work through Johann's thick accent. "Isn't the CZC responsible for schools and such as part of the lease agreement with the government?"

Gus shook his head. "No, the agreement only covered the existing services with a rider to expand as the population grows. Not a completely new colony where such services didn't already exist. A good lawyer could have fought it in court to cover the colony as well after, oh, ten years of litigation. Instead, Grego sold off the mining interests on Zeta to help Johann's people become self-sufficient and not need any help from Big Brother. Grego can be generous, but never stupid, and he has to justify almost every paperclip to the home office. Besides, the Freyans bought this land from the government, so the CZC doesn't have any lease clause allowing them to come here and exploit the natural resources. At least, not anymore."

Sylvinski was about to ask another question when somebody rushed in and whispered in Johann's ear. Not much for standing on ceremony, he thought.

"Chentlemen, I haff chust been told dot das *Luftauto*...ah...aircar dot Brünnhilde took vas discovered in die far east on Beta Continent. Brünnhilde vas not dere vit' it."

"Would you like to step up the search," Gus asked. "Send more of your people to work with the ZNPF?"

"Nein, Gus," Johann said. "Brünnhilde ist young, but she ist a Magni-Freyan. Fery strong *und* capable." Johann explained about the Freyan tradition of going off into the wilderness as a rite of passage. "On Freya only die, ah, boys do dis. For my people dere ist no point in making such exclusionary rules. Ve are confident dot she vill be vell vhen ve find her."

Sylvinski was a bit scandalized. "You seem a bit blasé about this missing girl."

Johann smiled. Magni-Freyan teeth were a bit frightening to the uninitiated. "Dot little girl could bend an inch t'ick iron bar in half, Herr Commissar. After die life ve haff had dis is not so frightening."

Sylvinski was impressed and let curiosity overcome political tact. "If I may inquire, what exactly was done to your ancestors?"

"Herr Brannhard, perhaps it vould be best if you explained."

Gus nodded. "I read the report that Morgan Holloway gave the governor when he first proposed the purchase of land for Johann's people."

Gus explained how several Terro-human genes were spliced into the genetic makeup of as-yet unborn children. Among these were mutations that, if properly managed, would be very beneficial. One such genetic sequence improved their vision by adding new cones in the optic makeup, allowing for greater color perception, as well as adjusting the vision for 20/10 and even 20/5. The exact reason for this modification was not known. Gus supposed that the rogue scientists simply took advantage of the situation to try a few things out.

Next, they added an LRP5 mutation to increase bone density to the highest degree. This, at least, would be beneficial on a high-gravity planet. Fortunately, the scientists also designed a stopgap measure to prevent the development of boney protrusions often associated with the mutated gene.

To keep them working under harsh conditions, the MCR1 gene was introduced to give the Freyans increased pain tolerance. This would allow then to continue working even if injured as long as the injury was not too severe.

The DEC2 gene reduced the Freyans' need to sleep. This was to allow them to work much longer than normal humans. On average, Johann only needed five hours of sleep a night to feel fully refreshed for the next day's labors.

Additionally, a percentage of the Freyan's blood was given a sort of mild sickle-cell to boost the immunity to diseases and infection. Workers resistant to illness would be more productive.

Perhaps most importantly, the proteins myostatin and activin A, which regulate muscle development, were mostly suppressed to allow nearly unchecked muscle growth. Freyans so treated would develop extreme musculature even without heavy resistance training.

"Vun t'ing die demon doctors did not account for ist our greater regenerative properties. Ve can recofer from many extreme inchuries," Johann added. Sylvinski was slightly dubious until Johann explained how Rheiner had survived multiple gunshot wounds and direct exposure to the vacuum of space and was fully recovered in three weeks. Gus backed the Bürgermeister.

"Good God!" Sylvinski was almost aghast at the implications. An army of such people would be a nearly unstoppable force. "I don't want to be indelicate, but…"

"Vhy do our faces look as dey do?" Johann finished the sentence. "Dot ve are not sure of. I suspect it vas an after t'ought to make us easy to spot should ve escape. Rheiner vas die first to look much like our ancestors und vas able to escape fairly easily. Nobody took a second glance at him."

"Oh. Thank you for that, but I was wondering why you all speak German? It is almost a dead language on Terra. I know of only one planet where it is still used."

"Ach, Herr Commissar," Johann said. "Many of die oferseers dot verked vit' us vere orichinally from Heimdall. It vas simply easier for dem to teach us Deutsch instead of Lingua Terra. Ve haff a slightly different dialect due to die Sosti influence."

"Sosti…oh, right, the native tongue of Freya. Interesting," Sylvinski said. "Was Heimdall responsible for part of your compensation?"

This confused Johann. "Vhy should die actions of a few reflect on an entire planet?"

"Every world has its criminal element," Gus explained. "These particular mutts just happened to have immigrated from Heimdall instead of Terra."

* * *

After fending off several suitors, Janice requested to stay in one of the rooms Johann had provided for the visiting dignitaries. The Bürgermeister even provided an all-female escort. It was quite a change from how things went on Terra. Normally, men would either ignore her or treat her like a kid sister. A few of the better class ignored her birthmark, but none seemed particularly interested in developing a committed relationship with her. Once, she used concealing makeup to hide the mark and went to a lounge. More men seemed interested in her that way, yet she couldn't help but think they would run off if she removed the concealing cream.

Then she met Buck Trask, who wasn't the least put off by the mark. He seemed genuine in his interest, at least. Still, she couldn't help thinking that he might have an ulterior motive for spending time with her.

What that was she couldn't even begin to imagine.

Janice had virtually no influence over Supervisor Sylvinski. In fact, she had never even met the Supervisor until this assignment came up. Even if she had any ability to influence Sylvinski, what would that do for a captain of the FBCI? The Supervisor had no ability to affect the career of anybody in the Federation Bureau of Criminal Investigation or any other law-enforcement officer beyond making a positive or negative report about their work, most of which was usually ignored by the agencies involved.

That brought her to considering the possibility that Trask was interested in her *for* her. That opened the way for new problems. If they were to enter into a relationship, would he be willing to return to Terra with her or would he expect her to stay on Zarathustra with him?

Actually, the little she saw of this world made her consider staying on. Mallorysport was a thriving metropolis, though nowhere near as large as Sydney or Johannesburg. There were exotic animals, cleaner air and, from what she had heard from the commissioner's rants, no taxes.

She sat down and gave some hard thought to Trask. If she stayed on Zarathustra and Trask's interest in her was less serious than she hoped, would she still be willing to stay on a colony world? Equally important, what if Trask was a workaholic type who stayed long hours at the office? He had already cancelled one date due to his work. Then there was his career. Law enforcement of any kind was a dangerous vocation. Even if they got married and settled down, she could end up a widow in very short order.

Janice's thoughts were interrupted by a knock at the door. "Come in. It's not locked."

One of the Freyan women who escorted Janice to her room entered. She recognized the visitor as Jutta. "You should keep the door locked, *Fräulein* Goodfellow."

"Please, call me Janice. If I may say so, your command of Lingua Terra is very good."

Jutta nodded. " Danke. I worked in administration as a secretary. There I was exposed to immigrants from other worlds who did not speak

German." She rubbed her neck absently. "They made me wear a control collar while I worked there to make certain I didn't give away what they were doing, not that I would have known these men weren't a part of the slaver's operation. I will say I was treated well otherwise. Slightly better food and nobody tried to chase me around the desk." Jutta noticed the curious look on Janice's face and laughed. "Some men are not too choosy about who they mate with so long as they mate with someone, or something. I have heard stories of Terros that, um, partnered with Khooghra females."

"Oh, Ghu!" Like almost everybody, Janice knew the reputation of the Khooghra was less than flattering. "That borders on bestiality."

"Terros who take such liberties are charged with crimes as Khooghras are considered incompetent aborigines with the lowest recorded mentation of any human race," Jutta said. "And believe it or not, a few men did make a pass at me back on Magni."

Janice recalled from her history classes that there was a woman named Julia Pastrana who had been dubbed the ugliest woman on Earth. She suffered from hypertrichosis and gingival hyperplasia. She looked very apelike, in fact, yet she received numerous marriage proposals. Jutta was far more attractive than poor Julia Pastrana.

"No, actually, I can believe it," Janice said seriously. "On Terra my birthmark is considered something of a disfigurement." Now it was Jutta's turn to be surprised. "Really. Most Terrans have such marks removed."

"But you did not." Jutta nodded. "Perhaps you knew in some way that it made you special?"

"Well, my grandmother always said it was a good sign though she didn't explain why," Janice said. "She was from Freya so I am one quarter Freyan."

Jutta's eyes went wide. "You are? That is fantastic!"

Janice decided it might be best to change the subject. "Oh, did you want something?"

"Ach! I almost forgot. You rooms are ready for you now."

"Rooms?" Janice looked about at her current lodgings. It would be considered a suite in a Terran hotel. "I thought this was it."

Jutta shook her head. "No, this was just a temporary waiting place while we made up something suitable for you. If you will come with me?"

Gus had cautioned Janice about being a prima donna while adding she should also go along with whatever the Magni-Freyans wanted… within reason.

"Okay. I'll just get my things…"

"I will carry that for you." Jutta grabbed the suitcase and steamer trunk. The suitcase wasn't too heavy as it was only clothing but the steamer weighed around forty kilos, which was why it had wheels at one end for easy transport. Jutta either didn't notice or just ignored the wheels and hefted the trunk like it was filled with feathers.

"Oh, you don't have to do that—"

Jutta shook her head. "It is my honor."

Outside of the room Janice and Jutta met up with the other three women who formed the escort party. Their names were Arla, Delia and Kirsten. Kirsten, the largest, took the lead with the rest walking behind Janice. They took her security very seriously.

"Jutta, is all of this really necessary," Janice asked. "Your people seem very nice. You don't think I will be attacked, do you?"

Jutta grinned. "My lady, there is attacked, then there is *attacked.* Many of the crimes against women are against our ways, even more so than on Freya. Partly because the strength difference between men and women is very slight among the Magni-Freyans. A suitor is on guard against annoying the focus of his interest for fear of what she could do if annoyed. And also partly because our laws are very strict in this matter. Those convicted of rape are put to death. We don't want that kind of man, or woman, for that matter, making life harder for the rest of us.

"In your case, we are just keeping the men back to a respectful distance. We don't want another incident like earlier today."

The incident was the result of Gus Brannhard interfering with a young man, Siegfried, from giving Janice his bracelet. Unknown to Gus or Janice, such interference was considered provocation to a fight. While Gus was a fairly large and strong man as Terrans go, Siegfried would have ripped his head off had not Johann stepped in.

Janice shivered at the recollection. "No, I don't want anybody getting hurt. Not me, either."

Kirsten laughed. "You? Get hurt? Nein! Right now you are die safest *Fräulein* on Zarat'ustra. Effery man in Neu Freya vould face a damnt'ing naked to protect you."

"*Ja*," Delia agreed. "Die vun vit' die Mark of die Gods ist sacred to all Freyans. Dot includes ve Magni-Freyans. It giffs you great power. Der ist also some responsibility."

Janice felt a bit crestfallen. "So, the young men here want to, what, marry me because of the power I am supposed to have?"

"*Nein*!" All four women said in harmony. Jutta continued. "Any Freyan man you married would be in your shadow. He would be expected to obey your every whim and even die, if necessary, to protect you. Does that sound like a prize you would want to win?"

Janice admitted she wouldn't. "Then why all the trouble with the bracelet?"

"You are an attractif vomen in a city of gorillas, *Fräulein*," Delia said. "You vould haff attractif *Kinder*. Die Mark indicates dot die gods vould approve of you und any union you entered into vit' a Magni-Freyan man."

"Gorillas? Oh, no! You look nothing like that. Who told you such a thing?"

"The Overseers on Magni," Jutta said.

"Have you ever seen a gorilla? I mean a picture of one?" The women admitted they had not. Janice pulled out her data pad and called up her encyclopedia. "This is what a Terran gorilla looks like."

Everybody looked at the screen. They were silent for so long Janice became worried. Then Jutta started laughing.

Janice was confused. "What is so funny?"

"We knew that being called gorillas by the Masters was supposed to be an insult, but never had a frame of reference before," Jutta explained. "Now we do."

"And you are not angry about it?"

"Ach, *ja*, ve are fery angry," Delia said. "But vhat ken ve do about it? Die Masters are light-years avay, many in Prison House on Terra, or possibly *tot*, um, dead. But die gorilla ist so cute! It looks a bit like a fery big kolph, vhich many Freyans keep as pets."

"Dot doesn't mean ve vouldn't take revenge on die Masters if dey effer came to *Neu* Freya," Kirstin added.

The women discussed the gorilla and wondered if it were possible to get one for a pet. Janice couldn't help admiring the emotional strength of the Magni-Freyans. After centuries of abuse to have a sense of humor about it was amazing.

The rooms she was escorted to amounted to a presidential suite. Janice was incredulous. Her apartment on Terra wasn't half as big. "This is too much!"

The Magni-Freyan women looked around. It was decorated in high Freyan style with wood furniture and furs. A few wood carvings for decoration and a marble bust of a man's head accounted for all the non-essential décor.

"Oh, my! This is very nice." Janice looked around and spotted the wet bar. "This must be somebody's home! I can't move in and take over."

"It vas meant for Prince Morgan, but he has a kestle on Beta und rarely stays ofer night." Kirsten explained. "But ve kept die apartment ready chust in case."

"Prince Morgan?"

Jutta tapped the bust. "This is his image. It was he who freed us from the masters on Magni."

"I can't…"

"He would insist on it. He is of Freya as well."

Janice was beginning to feel boxed in. She couldn't outright refuse the Magni-Freyans' hospitality as it could provoke an interstellar political incident. Supervisor Sylvinski cautioned everybody to mind the local customs before leaving Mallorysport. Janice found herself wishing she had listened more closely to her grandmother's stories of Freya.

"Uh, if you are certain, um, Prince Morgan won't mind…."

"He vould insist on it," Delia said. "It vill be a great honor for him."

"Could Dana stay with me here?"

"You may invite anybody you wish to stay as long as you like." Jutta winked. "There are several men in town that would happily volunteer to be your consort."

Janice blushed so deeply it almost obscured the birthmark.

XXII

Jack cursed softly under his breath. With Betty in the office he wasn't comfortable expressing his ire out loud even though he had, on occasion, heard similar language from her. Betty didn't hear the specifics but got the gist.

"Problem, Jack?"

"Rheiner and Cinda found the aircar that Magni-Freyan girl borrowed in the Keaton province about two hundred miles in from the eastern shore," Jack said. "The girl wasn't with it. Her footprints were crossed with that of a damnthing's tracks, which isn't good."

"Oh, Ghu!" Betty exclaimed. "Wait, as a Magni-Freyan isn't she able to handle a damnthing?"

Under other circumstances, Jack might have laughed. This was too grim to be funny. "A damnthing is about two tons of pure mean. Even the strongest Magni-Freyan couldn't stand up to that empty-handed. I understand that this Brünnhilde might have a .500 Magnum pistol with her, but that isn't very good protection against a charging damnthing. It took two shots from my 12.7 Express to drop the one that came on my property a few years ago."

Now Betty was confused. "Didn't Maid Marian kill one with her bow and arrows?"

"With about two dozen Fuzzies on Curtyses backing her up. And she was able to hit both eyes. William Tell would have had a hard time competing with that kind of accuracy. The Freyans on Magni were bred for strength and endurance and, as Rheiner demonstrated on the slaver's ship, the ability to recover from almost anything that didn't kill them outright. But they never so much as looked at a gun until Morgan freed them. I doubt this Brünnhilde could hit the broad side of a barn standing inside of it."

"Can she outrun a damnthing?"

Jack considered and said he thought not. "I clocked one doing almost forty miles an hour for a short distance. They can go fast, but not for long. A highly trained human athlete can do around thirty, and then only when raised on a high-gravity world. I don't think a Freyan could go any faster though they might be able to go longer in Zarathustran gravity. But for how long? The damnthing could easily run her down. Even if she got away initially, moving all that muscle on two legs would likely sap her strength allowing the damnthing, or another opportunistic predator, to catch her. I think she could manage a bush goblin well enough, but anything larger and she'll be in trouble."

Betty looked concerned. "So, what are we doing about it?"

"Piet is already diverting some ZNPF troopers to that area," Jack said. "They'll start at the downed airship then spiral out in wider circles. They will also use their sound systems to call out for her. That should frighten away some of the smaller predators though it will attract the larger ones, hopefully away from Brünnhilde."

Betty shook her head. "Boy, I would hate to be on the business end of the hiding she'll get when she is recovered and sent back home."

"Mainline Freyans don't use corporal punishment as a rule," Jack said. "Especially not the altered ones. With their thick skin and rock-hard muscle, I doubt it would be very effective, anyway. According to Morgan they see anything like that as following the example of the overseers. They want nothing to do with that."

A beep from the comscreen interrupted the conversation.

"Gus, how is the visit to Neu Freya coming along?"

"Not too badly, so far," Gus said. "Supervisor Sylvinski is behaving himself and not annoying Johann and company, too badly. He must have learned better manners after his initial meeting with Ben."

"And the woman…Janice?...is she keeping her cool about the whole favorite of the gods thing?"

"As far as I know," Gus said. "They have her set up in the penthouse of a hotel here that used to be a warehouse. She has four female guards so she shouldn't have to worry about bracelets flying at her from every direction."

Jack peered more closely at the screen image. "Is that a shiner? How did that happen?"

Gus absently put a hand to his left eye. "I bracelet-blocked one of the Magni-Freyans. Since my head is still attached, I think the punch was an accident."

"How does somebody punch you by accident?" Betty asked, from behind Jack.

Gus grimaced. "The boy was rushing forward with the bracelet when I stepped in front of him. He tried to stop short and his hand went up, the one holding the bracelet, and pow! I can't be certain, but I think he was a little impressed that I stayed on my feet. All the same, I'm getting an X-ray to make sure he didn't break anything."

Jack stifled a chuckle. Only somebody like Gus could take a hit like that and stay conscious.

"Oh, and some young buck by the name of Wolfgar wants to know when he can come out for more boxing lessons." Gus looked dubious. "Do we really need to teach these people how to do more damage?"

"It is about discipline and control. Besides, nobody outside of Neu Freya will try to pick a fight with one of these guys. None with any sense, anyway. So, did you call just to shoot the…um…time of day or was there something else?"

Gus nodded. "Have you heard from Morgan?"

"Not since he got back and picked up the veridicator," Jack said. "I think he is out hunting down those…um…people we spoke about earlier." It wouldn't do to discuss the counterfeit sunstones and the potential damage to the market on an open frequency. "We haven't spoken since."

"Well, if you do hear from him tell him to get his ass over to Neu Freya ASAP. Sylvinski is making noises about this colony being recognized by the Freyan monarchy."

Jack said, "I thought you settled that with the precedent of the Thoran colony."

"Only for the moment. His lawyer, Clarence Burr, informed him that the colony has to be recognized by their home world as a vassal state."

Jack was surprised. "You didn't already know that?"

"Of course, I did," Gus said. "But Sylvinski can do his own damned research. Which it looks like he did. I need to speak with Morgan to see if he has any documentation to back the new colony up."

Jack felt the stirrings of dread. "And if he doesn't have anything?"

Gus wasn't certain and said so. "The commission might try to invalidate the sale of Zeta and require the colony to submit to Federation law without the protections a sanctioned colony would have. That means they could be drafted into the military, if the excrement strikes the wind generator on some planet or planets."

Jack recalled Rheiner's example of durability and recuperation. The Federation military forces would like nothing better than to fill their ranks with such men and women. Any one of the Magni-Freyans would be worth five times his weight in Marines; and they weighed a lot. While the Federation did not currently draft people, the power to do so was still on the books. So if something like the Isis Insurrection were to pop up....

"I will send him your way the nanosecond I hear from him, Gus," Jack said. "I would hate to see these people released from one kind of slavery, only to be dragged into another."

"One other thing," Gus added. "Any word on that Magni-Freyan girl who got herself lost over there?"

"Not yet. Rheiner Sostreus and Cinda Dawn are out looking, as are a fair number of the ZNPF. The problems are that it is a lot of real estate to cover and the infra-red scanners get confused by the local fauna. Bush goblins throw about as much heat as a fair sized human. Goofers traveling in a pack cause the same problem. Fuzzies, too, for that matter."

"Yeah, I can imagine. The upside is that anything short of a zarawolf won't present too much trouble for her. Tunnel worms won't be able to dig through her super-dense musculature, either, according to the doctor at the hospital I spoke with. All the same, her parents are concerned. This is the first time anything like this has happened to any of them. Oh, I almost forgot; Sylvinski is sending one of his people here over to the Rez. A Dana Alexander. She'll be sniffing around the files."

Jack nodded. "I expected that sooner or later. Why didn't he take her out there first?"

"I suspect he was going to have her root around in the Rathaus paperwork." Gus chuckled a bit. "After the reception Miss Goodfellow received, I think he just doesn't want to risk the Freyans finding something special about her, too."

* * *

Outside of Jack's office, Little Fuzzy and Emily Dickinson overheard the conversation between their pappy and Pappy Gus.

"Big One lost? We go help find."

"We need to know where she got lost, Little Fuzzy," Emily Dickinson said. "We will need to see a map and find out how far away she might be."

Little Fuzzy nodded. Map reading was another one of the skills taught at the reservation school. Little Fuzzy had become very conversant in that area, after he was lost once himself.

"I ask Pappy Jack where Big One is lost and find on map. Then we go and help."

Jack Holloway explained to Little Fuzzy that it was far-far to where Brünnhilde was believed to be. He opened a map on the viewscreen.

"This is where we are, a couple hundred miles from the western ocean," Jack explained, using a laser pointer to indicate the location. He set the image to zoom in on where he was pointing. The school and the ZNPF buildings came into view.

Little Fuzzy had seen this done before but was still impressed.

"Now, we zoom back out." The image shrank until the entire continent was visible. Jack placed the pointer on the east coast of the continent. "Rheiner and Cinda found the aircar around this area. This is a few thousand miles from where we are right now. On dog mounts it would take weeks, maybe even months, to get out there."

Little Fuzzy struggled with the concept of "thousands." When Fuzzies were first discovered, they could count to five, then to twenty-five. Anything more was "many," then "many-many." In the years since the school was started up, Fuzzies, while adept at the physical sciences involving fletching, smithing and even small construction, abstractions like hundreds and thousands came slowly. It wasn't something they could readily see or touch.

Emily Dickinson solved this by setting up tins of XT3, first in stacks of five, then stacks of twenty-five, then several stacks equaling a hundred. She also arranged for a recording of human children counting to one hundred to be played for them. She hadn't gotten to numbers greater than one hundred herself, yet.

"A thousand is two hands of a hundred," Jack explained. Little Fuzzy looked at his hands then mentally bridged the gap. Emily Dickinson was having much the same trouble. While her grammar and word knowledge far surpassed any other Fuzzy, she was a Fuzzy herself and had some difficulty grasping the higher mathematics.

"Not ride dogs there," Little Fuzzy countered. "Take aircars then look with dogs."

Emily Dickinson cringed at the suggestion. The thought of being in any motor vehicle still frightened her.

"We don't have more than a few aircars available, right now, Little Fuzzy."

Little Fuzzy thought hard. If Unka Morgan were there he could take many-many Fuzzies and dogs fast-fast in his yacht. But Unka Morgan was away.

"Hokay. Then take me and Emily Dickinson and Mike and Mitzi and Mama Fuzzee and Baby Fuzzee and Cinderella and Ko-Ko to aircar place. We can look from there. Follow tracks. Talk to other Fuzzee there. We go in small groups with police."

Emily looked like she wanted to run and hide. Jack saw this and hesitated. Besides, he didn't want to put his whole family at risk. Out east the ZNPF hadn't gotten around to clearing out some of the more dangerous fauna yet. There were way more damnthings, and even a few harpies still flying around. After the rise in the goofer population, Ben Rainsford had called a moratorium on harpy season on Beta.

Jack considered the risks, then thought about the Fuzzies training at the school and the better equipment they could carry. Besides, his Fuzzies were all adults, except for Baby Fuzzy and he was coming up fast. Adults were expected to shift for themselves, not be pampered like some pets.

"Hokay, Little Fuzzy," Jack said. "I'll get one of the officers to take you and as many Fuzzies as he can in a troop transport next shift change. Make sure everybody has a radio and a rifle. If something bad comes along, you hide fast and shoot only if necessary. No point attracting a damnthing if you don't have to." Jack thought it over for a moment. "On second thought, during shift change I can arrange for each patrol car to take a couple Fuzzies with their dogs out with them like you suggested. If you and Emily are ready to go, Unka George can take you two out."

Little Fuzzy was excited, while Emily Dickinson was horrified. The idea of flying out in an aircar made her feel sick to her stomach. Since her arrival on the Rez she hadn't gone anywhere that a dog mount couldn't take her.

According to Dr. Mallin, Emily Dickinson's case was unique among Fuzzies. Unlike the natural fear of a damnthing or a harpy, the fear that a motor vehicle could crash was less rational. Fuzzies, to date, were the most rational people he had ever studied, almost immune to many of the psychosis that affected more advanced sapient species.

Little Fuzzy noticed that Emily was shaking and tried to console her. "I go with Pappy Jack in aircar many-many times. I even went to the little moon in Navy shuttle an' fly in Unka Morgan's big-big aircar…um… yacht. Pappy Jack not let bad things happen to us."

Emily understood and still she was frightened at the prospect of getting into an aircar and flying out to the east coast. The accident that made her forget the Lingua Fuzzy still replayed itself in her nightmares. The brain damage she suffered from the crash that destroyed her native tongue also made it difficult for her to relearn the language of her people.

Dr. Mallin had suggested that she try to overcome this phobia by using very small transport devices and working her way up. She started with a hover board. Ko-Ko, who was very adept at the use of this children's toy, demonstrated how easy it was to use and even did some fancy tricks he learned from the viewscreen. It took Emily several tries before she could stay on it for more than a few seconds.

"Emily, you don't have to go if you don't want to," Jack said softly. "The others will understand."

Emily looked first at Pappy Jack, then at Little Fuzzy. She saw sympathy and understanding there. "No. I will go. But I will sit in back with my eyes shut."

Jack was impressed and said so. It was easy to do a thing you were not afraid of, but it took real courage to do something even when it scared the Niflheim out of you.

XXIII

Brünnhilde grimaced as she ate the XT3 from the tin. Her plan was to make every other meal the power bars or whatever she could find through foraging, and the alternate meals the vile XT3. She recognized the dietetic value of the stuff just as she knew her Magni-Freyan body required a lot of nutrition. She also knew that if she ate all the food she liked first, she would eventually have nothing but the XT3 for later. Better to pace herself on both counts.

Off in the distance she could see a damnthing again. It was a large and unpleasant carnivore, about the size of a Terran rhinoceros, which had a single horn on its forehead and one on either side of the lower jaw. She didn't know if it was the same or a different one. Either way, she wanted to avoid getting its attention. Earlier she found an ironwood tree branch and, with great difficulty even with her strength, fashioned a spear. She didn't bother trying to make a spearhead out of stone; the ironwood was named for its phenomenal strength and hardness. It was a painstaking chore just to whittle the end into a point.

Like the school on the Fuzzy Reservation, Prince Morgan had set up a school to teach the Magni-Freyans how to survive on their own, as well as teach them such skills as were denied them back when they were still slaves.

Not every Magni-Freyan had worked in mines. Some worked in administrative offices, although with control collars to insure their obedience. Others worked in the hydroponics and carniculture labs that supplied most of the food for the Magni-Freyans. A special few worked in the repair shop for maintaining the heavy mining equipment.

Brünnhilde's mother, Ernestine, made and repaired the clothing the miners used. Her father was a heavy equipment operator who dug the new tunnels in the Magnian earth. Brünnhilde was apprenticed to her mother when Prince Morgan had set them free. She was almost twelve years old at that time and had worked in the mines for three years before that.

There were still a number of skills needed for running a colony that the Magni Overseers did not provide. To help fill in the gaps, Morgan and Victor Grego arranged for teaching machines, often used on new colony worlds until living teachers could be brought in, and instructional videos to be used in Neu Freya. Brünnhilde made good use of those resources.

The meal, such as it was, finished, Brünnhilde buried the empty tin. As an afterthought, she placed a heavy rock over the filled in dirt to be sure some poor animal didn't dig it up and cut itself on it. Checking her compass, she again proceeded west. The idea of meeting some Fuzzies was no longer her main concern. She wanted to find civilization, a hot bath and a good meal, not necessarily in that order.

With her superior eyesight she scanned the horizon. Tall grass, an occasional featherleaf tree and a whole lot of nothing awaited her in the direction she was going. She was hoping to spot a lake or river. She would be out of water soon and needed to replenish.

Grumbling at the situation, for which she gave herself all the blame, Brünnhilde continued her trek through the willowgrass. She wanted to run or even jump. Magnians could leap a good distance in the lower gravity of Zarathustra. Doing so, she realized, might cause her to land or trip on some sort of local wildlife.

She didn't fear much where small animals were concerned. Unfortunately, there could be something bigger, like a sleeping zarawolf or bush goblin or, worse yet, a nest of tunnel worms. She wasn't certain even her thick skin and solid muscle would be enough to protect her from that.

From the little she remembered of Beta Continent from the teaching machine, Brünnhilde knew that there would be some small villages around the Rez, and a few abandoned ones in Fuzzy territory. Little to nothing would be found this far to the east. So, with one hand on the .500 Magnum and the other holding the spear, she made her way west through the veldt.

* * *

Junktown had two major sections: the clapboard buildings and the economy housing. Due to the efforts of Victor Grego and Clancy Slade, the clapboard part was shrinking while the economy housing was expanding. A minor section of Junktown consisted of single occupant pods that were portable and almost completely self-sufficient. Solar powered units equipped with sanitation facilities, mini-kitchens and sleeping cots that could be hooked up to a ground roller for easy transport. Not that anybody in any section of Junktown could afford such a vehicle.

Arthur Twopersons lay comfortably on his cot watching the viewscreen, one of the few possessions he was able to keep after he lost his livelihood in Mortgageville. On the news feed there was still a lot of talk about the bank bombing in Mallorysport and the possible cause. Speculation arose that it was a response to the lease deal for the unseated lands and the Chartered Zarathustra Company. Some people were still unhappy with the lease deal between the Colonial Government and the Charterless Zarathustra Company. Especially in Junktown, where a lot of folks had hoped to run out and lay claim to some undeveloped real estate.

In fairness to the Governor, the lease deal kept the planet going without taxes. Nobody could complain about that except some members of the Legislature. No taxes, but no land on which to build a new life. That part hit the residents of Junktown the hardest.

Many of the Junktownies were people who came in when the CZC was still hiring. At least they were when the notices on the job boards of other worlds were posted. But the transmission of information was slow in the Federation and often out of date by the time any news or data hit the next world. As a result, hundreds of people arrived on Zarathustra only to discover that all the jobs were taken.

The CZC did what they could to assist the newcomers. Some were given passage back to Gimli, the next closest world where jobs, if not high-paying, were available. A few people, considered good risks, were set up in small businesses on the edge of Mallorysport. These failed to thrive as the CZC could produce almost anything faster and cheaper, even though Victor Grego tried to curtail the competition from the

Company wherever possible. Within three years the last business closed its doors and the area became known as Mortgageville, after the bank had no choice but to foreclose on all of them.

Arthur grunted in annoyance and shut the screen off. The pod, provided for Arthur by Clancy Slade as compensation for work he did on Clancy's new home, was equipped with a viewscreen, comscreen, mini-fridge and even a small computer. All of the equipment and amenities were built into the pod to prevent theft or piecing them out for quick cash. This protected the occupants from both burglars and themselves.

Arthur sat up on the cot and pulled a beer out of the fridge. The can was old-style instead of self-cooling. Arthur was only willing to spend so much in his circumstances. Stuck to the fridge with a magnetic holder was a flyer calling for support for the Martianist cause. They didn't pay anything, of course, but there was always food and drink at the meetings.

Arthur had gone to one of the Martianist seminars. What struck Arthur as odd, besides the strange incense they used, were the peculiar questions they asked under veridication. Some questions he recognized as psychological tests. One in particular really stood out: Are you connected with law enforcement? Anybody that came up red for any reason was ushered out and never seen again.

After the questions came the sales pitch, Arthur was ready to leave by that time but he was getting hungry and had already cadged three free meals from the Soup Kitchen that week. The free eats promised after the spiel kept Junktownies from walking out. Not that the seminar was dull.

The main speaker was a man named John Carter. Arthur heard somewhere that a lot of Mars Colony residents took their names from books like *John Carter of Mars* and *The Martian Chronicles*, both written by long-dead authors from Terra. Still, the speaker was not boring and had given Arthur something to think about.

John Carter started out by introducing the concept that all of mankind originated from Mars. DNA comparisons with samples taken from the mummified remains discovered on Mars and living Terro-humans showed surprisingly little difference. Moreover, Freyan DNA was closer to the Martian DNA than that of Terro-humans.

That little factoid suggested that Martians settled on Freya untold thousands of years earlier. One person in the audience had argued that the Terrans should have been a closer match, since it was much easier to travel within the solar system than traverse interstellar space. Carter smiled at that and pointed out that Terra had something Freya did not: a sapient race already in residence. These creatures somehow interbred with the Martians, adding traces of their DNA to the genome. Freyan Martians were therefore purer than the Terran stock. This also explained why the Freyan women seemed so much more beautiful than Terran women. A few women snorted at that and shook their heads, though none spoke up to argue the point.

As the speaker continued, Arthur found himself nodding in agreement. Everything Carter said made sense to him. He didn't even wonder how Martians could have made it all the way out to Freya in the first place. After the lecture, things got a little hazy in Arthur's memory. He recalled being given some of the incense that he was now burning in the pod, and a box that he was not to open for a few days.

After finishing his first beer, Arthur decided to splurge and have a second. On average he could only afford one six-pack a week. Lying back, he popped the top, then reached for the bag of pretzels in the cabinet above the cot. Almost everything was in ready reach in the tight confines of the pod. While there was talk of newer, larger pods, they were intended for multi-person occupancy with space determined by the number of residents.

The comscreen beeped. Arthur reached over and tapped the answer button. After a brief explosion of Technicolor, the screen resolved into an image of a green man with four arms.

"Arthur. Carter. Thoris. Tarkis. Helium. Engage."

Arthur's face relaxed into a vacant look. He sat up, opened a drawer, and then extracted a box, such as one that might contain new shoes. Box tucked under his left arm, Arthur left the pod. In stocking feet he walked to the midpoint between Podville and the clapboard constructs. There he stopped and took the box in both hands.

"Restore Mars!" Arthur yelled, then opened the box.

The explosion instantly killed and all but vaporized the body of Arthur Twopersons. The nearby pods, made mostly of polysteel and duraplas, did not suffer any real damage from the blast. However, the pods that were only held in place by weight atop locked wheels, failed to remain anchored in their positions and tumbled over, sometimes rolling a short distance. The pods could take such abuse easily. The people inside of them did not fare quite so well.

The shanty town constructs were instantly blown apart and in many instances caught fire. Dozens of the occupants died instantly. Others lingered on a while before fire control vehicles and ambulances arrived only to die on the way to the hospital.

The police arrived on the heels of the ambulances and provided what assistance they could. There would be time for investigating and interviewing witnesses later.

* * *

"Restore Mars!"

The viewscreen filled with light and sound in the computer simulated rendition of the explosion in Junktown. "There you have it, according to eyewitness accounts and police forensic evidence interpretation. The individual who set off the bomb was identified as Arthur Twopersons, a Junktown resident in the section known as Podville. Current estimates have it at seventy-three people dead, forty-seven seriously wounded and another nineteen with minor injuries. Our people on the scene are currently barred from the bomb site as there is concern that another bomb could be in the area—"

Ben Rainsford turned off the viewscreen and shook his head. This time there would be no way to keep the story quiet. Already, Marshal Fane was ordering a stepped up presence in Mallorysport, with video-drones buzzing about looking for any suspicious activity.

Suspicious activity? Ben grunted softly to himself. Not a lot is suspicious about a man who enters a bank until the whole thing blows up. That man in Junktown would have been fairly conspicuous walking around without his hat and shoes anywhere else except for Junktown where any number of people might be missing such items.

The real problem, of course, was that now it was out that Martianists were behind the bombings. Gerd van Riebeek once joked that Ruth was a closet Martianist. He would have to be very careful about making another such jest now. Citizens would be out for blood and almost every last one over the age of sixteen carried a gun of one type or another. Even in Junktown, where money was as scarce as hen's teeth, everybody was armed. The smallest spark could ignite a powder keg of hate, bloodlust and revenge. Anyone even expressing a sympathetic word for the Martianists could find themselves hanging from an ironwood tree before anybody could even think about stopping them.

Ben looked out from his terrace and took in the city. At any moment it could erupt with violence. And what would that serve? Only the Martianist agenda of dividing the planet and setting people against their neighbors. There would be the demonstrations, riots, slanted news coverage and even victims, real or setups, blaming the other side. People who didn't care a goofer's whisker about the Martianist cause would be rallying behind them just to be a part of something.

The intercom buzzed. Victor Grego was waiting in the outer office. Ben had him sent right in. The two men shook hands then took seats on the terrace.

"Victor, you usually give me some advance warning when you plan to come over," Ben said.

"I was just coming from the news station and thought you would want to hear this straight away," Grego said. "Hey, where's the kids?"

"I sent Flora and Fauna off to the Rez as soon as I heard about the second bomb," Ben said with a grimace. "I am tempted to issue a statement advising everybody with a Fuzzy to do the same."

Grego took out a cigarette and lit it. It was a stalling tactic to allow him a moment to think. "I don't think that is feasible, Ben. Jack has a pretty heavy load as it is. How many thousands of Fuzzies have been adopted and are living in Mallorysport?" Ben admitted he didn't know. "Mrs. Pendarvis or Ruth van Riebeek could give you an exact count, I would wager. Jack's staff is equipped to deal with the slow trickle of incoming Fuzzies and the slower trickle of Fuzzy adoptions. Dumping several thousand Fuzzies on him would—"

"I know!" Ben interrupted. "I couldn't do it anyway. I don't have the authority to order innocent people to surrender their Fuzzies. Not even for their own good. Niflheim! I couldn't even order the Fuzzies to go, if they don't want to."

"And you can bet, they wouldn't want to," Grego added. "They would instead want to stay and help fight the bad Big Ones." He threw up his hands in disgust. "Remember that debacle in northern Beta when the Reservation Fuzzies wanted to rescue Jack from the Jin-f'ke?"

"Morgan was lucky Flora and Fauna weren't hurt, or I would've... well, I couldn't challenge him to a duel. He'd slaughter me. And governors don't duel anyway. But I could sic Gus on him. Gus assured me that there were oomphty laws and regulations Morgan violated. I could bury him so deep in litigation he would never see sunlight again."

And Jack Holloway wouldn't lift a finger to help no matter how much he might want to, Grego thought. *Morgan dug his own hole and Jack couldn't fix it for him. A man stood up for himself. Period.*

"So, what did you want to see me about," Ben asked.

"Oh, right. I have ordered all of the CZC news outlets to soft-pedal the bombings and no mention of Martianist involvement will be made until Marshal Fane okays it. H.I.N. is agreeing to go along with us. I can't speak for any of the other newsfeeds."

Ben thanked Grego for that and thanked Ghu that there were no Streamers around to catch the incidents themselves.

"Streamers are just hopped up paparazzi. They go where the most action is. A random bank or Junktown wouldn't hold any interest for them. Until now."

Ben nodded. "That brings us to the next question: why Junktown?"

Grego thought for a moment then said, "We were able to hush up any Martianist involvement with the bank. I control the bank, hence any video footage inside of it. Nobody has any such control over Junktown. The people there were targeted for no other reason than it was a tragedy we couldn't contain. Even with my people in the news services playing it down, this was going to get out and go big sooner or later."

"Damnit, you're right." Ben got up and went back in his office and called Ned Foster. "Ned, I need you to get any and all warrants so you can to interrogate, investigate, and search every Martianist and their properties. Tell Judge Pendarvis that I will call a planetary emergency if I have to. I want these terrorists found and I bet some of them are members in good standing with the mainstream members."

Grego stood at the entrance and watched. The last time Ben was that hot for anything it was himself, and only Gus had been able to talk Ben out of going after the CZC. This time everybody would be onboard. He almost pitied the terrorists.

XXIV

The sound of the land rovers frightened away every small animal in their path. A damnthing, initially attracted by the noise, received a few shots from a .30-30 and was sufficiently discouraged as to not charge the caravan.

"Lucky for us, that was a young one," Bo said. "If he had reached full growth, he might've been more aggressive."

Weaver watched as the damnthing trotted away. "Don't be too sure we've seen the last of him. Damnthings have been known to circle back on their prey and take them by surprise from behind."

Clem watched as the brute first moved away, then slowly started to curve around. "Yup. He's doin' it, all right, Weave."

"Bo, get out the elephant gun. You should've kept it handy for something like this anyway."

Bo crawled back to the boot, extracted the CZC 550 bolt-action rifle and chambered a .600 round. He watched as the damnthing moved in a full circle behind the ground rollers. The huge beast moved with surprising stealth belying its monstrous bulk. When it felt it was close enough, the damnthing charged. That was the moment Bo pulled the trigger.

Bo didn't wait to see if he did any damage. Instead he quickly, deftly, chambered a second round and took aim. Now he could see the blood pouring from the first shot over the beast's left eye. The second round went into the head just above and to the left of the single horn. That finished it.

"It must have a brain the size of a pea to keep coming after that first hit!" Weaver cried out. "All stop! Bo, Clem, go skin that bastard and keep the primary horn and the hide."

"What the Niflheim for?" Bo protested. "It'll stink all the way to Terra."

"I have some instant tanning fluid we can spray on it. A few skins might help us sell our story about being prospectors. They live off the land a lot of the time and trade in furs and leather to stay afloat, while they keep looking for that big strike. This will just add to our credibility."

Bo and Clem grumbled but did as they were instructed. The carcass was left where it lay for the scavengers to feast on.

"Let's get some distance from this before the varmints come to dinner," Weaver ordered. "Everybody keep your head on a swivel. If we can bag a few more hides it will be all the better for us. We can use the money from selling them if nothing else."

"Fine," Bo said, "But we put them on the rear vehicle. No point in stinking up the whole caravan."

* * *

"This new footage clearly identifies the suicide bomber in Junktown as Arthur Twopersons, an unemployed finish carpenter—"

John Carter shut off the screen. "I can't believe our luck! A Streamer was in Junktown just as Twopersons activated."

"What was a Streamer doing in Junktown, anyway," Tars Tarkas wondered aloud.

"Probably looking for a low-rent prostitute," Dejah Thoris said. "Junktowners come in every stripe and do whatever they can to scrape by."

"Junktown*ies*," Tars corrected. "They are called Junktownies by the locals."

"He-she-it could have been there doing a documentary on the sex life of a land-prawn, for all I care," Carter interrupted. He was unaware that land-prawns were parthenogenetic females and thus had no sex life, nor would he have cared had he known. "The point is that the conditioning worked and we got our sound bite on the news. No more sending true believers out to die. We can use the castoffs of humanity to get our message and demands out in the public eye. I only wish we had succeeded before sending out Carthoris."

Everybody around the conference table nodded in agreement. Carthoris Carter had been a true believer, willing to sacrifice his life for the cause. His loss was felt by all.

"Now we can get started in earnest," John Carter continued. "We will send out three, ah, converts at random locations in the city. No playgrounds or schools or hospitals. That would only serve to make the locals more determined to defy us. Going after children or the infirm would make us appear to be bullies."

"What about the Fuzzies?" Kantos Kan suggested. "The people of this planet love Fuzzies more than anything."

John Carter shook his head. "No better, possibly even worse, than going after children. I have never seen any alien race that engendered so much affection from humans as these Fuzzies. And I have been to Loki."

Lokians were a fawn-like species that barely even had a concept of violence and none of slavery until humans set down on their planet. That was when Anton Gerrick masterminded a scheme to enslave the defenseless Lokians and work them to death in his mines. Over twenty thousand of the helpless natives died as a result.

Garrick, finally arrested on Fenris, was eventually taken back to Loki and hung in public to show the Lokians that even Terrans were not above the law. Nobody in the Martianist council wanted to end up like Anton Garrick.

"Okay," Tars Tarkis spoke up. "No children, patients or Fuzzies. I am actually a bit relieved by that."

"As am I," Dejah Thoris added. "Where are we on the abduction schedule? Has our target made himself visible, yet?"

Carter shook his head. "He vanished almost as quickly as he appeared. I have several members keeping watch for his return. Then we can grab him up."

Dejah nodded. "So what do we target for our next strike? It will have to be big."

"Indeed," Carter said with a smile. "And what are the biggest, most important targets, outside of anything relating to Fuzzies?"

It was as if somebody threw a switch. The lights came on in everybody's eyes.

* * *

The police cordon around the bombsite in Junktown began to attract as much attention as the original explosion. Streamers almost tripped over each other trying to get footage of the affair. To keep the voyeuristic public at bay, extra personnel were needed to man the barriers. As it was, there was only a skeleton crew working the perimeter. Chief Carr, watching the area on spyeye in his office, was hard put to find bodies to fill the positions until Officer Sullivan made a surprising suggestion.

"Why not? There are a lot of down-and-out cops and military men and women who live there. Why not hire them to guard the perimeter?"

Sullivan's partner, Officer Gilbert, agreed. "We actually kill two birds with one stone, Chief."

Chief Carr was uncertain. "How so?"

"Nobody will be more motivated to protect Junktown than the people who live there," Sullivan said. "Junktown is the last stop before being completely homeless. The housing is on par with a cardboard box, true, but when it is all you have, you fight to keep it."

"And," Gilbert chimed in, "if we hire people in Junktown to protect the crime scene, they will be paid, oh, rookie rate, I would guess. Not a lot, true, but a start toward getting them back on their feet."

Chief Carr sat back in his chair. "I won't say all, but a lot of the Junktownies are petty thieves, muggers, hookers and grifters. How do we find an honest enough crew to work with down there?"

"Veridicate the volunteers," Sullivan said.

"Yeah," Gilbert said. "If they refuse or don't pass, we don't take them on. You know, some of the ex-cops in Junktown were on the rolls until the Fuzzy Trial. Then you and Marshal Fane cleaned house and a whole lot of cops got axed."

"Some might see this as a chance to get back in uniform," Sullivan finished.

That knocked Carr back a bit. Generally, when a cop was cashiered for cause—that was the end of it. But Zarathustra was a young colony world, with limited amount of qualified personnel to fill the ranks. Maybe some of the cops who were kicked out could be brought back in, provided they hadn't committed any out-and-out felonies and passed veridication. They would start back on the bottom. Rookie status and pay and extended probation with periodic veridication to make sure they were staying on course.

"I'll have to sell the idea to Marshal Fane. I think it'll take a lot of fast talking."

"The marshal is a good guy," Gilbert said.

"Keeps a well-stocked wet bar in his office, too," Sullivan added. Carr raised an eyebrow. "We were in on the brainstorming session in his office during the Fuzzy Slaver case. Remember?"

"Now you mention it, I do. But don't talk that up too much. People might get the wrong idea."

* * *

Hugh Lennon had been wrestling with his conscience ever since he met with Supervisor Sylvinski. Messing around with a political climber didn't bother him at all. Dealing with people of that stripe was par for the course in the galaxy of big business. At least Sylvinski didn't seem as slimy as some he had dealt with in the past. Ambitious, sure, but by the book.

What bothered the Magnian was his own conduct: Basically, he'd sicced a pain in the ass bureaucrat on the Magni-Freyans. And that was what he found upsetting.

As a board member, Lennon was part of the organization that kept the Magni-Freyans enslaved to work in the mines. Like many others in the Chartered Magni Company, he had no knowledge of the slavery happening right under his nose. Only the men and women who needed to know, knew. Lennon hadn't, so he didn't.

It was the simple fact that he was an unwitting coconspirator in the operation, not to mention the act itself that bothered him. When John Morgan—correction, John Morgan Holloway—exposed everything and brought in the Feds, Lennon was a strong proponent of compensating the Freyans and the first to testify against the involved parties. He even pushed for more money in damages, and even nominated Morgan Holloway for chairman of the board. Morgan had to refuse as he was not going to stay on Magni.

The Magni-Freyans didn't deserve the harassment he sent their way.

Lennon paced back and forth in his quarters until he worked his way through to the other end of his thoughts. He came to what could be a very dangerous decision…for him.

* * *

Betty closed the file drawer, then opened the one below it. Next to her stood Dana Alexander from the Terran Commission. Dana was short, almost tiny in comparison to Betty's five-foot five-inch frame. She had stood on her toes while looking through the top drawer of the file cabinet.

"Find anything interesting, ladies?" Both women turned to see Jack Holloway in the doorway to the office. He took off his gun belt and hat, then said, "Why don't you two break for lunch? Miss Alexander, you can have me tarred and feathered on a full stomach."

Dana laughed. "Commissioner Holloway, nobody uses tar and feathers anymore. We seal them up in carbonite."

Betty laughed at Jack's visible confusion. "She's joking, Jack. She pulled that out of an old space-opera movie from, what, First Century, Atomic Era?"

Dana nodded. "I dated a guy who loved the old flatties. I am afraid I got hooked on them as well, if not the guy." She nodded at the filing cabinet. "Somebody has been sprucing up the files."

"That would be me," Betty said. "Just organizing. No creative reorganizing. The only thing the Native Affairs Office has to hide is the shabby filing system they have here. Had."

"I will have to look more closely at everything later," Dana said. "For now, I am content to see I won't have any trouble finding my way around. Lunch sounds good."

"Me, too." Betty grabbed her light jacket from a hook on the wall. "Jack….um, Commissioner Holloway, I'll take Miss Alexander over to El Cantina to try some of the local fare."

"Sure thing. Oh, could you bring me back a sandwich?"

"You got it, Boss."

El Cantina, another new construction on the Rez, was built in response to the need for an on-site eatery. The undersized kitchen in the ZNPF barracks was too small for the growing number of officers. Additionally, a building full of bachelor cops lacked for many with a skill in creative gastronomy.

Conveniently located between Jack's office building and the ZNPF barracks, it was a short walk for the two women. From the outside the Cantina looked like something from Old Mexico. Designed by Officer Carlos "Chico" Hernandez, who fancied himself full-blooded Mexican despite DNA tests to the contrary, El Cantina had the flavor of a bar he once saw in southern Mexico before he immigrated to Zarathustra ten years earlier. Chico even went so far as to set up an outdoor barbeque grill.

Betty led the way into the cantina and chose a quiet corner away from the ZNPF cops so they could talk. A robot, Little Fuzzy's idea as the Fuzzies were all amazed that a made-thing could be so smart, took their order and transmitted it to the chef who was very human and not a policeman.

The two women chatted while they waited for their orders, first about what Dana had and hadn't tried of the local fare, then Betty pumped her for some Terran gossip. Just before the robot returned with the meals, Betty decided to be straightforward with Dana.

"So, have you found anything interesting in Jack's files?"

"No, and I don't expect to," Dana said as she accepted her order from the robot. "Especially not after the whitewashing you gave them."

Betty was taken completely by surprise with that remark. "What do you mean? I just made them better organized."

Dana inspected her roast banjo bird sandwich before answering. "Forensic accounting is my field. I go through people's files almost every day. After a while I learned to spot quirks in how the filing was done. Before I came out to…um, what do you call this?"

"The Fuzzies call it 'The Wonderful Place' in their language. We Big Ones call it the Fuzzy Reservation—or the Rez, now."

"Right." Dana tried a small bite then took a mouthful. "This is good. Kind of like a cross between ham and turkey. Before I came out to the Rez, your Mr. Grego allowed me to do a little snooping in his files. I got the impression that it was getting to be something of a regular occurrence for him."

Betty laughed. "I guess in a way it is. First the Navy put a spy in the Company, Ruth Ortheris, then John Morgan came in after buying up a lot of Company stock and went through everything. That is how he met Akira, his new wife, and now you. I guess he'll install a revolving door to speed things up."

Dana couldn't be certain if Betty was joking about the door. "Um, okay, well, the files in Commissioner Holloway's office were organized just like the files at the CZC. Color coded tabs, drawers labeled for contents, a notebook with cross-referencing charts...how long did it take you to get it all fleshed out?"

Betty sighed in resignation. "Not as long as you might think. Jack and Piet keep things pretty organized. Jack ran his father's business back on Terra and Piet was a police chief before retirement was forced on him. Injured in the line of duty. The notebook and labels were all me, though."

"Well, even Supervisor Sylvinski isn't looking to catch Jack with his hand in the cookie jar," Dana admitted. "Captain Trask allowed us to go through his background checks on all the big players and he could see that Jack was a stickler for doing what he thought was right...and that he has been known to shoot a lot of people."

Betty shook her head and laughed. "He assured me that every person he ever shot had it coming. And there were a few he thought he should have shot and didn't. Leonard Kellogg, for instance."

"Ah, yes, I read about that on the datastream." Dana spotted a Fuzzy coming in the cantina. "Shooting would have been too good for any monster that would harm a Fuzzy."

"Ha! I think you and Jack will get along if you give him a chance," Betty said. "Just so long as you don't get along too well."

Dana still wasn't sure if Betty was joking or not. Better not to find out the hard way, she decided.

"If you don't mind my asking, why did your supervisor send you here, if he doesn't expect to find anything damaging?" Betty inquired between bites of her sandwich. "Weren't you out on Zeta with him?"

Dana nodded. "He decided my talents were wasted there. Privately, I think he was concerned that the Magni-Freyans would take a special interest in me, like they did Janice." Dana explained the situation with the birthmark. Betty didn't bother explaining she already knew about it. "With Janice being treated like Ghu's favorite daughter, Supervisor Sylvinski was feeling overshadowed and didn't like it."

"Why not just send Janice back to Alpha?"

Dana shook her head. "Mr. Brannhard suggested that it might cause a riot if their special woman vanished too quickly. The boss was smart enough to see the wisdom in that and decided to get me out of there before I became too popular or something."

"Humph. Some men have very fragile egos," Betty said.

"Oh? Does Commissioner Holloway?"

Betty had never given that any thought before. On reflection she realized Jack's ego was very healthy. "He is what they used to call a man's man before the term was retooled for a different meaning. Jack is one-hundred percent self-sufficient and self-reliant. He doesn't need anybody to prop him up and if I was in Miss Goodfellow's situation he would just tell me to enjoy it while it lasts. Nothing much threatens him emotionally, and anything that ever did physically is likely dead and buried now."

"Nothing emotionally?" Dana asked. "Doesn't he love you, his son and his Fuzzies?"

Betty recalled hearing that Jack was a wreck when Little Fuzzy was lost and believed dead. His drinking went way up to Gus Brannhard levels, which no man other than Gus could get away with. But he recovered even before Little Fuzzy was found.

"Okay, maybe he has the some vulnerabilities in that area," Betty admitted, "but he isn't threatened by the possibilities the way a lot of people are. I like to think he would be terribly upset if he lost me. Still, he recovered from losing his wife on Freya."

"Are you sure about that?"

Betty was surprised by the question. "What do you mean?"

"Well, he is seventy-seven and hasn't been married since, has he?"

Dana made a very good point. “Have you seen any photos of his first wife?”

“Oh, yes. He kept an old style hard-copy photo album and showed it to me and Morgan. Adonitia was a tiny thing standing next to him. Blonde like all of the Freyan people, petite to supermodel thinness. Lovely, of course. The whole damn planet could be supermodels.”

Dana thought she might be entering dangerous territory. “Do you think anything about you reminds him of her?”

“Hmm.” Betty thought it over. “I don’t think so. I am taller, darker, a bit more robust, though I’ll deck Jack if he ever says that. Personality wise, I have no way of knowing. Adonitia died in childbirth so even Morgan wouldn’t know.”

“How long have you two been keeping company? Oh, that really isn’t any of my business….”

Betty waved that off. “It’s fine. About two years, now.”

Dana debated whether to say anything. Caution lost the battle. “And the age difference doesn’t bother either of you?”

Betty looked amused. “Jack can hold his own against anybody half his age. His strength and energy is easily that of a thirty-year-old. I am not bothered at all. I think he might be…a little.”

XXV

The paperwork was in order, the argument compelling, and the bench warrant properly worded. Chief Justice Pendarvis could see no justification for denying Clarence Burr's petition. Ned Foster fought it the whole way, brilliantly, in fact, but the law was the law and there was no way around it.

"You have your court order, Mr. Burr," Judge Pendarvis said. "However, I am going to limit the scope of the questions you can ask while the Deputy Governor is being veridicated."

"How so, Your Honor?" Burr asked.

Judge Pendarvis held up a hand and counted off as he explained. "You will only question him in the presence of council. That means you may have to wait for Chief Prosecutor Brannhard to return from Zeta Continent if that is who the suspect chooses to represent him.

"You will limit your questions to the facts of the charges against him. No digging into his private life whatsoever.

"The entire interrogation will be recorded on video for my review. If I find you overstepped, well, you are in my jurisdiction and I will take the appropriate action.

"You will also have Captain Trask on hand. As the senior FBCI agent on Zarathustra, and since the crime would now be considered multi-planetary, he has to be involved if there is an arrest.

"Finally, this will all be kept confidential. If the video is leaked, or a transcript is posted to the datastream or if you so much as whisper it to another person, news services especially, I will hold you in contempt of court. And as Mr. Foster can tell you, the law on this world hasn't evolved to the point where there is a time limit on how long I can hold you for contempt. Understood?"

"Yes, Your Honor," Burr said. Inside he was seething at the limitations imposed on him. On Terra he would have a good deal more leeway.

"I will inform Deputy Governor Takagashi to expect a visit from Mr. Burr and company, Your Honor," Ned Foster said.

Judge Pendarvis weighed that for a moment and decided it wouldn't violate any statutes. Juan Takagashi had to already know what was coming, anyway.

"Very well, gentlemen," Judge Pendarvis said as he raised his gavel. "We are adjourned."

The gavel sounded like a gunshot in the close confines of the judge's chambers.

* * *

"...and there is nothing I can do to block it?"

"I'm afraid not, Governor," Ned Foster said. It fell to him to be the bearer of bad tidings where Juan Takagashi was concerned. It would not have been kosher for the Deputy Governor to ask Ben Rainsford for help, even if Ben could provide it. So, Ned took it upon himself to inform the Governor that his deputy would have to submit to veridicated interrogation. "The Chief Justice works for the Federation judiciary. As such he only answers to them. This was set up to keep colonial governors from taking too many liberties."

"Like protecting a possibly corrupt government official?" Ben shook his head. "How did Nick Emmert get away with it for so long?"

"It helped that Ham O'Brien was in Emmert's pocket," Ned said. "Judges don't investigate crimes or file charges. That's what the police and prosecutors are for. It is also why they were sent to Terra to be tried by the Space Navy. Chief Justices don't oversee the prosecution of colonial governors, either. This is to keep said governors from bringing pressure on them."

Ben sat down at his desk and thought it over. "If I was ever charged with a crime I would be sent to Terra? Ghu! That would almost be worse than the guilty verdict itself."

Ned agreed. Terra was no fit place for anybody anymore. "However, the Chief Justice clearly doesn't like what is going on. He had no legal option other than to grant the request, but he added a stipulation to buy us some time."

Ben's head snapped up. "Stipulation?"

"Yes. The Deputy Governor can only be interrogated in the presence of counsel. On this planet that means Chief Colonial Prosecutor Gus Brannhard. That is his other hat, acting as defense for you and Mr. Takagashi."

Ben smiled. "And Gus is currently shepherding Sylvinski and company over on Zeta. Can he be compelled to return early to deal with this?"

"Only if the Chief Justice thinks Gus is purposely delaying his return in order to keep Mr. Takagashi out of the chair," Ned said. "And then, only if Burr and company file a complaint. This is where they are backed into a corner. Gus is on Zeta to assist Sylvinski. No doubt Sylvinski is behind charging Juan. Yet, he can't just ask Gus to return to Mallorysport to get things rolling without revealing that he is the one who started the trouble. No law against it, mind you, but he wouldn't want to look like he was creating problems just to have something to report when he gets back to Terra."

Ben sighed. "If I knew all this was coming I would have never let Commodore Napier put me in this job. This world needs an experienced planetary administrator."

"Don't sell yourself short, Governor," Ned said. "You have done a bang-up job. And if I may, I would like to point out that you are replacing an experienced planetary administrator who had his hand shoulder deep in the cookie jar."

Ben snorted. "Commodore Napier said much the same thing."

* * *

Parsec Paul sat at his usual booth in The Soup Kitchen. He was feeling particularly happy with his current state of affairs. He had some real money for a change and made good on all of the free meals he had received from Clancy Slade's establishment. He even had the foresight to pay for his future meals, at least for a while. Clancy insisted that it wasn't necessary but Parsec wouldn't hear of it.

"It is one thing to accept help when one needs it, Mr. Slade," Parsec Paul said. "It is quite another not to make good on one's debts when he has the means to do so."

Clancy could see that he wasn't going to get anywhere arguing and accepted the money. Later, he decided to put it where Parsec would "find" it and recover his fortunes. Clancy even added some so that the amount would be different so that Parsec wouldn't get wise, assuming his addled mind was capable of making such a connection.

Parsec had just sat down to his first veldbeest steak in over a month when a tall blond man entered The Soup Kitchen. The face was new to him, which was odd as Parsec Paul knew almost everybody on the east side of Mallorysport. The man also seemed to be looking around for something.

"Hey, kid, come pop a squat and I'll stand you for a dinner," Parsec said. It felt good to be the one buying dinner for somebody else for a change.

The man hesitated then accepted Parsec's offer. He held out his hand and introduced himself as Merlin of Freya. Parsec grasped the man's fore-arm in the typical Freyan fashion, surprising Merlin.

"You have been to Freya," Merlin said. It was a statement, not a question.

"Oh, sure, sonny," Parsec replied. "I can't remember when but I sure as Niflheim remember all those lovely women. It would take a lot more brain damage than I've got to forget something like that."

Merlin smiled in genuine mirth. "Oddly enough, my people find Terran women equally fascinating. I think it is the seemingly infinite variety they come in. Freyan women are almost universally blonde with blue eyes."

Parsec laughed. "We all want that which is new and different. So, what brings you to this part of the galaxy?"

"Just wanted to get out and see the universe," Merlin answered. "I didn't figure on how expensive it would be. A taxi pilot told me I could get a good meal here and square it with the owner when, and if, I was able to later."

The waitress brought over Parsec Paul's bread basket and spotted the new arrival. "What about you, Stud? What would you like to wrap yourself around?"

"Ellen, the boy is from Freya," Parsec said. "He don't talk no Z Street lingo." He turned to Merlin. "What'll you have, kid?"

Merlin, who actually did understand Lingua Terran slang, asked for what Parsec was having.

"Merlin, I am having one of my rare good days when my rockets are all firing at once," Parsec said between bites. "You're here for something more than a good meal. In fact, I think you are looking for some*body*."

Merlin nodded. "I heard about somebody moving some, ah, valuable merchandise on the sly and I'm trying to track him down. I was told a man named Hans Gunderson might have a line on Paxton, and that he comes here often."

"Gunderson? Um...Oh, yeah! Gunner! Sorry kid, but that's a dead end."

Merlin looked crestfallen. "Why is that?"

Parsec Paul let out a long breath. "He was in one of the clapboard shanties that went all blowie-uppie the other day," Parsec said with a sigh. "I had to identify some of the bodies. My shanty was next to his. I would have been there if I hadn't been set up with a room in town by the cops. Real shame. He was telling me the other day that he was getting out of Junktown and heading back to, oh, what planet was he from...No matter. He won't be heading there anymore. Damned bomber. Second one this week." Parsec related his story about how a nice young man had given him money and a place to stay then died in the bank bombing incident. While he spoke the waitress returned with Merlin's order.

Merlin became very interested in his steak. Parsec noticed this and kept talking. "I don't know what kind of *merch* you think Gunner had a line on, but I can tell you where he usually kept it. Junktown is no place to store anything valuable, y'know."

Merlin's head snapped up and he looked at Parsec Paul with wide eyes. "How do you know?"

"Mostly Junktownies look out for each other. Sometimes for mutual protection. When Gunner first landed in Junktown, after losing his ranching gig, I looked out for him and taught him the ropes." Parsec raised his fork to eye level and pointed it in Merlin's direction as if to underscore his point. "Newbies in JT can get eaten alive in short order without some help. I became his pappy, so to speak, so he trusted me with everything. I trusted him, too. Never regretted it."

Merlin attacked his steak. Between bites he asked questions. "Are you planning on getting to his…his stash?"

Parsec shrugged. "Sure, why not. Won't make any difference to ol' Gunner, now. You willing to go fifty-fifty on whatever is there?"

Merlin nodded vigorously. "Agreed, provided it isn't any kind of contraband. I hear the locals can be very particular about that. But why not go yourself?"

Parsec Paul thought for a moment. "Well, at first, it was because I didn't remember it. I could leave right now and forget all about it before I got there. But you won't, and all the Freyans I ever met were upright straightforward types. I figure I can trust you." He shrugged. "And if not, odds are I'll forget all about it. Trust is all I have to work with, sonny."

"I vow it will not be misplaced with me, Parsec Paul."

* * *

The ravine looked to be about ten meters across. Down at the bottom was a rushing river that looked too dangerous to cross. Magni-Freyans were not good swimmers: no opportunity to learn on Magni and their dense muscle made a better anchor than a floatation device. Brünnhilde weighed her options. Nobody from Freya or Terra could possibly make that jump in Zarathustra's gravity. As a Magni-Freyan, the gravity worked in her favor, but she had never attempted to make such a leap before—not on Magni and not on Zarathustra.

Brünnhilde looked about. There was nothing she could fashion into a bridge except for a downed tree and even enhanced Magnian muscle wouldn't be able to move it and place it across the ravine. The big tree looked to be ironwood and she wouldn't be able to break off any branches big enough to serve, either.

Brünnhilde grimaced. She would have to try to jump the ravine. First she would see if it were possible. She turned away from the ravine and started running. When she hit her top speed she jumped. After she landed she set her pack down to mark the spot then paced back to where she leapt. It looked like roughly nine meters. At least a meter short. She returned to her starting position and tried again. This time she landed about a meter and a half past the pack.

"Okay, I can make the jump but only if I don't have my pack on," Brünnhilde said aloud. Leaving the pack behind was not an option. While she rested up for the next jump, she put everything she had into the pack then pulled out the rope. She then tied the backpack straps with the end of the rope. After a very quick meal of XT3 and water, she tested the weight of the pack and the strength of the rope. It should do.

At the very edge of the ravine, Brünnhilde started swinging the pack with the rope feeding the line with each rotation. When she was confident she had the right velocity, she flung the pack over the ravine. She might have been able to simply toss it across, but she had no way of being sure she could do so safely, so she decided to use the rope. That way, she could get more power into the launch, and pull the pack back if it missed the other side. As it was, she needn't have worried. The pack came to the ground a good ten meters past the edge of the ravine. Then she threw the spear and it stabbed the ground inches from the pack. The accuracy of the spear was the result of luck, not skill. Her people had no experience with any kind of weapon beyond a pick or a sledgehammer.

Again, Brünnhilde took a moment to rest; she wanted to be at the very top of her game for the leap. Magni-Freyan vitality was not endless, and she was going to have to push herself hard to be sure she would safely make the jump.

When she felt she was ready, she stepped well back from the edge to give herself the necessary running space. After a few deep breaths, Brünnhilde started running as fast as she could. A foot short of the edge she jumped. She tried not to look down as she flew over the ravine. Just as she feared she wouldn't make it, her feet came down on solid earth. She rolled to absorb the impact, then quickly got back on her feet. Breathing hard, more from the exhilaration than the effort, Brünnhilde recovered her gear and turned to go. Then she stopped.

No more than fifty meters away was a damnthing. Brünnhilde couldn't be sure of its age, though the animal looked fairly old. That was bad—age meant experience.

The damnthing didn't move at first. It stood over its most recent kill and looked at her as if appraising whether or not she would be worth the effort. On a full stomach it would be curious more than hungry. That could mean it would be slower, not that it would be any less dangerous.

Brünnhilde reached for the .500 Magnum she kept at her side only to remember she had put it in the backpack with everything else.

"Well, this sucks."

* * *

The ground rollers worked their way through the tall grass at considerably less than hair-raising speed. While the vehicles could never match the super-sonic velocity of the aircars, they were capable of going over 200 kilometers per hour. In the wilds of Beta Continent where the ground was unpaved and far from uniformly, it was ill advised to race along at break neck speeds. Forty miles per hour was considered the top safe rate. One needed time to spot a potential hazard and react appropriately.

Weaver understood all of this yet quietly fumed at how long the journey would take at the speed they were going. Clem, at the controls, was more comfortable at the lower velocities. Bo sat in the back on the high seat so he could watch the terrain ahead and be ready for any dangerous fauna.

"Slow down, Clem," Bo called out. "I see something ahead."

Weaver straightened up in his seat. At this point, he was up for anything to break the monotony of the ride. "What is it?"

Bo shielded his eyes from the sun and squinted. "Can't be certain. We'll have to get closer."

"We wouldn't have to if you hadn't lost the field glasses," Weaver groused. "Fine, get your rifle ready in case it's something mean and evil."

"Already, ready." Bo grabbed the only rifle with a scope hoping to get a clear view. It took several seconds of adjustment to get the range then he had to reconcile what he saw with what he knew. As they crept closer he finally realized he was looking at the back end of a damnthing. It was rare to see one from that angle as they tended to draw attention by coming toward the viewer.

"It's a damnthing. I think it has something cornered at that ravine coming up."

"Ravine?" Clem looked at Weaver. "We could have just taken the route we know. No, you wanted us to take a new one."

"If somebody found out about us and figured out our original route we would all be in cages right about now," Weaver countered. "Better a long route back and a chance to get off-world in one piece than a quick path to a public execution."

Clem had no response to that so he kept silent and watched as the damnthing drew nearer. Above, Bo took aim with his Baldurtech 10mm repeater rifle. He fired a round into the damnthing's backside hoping to spook it into running into the ravine.

XXVI

The damnthing stomped a hoof on the ground and kicked up small clouds of dust and dirt. Brünnhilde didn't need to be an expert on local zoology to know that meant it was getting ready to charge. She might be able to outrun the beast in a sprint, but long term it would eventually run her down. She doubted she would have a chance to get her gun out of the pack. She considered possibly grabbing the spear and meeting it head on. She didn't like that plan either.

Her best bet was to hope it would charge straight at her and then she could dodge and let the monster run over the edge into the ravine. She didn't know if even a fall that far down could kill it, and she didn't care. As long as the damnthing couldn't climb back up and get her she was good.

Then she heard the shot.

Brünnhilde used every colorful metaphor she learned from the Overseers when the damnthing lurched forward in surprise. The beast came at her at full speed. When she couldn't risk waiting any longer, she leaped straight up into the air over the damnthing and landed behind him just as another shot rang out. Then she collapsed unconscious.

* * *

"What the Niflheim was that second shot for?" Weaver yelled. "The damned thing was already going where you wanted it."

"Damnthings are a lot more agile than their size and bulk would suggest," Bo yelled back. "I figured a little extra incentive to keep going straight would finish the job. It worked; that 'thing went into the ravine like a good little monster. I wasn't expecting anything to get in my way."

"What the hell was that, anyway," Clem asked. "It jumped a good three meters straight up and over the damnthing. No veldbeest or zarabuck could do that."

"I think it stood on two legs," Bo said. "We should go take a look at it. It might be something new for the xenozoology books. We could get credited for discovering it."

"Yeah, right," Weaver said sarcastically. "We'll be the most famous people on Death Row." Weaver kept his eye on the downed figure as they approached. The closer they got the more worried he became. "That ain't no animal. It looks like a man."

The ground rollers stopped and everybody got out to see if the "man" was still alive. Mai, who had been in the second vehicle, got there first.

Bo reached the fallen figure next. "This isn't a man. It's a girl."

"What do you mean it's a girl?" Weaver shot back.

"Didn't your parents ever have The Talk with you?" Mai said as she checked the neck for a pulse. "She's alive. Looks like the bullet creased her skull. I'm surprised it didn't blow it off."

"What'll we do, Weave?" Clem was getting worried.

Mai stood up and faced the men. "We take her with us and try to keep her alive. We don't need a murder rap on top of everything else."

Weaver was still looking at the unconscious body. "Are you sure that's a girl? I knew body builders on Odin who would have traded ten years off their lives for a build like that."

Mai looked disgusted and made an obscene gesture at Weaver. "Bo, you shot her, so help Clem get her into the supply truck."

"What about the supplies," Clem asked. "He…she looks like she'll take up a lot of space."

Mai rolled her eyes. "We have lots of room since Weaver had us destroy all those cages and use up the anesthezine gas. I'll make a bed out of the tents for her. Ghu! Somebody get the damned medical kit! It is amazing blood isn't shooting out of her head like a geyser."

"What's amazing is that her head is still on her shoulders," one of the others said. "I saw a zarabuck shot with a BT 10; took out half the neck. At the minimum this little lady should have lost the top of her skull. She must be made of some very stern stuff."

Bo and Clem struggled to lift the unconscious girl until Lars came over and carried her to the ground roller.

"Damn, she's heavy!" Bo exclaimed.

Mai followed. The three men watched with amazement.

"I would wager she is from some heavy gravity world, like Modi,"

Clem said. "She is easily as big as Lars and that is where he came from."

"With a build like that, I can believe it," Weaver added. "Okay, this was an accident. We were aiming for the damnthing and she, um, jumped in the way. We get her to the first town we come to, make out a statement and get goin' again."

"What if they veridicate us?"

"Clem, those things don't grow on trees," Weaver said. "Not every little Podunk town and village will have an expensive piece of hardware like that. Even if they do, they will just ask about what happened here. Just to play it safe, I'll volunteer to be questioned. One of you start feeling guilty while in the seat, and you might give a false positive."

"Can that really happen?" Bo asked.

"Don't know, don't care," Weaver shot back. "I am not going to take that chance."

"What about the damnthing?"

Weaver turned to look where it had been, surprised at himself he would forget about something that large and dangerous. "It's in the ravine, right? Well, unless climbing is one of its hidden talents, it's no longer our problem. Let's get moving before something else comes along."

* * *

The warehouse looked to be abandoned, as it should have, since it was in Mortgageville. Jason Roberts entered with his sidekick, the Fuzzy Mike Hammer. For the past few days he had been shaking down every mook, skel and hump in Mallorysport looking for a line on the Martianists. He found a flyer stating they were having a meet and greet in Mortgageville and would provide snacks. The date on the flyer made it clear that he missed the meeting by a couple days. Instead he hoped to pick up any clues that may have been left behind.

Then, along the way he accidently overheard a conversation in one of the seedier dives near Junktown that somebody named Ulysses Paxton had left planet with a chest full of sunstones. The conversation was between a Dick Domino and Affanita Goncalo. Jason didn't know their names at first so he snapped a digital photo from his artificial hand and looked them up afterwards. He wasn't looking for sunstone thieves at the moment, but one simply didn't ignore a lead on such a thing.

Dick Domino—amazingly enough that was his real name—was telling Affanita about the chest of stones taken off-world by Paxton and how he heard that it might be connected to the counterfeit sunstones floating around last year. As to how this Paxton person managed to get, let alone smuggle, so many stones at once was a mystery. Most likely somebody on one of the space liners was bribable.

The conversation devolved into a "where do you think he is now that he's filthy rich" topic. Jason didn't get anything else useful and left. Paxton was long gone by now, but might have left something useful behind. There were a lot of warehouses in Mortgageville. Jason could only hope to get lucky.

The name gnawed at Jason. Ulysses was more common a given name, than it used to be, and Paxton, while not as common as Gonzales, Wong or Smith, was far from unique. It was the combination of the two names that ate at the back of Jason's mind. He considered asking Mike Hammer and discarded the idea. What would a Fuzzy know about a human being he never met?

After Jason had lost his arm and took the artificial option rather than re-growing it, he spent a lot of sols having after-market extras installed. The sono-stunner he had removed when he learned of the danger to Fuzzies. He replaced the stunner with a powerful flashlight capable of blinding an opponent. Here, in the third warehouse he had broken into, he used it to find his way through the darkness.

Technically, Jason and Mike were trespassing. Mortgageville was owned by the CZC, after Hugo Ingermann fled the planet with a quarter million sols worth of stolen sunstones. If he were caught, he would ask for Leslie Coombes for a little assistance. Coombes seemed like the kind of man who would help somebody who had once helped him.

Jason felt a tugging at his pants leg. He looked down to see Mike Hammer holding a finger over his mouth. Jason nodded. He needed to be quiet. He also turned off the flashlight. No point giving away his position, if there was a less than friendly individual in the warehouse with them.

Mike Hammer didn't need a flashlight to work in the dark. While Fuzzies were not nocturnal as a rule, their night vision was almost as good as a cat's. When it came to the five senses, Fuzzies had Terrans beat all to Niflheim.

"Do you see anything, Mike?" Jason whispered.

Mike Hammer peered into the darkness then pointed, though Jason couldn't see the gesture. "Not see. Hear. Noise come from that way."

Jason cursed under his breath for not investing in night-sight goggles. Instead he had leaned on his built-in flashlight. He made a mental note to correct that oversight, if his own stupidity didn't get them both killed. With a hand on Mike's shoulder, his human hand, he stayed hunched down and followed the Fuzzy as quietly as he could.

The pair silently approached the sound and Jason noticed it was getting easier to see. Whoever it was rooting around in the warehouse hadn't worried about using a light of some kind. Mike, still in the lead, looked around a corner then stepped back.

"It's a Big One, Boss," Mike Hammer said. "Male, around six two, light skinned, husky built without being fat."

Jason couldn't help feeling proud of Mike. He doubted another Fuzzy outside of the police Fuzzies could make a description like that. Silently, he gave some of the credit to Mickey Spillane.

"I make noise. You sneak up from behind, Boss."

Jason smiled at Mike, taking a page from one of Spillane's books. "One change; I'll make the noise, and you sneak up behind. You are way stealthier than I am."

Mike Hammer nodded. Fuzzies were very pragmatic about that sort of thing. Mike vanished into the darkness and Jason moved forward. The man was crouched over something with his flashlight. Mike Hammer was still out of sight.

Jason decided to take the direct approach. "Find anything interesting?"

The man's head shot up and faster than Jason thought possible, a large caliber gun appeared in his hand. Part of his mind couldn't help noticing that the gun was a Baldurtech .457 Magnum, an experimental design intended to be a midpoint between a .454 and a .500. The man held it single-handed, something that could fracture a wrist or even bounce the gun off the user's head if he wasn't used to it. This was a two-handed firearm for the vast majority of people. This man held it easily with a steady hand. One pull of the trigger and it would put a hole in Jason that a Curtys could jump through without touching sides.

"I don't suppose I would get anywhere by asking you to put that thing away?" Jason kept his hands in front of him so as not to spook the nice man with the really big gun. Another part of his mind was racing, considering possible ways of diffusing the situation. And one tiny section said the man was somehow familiar to him.

"Why are you here?" demanded the man.

Not "who are you," Jason thought, and he doesn't seem the least bit shaken. *It's like he owns the place.* "Oh, just doing a little scavenging. You never know what somebody might have left behind when they abandon a place like this."

"I very much doubt that." The man stood up. He was about to speak again when he was interrupted.

"Grab some sky, Mack." Mike Hammer had appeared out of nowhere. He held a custom .38 Special and it was aimed at the broad of the man's back.

Jason suppressed the urge to laugh. Mike was using a line from one of his detective novels. "I would do as he says, uh, Mack. I'm his pappy and he takes a very dim view of people putting holes in me."

"Got that right, Boss," Mike Hammer added.

The man lowered his gun and gently set it on the floor then straightened up. Jason ordered him to kick it over to him and the man complied. Mike walked around the man, being sure to keep the gun trained on him and walked over to stand next to Jason.

"Let's get the intros out of the way," Jason said. "What's your name?"

"Merlin."

"Just Merlin? Nothing else like Smith or Gaspass?" Jason asked.

Mike Hammer said, "Not Merlin."

Jason looked down at the Fuzzy, "What do you mean?"

Mike put his gun away in a holster somewhere under his natural fur. "Not Merlin. Smell like Mistah Morgan."

That was it. Jason did some business with John Morgan back when he first made planet fall. The blond hair and dark warehouse threw him.

"Mr. Morgan? What gives?"

Morgan grimaced. "I go by Holloway, now. When I'm not Merlin, of course. I am trying to track down a counterfeit sunstone ring. Fakes were flooding the Terra market. Maybe other planets as well."

"Oh, then you must be tracking Ulysses Paxton," Jason said. "I am actually on a different case but I tripped over some intel on the sunstone operation and couldn't help chasing it down."

"Ulysses Paxton? Who is that?"

"That Big One from Terra who went to Mars," Mike said. The two men looked at the Fuzzy quizzically. "He in not-so story by…"

"Edgar Rice Burroughs," Jason said. Now he recalled where he had heard, or more to the point *read*, the name.

That started a heated conversation between Jason and Morgan/Merlin. The final conclusions were: 1. Paxton must be a Martianist. 2. He took the stones to Terra to get up money for the Martianists. 3. That was how the extremists were supporting the bombing attacks on Zarathustra.

"This had to be where he either found the stones or stored them," Morgan said. He went back to where Jason had found him and picked something up. He then held out his hand for Jason and Mike to see. They looked like pebbles. There was also a bank bag stuffed with sol notes.

Jason wasn't sure what he was looking at. "I don't get it. What are those?"

"Counterfeit sunstones that have depleted their charge." Mike came closer for a better look and Morgan pulled them away and dropped them into his shirt pocket. "Sorry, Mike. These might have a residual radioactive signature and we can't risk it hurting you."

Mike nodded. "I unnastand, Mistah Morgan."

Morgan absently noticed that Mike easily pronounced the "R" sound in Merlin and Morgan, yet insisted on saying "Mistah." Force of habit or maybe he was emulating a character in one of the detective novels he read?

"Okay," Jason said. "We now know: the who and the why. Now, we need: the where and the what, next."

"Who are you working for, if I may inquire," Morgan asked.

"Huh? Oh, I was just tracking this down out of my sense of civic duty." Jason related his conversation with Parsec Paul and his conclusions at the time. "This one is off the books."

"Until now," Morgan said. "You are on my clock at your usual rate. Bill me for the time you've already put in. I should have gone to you in the first place. My only experience as a detective was tracking down my father. In fact, we both should have started with Parsec Paul, it seems. It was he who…gave me the skinny on this stash."

Morgan picked up some of the local slang, I see. "Yeah, when Paul is firing on all thrusters he is totally plugged in to everything that goes on in Mallorysport," Jason said. "What about the bag?"

"This must be Gunner's money," Morgan explained about Gunner and his conversation with Parsec Paul. "Now with Gunner dead, there is no point trying to open a case against him for moving ersatz stones. And the money wasn't technically stolen. My agreement with Paul was that he gets half of whatever I find here." Morgan tossed the bag to Jason. "See that he gets this and tell him it's his cut. I don't need the money. You can take ten percent for yourself and Mike as a courier fee."

"No problem, Boss," Jason said. "Just one question."

"What's that?"

"What's with the hair?"

XXVII

The aircar hovered at the edge of the *Neu* Freya security net. In the aircar sat Hugh Lennon, waiting for clearance to enter. Unlike his usual travels, this time he piloted himself instead of having a chauffeur do the work. He was here on private business and wanted to be sure it stayed that way.

"Please state die nature of your fisit, sir."

Hugh stared at the radio speaker in mild annoyance. Hitting it would serve no purpose and most likely destroy it. Magnians learned at a young age that many things were too fragile to withstand a temper tantrum.

"I need to speak with…um…" What was the word they used for their leader? "…with your Bürgermeister. Is he available? If not, I am willing to wait."

The speaker was silent for several minutes. Lennon began to worry that his wait would be a long one. Finally, he was given permission to enter *Neu* Freya air space and directed where to set down his vehicle.

Once on the ground, Lennon was met by a team of very powerful looking men, at least he thought they were men, wearing helmets with darkened faceplates. Internally, he shuddered at the thought of what those helmets concealed.

"You vill come vit' us, Herr Lennon," said the one with the sergeant chevrons on his sleeves. Without comment the Magnian allowed himself to be escorted. Not that he thought he could do anything about it if he wanted to. He knew that the Freyan slaves had been bred to be far stronger than a normal Magnian. Lennon doubted he could handle a single Magni-Freyan, let alone all six escorts.

Lennon was taken to a building with "RATHAUS" in big block letters above the entrance. He assumed it had to be some sort of local government building and cursed himself for not taking the time to pick up some German before coming here.

"Der Bürgermeister vill be vit' you momentarily, Herr Lennon," the Sergeant explained.

Herr Lennon, Lennon thought. "Herr" was a respectful address. Lennon thought he hardly deserved such civility. "Thank you, Herr…?"

"Wolfram," the Sergeant supplied.

Everybody remained silent after that. Lennon wasn't the type to engage in small talk and his escort wasn't the least bit chatty. When the doors to the Bürgermeister's office opened, a couple of unaltered humans walked out. One he recognized as Gus Brannhard. He pretended not to recognize Supervisor Sylvinski, as he walked by. Sylvinski did likewise.

A burly man sitting at a desk gestured for the party to enter. Lennon found he was relieved instead of apprehensive though he didn't understand why.

"*Dis ist Herr Lennon, ja?*"

"*Jawohl, Herr Bürgermeister.*"

"Und has he been checked for veapons?"

"*Jawohl!*"

The Bürgermeister nodded, then gestured for the security team to leave.

"Herr Lennon, I am Johann Torseus, Bürgermeister of Neu Freya," Johann said. "How may I be of service?"

So, so polite! "I…well, this may seem strange, but I am here to issue a formal apology for how you were treated by the Chartered Magni Cooperative, Herr…um, do I address you as Herr Torseus or Herr Bürgermeister?"

Johann smiled. "Johann vill do for now, Herr Lennon."

"Then please call me Hugh."

"*Sehr gut.*" Johann indicated a sofa chair with a fur draped on the backing. "*Bitte*, haff a seat."

The two men sat in chairs facing each other. Between them was a table with something like a chessboard on it. Instead of being eight squares in both directions, it had twelve.

"*Drahlm'toq*," Johann said. "A game much like Terran chess dot ist played on Freya. I learned how to play from mein faht'er."

"Oh. I play chess. I never heard of this...*Drahlm'toq*."

"So, you vant to make a formal apology? Ist dis from die Chartered Magni Company, or from you personally?"

Hugh leaned forward. He didn't know what he expected when he decided to come to Neu Freya. He also didn't expect the Bürgermeister to smell of some unfamiliar flower. The scent was pleasant and would make a good perfume for women.

"For now, I speak for myself, though I have considerable holdings in the CMC."

Johann nodded his understanding. Lennon thought the Bürgermeister's head was going to fall off. "Ve vere giffen an apology vhen ve left Magni. Prince—ehhh—Herr Morgan drafted die vording himself."

John Morgan, Lennon recalled, bought controlling interest in the CMC when word of the slave racket was made public and the stock plummeted. Lennon took the opportunity to likewise increase his own holdings in the company. He was confident that it would rebound and make him another small fortune. It paid off even better than he expected under Morgan's—correction—Holloway's leadership.

Johann pointed to a framed document on a wall. "Dot ist die official apology made by die CMC." Johann peered at it for a moment before turning back to Lennon. "I chust realized dot yours ist die largest signature."

Lennon nodded. "There was a lot of discussion in the boardroom about whether or not to sign. Some thought that such an act would be an admission of guilt from the members who knew nothing of what was going on practically under their feet. I was first to sign to get the ball rolling. If you know anything of Terran history, I fancied myself as something of a John Hancock when I signed. His was the largest signature on an old document."

"Och! Die Declaration of Independence, *ja*? Do not look so surprised, Hugh. Ve haff all been studying Terran history as vell as dot of Freya."

There was a polite, by Magni standards, knock at the door. Johann opened the door and allowed a woman to enter with a tray of steins. "*Danke*, Gertrude. Ve may need refills." Johann returned to his seat after setting the tray down on his desk and carried the steins back to his seat. He offered one to Lennon.

"Freyan ale," Johann explained. "Haff you efer tried it?" Lennon admitted he had not. "Den I t'ink you vill be delighted. None of mein pipple had efer had alcohol of any kind until ve vere freed."

The two men drained their steins and ordered refills. The ale relaxed Lennon to the point that he felt he could ask more serious questions. "Herr...Johann, what was your life like in the mines of Magni?"

Johann considered the question before speaking. "It vas hard verk. Ve toiled up to sixteen hours a day. If ve tried to refuse, food und *wasser* vas cut off."

"Gods! How did you survive in that hell hole? Were the Overseers cruel?"

Johann leaned back in his chair and took a long drink from his stein. "Do you mean vere ve vhipped? Nein. Die chenetic manipulation ve vere giffen made our hides fery tough. Almost like leat'er. Vhips vould haff been less den effective as a means of controlling or punishing us. Nein. For dot dey had die collars. If vun of us became, ah, difficult, ve vould get a nasty electrical shock. Our skin is tough, but der are limits, after all." Johann pulled down the collar of his shirt to show what appeared to be electrical burn scar tissue on the side of his neck. It was faint but visible.

Lennon blanched at the very idea of treating an intelligent being in such a manner. He found himself staring at the scar tissue and switched the topic. "Was…was the food…um…?"

"Ve vere vell fed," Johann finished. "Dey vanted us strong to verk die mines, so dey gafe us goot food und *wasser*. Ve vere often giffen XT t'ree, vhich I t'ink vas cruel und unusual. Ve neffer allowed die *Kinder* to eat dot stuff. But ve vere neffer starfed as long as ve verked."

"Were there any…incidents with the guards?"

Johann was confused for a moment then realized what Lennon was trying to say. "You mean vere die *Fräulein*s raped?" Johann made a choking sound that Lennon realized was laughter. "It vas tried only vunce dot

I know of. An Oferseer t'ought he could molest Inga, a *Fräulein* who ist fery small compared to die rest of us. It did not go vell for her attacker. She broke his arm, smashed his face und fractured seferal ribs. Och, do not vorry. She vas not punished for defending herself. In fact, die ot'er Oferseers insisted she get a medical exam und ve neffer saw die attacker again."

Lennon nodded. "No quicker way to get a people to stage an uprising than to abuse their women and children. What about the living quarters? Did you have any or did you sleep where you worked?"

"Ve had a barracks of sorts. Beds on die floor, but dey were made of memory foam so ve vere at least comfortable at night. Und ve had *Sonntag*...eh...Sunday off. Dot vas vhen ve ...eh...socialized vit' each ot'er."

"Gods! They could have at least given you better living conditions."

"Efen a nice cage ist still a cage. Vhould you enjoy being locked in a cage efen if it vere nicer den die home you haff now?"

Lennon considered his mansions on Magni and Odin, which were lavish in the extreme, then thought about never being able to leave them. He had to admit he wouldn't like it at all.

"*Jawohl.* Hugh, vhy are you really here? Prince Morgan...ehh... Herr Hollovay made a goot deal vit' die CMC. Ve are content vit' our *neu* situation. Vhat do you t'ink vill heppen now dot you are here?"

Lennon started to speak then stopped. *What am I doing here? There was nothing he could do to further make up for what was done to the Magni-Freyans. They didn't need money. They had their freedom, and those who were responsible were dealt with by the Federation. What was I thinking when I decided to come out to this place?*

"I must confess, I don't know," Lennon said. "I just felt that I had to. I never knew what was happening to you and yours, yet I can't help feeling responsible."

Johann nodded. "Slafery ist a terrible t'ing. Not just for die slafes. Men of conscience find dot it eats avay at dere souls."

Johann stood and went to a cupboard. Lennon knew that the wall unit was actually called a "*schrank*" in old German. This one was beautiful.

Hand carved from, presumably, local wood, stained and lacquered; Lennon was impressed with the workmanship.

Johann returned to his chair and held out what he had taken from the *schrank*. It was a set of manacles. Lennon actually cringed inside looking at them.

"Vhen an oferseer t'ought ve needed a lesson, ve vere chained vit' dese. Den ve vere placed in a small dark room for as long as dey t'ought ve needed to learn our lesson. Please take dese." Johann held out the chains. "Take dese beck vit' you."

"To remember what was done to you?"

Johann shook his head. "Nein. To remember dot now ve are free und vill never vear dese again. Remember to nefer let such a t'ing heppen again."

Lennon accepted the manacles. They were much heavier than simple polysteel. Micro-collapsium laminated he realized. Expensive, yet immune to rust or metal fatigue, and absolutely unbreakable—even for a Magni-Freyan. He tried to say something but his voice failed him.

"Now, it is time for die mid-day meal. Come choin us, meet more of my people und see dot ve are heppy here," Johann said. "Ach, best vie put dot in a bag." He indicated the manacles.

"I...won't some of your people object to me being there? For what I may represent to them?"

Johann made the choking sound again. "If you truly feared dot, you vould not be here at all. Some might object, but dey vill stay politely silent."

Lennon was overcome by the emotions running through his body. He thought of all the Freyans had endured and yet they were ready to sit at the same table as one who represented their captivity. Another thought came to him and almost stunned him into immobility: *What I was going to do to those Fuzzies!*

XXVIII

It was the first time since the Fuzzy Slaver business that everybody crowded into Marshal Fane's offices. Most of the same people were in attendance: Jack Holloway, Victor Grego, Leslie Coombes, Captain Trask, Chief Carr, Officers Gilbert and Sullivan and even Ben Rainsford were there. Gus Brannhard was still on Zeta Continent with the Commission. John Morgan and Jason Roberts were the last to show up.

"Morgan, what is this all about?" Jack demanded. He was still in ill temper due to the Commission representative, Dana Alexander, who was still going through his files. Not that he faulted her for it, she was given a job to do and she was doing diligently. She was into the financial reports when Jack was called away. "And what happened to your hair?"

"I'll explain later, Pa. Victor, if I may bring everybody in on our little problem," Morgan asked.

Grego nodded though he was inwardly annoyed that Morgan would put him on the spot in front of everybody.

"Thank you. Gentlemen, as only a few of you know, there have been counterfeit sunstones popping up on Terra, and maybe even on Thor, Odin, Baldur and who knows where else. With Mr. Roberts' assistance, we believe we know who distributed the fake sunstones."

Marshal Fane nodded. "Excellent, though I would have liked being brought into the loop sooner. What is everybody else here for?"

"We believe the fakes were sold off to bankroll the Martianist extremists who have recently been causing so much trouble." Morgan outlined the A to B of how the stones left Zarathustra and why they believed the Martianists were involved.

"Ulysses Paxton, eh?" Trask mulled it over. "It could be a coincidence."

"With the sudden appearance on Zarathustra of the Martianists?" Officer Gilbert said. "Separately, those are not common names. Together, too much to call it a coincidence. I have only ever met one Paxton, and never a Ulysses."

"This duck is quacking," Sullivan added.

"I agree," Jason said. "It all fits the timeline. In fact, there is just enough time to take the sunstones to Terra, sell them off, then have the Martianists come straight back here. It even gives them a month's worth of cushion."

"Okay, fine," Ben said. "But what do they want? We are a long way from Mars and not yet important enough as a colony to rate this kind of attention."

"What they want is fairly obvious," Leslie Coombes spoke up. "They want the so-called Fuzzy Rocket. We managed to prove that Fuzzies never flew the damned thing, so that leaves only one viable possibility, at least, to these people."

"Gods and monsters," Jack said. "More trouble because of that Ghu-damned rocket? I thought the military had it hauled away. It could be in a black hole by now for all we know."

"Can we just ask Commodore Napier to bring it back?" Ben asked.

The consensus was a flat 'no.'

"The Commodore won't waste heavy ammunition on a small problem," Marshal Fane said. "He hauled away the rocket with a situation like this in mind. The last thing he will want to do is give the Martianists the rocket just so they can say, 'Look here! Proof that Martians had space flight! We were right all along. Terra was settled by Mars.' The political fallout would be bad enough. This could start a sort of civil war."

"Okay, so we can't give them the rocket," Jack said. "What else is there?"

"Easy," Grego spoke. "We give them what they want."

* * *

Juan Jimenez re-read the report for the third time. Minor damage to the ozone shield that screened out the more harmful solar and cosmic rays. The worst of the damage was above Alpha Continent. That made sense as most of the traffic coming and going from the planet was near Mallorysport space terminal.

As it stood for now, the ozone layer could rebuild itself in a few short years if all space traffic ceased. *That isn't going to happen as long as the planet needs interstellar trade,* Juan reflected. He turned and switched on the comscreen.

The screen resolved into the image of Victor Grego. "Juan, I was just about to call you."

"Oh? What about, Victor?"

"It's your deci-sol, Juan. You go first."

Juan explained the minor damage to the ozone layer and the potential pitfalls of letting it continue. "Back on Terra, after World War III, the ozone layer was almost completely destroyed, causing skin cancer and a host of other problems. I think it could cause trouble for the indigenous flora and fauna."

"Like the Fuzzies," Grego added. "Okay, you're the scientist here. What do you suggest?"

"We need to set up a series of lightning generators on contragravity platforms and send them to the areas where the layer is thinnest. It will be somewhat pricey—"

"Cheaper than letting the planet burn," Grego finished. "I'll authorize the start-up and get Joe Vergano busy on it. What exactly will these lightning generators do?"

"The electrical discharge will create new ozone. Even with hundreds of units up there, it will take years to rebuild the layer, considering that we'll still have to allow space travel in and out of the atmosphere. We should look into a way of limiting that."

Grego agreed. "I'll have to discuss this with the Governor, of course, but he's a naturalist. He should be willing to go along."

Juan agreed. "You said you were going to call me?"

"Oh, yes, I need you to get that, ah, relic out of mothballs. There are some people in town that will be very entertained by it."

"The relic? Oh, you mean—"

"Not out loud, Juan," Grego cautioned. "You never know who might be listening in."

Juan nodded. Normally, CZC internal communications were one hundred percent secure. However, that depended on the people in the

CZC not being compromised in some way. The latest troubles suggested that might not be safe to assume.

"Understood, Victor."

* * *

"I guess I just assumed you would be good at tracking," Cinda said.

Cinda and Rheiner looked around the downed aircar in search of some sign to show what direction Brünnhilde took when she set out on her own. The girl left without leaving a note or even a bunch of rocks forming an arrow to show which way she had gone.

Rheiner shook his head. "In die mines ve had no need of dot skill set. Lifting, carrying, und svinging a pick-axe in areas dot a robot could not be trusted to maneuver in vas our required abilities. Some of our young hafe been learning some tracking und forest craft. I haff been ot'ervise engaged."

Cinda understood. As former slaves, the education of the Magni-Freyans was very limited. Much of what they learned, after their emancipation, happened on the hyperspace crafts during the time they traveled to Zarathustra, and the accelerated training they received since setting up Neu Freya. Tracking would have been low on the list.

"Don't you know how to track?" Rheiner asked.

It was a fair question. Cinda admitted she had been too involved in her studies to pick up that bit of education. "Yet, how hard can it be? Your people are a bit…robust and should leave fairly deep imprints in the ground."

"True," Rheiner admitted. His own five-foot, eight-inch frame weighed well over three hundred pounds, with only three point nine percent body fat. "What about ot'er animals dot valk ofer dose tracks? Or vind blowing dirt ofer dem? Ve are fortunate it hasn't rained."

Rheiner could be somewhat infuriating when he made perfectly logical sense.

"Mummy Cinda, we can find track."

Cinda looked down at James Hutton and mentally kicked herself. Fuzzies were among the finest trackers in the known universe. "You are right, James. See if you and Sarah can find something, please."

James Hutton and Sarah Balfour looked around for any signs of footprints while Rheiner released their dogs from their safety harnesses. After attending to some overdue business, the dogs went to stand near their masters. The Fuzzies quickly equipped their mounts with saddles, harness and hackamore bridle, then mounted. Once set, they went over to the downed aircar.

Rheiner was confused. "Vhy dey go to aircar?"

Cindy thought for a second then it hit her. "The dogs are getting Brünnhilde's scent from the seat. A Curtys can't follow a scent as well as a bloodhound. Still, I hear they are competent trackers and will help the Fuzzies. Don't they use dogs on Freya?"

Rheiner shrugged. "I don't know. I haff neffer been dere. I t'ink dey haff somet'ing volf-like. I don't know if it ist domesticated."

Cinda mentally kicked herself again. Rheiner had been raised in the mines of Magni, hidden away from the Overseers, so that they wouldn't see his face. The only other planets he had actually set foot on were Gimli and Zarathustra. Everything he knew about Freya would have come from handed-down stories and teaching machines.

"Dogs are great trackers, in general, having a sense of smell hundreds of times more sensitive than humans. Or Fuzzies, for that matter."

Rheiner nodded. "So, ve follow dem in die aircar vhile die Fuzzies und dogs...*hunde*! I neffer connected die vord vit' die animal before. Dey don't haff dogs on Magni, eit'er. So ve follow dem vhile dey do die tracking. Ve can vatch out for dangerous animals und terrain, also."

"Sounds like a plan…I think the dogs have the scent. We better hurry before they get out of sight."

* * *

"We should make camp here," Cindy Tezza said. "According to the sat-feed there is a troop of Fuzzies heading this way. We will want to be well hidden by then."

"A furry."

"A what?"

"A furry of Fuzzies," Erena Taylor explained. "A group of Fuzzies is called a furry. Like a pride of lions, a murder of crows or a pack of wolves."

"That's a new one on me, too," Kealani admitted as she pulled out the fibroid tent from the ground roller. "Is this a new term?"

Erena grabbed the other side of the tent and helped open it. "It was coined during the whole Jin-f'ke fiasco. Some guy suggested it to Commissioner Holloway and it stuck."

Kealani made a mental note to do more background research of Fuzzies in general. All she knew about the Jin-f'ke was that they were a northern community that was somewhat xenophobic. She had missed any mention of the fiasco Erena mentioned.

"Do you need any help with the tent?"

"Nope," Erena said. "This is one of those fancy self-erecting jobs. Does everything save for loading and unloading from the ground roller. Watch this." Erena found the button pad on the tent and pressed the blue button. The tent unfolded itself and formed an oblong shape roughly three by four meters in width and length.

"Inside it has a ground pad, so we don't have to put our sleeping bags on the dirt. The fibroid weave is lighter than silk and stronger than steel. None of the local fauna will be able to get in as long as we keep the flap sealed."

"Will it stop a damnthing?" Kealani asked.

"Have you ever seen a damnthing?"

Kealani admitted she hadn't, save for computer images.

"Well," Erena said, "they are like a cross between a bison and a rhino and ten times as mean. The horn won't pierce the fibroid weave at all. That won't stop us from getting trampled, though."

"The Fuzzies are getting closer," Cindy said. "Rockthrower, Maid Marian, come over here."

The two Fuzzies complied.

"Now we must be very quiet and not let the other Fuzzies know we are here."

This confused the Fuzzies. "Why not make friends? Not understand."

Cindy thought a moment before answering. "We want to see what

Fuzzies do when no Big Ones are around. Learn new things about Fuzzies."

"Maid Marian not Big One. I not Big One. Why can't make friends?"

"You have been with Big Ones a long time," Cindy explained. "So you know more things. Maybe after we watch Fuzzies for a few days, then we can go make friends. Until then we need to be very quiet. The dogs, too." The Fuzzies weren't happy though they believed their Big Ones to be very wise so they agreed.

"So you do plan on interacting with the Fuzzies?" Erena asked. "I thought this was strictly look and see."

"Watching is the larger part of what we will do here," Kealani said. "Observe their culture and rituals, religious rites and so on."

"According to Dr. Mallin, the Fuzzies don't seem to have any religion," Cindy said. "We believe they haven't evolved to that point as a culture, yet."

Kealani was surprised. "No religion at all? I don't think I ever heard of such a thing. There are some Terran cultures that had a religion, then eventually abandoned it, usually in favor of a new religion. Every other human species has some sort of religion. Thorans worship Ghu, Freyans have a host of gods, not unlike the Norse pantheon, and Lokians have a sort of earth- and sun-centered religion."

"If the Fuzzies hang around with us long enough, they might pick up some of our bad habits," Erena said, with some irony.

"If not want Fuzzies to know we here, best to not make talk and get down behind tall grass," Maid Marian suggested. "Fuzzee have good ears."

Everybody got down quickly. Kealani set up the spy cameras and sent them out in different directions so she could record everything from multiple angles. As an afterthought, she sent a couple off behind them, just in case something unpleasant came along. She observed the camera feeds on her data pad.

"What about the ground roller?" Cindy asked.

Erena said something in Sheshan and crawled back to the ground roller on hands and knees. There she tapped a series of commands into the dashboard computer. The ground roller, originally designed for military use, was equipped with a simple camouflage cover. Unlike the stealth suits used by field soldiers, the ground roller had no need of being invisible. It just had to look like some other innocuous stationary object. In this instance, Erena went with the simplest and most convincing disguise she could think of.

A panel between the rearmost seat and the boot opened up and a fibroid weave canapé came out and formed around the ground roller. Monofilament wires provided the lift and thrust to form the tarp in the rough shape of a large boulder. Erena hoped the Fuzzies didn't notice the movement of the tarp as it settled into place.

XXIX

It was a world of light flashes and pain. When Brünnhilde tried to open her eyes, the pain became more intense, more real. Yet, she had to open her eyes, had to see where she was and find out what had happened to her.

With a hand shielding her eyes from most of the brightness, Brünnhilde looked about and tried to get an idea about her surroundings. She was in the back of a ground roller and it was moving. The top was down, which was why it was so bright.

As the pains subsided, from swords being driven through her skull to simply small daggers poking around in her brain, she looked around to see three people in the ground roller in front of her. She had no idea who these people were or where they were going. There was the possibility that they were responsible for the horrible headache she was experiencing. She decided to play dead and see if she could learn anything.

Mai looked back and saw that the injured woman was still out. The bandage around her head seemed to be doing its job. At least there wasn't any blood soaking though it.

"I can't believe she is still alive," Mai said. "Have you ever heard of anybody taking a shot like that and surviving?"

The woman next to Mai, Consuela, shook her head. "That bullet should have taken off the left side of her cranium. I've seen Bo practice on rocks with that BT 10 of his. The rocks didn't fare as well as that little lady back there."

The driver, Estefan, looked back. "Are you two going to go on and on about how impressed you are with Muscle Girl all day? Did it occur to either of you that Bo had a bad round in the chamber, and that it didn't have as much force as normal? She just got very lucky."

That made sense to the two women and Consuela said so. Mai went along though she had her doubts.

"I hope she wakes up soon," Mai said. "She might have a concussion."

"If so," Estefan said, "then she got off light. Me, I'm just as happy she is staying unconscious. Otherwise she might get a little too curious for our own good."

"Don't you start making any plans for her, Este," Mai said. "We take her to a town with medical aid and that's that."

"Frankly, the sooner we drop her off the better for all of us," Consuela said. "Eddie has been looking at her in an unsettling way. I don't want to risk him trying to take advantage of her while she is unconscious."

"Oh? What about after she wakes up," Estefan said. "And I've known Lars for a while. He always behaves himself around the ladies. I think he is afraid of breaking somebody. If he catches Eddie doing anything he'll rip his head off. For real."

"Do you really think any man could try something, when she's awake and can defend herself?" Mai responded, jerking her head to indicate the unconscious girl in the back. "I'll bet she could remove parts he would rather not be without. Even with that muscle bound lout Lars."

Consuela and Estefan agreed with that.

"What worries me the most is *if* she will ever wake up."

"Weaver probably hopes she doesn't," Estefan said. "He's afraid somebody will slip and let on about the Fuzzy poaching. If she does find out about that, well, Bo will get another shot at her."

"Shut up!" Mai yelled. "What if she had woken up, just as you were saying that? I never liked what was going on out here and I for damned sure don't want anybody else getting hurt because of it." She looked back at Brünnhilde and shook her head. "This poor girl was probably lost and had the bad luck to run into us."

"Hey, Bo didn't shoot her on purpose." Estefan was getting nervous. Poaching Fuzzies was one thing. Killing a Terro was a whole different ball of wax. "It was an accident, plain and simple. And it ain't like we just left her there. We're going to get her help."

"If she never ran into us. she wouldn't have been hurt in the first place." Mai said.

"Or the damnthing would have had her for lunch," Estefan countered. "Nobody, man or woman, high-gee or low-gee planet of origin, survives one-on-one with a damnthing barehanded. Getting shot in the head didn't do her any favors, but I'll take that over getting gored and eaten."

Mai looked back again. "I'll bet she is a competition bodybuilder. That means she'll have to get that scar removed or it could ruin her career."

"If she is a bodybuilder," Consuela countered, "she might be from a high-gravity planet. I saw a family from Rama, a planet with one point, two gees. They were all thick and squat and looked like they could punch out an Ulleran. Sleeping Beauty back there might be from Rama or Modi. They are not usually that well-defined, but some weight-train to get the cut and definition. I think it makes them more flexible."

"Modi." Estefan considered it and it made sense. "Okay. So she might be from a high-gee planet like Lars. What the Niflheim is she doing in the armpit of nowhere? We're hundreds, if not thousands of miles, from the nearest village or settlement."

Mai and Consuela thought on that. They both came up dry.

* * *

As Brünnhilde listened, her headache faded to a dull throbbing. She touched the side of her head and felt the bandage there. She recalled the loud noise she heard before losing consciousness. *I got shot*, she thought. As the conversation continued she caught word of Fuzzy poaching. Her temper flared up and she considered doing something rash, then reason took over. *I can't fight these people barehanded. They obviously have guns and outnumber me. One of them sounds like she is protecting me.*

When the conversation turned to how she got herself stranded in the middle of nowhere, she decided it was time to 'wake up.' She sat up only to suffer another blinding flash of pain in her head. She made an agonized sound and Mai looked back.

"Oh, dear, you shouldn't be sitting up like that," Mai warned. "That is a nasty injury and you might have a concussion."

Brünnhilde didn't know what a concussion was as, to the best of her knowledge, none of her people ever had one before. It might explain the blinding pain she felt, though. She took a few deep breaths and waited for the pain to fade, which it did, although a dull ache stayed with her.

"I'll be fine," Brünnhilde said through gritted teeth. "Vhat…um… what happened to me?"

Mai, Estefan and Consuela exchanged glances, then Mai explained about the accidental gunshot. "You appeared out of nowhere just as Bo pulled the trigger. It wasn't intentional."

Brünnhilde recalled jumping over the damnthing as it charged toward her. The bulk of the beast would have hidden her from the shooter, Bo, and nobody could have expected her to leap over the damnthing the way she did.

"I understand. It vas…was an accident. *Danke*…thank you for patching me up. Can you tell me where we are?"

"About three hundred miles west of where we picked you up," Estefan offered. "We drove through the night so we could get you to a medical facility as soon as possible."

Brünnhilde wasn't certain she believed the man. While maybe they didn't shoot her on purpose, she did hear them mention something about how they were Fuzzy poachers. She decided to be very cagey with these people. "How far are we from this medical center?"

"We don't really know," Consuela said. "We had to take a different route back from our…um…dig site. We neglected to bring maps that show villages and such in this section of Beta. We mostly have topographic maps. You know, the kind that shows terrain features and elevations and bodies of water? For some reason that ravine where we found you wasn't on it. It might be a new terrain feature caused by an earthquake or something."

"True, it wasn't on my data pad map, either," Brünnhilde said.

"Hey!" Estefan became excited. "You have a data pad? With satellite feed maps?"

"Ja…yes," Brünnhilde nodded. "But the charge ran out well before I got to the ravine. I forgot to charge it before I left."

"Maybe we can charge it from the ground roller's power bank." Mai suggested. "Your backpack is back there, I think. Did we leave it in the other roller?"

"No, here it is," Brünnhilde opened the pack and rooted around inside of it. Her gun was still there, meaning nobody bothered to steal any of her gear. That was a big relief. "Ach, nein! The 'pad is cracked. That must have happened when I threw the pack across the ravine." She mentally cursed herself for putting the gun in the pack right next to the data pad. The screen could be replaced when she returned home but it was useless in the meantime.

"Too bad," Consuela said. "By the way, I hope you don't mind my asking, but where are you from? You have a German accent, but it doesn't quite sound Heimdallian."

"Oh, uh, my family has a place on N…Zeta Continent. Before that we lived on Magni." *No point in giving these people my whole life story*, she thought.

"Magni? That explains it," Estefan said. "That is a high-gee planet." Mai threw him a nasty glare.

Brünnhilde absently glanced down at herself. "Yes, that is why I am so musclebound."

"I mean no offense," Estefan said. "I mean that explains how you were able to jump over that damnthing when you got shot. Only somebody from Modi would be stronger than you."

Brünnhilde refrained from correcting the man. The genetic engineering the Magni-Freyans underwent actually made them even stronger than a Modian. She decided it might be better if they underestimated her, even if only a little bit. Distrust of anybody that wasn't another Magni-Freyan came easily to her people. Prince Morgan was virtually the only exception to that rule.

"So we don't know how long it could be before we find a village?"

"Afraid not," Mai said. "For all we know we passed any number of settlements missing them by ten or twenty miles or more."

Scheisse! I have to get away from these people, Brünnhilde thought, *but how?*

XXX

"…if she consummates this unholy union, she will become like her unnatural spouse, doomed to walk the Earth in search of the flesh of the living to sustain her."

"Oh, God, we have to find her and destroy her…her husband. But how do we find them?"

"He will seek out cool dark places where he can hide and retard the slow decay of his undead body. Once we find them, his head must be destroyed. It is the only way he can be killed. While he can move about in the day, he shuns the sun."

"The police won't believe us if we go to them, Doctor. I'll have to—"

"We interrupt *The Zombie's Bride* for this important news update. The Martianists who recently claimed responsibility for the terror attacks on a Mallorysport Bank and Junktown have issued this warning. Today, at 1800 hours, they will strike at three undisclosed locations if their demands are not met. These demands have been sent to the office of the Colonial Governor, Bennett Rainsford. The Governor has not been available for comment. CZCTV will follow up on this story as it develops. We now return you to *The Zombie's Bride*."

The father turned down the sound and addressed his family.

"Nobody goes out tonight. We stay here away from potential targets."

"Dad, what is a terror attack?"

"It is when bad people do very bad things to get their way."

"It is like blackmail, Timmy," added his mother.

"Would they do the bad thing here? To us?"

The father strapped on his gun belt and checked the chamber in the pistol. "Not if I have anything to say about it."

* * *

Colonial Governor Bennett Rainsford fought hard to not yell at the comscreen: "I thought you were going to keep this sort of thing off the networks, Victor."

On the screen, Grego nodded. "This message went out to every outlet, even the ones Morgan and I have no control over. My people had to broadcast it to maintain their credibility. Once the public stops trusting you, it can take years, if ever, to get that trust back. Slanted news reporting went out way back in the late First Century A. E. when the populace got tired of the news services shilling for political figures."

"The first two bombings were just to show us how serious they are. I wish we had an idea where they were planning to hit next," Marshal Fane said. "With no idea of where or who, there isn't a lot we can do."

"We can impose a curfew. Everybody home by 1730," Ben said. "I know it is a short-term fix that only protects people, not property, but it's all I can think of right away."

The Marshal shook his head. "That's assuming these Martianists don't just decide to go all blowie-uppie an hour early. Remember, these are not sane people we are dealing with. These mutts think the entire Terro-human race, and Freyans, came from Mars and that somehow we lost touch with our Martian origins. And it's their sacred duty to enlighten us."

Ben grunted. He knew that there was actually some basis for the belief, even if he didn't subscribe to it himself. "We need to get them out in the open and deal with them straight on."

"Any ideas how we can swing that?" Grego asked. "Almost by definition, Khooghras like these work from the shadows. Remember the Isis Insurrection? Those fanatical maniacs used suicide bombers left and right before the Feds declared martial law and brought the fighting into the open."

"Only by capturing a terrorist with a dud strapped to his back, and putting him under veridication," Marshal Fane added. "We don't have a Martianist with a malfunctioning bomb to question. Yet."

"Okay, I have been down this road long enough that I can see you have something in the works, Victor."

"I do. It is being delivered to the park as we speak."

"You mean…?"

"Yes. With a few added extras."

Marshal Fane smiled wide. "Oh, yes. That should buy us some time."

* * *

"Well, my boss won't like it, but I can't find anything wrong with your files or finances."

Jack released a long mental sigh. He hoped he didn't look too relieved. "I could have told you that and saved you a three-hour trip, Miss Alexander."

Dana laughed. "That is what they all say, Commissioner Holloway; at least the ones who didn't get caught with their hand in the cookie jar. Actually, you could put in for compensation for the land you turned over to the Reservation. The addition to your home being paid for by your Fuzzies is a bit unusual. I never heard of anything like that, but as I see it the Fuzzies are your family and they used their own funds. I can't think of any rule that violates."

Jack thought it over and realized that Fuzzies were very different from all the other alien humans. *No Terro would ever adopt a Khooghra, for example, and make him part of the family. Thorans, while accepting of Terros and happy for the technology they brought, were rather sticky on the idea of Thorans raising Thorans and keeping them pure, at least culturally. A Lokian might have been a good candidate, if their species hadn't been enslaved and worked to death in the mines. While Lokians don't hold a grudge, the very concept is alien to them; their memories are long and slow to accept change.*

"I think Gus Brannhard will be thrilled to hear this," Jack said. "A new precedent is every lawyer's dream and nightmare, depending on which way the precedent falls. Now, what do you think your boss will say?"

Dana shrugged. "That I did my job. I know he is a bit overbearing and even obnoxious; he hasn't been out in the field in years, so he is somewhat rusty on the etiquette. However, he is basically honest. He wouldn't stand for any of his people inventing a problem where none exists."

Jack pulled out his pipe, packed it, then lit it up. "Instead he will just jump on any little thing he can. Well, if he wants to pick nits, he is welcome to it. I have been to a lot of planets—"

"There's an understatement," Betty said.

"…and dealt with a lot of government types over the years," Jack continued. "What we have here is probably the most honest and diligent ruling body I have ever seen or even heard of. Your Supervisor Sylvinski is going to have to dig mighty deep to find anything of interest."

Dana looked anxious. "Um, I shouldn't say anything but he thinks he found something already."

It was Betty who responded instead of Jack. "Really? Like what?"

Jack chuckled. "She is talking about Juan Takagashi's time on Odin. Don't look so surprised, Miss Alexander. Ben, that is, Colonial Governor Rainsford, filled me in as soon as he heard about it. He's a little worried but he seems to think worrying about things is part of the job description."

"Hmm…do you think Deputy Governor Takagashi did anything while on Odin?"

She's fishing, Jack thought. "Oh, I am sure he did plenty. His job, mostly, though I suspect he had an active social life."

Dana looked confused for a moment, then smiled. She understood what Jack was doing. "Well, I hope it works out well for you folks here. Any government as intent as you folks on protecting the natives is all right with me."

I wonder if it is safe to believe that? Jack asked himself.

* * *

If a drawback could be said to apply to anthropology, it is the fascination with people of different cultures. When in the vicinity of an interesting person from a different culture, especially one with as diverse a background as Cindy Tezza, Kealani couldn't help asking questions.

"So Heimdall was settled entirely by people with a significant Germanic heritage?"

Cindy nodded. She had to finish swallowing before speaking. "Ach, these cold rations are so bland. Ja, the planet was originally settled by wealthy German businessmen. They wanted to recreate Old Germany from before the Great Wars. The company discovered the planet and filed the claim, and since it was a Class III uninhabited world they were able to get the charter that gave them the monopoly on it."

"Oh, like Zarathustra was before we discovered the Fuzzies," Erena added.

"Ja, and they commissioned the construction for several little hamlets based on old German villages. Eventually a city much like Mallorysport, called Neu Stuttgart, rose up. Herr Wagner, very old by that point but still in control of the Chartered Heimdall Company, had the buildings based on those of Old Stuttgart after the reconstruction era following World War II. Heimdall is a beautiful world much like pre-war Terra and there was some concern over too much immigration to there, so before he died Herr Wagner created a Constitution that required all immigrants to have a Germanic heritage of no less than fifty percent. Every applicant is given a DNA test to verify it."

"Isn't it illegal to bar immigrants that way?" Kealani asked. "I would think that the Federation would have rules against that sort of thing."

"They used to," Erena said. "Until Hiawatha was established by persons of North and South American aborigine descent. They fought to create a new homeland to get back what they lost when the Europeans invaded the Americas. They put similar restrictions on immigration, too. Later, when Amadioha was discovered by people of predominantly African descent, they set up the same kind of rules. Amadioha is a very hot and bright world, so, really, only people with very dark skin could thrive there anyway."

"Amadioha?" Kealani thought for a moment. "Oh, yes, named for one of the African gods of thunder and lightning." She turned back to Cindy. "I understand you were a datastream model before becoming a psychologist. If you don't mind my asking, how did you get into, uh, that sort of thing? Didn't it make you nervous to be photographed in the nude and have the photos sent out all over the Federation?"

"I admit," Erena said, "I'm curious about that as well."

Cindy laughed. "Heimdall's culture was mostly based on Old Germany. The German people were not so embarrassed by such things, as many other cultures. I started fairly young doing family photos with my sister, Jenny. Later, when the family farm fell on hard times, Jenny and I started doing semi-nudes, then later full nudes. I actually enjoyed it. It was liberating and fun for me. We were able to bail out the farm and even save some money. Until the tax people got involved." Cindy sighed. "Those were some very bad times and one of the reasons I relocated to Zarathustra. A world without taxes is like heaven to me."

"I wouldn't count on that lasting forever," Erena said. "A tax-free planet will bring in all kinds of people. As the population grows the ability for the CZC to maintain the planetary services will become stretched and, eventually break. I understand that Colonial Governor Rainsford is trying to raise money and bank it against that eventuality."

Kealani became interested. "How is he doing that without taxes?"

"For one thing, he is leasing a sizeable tract of land on Alpha about twenty kilometers away from Mallorysport to the military," Erena continued. "There are also the fines for trespassing on the Rez, not that that is any kind of big money. And I read that he sold Zeta Continent for fifty million sols. It caused a lot of ruckus with the people who wanted to get some land and had it blocked by the CZC lease agreement."

Kealani held up a hand for silence and pointed to the screen on the data pad. The hidden cameras outside of the camouflaged enclosure were set to keep a lock on the Fuzzies as they passed through the region. They also caught a bush goblin hiding in the nearby brush.

"We have to warn them or shoot the goblin," Erena said. She was getting agitated. Cindy was all for helping the Fuzzies even if it meant contaminating the observation data.

Kealani was torn. She wanted to help the Fuzzies but the first rule of anthropology was to observe, not interact with the subjects. There was another issue as well. "Do we have the right to interfere? This is Fuzzy land. We are outsiders."

Erena pulled out her radio and sent a signal to the ZNPF. "We are the observation team on the Rez. There is a bush goblin about to attack a tribe of Fuzzies. Do we have clearance to get involved?"

Major George Lunt's voice came back over the channel. "How many Fuzzies?" Kealani indicated there were ten adults and two juveniles. This was an unusually large clan as Fuzzies went. "Hold your position. The Fuzzies will handle this all by themselves." All three of the women were surprised. A bush goblin would be dangerous even for a full-grown Terro. Erena pointed this out.

Major Lunt explained, "Bush goblins, what Fuzzies call 'screamers,' are a problem for smaller groups. A group the size you are talking about will be more than the goblin will want to take on at once. Unless it is really hungry, it will go look for dinner elsewhere."

"What if it is really hungry?" Kealani asked. "A bush goblin is twice the height and four times the weight of an adult Fuzzy. Not to mention it is all teeth and claws."

"We have observed the Fuzzies in that area with mobile spy cameras," Major Lunt responded. "They'll know what to do."

Kealani and Cindy both started talking at once asking if they could get copies of the footage. Major Lunt said that if it was okay with the Commissioner, he would make duplicates of everything they had.

"I would like any copies you could give me as well, ladies. Have to go. Shift change. Let me know how this turns out."

The three women sat processing what they heard. Erena spoke first in a whisper. "It wasn't that long ago they were exterminating the harpies to protect the Fuzzies. I can't believe we shouldn't help them."

Kealani thought about it. "Commissioner Holloway must want the wild Fuzzies to develop without Big Brother watching out for them. Most of the Fuzzies at the Rez school came in under their own power. Some were recruited by other Fuzzies, but the ZNPF doesn't go out and grab them up."

Cindy nodded. "Ja, that makes sense. Fuzzies brought in by force could be traumatized by the experience. Out here, well away from Terro-human interference, their culture can grow organically. Removing the harpies only allows them to do so. No Fuzzy would be a match for one of those monsters. On the ground they know how to hide from damnthings, bush goblins and other predators."

"This also keeps their entire race from becoming dependent on us Big Ones," Kealani added. "Yggdrasil Khooghras that camp near Terran settlements are little more than beggars wanting metal spearheads, matches and such. Many no longer know how to make fire using from flint." Kealani looked at the screen and observed the Fuzzies getting closer to where the bush goblin crouched. "It may seem terrible, but in the long run Commissioner Holloway is correct. Better to not make the entire race dependent on us."

XXXI

Red Eye raised his weapon into the air to indicate that he wanted the tribe to halt. He sniffed the air and the rest did the same. He slowly backed up to speak with the others.

"Screamer ahead." The others nodded. One, Tree Chopper, suggested that they make run fast away. Red Eye said no. "Screamer fast-fast. We run, it chase us. Kill slow ones. Hurt Foot not get away."

Hurt Foot, so called after falling from a tree while gathering fruit and injuring an ankle, which the Fuzzies had no word for, was Tree Chopper's mate.

"We make screamer dead," Tree Chopper declared. He hefted his *coup-de-poing* axe ready to face the threat.

Red Eye nodded. "Tree Chopper, Fruitfinder, Spear Thrower and Runs Fast come with me. Hurt Foot will stay back with young ones. Fisher and Maker will go to Moon's right hand and Rock Thrower and Pale Fur go to Moon's left hand."

Nobody argued. Red Eye was the Wise One of the clan and everybody always did as the Wise One directed.

* * *

"The Fuzzies are splitting up," Erena said.

Each woman was glued to her transmission view pad. On the screens, each showing a different angle, the Fuzzies were separating into smaller units and moving off in different directions.

"They are going to attack it on three sides," Kealani said. "The group in front will distract the, um, screamer while the other two groups get into position on the flanks."

"Why not attack it from behind as well," Cindy asked.

"Not enough Fuzzies to cover all sides effectively," Erena suggested. "And it gives the goblin an escape route."

Kealani nodded. "Sure. If they can drive it away, all the better. The Fuzzies just want to be safe, not kill and eat it."

"Screamer not good to eat," Maid Marian added. "Pappy Jack shoot one near Wonderful Place and let Fuzzies eat it. Not good." She made the same face that children across the universe made when forced to take a spoonful of cod liver oil.

"Coming from a Fuzzy," Erena said with a smile, "a species that actually likes XT3 that is saying something!"

"Oh, the attack has started," Cindy said holding up her screen.

* * *

"I don't get it. The tracks just lead up to that boulder, then stop."

Cutter inspected the tracks more carefully. "These look real, not something to mislead any potential followers."

"Like us?"

Cutter nodded. "I wouldn't be surprised if these Sheilas expected us to follow, Cody. But these tracks look real enough…."

"Maybe the tracks are. I'll bet the boulder isn't," the third man said. He sounded like he had a bad cold due to the heavy bandage on his nose.

"Whattaya mean, Kev," Cutter asked.

"Back when I was in the Space Infantry we used fibroid weave covers to disguise the ground rollers," Kev explained. "We couldn't do anything about the tanks when they were airborne but on the ground we could make them look like boulders, small hills, even a copse of trees."

Cody rolled his eyes. "Why do they have to put 'space' in front of everything that leaves Terra?"

Kev ignored the comment. "That ground vehicle we saw outside of the pub was retired military issue or I'm a bat-winged Gimlian."

Cutter inspected the boulder from a respectful distance. "Fibroid weave, huh? Impervious to small arms fire and cutting tools?"

Kev nodded. "Very."

Cutter swore. "Can they see us out here?"

Kev thought for a minute. "Through the weave, no. But if they have any external cameras or spy-eyes, well, we're blown for sure."

"So if they do come out they could do it with guns a-blazin'," Cody added. "I'm plenty mad about my nose, but not enough to be an easy target."

Cutter thought about it. "Why would they have cameras set up while they hide under cover? What would they be looking at? They couldn't have expected us to follow them."

"One of them had a CZC patch on her sleeve. The one who pulled the gun on you, Cutter," Kev recalled. "And the other one spoke German. That girl who clobbered me an' Cody was some sort of expert in some school of martial arts. An unusual pairing, don't you think?"

Cutter literally smacked his forehead. "Anthropology students with a CZC escort. They must be doing some work for Science Division."

"That's it. I'm out," Cody said. "Smacking around some Sheilas for some payback is one thing. Getting on the bad side of the CZC is a whole different critter. I say we accept our beatings and get the Niflheim out of here."

"We don't know that they are out here for the CZC," Cutter argued. "Lots of people wear shirts and jackets with CZC patches. Even in Junktown, and we know they ain't workin' for the CZC. I say we wait until they come out then get some payback."

Kev shook his head. "What do you care? That woman never laid a finger on you."

"No, but the other one pointed a gun right in my face. I don't take that sitting down. Wait…can they hear us in there?"

Cody said no. "Virtually soundproof. Works both ways. You need some very sensitive equipment to hear through that stuff."

"Good. Good. We'll just hope they don't know we're here and wait," Cutter said. "We can hide behind one of these real boulders."

"How do we know that is a fake boulder," Kev asked. "We haven't even touched it to check."

"The tracks are a dead giveaway," Cody said as he pointed to the ground near the boulder. "A real rock that size would need some serious contragravity to move, which is the only way it would be sitting on top of those tracks. You see any construction going on around here? And touching it could start an alarm inside. If those women don't know we are here already, that would tell them pretty damned quick. Trust me, it's a camouflage job. I've seen lots of them in my time. The boulder designs come in three basic layouts; this is the most common one, now that I think about it."

"I dunno." Kev looked the boulder over. "The patch might not mean anything, but this kind of gear should. Whatever these Sheilas are out here doing, there is some serious scratch behind them. On this planet that means the CZC. The CZC could disappear all of us very easily. Legally or otherwise."

Cutter smiled wide. "Only if they catch us."

* * *

Sylvinski had already decided he saw enough of Neu Freya and wanted a graceful way to make his departure when Johann Torseus insisted that he stay to see the live theatrical performance of *The Gnarly Man*. Intrigued, he asked if the play was of Freyan origin.

"Ach, nein! Dis ist from an old story from Terra. Ve haff had fery little exposure to Freyan culture beyond vhat ve handed down in der mines."

"Oh, I should have realized that. So, all the performers will be your countrymen, I take it."

Johann shook his head displaying an interesting work of the muscles on his thick neck. "Nein, only vun of die actors vill be a Magni-Freyan. Die rest are from Mallorysport." Johann noticed the look of surprise on Supervisor Sylvinski's face. "Not all of mine pipple chose to be isolated here on Neu Freya. A few go out to see more of Terran culture for demselves. Drugi vas ofer in Mallorysport sightseeing. He vore a long coat...hat und large sunglasses to disguise himself. *Dere*, he attended an audition for dis play not realizing dot dey vere looking for pipple. He t'aught it vas a rehearsal. Vell, die, um, producer? Ja, he saw Drugi and noticed his build, die coat could not conceal dot, und asked him to come up on die stage. Vell, as you might imagine, dey got a *gute* look at him and die producer almost vept vit' joy.

"Drugi vas treated to a crash course in acting, somet'ing many of us haff a knack for, as it turned out, und vas cast in die lead."

The Supervisor couldn't imagine what part this Drugi could be portraying in a Terran play until he recalled Caliban from *The Tempest*.

Maybe this play was another of Shakespeare's lesser known works. He asked Gus about it.

"No, not Shakespeare by about half a millennia or so," Gus said. "I read the story when I was young but I won't spoil any of it for you."

As a visiting dignitary the Supervisor was given a balcony from which to watch the play. It was a good seat, although he noticed with some small chagrin that Janice Goodfellow was in another balcony with a significant entourage of female, at least he thought they were all women, guards.

The play started with a scene at a carnival or circus. A Tri-D projector provided the background canvas so only a few solid props were required. The play opened with a woman walking through the sideshow, made more realistic with the background moving with her and the hidden conveyor belt she walked on, until she came upon the sideshow beast man.

Sylvinski studied the "beast man's" face and spotted some changes from the norm. While the Magni-Freyans possessed a physique that could readily pass for a Neanderthal's, there were significant differences in the face. For this, Drugi needed makeup and prosthetic teeth. In Act IV, when Drugi's character grabbed and swung around one of the other actors as a makeshift weapon, there was no need for a special harness to relieve the man's weight: Drugi managed it with his own strength. For safety reasons, Sylvinski imagined that the actor wore special padding and much of the background was similarly padded.

After the play the Supervisor insisted on going down to meet the cast.

"I was very impressed with your performance, young man," Sylvinski complimented Drugi. "Have you considered doing other plays in the future?"

"I don't know," Drugi said in somewhat better Lingua Terra than most of his brethren. "I expect to be very typecast. I can't exactly pass as mainline Terran or Freyan."

"Bah! Most actors are forced into a certain mold. I can think of a few roles you would still be suited for."

Drugi raised an eyebrow. "Oh? Such as?"

"Why not play Mr. Hyde? In the book he is described much like you. Or Caliban. In fact, if a production of *Frankenstein* came around it wouldn't take much for you to do Igor!" Sylvinski became so animated about the ideas he was coming up with that he neglected to consider the possibility that Drugi might take offense. "There are also documentary films about prehistoric man. You just did a Neanderthal on stage; why not on film?"

Instead of taking offense, Drugi's interest was piqued. "Ja, I have read *The Strange Case of Dr. Jekyll and Mr. Hyde*. And *Frankenstein*. There was no Igor in the book."

"Some plays are based on the movies, instead of the books," Sylvinski said. "*Lord of the Rings*! You would make a fantastic dwarf!"

Gus watched the byplay with some amusement. There must be a movie mogul hiding under all that bureaucratic bluster. Still, he had to agree: Drugi could have a real future playing those kinds of roles. He recalled a Thoran bard who did a few Wolfman movies. By Thoran standards he made enough sols to be set for life. None of that was really important to the Thoran, of course. They were motivated by loyalty and honor. However, anything that distracted Sylvinski from being a bureaucratic pain in the lower posterior was welcome and even encouraged.

The Supervisor wrote something on the back of one of his Terran business cards. "This is my screen-com where I am staying. If you come up with any other acting work…gigs, I think they are called…let me know! I plan on being in the front row next time."

Drugi promised he would before being pulled away to meet with Janice Goodfellow. It would be the height of disrespect to ignore one marked by the gods.

Gus pulled the Supervisor off to the side. "Are you really that impressed with Drugi's performance?"

"Absolutely! Gus…Mr. Brannhard, I was not born to this job where my main function is to annoy the hell out of people."

"Niflheim," Gus said in a seeming non-sequitur.

Sylvinski paused. "Come again?"

"Out in the colonies we say Niflheim instead of hell," Gus explained. "If you had ever been there you would understand."

"Oh, thank you. As I was saying, in my youth I tried my hand at acting. Sadly, I just don't emote well. Drugi is a bit on the rough side, certainly, but I can see he has great potential. All the more impressive when you consider his background. Ghu, I almost wish I could be his manager!"

"You surprise me, Supervisor."

Sylvinski looked up at Gus and shook his head. "Yeah, I know. I came in like a cosmic storm and started acting like a four-star bastard the second I hit planetside. And, I will admit, it isn't all an act. Sadly, that is how things get done in my business. I will also admit that I think I will be going back to Terra without a head on a platter to pass around to my higher ups. This Neu Freya affair shows that your people have a lot of heart. We could use more folks in the government like that on Terra. Every single lead we chased down has ended up going nowhere. But I still have to go through the motions and give it all I have. If I miss something it'll come back to bite me in the ass. It wouldn't reflect well on my team, either."

Gus was a little stunned. "I am surprised you said all that."

"So am I," Sylvinski shrugged. "You realize of course, this is still war, of a sort."

"I do. Shall we discuss it further at the *Gasthaus*? The Magni-Freyans have some excellent house brews."

Sylvinski shook his head. "I can't for three reasons: One, I have to maintain appearances. I can't look like I was compromised. This would work against your little government here as well, especially if I have to turn in a favorable report.

"Two, I can't afford to get chummy with anybody I might have to lower the boom on. It makes things awkward."

Gus nodded. "And three?"

"Your reputation as a two-fisted no-holds-barred drinker is well established on this world. I am not about to let you drink me under the table."

* * *

Janice Goodfellow, with the aid of her "escorts," managed to fend off several more proposals of marriage. She did consent to do a number of blessings, mostly on pregnant women hoping for children that would look more "normal." She finally managed to excuse herself so she could meet the cast of the play.

The cast members, all Terro-humans except for Drugi, were far less impressed with her status as one marked by the gods than the Magni-Freyans. However, as she was being accorded the status of virtual royalty, the actors all considered it good luck to have her there.

Drugi, to his credit, did not gush in the manner of most of the men she had met in Neu Freya. He did ask her opinion on trying for the roles that Supervisor Sylvinski suggested.

"I know very little about stage and screen, Herr…"

"Please, Blessed One, just Drugi."

Janice smiled. "Drugi, I think your performance was excellent and you should be great at any role you turn your hand to. Are there more Magni-Freyan actors?"

"I am the only one, thus far," Drugi admitted.

"Well, your people should be encouraged to try new things. I know of your background and that you have little experience in this area, but might there might be others who share your passion? Why not try to create your own acting troupe and do roles that you wouldn't have to be typecast in? If everybody on stage is Magni-Freyan you wouldn't stand out as something different." Janice thought for a brief second. "Oh, I hope that didn't sound condescending or insulting."

Drugi smiled wide. "Not at all, Blessed One. I think you have made an excellent suggestion."

"I am so glad." Janice pulled out a small notebook from her purse. "Could I get your autograph, and maybe a photo with you?"

Drugi's eyes went wide. "Autograph?"

"It is something we Terros do. We like a remembrance of great or famous people. I think you will go far."

"Yes, certainly. In fact, I would also like your autograph and a photo!"

With that the floodgates were opened and everybody wanted Janice's autograph and asked her to stand for a photograph with them. Some tried to give her offerings, which she politely refused. Noticing that everybody seemed more interested in her than the actors, she suggested that she do a pose with the entire cast and made a show of getting all of their autographs. That started the audience doing the same.

In the wings Sylvinski watched as Janice mingled with the actors and audience. She was doing a good job of balancing her position as the Blessed One and working the room. *She might have a real future in politics*, he thought. It would be a shame that she wouldn't be able to work with the Magni-Freyans as an ambassador. Her special status would give her too much influence which could open the door for hostilities later on.

XXXII

"Is everybody in position?"

Tars Tarkis looked at his viewscreen. On the screen was a map of Mallorysport with three red dots moving on it. "Almost, John. Alpha is on slow approach toward Government House, Beta is in position at the spaceport and Gamma is wandering around Science Center."

A considerable amount of discussion had gone into selecting the targets for their next strike. The policy of avoiding harming children and Fuzzies made it difficult. Fuzzies were practically everywhere, although children were fairly contained by comparison. It was decided that Fuzzies may be an unavoidable casualty, though they could limit the scope of the collateral damage. The park and Fuzzy night club were out, for example. So was the hospital as it would have children as well. Government House only had Rainsford's two Fuzzies and the police Fuzzies. Word was that they had been sent to the Rez for their own safety. That made the government building a relatively safe target.

The business area of the spaceport was also considered. Security there would have made it impossible to slip a bomb into it. Dogs and Fuzzies were now checking anybody who entered the terminal. The luggage area was similarly defended. It was decided an aircar making a dive for the shuttle area would be most effective.

For the Science Division, the Martianists got lucky. One of the employees there, a custodian, came to a meeting and was "indoctrinated" to the cause with the same gas used on Arthur Twopersons. With his CZC credentials and access to toxic chemicals, an actual bomb would be unnecessary; he would simply be programmed to mix up a nasty concoction and run it through the air conditioning system. Something simple, like chlorine and ammonia, would get the job done in a rather spectacular fashion.

"And our man at the park?"

"Watching and waiting to see if they bring it."

John Carter nodded. “Good. Inform me the second J’ohnn J’onzz calls. I’ll be in the conference room.”

* * *

Victor Grego sat in the vault inspecting the chest of worthless rocks. Next to him stood Morgan Holloway. “So, only a few more faux sunstones are likely to be roaming around out there, likely on some poor women’s fingers.” Grego shook his head. “The poor bastards that put it there will be in a lot of trouble with their new fiancées when the stones stops glowing.”

“It is possible that a number of other stones left the planet through other, ah, enterprising individuals,” Morgan pointed out. “I doubt anyone else would have managed to pull off this kind of quantity, though. The real question would be: Does anybody else know how to create these fakes?”

That gave Grego pause. If word got out, everybody and his kid sister could be out irradiating jellyfish fossils and trying to pass them off as the real thing. The problem was that anything one person could do, sooner or later, somebody else could do as well. The genie was out of the bottle and nobody would be able to stuff him back in. Grego came to a decision. “By the end of the day, everybody on Zarathustra will know how to create fake sunstones.”

Morgan was surprised. “What? How?”

“Simple: we are going to tell them.”

Morgan watched Grego’s face and could see he was serious. He gave it some thought and put it together: “I get it. If everybody can make them, there will be no market for them. And the faint radiation they emit will make them easy to spot.”

“Exactly. Jewelers will all be given Geiger counters, at company expense, so they can spot the fakes if anybody tries to sell them.”

”And we can have a sale on the Geiger counters at the company stores for everybody else,” Morgan added. “We might even show a profit on this.”

Grego smiled. “That one got past me, but it is a good idea. If everybody has a Geiger counter then nobody can be taken for a pigeon on the street. I'll call Henry Stensen and see if he can miniaturize them down to wristwatch size."

"Why not build them into wristwatches? Fashionable and functional. This will be bigger than the Fuzzy Flush."

The two discussed it for a moment, then something else occurred to Grego. "These Martianists sold these fake stones off to finance their efforts here, right?"

Morgan shrugged. "That is the working theory."

Grego turned back to the chest. "You could get a couple dozen travel tickets with lots of luggage, and even buy a house with lots left over with just a million sols."

"About half that, I would hazard," Morgan said. "What are you getting at?"

"It would be pretty risky just selling that much. Why risk it to sell off all of these? As I understand it, these Martianists only care about money insofar as it is needed to Martioform Mars to its ancient, more viable state. But this much would be about a fraction of a drop compared to what they need. That is why they seek to become a political power."

"Right. To get the necessary influence to force the Federation to foot the bill for Mars' restoration."

"Getting caught passing off this many ersatz stones would work against them in public opinion. Why risk it for a few million sols?"

"Well, more than a few...."

Grego shook his head. "It doesn't matter how much as long as it doesn't get the job done. Terra-Baldur-Marduk Spacelines doesn't have the wherewithal to pull off a job like restoring an entire planet. Not without going bankrupt afterwards. So why risk it?"

Morgan thought for a moment. "There must be something else they believed they needed that was worth the risk. With that much money they could buy a...Niflheim!"

Grego nodded. "I see we are of like minds."

"Okay, but hold off on the announcement until the end of the week."

"Oh? Why?"

"Because if we have any hope of catching these Khooghras they will have to still be making fakes. If the whole planet knows how to do that, it will be worse than finding a needle in a haystack."

* * *

"A thought just occurred to me and I feel pretty foolish it didn't kick in a lot sooner," Marshal Fane said.

In the room with him were Chief Steefer, Major Lansky, both on loan from the CZC to oversee the security for the transfer of the relic, Police Chief Frank Carr and, of course, Governor Rainsford. Carr asked what it was.

"Well, once we drop off this, ah, relic these sons-of Khooghras want, how the Niflheim do they expect to get it off-planet?"

Everybody looked at the Marshal. The expressions on their faces said that they had missed that detail as well.

"After all, it is somewhat bigger than a breadbox."

Rainsford hit the intercom button. "Francine, I need you to put in a call to Commodore Napier. Tell the Navy operator that it is urgent. When you get through to him, pipe it to the big viewscreen in my office."

"Yes, sir."

Major Lansky looked like he wanted to slap himself in the forehead. "Of course, they will need a ship to haul it away. A big one at that."

"A mega-freighter, like they use to carry guano from Yggdrasil to Terra," Marshal Fane added. "You think maybe they hijacked one?"

"I think they bought one," Chief Steefer said. He explained about the value of the fake sunstones and Morgan's theory on who sold them.

"Commodore Napier on line one and Mister Grego on line two, Governor," Francine's voice announced from the intercom.

"Split screen, Francine."

Commodore Napier appeared on the left side of the screen, Grego and Morgan on the right.

Rainsford shook his hands at the screen, which was reciprocated. "Commodore, I believe we may have a cloaked ship tooling around in Zarathustran space."

Grego supported the Governor, and explained why.

Napier swore under his breath.

"Does every Khooghra with a spaceship have that damned cloaking paint?"

Everybody recalled the Fuzzy Slavers who used the black cloaking paint on their ships. They were visible through telescopes, but only if they blocked out the stars behind them.

"There has to be another method of spotting them," Lansky said without thinking. Never having been a military man he wasn't conditioned not to speak in the presence of a field grade officer without first being addressed. Chief Steefer threw a warning glance at the Lansky, then realized he might be on to something.

"Sir! Detection equipment is designed to spot objects in space by their mass and any electromagnetic fields, yes?" Chief Steefer asked.

"Among other things, Chief," the Commodore replied. "The cloaking paint baffles the mass and electromagnetic fields all hyperspace ships generate while powered up. It also obscures any vibratory actions."

"What about gamma emissions?" Everybody turned their attention to Morgan Holloway on the screen. "I have spent a great deal of time bouncing from world to world and know a bit about normal and hyperspace travel. Ships leave a faint trail of gamma energy in their wake."

"Gamma energy disappears instantly," Napier pointed out. As a Navy man he knew a thing or two about space travel as well. "We don't have the equipment on Xerxes that could track anything like that."

Rainsford turned to Morgan. "Do you have anything like that on your yacht?"

Morgan looked chagrinned. "My regular yacht is back on Terra right now. The ship I have here is basically a stripped down showroom model. But even if the *Adonitia* were here, it doesn't have that kind of detection array."

"Mining ships!" Grego burst out. "The CZC has automated mining drone ships in the asteroid belt. They are designed to locate and acquire fissionable ore. I can send them your way."

"Won't the cloaking paint block that, too?" Marshal Fane asked.

Napier shook his head. "As far as I know, that can't be done. The gamma trail is created by the ship passing through the minute particulate matter in space. Something about the Dillinghams causes it. The eggheads on Terra have been trying to figure out why since the things were invented. Anyway, the gamma creation occurs outside of the ship and thus outside of the cloaking paint. I wish we thought of that during the slaver battle."

Lansky ignored Steefer's glare and said, "If you don't have the detection gear on Xerxes, what are the odds a Navy ship would have it?"

"Somewhere in the neighborhood of zero, Major," Commodore Napier admitted.

I'll bet he sends off a memo to Terra advising gamma detection arrays be installed on all navy ships, Rainsford thought.

"How long will it take to get the mining drones back into Z-space, Mr. Grego," Chief Steefer asked.

"One second, Chief." Grego stepped away from the screen for a bit longer than the promised second, then returned. "About twelve hours, Z-time. They are not equipped with Dillinghams so they don't get around all that quickly."

"We'll need somebody who can direct the drones in real time," Morgan said. "Is Damien Panaioli still on the payroll?"

"If he isn't already, he is now," Grego said as he vanished from the screen then returned a minute later. "Mr. Panaioli is available. He can remote direct the drones from here. As serendipity would have it, he was testing a ship commander game we are beta testing. He should be primed for the mission."

"Excellent," Rainsford said. "Commodore, Damien Panaioli was a key player in bringing down one of the slavers' ships last year. I trust you remember the plan we used with the remote controlled Fuzzy-bots."

Napier chuckled. "I'll be honest; I thought even the idea of Fuzzy robots was ridiculous, but I can't argue against the results. Would this Mr. Panaioli be interested in joining the Navy, by any chance?"

"I doubt it," Grego said. "He was given a General Discharge from the Army for, ah, some bad behavior." Grego didn't think it was his place to get into any specifics about Damien Panaioli's unfortunate past.

Napier shrugged. "We can be a bit flexible, if he decides to give it another go." The Commodore turned away from the screen to speak quietly with somebody out of range of the camera, then turned back. "My people have spotted the mining drone headed toward Zarathustra on long distance telemetry. The supposed freighter is still not coming up on our detection arrays. I'll screen back in a few hours when the drone is in range and Mr. Panaioli is in place. In fact, I would like him up here on Xerxes to operate the remotes. It will speed up the interface between his efforts and ours."

"I'll make it happen, Commodore," Grego said. Mentally he working out what kind of bonus he we need to entice Damien Panaioli to go to the far moon.

"Thank you, Commodore," Rainsford said. Napier vanished from the screen and Grego's side expanded to fill the gap. Now Morgan Holloway was also visible. "Victor, please let me know when Damien is ready."

"I'll be in constant communication with Chief Steefer." Grego made his goodbyes and the screen went dark.

Chief Steefer turned to Lansky. "Major, I'll oversee things from here. You can go to the staging area and fly over to the park with the relic."

Major Lansky gave a sharp "Yessir," nodded to the Marshal and the Governor and briskly left the room.

Frank Carr watched the Major leave, then said, "Lansky seems to be a bit sharper since his promotion. His uniform is parade perfect."

Chief Steefer smiled. "Finding Gus Brannhard in the CZC sublevels made the job more real for him, I think. Being trusted with a job like this will reinforce that sense of duty. Good thing, too. He'll be taking my position one day."

"I am surprised you didn't call in Jack Holloway on this," Marshal Fane said to Ben Rainsford.

"I would have liked to, but, really, this isn't his area of responsibility since none of the Fuzzies or any of his family are involved," Rainsford said. "He has enough on his plate with the Rez and locating that missing Freyan girl."

XXXIII

"I found it!"

Betty almost dropped the file she was holding when Jack came into the room holding a data pad. "Found what?"

Jack held up the pad. "I've been looking for the old video file showing me facing off against Phil Matedne. Miss Ancheta's father."

Betty shook her head as if in disbelief. "With everything else going on, you take the time to rummage through old videos?"

Jack paused, then shrugged. "George Lunt is overseeing the search for the girl, Ben hasn't called for help with those Martianist idiots, not that I could provide any, Kealani and company called George about a bush goblin threatening some Fuzzies, so they are all okay—"

"A bush goblin!" Betty looked shocked. "Isn't that dangerous for them, too?"

Jack shook his head. "Goblins are basically cowards. They don't attack groups of humans, and even shy away from jumping a single full-grown man. Three women would be more than it could handle... especially those three!"

Betty harrumphed, then went to see what was on the data pad. Jack tapped the screen and a much younger version of himself appeared with a shorter man facing each other. From their stance it was obvious they were preparing to spar or fight. Looking at the two men, Betty thought the other man was at a considerable disadvantage. Jack was at least eight inches taller and had a good sixty pounds on the smaller Phil Matedne.

"Look how dark your hair is!" Betty said, as she pointed at the screen. "Morgan really takes after you, doesn't he? He could be your twin."

"Pat, Jim and I were the only Black Irish in the family. Well, Ma had dark hair, but she was mostly German. The rest ran from sandy to strawberry blonde. But Morgan's hair...."

"Well, don't go coloring your coif," Betty said. "I like it as it is."

"No danger of that happening." The sound was turned off on the data pad, allowing Jack to provide his own voiceover. "Looks like I'll take the other guy's lunch money, doesn't it? Watch."

Something or someone signaled for the match to begin. Betty recognized the stance Jack assumed from seeing him in the gym practicing his boxing skills. The other man, Phil, assumed a martial stance. Jack moved in and tried a few jabs. Phil didn't even bother to block them. He just seemed to be somewhere else whenever a fist came near him.

"Wow! He's quick," Betty observed.

"You ain't seen nothing,' yet," Jack said. "Watch this."

On the screen Jack did a combination attack. His fists moved too fast for Betty to follow, yet Phil easily maneuvered around the assault, came in close and slapped Jack in the face before slipping away. The look on Jack's face was one of utter astonishment.

"I never saw that slap coming," Jack said. "Watch how he moves between my punches and lands three more hits before I even knew he was there. I wish I could have stayed on-planet long enough to learn more."

"You sound like you are proud of the way he smacked you around," Betty said. "Are you a closet masochist or something?"

"Not even a little bit. I respect his skills and ability. I've taken a few beatings in my life since I left Terra. Most notable examples include a retired boxer on Odin who worked me over pretty good, though I got a fair piece of him, too. On Thor one of the natives demonstrated his knowledge of the local martial arts—on me. I barely held my own until he got bored and laid me out. When I woke up he bought the first three rounds at the tavern. Not every Thoran is that good, by the way; Thrud's'dor was a master. I learned a lot from those bouts. It was well worth the aches and pains I had for the next few days."

"Didn't you take a beating on Freya?"

Jack snorted. "That doesn't count. I was taken by surprise by four men. After I got patched up I hunted each one down and had a little one-on-one playtime. That was the last time anybody tried anything like that. At least while I was on Freya. Now look at this." Jack held up the pad. "Phil Matedne just slapped me around like a cat playing with a mouse. I never laid a finger on him. There is no question in my mind that he could have killed me with a pinky finger had he felt the need. In that match he didn't belittle me, either. He just showed me I was in his house and he wasn't about to move out."

"Why didn't he use his feet? When I took Tae Kwan Do we used our feet at least as much as our hands," Betty said.

"He didn't need to, as you can see. Good thing for me. I watched him warm up with some kicks; this would have been a much shorter bout had he used them. You never mentioned you took Tae Kwan Do," Jack added accusingly.

Betty waved that away. "You men like to feel like the big strong protectors of us helpless little women-folk," she said with an old southern American accent. "Well, until I met your sister, I thought you were much the same. Now I know better."

"Good. I'll let you protect my frail old self, sometime...oh! Did you see that? He just stepped in and flicked my nose and was gone before I knew it happened."

Betty shook her head. Jack seemed almost giddy showing off how he was being played with by the much smaller man. "Didn't you feel like he was making fun of you?"

Jack shrugged. "Tagger warned me before the match that Phil was going to avoid doing any real damage while showing me what he could do. He was the one holding the camera, if you were wondering. I'll take a flick to the nose over several broken bones any day of the week. And remember, I was almost twice his size. My boxing coach back in college drummed into my head that getting beaten is only shameful if you don't learn from it. You better believe I was taking notes."

Betty folded her arms over her chest and said, "Hmm...are you showing me this because I was on your case about those three women going out with just two Fuzzies and their dogs?"

Jack shook his head. "Nah, I was just feeling a bit nostalgic. Now that you mention it, though, Kealani was one of Phil's students. Top of the class, I would wager. If she can do even half what Phil was capable of, I wouldn't want to mess with her. And anybody she meets out there in the bush would do well to think the same."

"And if they come across a damnthing?"

"Why do you think I mentioned Ray Pulver to them? He'll make sure they have the gear they need to survive out there."

* * *

"What do you think frightened off the bush goblin?"

Kealani and Cindy looked at the screen and were unable to see what spooked the goblin. "There might be something bigger and meaner out of range of the cameras."

Cindy agreed. "We should take a look around. If it is a damnthing we might have to do a little running ourselves."

"I don't think it is," Erena said. "Look at the Fuzzies. They are just standing there looking at that big boulder."

It took a second then everybody realized that they were inside the "boulder."

"We must have given ourselves away somehow." Kealani suggested. "That means this area is burned and we'll have to go farther east and find another group to observe."

"Not look at us," Maid Marion said. "Feel ground shake. Something big come near. Not damnthing."

Rockthrower agreed.

"Ground shake?" Erena felt the floor of the fibroid cover. "I didn't feel anything."

"Fuzzies are very sensitive to movements in the ground," Cindy said. "Dr. Mallin thinks it allows them to sense large predators in their vicinity. Otherwise they would have no hope of escaping should one come too close for them to get away."

Kealani looked at the Fuzzies. "Not a damnthing?" Both shook their heads, a habit they picked up from the Big Ones. "Do you know what it might be?"

"Feel like ground roller," Rockthrower said. "Like one we ride in."

Cindy swore softly in German. "Somebody else, maybe a miner, is coming through the area. Best we pack up and go."

Everybody agreed. They gathered up their equipment and recalled the remote cameras. Once everything, except the cameras outside of the cover, was loaded back into the ground roller, Erena tapped the button to collapse the camouflage.

* * *

"Look! The boulder is shrinking," observed Kev. "Keep your heads down and stay quiet. Remember, they have a couple Fuzzies with them."

Cutter looked confused. "Are you afraid of Fuzzies?"

Kev looked disgusted, then whispered, "Hardly, but I understand they have ears like a bat. You want to give us away, just keep flappin' those lips."

While Cutter fancied himself to be the leader of the trio, he knew when to follow orders and when to give them. Kev was the military expert of the group, having spent even more time in the Space Marines than he had, and as such couldn't be argued with in this instance.

The three men watched as the "boulder" collapsed and folded in on itself after creating an exit for the women, Fuzzies and dogs. They didn't appear to be wary of an ambush. The one in the CZC shirt looked around as if watching for something that might be hungry and not too particular where it got its protein from.

"Nobody said anything about dogs," Cody whispered. "I heard a Curtys can take a man's arm off with one bite."

Cutter nodded. "I don't know about that, but I've heard they are vicious when their masters, the Fuzzies, are threatened. On Baldur they use them as nanny dogs to protect people's children. They're strong, fast, and can rip a man to kibble quick, fast, and in a hurry."

"They also have super-hearing, damnit!" Kev whispered urgently. "Shut up or you'll find out just how much of their reputation is genuine."

The three men watched carefully from their hiding places as the women packed everything away. The Fuzzies they had been observing noticed the commotion and cautiously approached. When Redeye spotted Maid Marion and Rockthrower, he threw caution to the wind and approached.

"I don't like this," Cutter said in a soft whisper. "Three women and two Fuzzies I think we could handle. Even with the dogs. Now there's an entire tribe in the mix. We'll have to wait until the numbers are more favorable."

Cody was surprised. "You're afraid of a bunch of Fuzzies?"

"He's right," Kev said. "Unlike you, Cody, I watch the news. That band of Fuzzies up north slaughtered some slavers with very little assistance from us *homo s. terra* types. Small and primitive does not mean weak and defenseless. We either pack it in, which I am in favor of, or we watch and wait for a better opportunity."

Cutter was still determined to get some payback. "We wait. Fuzzies in these parts are still nomadic, or so I've heard. They shouldn't stick around long."

"Unless the ladies give them XT3," Cody countered. "Once they get a taste of that you can't chase them away." Under his breath he made a remark about the XT3 and how anybody who liked the stuff had to be crazy.

Kev took in the camp and equipment he already saw and did a mental estimate of what the ground roller could carry. Unlike the aircars that needed rocket propulsion, hence liquid or solid fuel, military ground rollers were equipped with nuclear powered engines. That meant no space would be wasted for additional fuel. Atomic batteries lasted for years if not decades in surface vehicles.

That left food for the women, Fuzzies and dogs, clothing, weapons, observation gear and the usual odds and ends of a campsite. Kev doubted the roller could carry more than four cases of additional XT3 without filling the seats and sitting on them. Fuzzies and dogs were quite comfortable with hunting for their own food in the wild, so what would be the point?

"One case would feed that mob of newcomers for a week," Kev estimated. "And the ladies wouldn't want to give out more than that in case they meet more Fuzzies along the way. Gifts for the natives. I would think the women would hand out some samples, maybe even an entire case, then tell them where they could get more. The Fuzzies would likely head west as fast as their little legs would take them. That done, the ladies would be on their way to the next observation point."

That made sense to the other two men.

"Then we will just wait here until they leave," Cutter said. "Let them get far enough away that they wouldn't spot us from behind, then follow their tracks."

Kev shrugged. "Fine."

Cody agreed. "Let's just hope none of those new Fuzzies spot us before they go."

XXXIV

The splitter maul came down and chunks of punk wood fell away in two directions. Brünnhilde collected the two halves, then split them again. She looked around and saw that all the wood had been chopped and collected an armful. The headaches that had plagued her were gone so she felt she could use some exercise. Mia tried to talk her out of it but Brünnhilde just laughed it off.

The wood would be for a campfire. Brünnhilde had never been out camping or even attended a cookout on Magni, as it was a tin-can colony without any kind of outdoor recreation possible. Of course, as a slave she would not have been allowed out for something like that anyway.

Since coming to Zarathustra, her people had all been too busy for such a frivolous activity. There were homes to build, mining interests to start up and a local government to establish. Besides, she had no concept of even a picnic prior to being freed.

There was another reason for being active: Brünnhilde might end up in a situation where she would have to fight her way out to escape the people who had collected her after she had been shot. If Weaver and company found out that she knew about their Fuzzy-slaving activities they might decide it wasn't prudent to leave her alive. Should it come to that, she wanted to be able to function at peak performance.

Another thing bothered her: if these people had been poaching Fuzzies, where were they? There was no way to hide any live Fuzzies in the ground-rollers. And there was no sign of any pelts, either, which was a huge relief for Brünnhilde. So what happened to them? Maybe the Fuzzies were turned over to other poachers, which didn't speak well for their ultimate fate.

Then there was her personal safety. So far nobody had tried to take liberties with her, at least. She didn't know if the men in the party were put off by her build, which many non-heavy-worlders would find unappealing, or if they feared her great strength if they did decide to try something. She hoped that they simply had better manners than to force themselves on her. If somebody tried something and she hurt or killed her assailant, the rest might decide to either kill her or leave her stranded in the wilderness.

One of the men in the group was a powerfully built man who rarely spoke. Nobody mentioned it, but it was possible the man, Lars, was from Modi or some other high-gee world. If so, his strength would very nearly equal or even exceed hers and if he got "frisky," things could get awkward for Brünnhilde.

The only person Brünnhilde trusted even a little bit was Mai. She acted like a protective big sister making sure none of the men got too chatty with her. Brünnhilde thought that Mai might not like the people she was with but was somehow trapped with them.

"Hilde, how much wood are you going to chop?"

Brünnhilde turned to see Mai coming toward her. "I just finished." She tossed the last few quarters to the woodpile thirty feet away. "I thought we could have a real big bonfire tonight."

Mai shook her head as if in disbelief. "To burn all of that, we would have a fire you could see from space. Way more than is needed for a campfire."

Brünnhilde looked at the pile. When properly stacked, it would have made a full cord of firewood. Even a full cord would have been far more than needed, not that Brünnhilde had any experience in this area.

"Oh. I didn't know. On Magni we didn't have camping or cookouts. And the trees in the terrarium couldn't be cut down unless they had wood rot or something. They were part of the natural air-scrubbing facility."

Mai nodded in understanding. Airless or toxic worlds would have Terran plants brought in to maintain a breathable ecosystem in the enclosures, as it was cheaper and more efficient than bringing oxygen in from off-world or extracting it from water. Most of them didn't have trees at first since it was cost prohibitive to ship in anything larger than a sapling.

"What kind of trees do they have on Magni?"

"All introduced hardwoods like oak and walnut. Some of the sturdier fruit bearing trees, too. Softwood, like pine, doesn't fare well on heavy gravity worlds. Even the hardwood trees grow shorter and wider. Plus we prefer trees that bear fruit and nuts. Nothing purely decorative as water is expensive to bring in from the asteroid belt. There are no indigenous plants or animals on Magni." Brünnhilde gently struck the stump she was using with the axe to wedge it there. A hard swing would have simply split the stump and then she would have to put the axe someplace else. "Maybe we could bring the wood with us. We might not find more deadfall on the way."

Mai considered it. There was a lot of empty cargo space since the original "cargo" had been left behind. "Sounds like a good idea to me. Hilde, do you think your people are still looking for you? It has been a while."

"And most people would assume that I had been eaten by now," Brünnhilde laughed. "No, they are out there, I am sure, if for no other reason than my father will want a fair chunk of my hide for taking the aircar without permission. I am not looking forward to that particular reunion, but I'll be glad to be found all the same. I dare say that you will be rid of me fairly soon."

"They must be very worried, with you taking off like that." Mai looked wistful. "I never had anybody that would have gotten worried about me like that."

"Didn't you have a family?"

Mai shook her head. "I was dropped off at the fire department as a newborn. I never knew my parents. So I was raised in the System here on Zarathustra. There were a number of foster homes; some were okay, others not so much. I won't go into details on that."

Brünnhilde was no expert at gauging ages of non-Magni-Freyans. Her best guess was that Mai was in her early twenties. That would mean she was abandoned early in the colony's history on Zarathustra.

While orphans were far from uncommon for her people back on Magni, due to work accidents in the mines or extreme punishment for those who wouldn't cooperate, the children would immediately be taken in by another family. None were left to fend for themselves.

"How did you hook up with Weaver and this bunch?"

Mai looked down at the ground for a moment before answering.

"I…left another foster home. Ran away, really. My foster father tried to take…liberties with me." Mai shuddered at the memory. "I came across Weaver as he was gathering up equipment to go sunstone prospecting. At least that is what he told me. I signed on as the cook. I didn't know until later what…"

Mai went silent. Brünnhilde considered what she already knew and had a good idea what was left unsaid. Mai had no idea that she was hooking up with Fuzzy slavers. That could mean she was in danger, too. However, this could be a trap to see if Brünnhilde knew about the poaching.

"Being around mostly men out in the wilderness is risky," Brünnhilde said. "Especially if you are young. Um…how old are you?"

"When I came out here I was fifteen," Mai admitted. "I told Weaver that I was eighteen so he would let me join. Now I wish I hadn't."

"Did they…?"

"Oh, no. Consuela took me under her wing. She made it very clear that she would shoot the family jewels off the first man that touched me without my consent."

Brünnhilde never heard of "family jewels" but was able to surmise the meaning. "Well, you can add me to your host of allies. We 'maidens' have to look out for each other."

Mai laughed at being characterized as "a maiden." "I haven't been that for a while, now. One of my foster fathers took care of that."

Brünnhilde was shocked by Mai's confession. While she knew little of home Freyan culture, among her own people such a thing would never happen. Even the overseers never took such liberties. Of course, the overseers never ventured to the slave quarters, so they'd never seen her. Had they seen her face, might things have been very different? However, among the Magni-Freyans children were treated with an almost religious reverence. Infant mortality was high among the slave class. Any man who tried something untoward would be unlikely to live long enough to repent.

"I am so sorry you went through that. What happened to the man that, um, did that to you?"

Mai looked like she wasn't certain whether to share any more. Finally she shrugged and said, "I got his gun one night when he was drunk and shot him with it. Then I ran like all Niflheim was after me. I don't even know if he survived or not. I lived in Junktown for a while, scavenging food and clothing. Things got a bit better when the Soup Kitchen opened. Better food and there was even a donation closet where people dropped off clothing and other stuff. It was around that time I joined up with Weaver and company." She sighed. "Now I wish I had just turned myself in."

Brünnhilde laid a gentle hand on Mai's shoulder. "You still can. When we get to a town with a medical center you could stay with me there. You can tell your story to the guardsmen…um…I mean police."

Mai shook her head. "They won't believe me. Nobody will."

"You can't be sure of that. I have heard of a machine that can tell if you are lying. Surely it would back you up."

"The verifier? I thought that was a myth police started to scare criminals into confessing. Even Weaver is afraid of it."

That gave Brünnhilde pause. She had never seen a verifier, if that is what it was really called, herself. Maybe it wasn't real after all.

"Well, even if it doesn't exist you'll have me for a, um…"

"Character witness?"

"Ja! That. Among my people that counts for much. Now, I think I need to get this firewood loaded. Maybe that big man, Lars, could help?"

Mai was surprised. "Are you getting sweet on the muscle man?"

Brünnhilde shook her head. "No, he just looks like this kind of work wouldn't bother him much." *And I won't become involved with any Fuzzy slavers*, she thought.

XXXV

The relic was brought in by contragravity barge to the outskirts of the Junktown. Originally, the Martianists wanted it brought to the park where the now famous duel between Jack and Morgan Holloway took place. Marshal Max Fane gave a flat "no."

"If something goes bad and the shooting starts, I don't want a lot of innocent bystanders getting killed." Governor Rainsford had to agree and backed the Marshal.

The Martianists' representative on the comscreen, wearing a disguise based on something from a Bradbury novel with a voice modulator, acquiesced, though not gracefully.

The barge settled down in the open field east of Mallorysport. This was the spot chosen by the Martianists since it was on the opposite side of the city from the newly installed Space Navy ground base. Although the base was not yet fully operational, the Martianist representative was clearly taking no chances.

Half a dozen people in costumes cribbed from the ancient television show *The Martian Chronicles* waited at the landing site. Gender was impossible to distinguish through the ornate masks and long robes.

Police Chief Frank Carr shook his head and laughed softly. "These mutts are just a little too infatuated with anything relating to Mars, even the fanciful fiction by Terran writers."

Chief Steefer rubbed his chin. "Well, according to them, we are all Martian descendants, so those ancient authors were just writing about 'The Old Country,' in a manner of speaking."

Carr agreed that made a sort of weird sense. A thought struck him. "I think we have just been played."

"Played?"

Chief Carr turned to Chief Steefer. "They never really wanted to collect this thing from the park. How would they get their freighter in to collect it? It was just smoke and mirrors to make us think we got one over on them. While we were watching the park for anything suspicious they were out here setting up Ghu-knows-what."

Chief Steefer thought it over and it made sense. He shrugged. "Does it really matter?"

Chief Carr grimaced. "Probably not."

* * *

With the barge settled down and the retractable ramp extended, the "Martian delegation" approached the relic. The ship, once thought to be the Fuzzy Rocket, gleamed in the early evening sunlight.

"By all the gods of Mars, it is beautiful," said the first to approach. He, or she, placed a gloved hand on the hull. "It is like touching the past glories of the Martian civilization."

"More like the glories to come," another said. "People will rally around us from all over the Federation when they see this ship: actual proof that our ancient forefathers made their way to the stars. It will galvanize the people to action! We will gain political power and, thus, the funds needed to restore the home world to its original glory."

"It will have to be inspected by experts," a third spoke up. "Not just members of the Cause."

The first one to touch it removed his hand from the hull and turned his attention to the rest. "Let's inspect the hell out of this ship before we call down the transport. It would be foolish not to expect it to be bugged with a homing device. More than likely several such devices. And mind what you say. It could have listening devices planted as well."

Everybody nodded and extracted gadgets of various sizes from pockets and pouches within the robes. The hatch, left open by the CZC techs, allowed easy entry into the rocket. Inside, the first thing they noticed is how clean everything was.

"It looks like everything was scrubbed down from top to bottom," one of them said. "Do you think they might have collected any trace amounts of Martian dirt or fossil microbes?"

Another tried to shake his, or her, head, But the mask prevented the full motion. "Artifacts are always cleaned up during analysis. It would be suspicious if they hadn't. No, they were clearing away any dirt from this world so they could get a clearer picture of what they had."

"Has anybody detected anything, yet?"

"I found a tracker under the console."

"Spy-bug in this, um, storage locker?"

Several bugs and tracking devices were located throughout the ship. All had been well camouflaged to appear to be part of the original construction.

"They *really* wanted to follow us remotely," a short one said. He held up his hand to show his discoveries. "I found seven tracers so far. I would have missed them entirely if not for the bug scanner. These people really know how to hide tracer." He considered dropping the spy devices on the floor and stepping on them, then thought better of it; it might mar the floor. Instead he simply threw them out the hatch. Who cared if they kept transmitting as long as they weren't on the ship?

By the time they were satisfied that all the tracers had been removed, they had collected twenty-seven of them. All were tossed out the hatch. That done, the apparent leader of the group extracted a small sphere from a pouch. It was fairly nondescript, looking like a large marble or small ball. Held between finger and thumb, the leader pressed the opposite ends.

"Everybody out," the leader ordered. "We don't want to be in here when this ship is collected."

Everybody filed out. The shorter person absently stepped on, and crushed, some of the electronic bugs that had been thrown out of the rocket.

* * *

Chief Carr looked at a screen and noticed several blips vanish. "Looks like they found at least some of the bugs and destroyed them," he said with annoyance. "If they found any, they likely found them all."

"I'll inform Mr. Grego," Chief Steefer said.

"I'll call Marshal Fane," Chief Carr said. "I don't think he's going to be very happy about all the bugs being neutralized."

Chief Steefer kept his face neutral. "I wouldn't worry too much about that."

* * *

On Xerxes everybody was on high alert. Naval and Marine personnel stood at battle readiness, prepared to move out at a moment's notice. Every interplanetary shuttle and combat cruiser was fully loaded and manned.

Sitting at the control station that had been sent up from the CZC was Damien Panaioli with his new bride Cortney. Both stared at screens with blips of light that represented a mining drone they each controlled.

"Enjoying the honeymoon, babe?"

Cortney laughed. "I didn't think it would be on an actual moon, honey."

Damien shrugged. "Well, when I proposed…"

"In front of all my co-workers at the CZC accounting department." Cortney said with a small giggle.

"Yup. And I brought pizza for everybody when I did it. Well, as you will recall, I did say that the sky was the limit for the honeymoon."

Cortney laughed again. "I think you surpassed that little limitation. The sky is about two hundred thousand miles from here, I think."

"Two hundred and ninety-six thousand, give or take a few thousand for the elliptical," said a new voice from behind them. It was Commodore Napier. "Darius is about half that. How are you two lovebirds making out over here?"

Damien nodded at the screen. "I am controlling six drones and Cortney has the other five."

"Eleven is all the CZC has out there?" Napier noted.

"These were all the CZC could get over here in time to do any good. Most of the drones are on the far side of the asteroid belt. Even at full burn it would take at least a day to get them here, and that's without an obstacle course of flying rocks in the way. More like two or three days to get through all that mess." Damien noticed the surprised look on the Commodore's face. "I was fully briefed by Murphy over in the control center back at the CZC. He wanted me to apologize for the limited resources we could send your way."

Napier nodded. He had also been briefed on Mr. Panaioli. Damien was a maverick who generally did whatever came to his mind, good or bad. He started a weekly barbecue on the roof of the CZC building, for example. He would buy all the food and fixings himself, then refuse any recompense from his co-workers. So his fellow employees set up a tip jar that was filled every week. What they didn't know is that Damien gave the tips to the Soup Kitchen to help the down and out.

Then there was the other side. Napier decided against looking into what had gotten Damien bounced from the Army. It wasn't anything too serious or he wouldn't have been given a General Discharge, which became honorable after six months. That left out treason, murder and gross insubordination…nothing that would keep Napier from allowing Mr. Panaioli on base for security reasons. That was all the commodore needed to know and left it at that.

Damien's supervisor, Murphy, was prepared to put a stop to the weekly cook-outs but word got to Mr. Grego that morale had improved, which translated to higher productivity, and quietly suggested to Murphy to let it be. Later, Damien pulled a prank on Mr. Grego. It was harmless enough; he disconnected the drive control cable in Grego's private aircar. The vehicle would start up and even engage the contragravity, but that was all. Nobody was placed in danger and Grego didn't miss anything important.

Instead of firing the prankster, Grego returned the prank. He never said what he did and Damien never discussed it, but there was a reduction in similar pranks for a few weeks.

Napier also learned that Damien had no filter in his dealings with people. Whether it be pauper or prince, he spoke the same to either party in plain talk that often bordered on disrespect. Only the way he spoke, generally tended to prompt amusement rather than ire. More than once he had been thanked for his candor.

Well, if that is how he can work better, he can be as outrageous as he likes, thought Napier, *as long as the crew doesn't try to emulate him.* "I confess to being surprised when I learned your wife had joined you."

Without glancing away from his viewscreen, Damien replied, "I like to think I am the best there is in this area, but I know my limitations. I could manage control of eight of the drones, at best. Cortney is almost as good as I am with the home games so I brought her along to help. Six I can manage without stressing myself. Cortney can handle the other five more than well enough. You do want optimal performance, yes?"

There it was: just a hint of impertinence while making a valid point. That wouldn't go over well with many in the military regardless of the service branch. Napier got the impression that Mr. Panaioli was actually on his best behavior. Well, the man wasn't in his Navy and as long as he performed well he could start singing bawdy songs in Sheshan for all Napier cared. He wanted results, not a spit-and-polish-by-the-book type who would do everything the Navy expected and still fail the mission.

"If you need anything, just ask," Napier said. "Ah, no alcohol allowed in the control room, in case you were thinking of that."

Damien shrugged. "I drink when playing. Not when working. Sir."

Was that a dig? "Good to know. I'll send the steward up to assist."

"Thank you, Commodore. Cortney, you might want to up the gain on the transmitter to that far drone."

"Can't the signal be picked up by whatever we're looking for?"

"Doesn't matter. These signals are all over the ether to control all the mining drones. As far as I know, while the bastards we are looking for can intercept the signals, they won't be able to decrypt them and find out what we are doing."

Cortney nodded, then she had another thought. "If there is a ship out there, won't they be able to track the movement of the drones?"

That set both Damien Panaioli and Commodore Napier back a bit. "Damn. Good point, honey. We should have the drones zigzag through the areas like they are looking for more ore. Set them down on an asteroid or two while we are at it."

The Commodore smiled and stepped away. He was satisfied that the mission was in good hands.

"I think I have something," Cortney said as she leaned closer to her control console. "Drone seven is detecting a string of microscopic gamma bursts moving in a straight line toward the planet."

Damien glanced at Cortney's console. "They're making a beeline for Mallorysport, Commodore."

Commodore Napier looked over Courtney's shoulder at the console. "Excellent." He moved to another station and quietly gave some instructions to the sailor manning it. The sailor gave a curt nod and got busy speaking quietly into a microphone and tapping buttons.

Napier returned to the Panaioli's console. "Excellent work. Please keep tracking the gamma trail."

"I wish I could be there when you nab these assholes," Damien said. Cortney gave him "the look" that told him to be mindful of his language.

Napier shook his head. "Who said we planned on capturing these… uh…assholes?"

XXXVI

With everything stowed away the three women, two Fuzzies and their dogs prepared to leave. They were held up by the tribe of Fuzzies that had come to investigate what all the commotion was about.

"They want to make talk with us," Rockthrower said. "Very curious. Is hokay?"

"Is hokay, Rockthrower." Cindy watched as the two Fuzzies went to talk to the tribe. She noticed that many were a bit skittish around the dogs.

"We should get going soon if we want to make a new camp before dark," Kealani said. She glanced at her watch then reminded herself for the umpteenth time that it was set for Terra Standard and not Z-time. *Next planet I go to I'll get a new watch before I leave the spaceport.*

Erena noticed Kealani's disgusted expression and told her it was a little past 1700 Z-time. "Didn't you start from another colony then go to Terra for your education?"

"Yes. Bathala." Kealani saw where Erena was headed. "Bathala is so close to Terra in terms of orbit and rotation that the years and days are virtually identical. This watch is from Bathala, yet I used it on Terra with only an adjustment to the local time zone. I understand that planets like that are rare."

Erena nodded. "What is, um, Bathala? What is Bathala like?"

"Mostly a water world with several strings of islands created by volcanic action. There is only one major land mass and it is roughly the size of Greenland. We call it 'The Continent.' On the island I am from, New Philippians, the weather is tropical, like Hawaii back on Terra."

"And you had to go to school on Terra?"

"Just college. Bathala hasn't been developed enough for a university, yet. There are some plans to get one started on The Continent since that has the highest population density, not to mention the real estate to spare. A lot of marine biologists have been there to study our aquatic life. The first university will likely be built around that subject."

"On Heimdall we have several universities," Cindy said. "I went to the one in Neu Stuttgart. Prince Heinrich University. That's where I started my initial training in psychology."

"Aunty Cindy," Rockthrower interrupted. "We give estefee to new friends? Is hokay?"

"Yes, Rockthrower. And tell them about the Wonderful Place. They may want to go there and see it for themselves."

"Hokay. You make friends with the other Big Ones?"

The three women were confused. There were no other Terro-humans about.

"Other Big Ones?' Erena asked.

"Yes. Behind big rock over there. Rockthrower and Maid Marian hear them talking. Not know what they say. They whisper."

Kealani took the strap off of the gun holster at her side. Erena picked up her M16L07 and acted like she was inspecting it. Cindy stood up and went to the ground roller and pretended to root around for something.

"Dammit, they're on to us."

"What? How can you tell?"

Cutter turned and eyed Kev. "That Fuzzy with them just pointed at this boulder we are hiding behind."

Cody pulled his pistol. "What we gonna do, Cutter?"

Cutter thought it over. "Nothing. Unless they come over here. Then we'll see. Hopefully, they'll just get in that 'roller and head off hoping we won't try to follow."

"Maybe we should just hit them now," Kev suggested. "They might decide to set up an ambush later on."

"Or maybe we should just forget about the whole thing," Cody said. "That woman could have killed Kev and me and settled for just knocking us around."

Cutter started to get mad and barely controlled his voice. "Do you want it getting around a tiny little woman got the best of both of you? And I didn't appreciate the dark one pointing a gun in my face. We need payback."

Kev shifted uncomfortably. "And what do we do when we catch them? Kill them? I don't go around killing people, especially women, just to save face."

"I'm with Kev on this," Cody said. "We got beat up. It's happened before and it will probably happen again. I'm not killing anybody over it."

Cutter gave it some thought. "No, not kill them. I just want an equal fight and put them in their place."

Kev snorted. "And when that little thing lays us out again, then what? Sitting in her chair she still got the best of us all by herself. You want to take on all three one on one?"

"Fine, I'll do the fighting. You two just keep the others busy."

Kev and Cody shared a thoughtful glance, then looked back at Cutter. Kev said, "I've seen you drop guys way bigger than you in a bar brawl, but this is different. That woman has skills."

"Have you forgotten? I was a Space Marine for twelve years. I hold a black belt in Tae Kwan Do. I can handle that little girl."

Cody was confused. "I never saw you use any Kung Fu in those brawls."

Cutter rolled his eyes. "Because that was fun fighting. I didn't need to kill anybody. But against a real, sober opponent you'll see a whole different fighting style out of me."

Kev and Cody thought it over. "Okay," Kev said. "We catch up and beat up some women. Then what? Wait for the cops to pick us up for assault and battery? When we started after these women our blood was up and adrenalin pumping. Now, I just don't see the point. We started this back at the tavern when we harassed them. Cody trying to get handsy with the Asian-looking one started this whole mess. We got off with what amounts to a warning. Fine. Consider me warned. I'm out."

Cutter turned his gaze to Cody. "And you?"

Cody seemed to be fighting with himself. "I would sure like some payback, but Kev is right. I shouldn't have tried to grab that girl. That wasn't the first time a woman hit me because of my poor behavior, but I think I will try to make it the last."

Cutter stood. "Well I won't stand for it. As soon as I catch up with them I'll give them all…"

"Why wait?"

The three men turned to find Kealani, Cindy and Erena along with Maid Marian and Rockthrower standing there. That meant three pistols, a quarrel of arrows and a boomerang aimed in their direction, plus the two large dogs backing them up.

"I won't bother asking why you three are following us," Kealani said. "The densest Khooghra on Yggdrasil could figure that one out. The question I have is what to do with you."

"We could just shoot them and leave the bodies for the local scavengers to deal with," Erena suggested. She threw a covert wink at Cindy so she would know it wasn't a serious idea.

Kev spoke up. "Ladies, you have nothing to worry about from me. Cody and I were just discussing heading back when you arrived."

"Yeah," Cody added. "I'm with Kev. And if it helps, I want to apologize for the way I acted back in town."

Kealani nodded. "Apology accepted, provided you get gone and don't follow us anymore." She turned to Cutter. "What about you, big guy?"

Cutter was too mad to think straight. "You aren't the one I want to settle with." He pointed at Erena. "My beef is with her." The three women were surprised. Cindy asked why. "I don't like having a gun shoved in my face. Kev and Cody earned the ass-whoopin' they got, but I was just standing at the bar."

"It was very clear that you were about to help your friends," Erena explained. "Besides, by keeping you out of it, I think I saved you from some serious injury."

Kev and Cody shared a knowing glance. Privately they agreed with Erena. Both of the men were still feeling the souvenirs from their previous encounter with Kealani.

"I don't care. Nobody points a gun in my face and gets away with it." With his left hand Cutter undid the buckle to his gun belt and let it fall. "What say we settle this old school?"

Before Erena could respond Kealani said, "You are at least twice her size. Hardly a fair fight."

Erena was about to say something, but was interrupted by Cutter. "Then give her an equalizer. That night stick should even things up a bit."

Erena glanced down at her equipment belt. A CZC standard issue nightstick had little use out in the wilderness. She only had it with her out of habit, since Chief Steefer insisted everybody carry one while on the job. Nightsticks had been replaced by sono-stunners until it became known that Fuzzies were deathly susceptible to sonic attack. In a situation where firearms could not be used and Fuzzies were nearby, the nightstick was the best option.

Erena took the nightstick in hand and gave her equipment belt to Cindy. "Fine. I got this."

Kealani and Cindy both looked worried. "That man must weigh at least 220 pounds and that tattoo on his forearm is the Semper Fidelis, the insignia of the Space Marines. *I* might have a hard time beating him. Are you sure you are up for this?"

Erena winked at Kealani. "I'm not saying it will be easy, but I like my chances, especially with the stick."

Cutter took several steps away from his gun belt into the open field away from the boulder. He wanted lots of room to move. There were a few rocks on the ground around him. These he kicked away to make sure he didn't step on one and lose his balance during the fight. He also didn't want to risk his opponent using them as weapons. "Ready when you are, sweetheart."

Erena removed her hat and jacket, since any loose clothing would allow her opponent to grab her. She considered removing the T-shirt; Cutter could grab the fabric and possibly overpower her. Then she thought better of it. This was supposed to be a fight, not a peep show.

The dogs growled as they watched Cutter close in on Erena. The Fuzzies had to restrain them to keep them out of it.

Fuzzies understood dueling and didn't discriminate by gender. In the wild the males and females were considered equal when it came to survival. The difference in size, however, was not lost on the Fuzzies.

"Fight not good," Maid Marian said. "Bad Big One big-big."

"Aunty Erena has stick," Rockthrower said. "Maybe help."

Maid Marian looked doubtful. However, as long as Aunty Kealani and Aunty Cindy didn't interfere, neither would she. "We wait. Watch other bad Big Ones. They make trouble, we make trouble for them." Maid Marian held up her bow for emphasis.

"This all our fault," Cody said softly. "We shouldn't have smoked that chuckleweed before going into town."

"Yours more than mine," Kev replied. Cody demanded to know why. "You were the one that tried to feel up the girl at the table. Still, there is no excuse for either of us."

"You think Cutter is gonna hurt that other girl much?"

Kev pulled out a cigarette and lit it. "I hope not. None of this should be happening. Back when we were in the Marines, Cutter would beat the Niflheim out of any of us for doing something like this. The Isis Resurrection did something to him, I think."

Cody nodded. "It did something to all of us."

The Isis Resurrection, so called because survivors of the Isis Insurrection, which was put down by Federation forces, managed to regroup and recruit new members and rebuild their army. This time they exported terrorists to neighboring planets as a warning to the Federation if they interfered with their planetary goals a second time. The plan blew up in their faces. Terrorism tends to be less effective when the targeted victims are all armed and willing to shoot back first. The Federation again quelled the rebellion and no planet would accept refugees from Isis, thus reducing the possibility of more terrorist activities.

Cutter faced Erena empty-handed. Somewhere in what was left of his conscience he felt a twinge of guilt. Not enough to call the fight off but he planned to hurt her just enough to make a point. During the Isis Resurrection a gun had been aimed at then Gunnery Sergeant William "Cutter" Blaskowski's face. He managed to avoid getting more than a few minor flesh wounds but the mark on his psyche never recovered. Nor did the unfortunate individuals who had wounded him in that battle.

Erena inspected her night stick carefully, as if making certain it wasn't cracked or otherwise damaged. It was the standard issue night stick used by the CZC security police force. It had the reinforced handle that came out at a ninety degree angle from the bottom end of the shaft, a CZC logo on the side and the silvery wires that crossed the top end. Unlike the original design used on Terra centuries before, this stick was made of a hard plastic that was nearly shatterproof.

"Are you going to keep eyeing your toy or are we going to get this started?" Cutter yelled.

"Oh, you know how us poor little women like to make men late for a party," Erena said back. "Okay, big boy. Let's dance."

XXXVII

The patrol squad car landed next to an aircar already settled on the ground. The hatch opened and Major George Lunt and Ahmed Khadra stepped out followed by two Fuzzies and their dogs. One of the Fuzzies, a female, appeared badly shaken.

Near the other aircar stood Rheiner, Cinda, Cinda's Fuzzies and their dogs. The Fuzzies ran over to the shaken female. James Hutton and Sarah Balfour joined Little Fuzzy in helping Emily Dickinson over to a small boulder to sit down. Rheiner watched with a critical eye.

"Herr Major, vhy bring more Fuzzies? Four vill not trek better den two, *nicht wahr*?"

George Lunt stepped well away from the Fuzzies and motioned Rheiner to follow. "Little Fuzzy insisted on joining the hunt and since you already spotted this…Brünnhilde? Brünnhilde's tracks, there was no point in dropping them off at some random point in the middle of nowhere." He nodded toward the Fuzzies. "Besides, I think Little Fuzzy has another agenda."

"Agenda?" Cinda echoed.

"Emily is deathly afraid of riding in any kind of motorized conveyance. I think Little Fuzzy wanted to join the search as a pretext of getting Emily to face her fears." George shook his head. "That little gal white-knuckled it the whole way here but never asked to be let out. It takes a lot of heart to do something that scary without a single peep."

Rheiner nodded. "Dere ist only vun t'ing my pipple are afraid of. I don't know if ve vould face it vit dot much grace. Okay. Die more die merrier."

"Excellent." George turned his attention to the ravine. "It's been a while since I last flew over this area. Where did that ravine come from?"

Cinda held up her data pad. "It doesn't show on any of the maps of this region. Has the CZC Science Center reported any earthquakes?"

"Not that anybody has mentioned to me, but Zarathustra is as tectonically active as any inhabitable world. Ahmed and I will take some photos and transmit them back to the Commissioner." George looked around. "Has she been following the ridgeline?"

"No, she was on the other side then she was over on this side," Cinda said.

George Lunt looked over at the ravine. It had to be at least ten meters across at the narrowest point. "Are you saying she jumped over that?"

"Ja. I t'ink she could do dot. A moment."

Rheiner stepped away from the group, marked the ground then stepped well back. George's jaw dropped as he watched Rheiner run forward then jump an impressive distance. Upon measuring the span it was determined he cleared eleven point three meters. At least a meter more than the span of the ravine.

"If I can make dot jump, I am sure Brünnhilde could as vell," Rheiner explained.

"So we can rule out the possibility that she fell into the ravine," George said as he walked over to the edge. "What the…!"

"Ja. Die damnt'ing vas der when ve got here."

George observed the beast at the bottom of the ravine. "It's limping. It must have broken its leg. Ahmed, bring the rifle."

Emily Dickinson shook for several minutes before she calmed down. Then she noticed the concerned looks on the faces of the other Fuzzies.

"I am fine now." Emily said sheepishly. "Shall we get busy looking for the missing girl?"

"Fire in the hole!"

The Fuzzies all covered their ears before the shot rang out. Jack had been concerned about the long-term effects of loud noises on the super sensitive ears of the Fuzzies. He spoke with Victor Grego about making some Fuzzy friendly ear protection. The placement of the Fuzzies' ears made it a bit of a challenge. In the meantime Jack ordered all scaled-down firearms for the Fuzzies be equipped with noise suppression modifications.

James and Sarah indicated the spot with blood on the ground. "Not know how Big One hurt."

Little Fuzzy looked at the marks on the ground. The placement of the hoof prints, the impression of a body on the dirt, the small amount of blood. Then he followed the damnthing's tracks to the edge of the ravine and found signs of the Big One near the rim. More blood, but no connecting trail between the two. He looked across the ravine and saw the widely spaced footprints.

"Big One make run fast an' jump over wide space, land and roll. Damnt'ing come to see. Big One jump high over damnt'ing and land there. Not know why it fall in open place. Not know what hurt Big One. Maybe hurt. Blood there is from Big One. Blood here from damnthing."

Sarah looked at the blood. "Maybe hurt while jump over by horn?"

The rest were unconvinced. When a damnthing attacked it was always messy. This was too neat.

"Maybe other Big Ones did somet'ing?" James suggested. He pointed at the footprints of at least four people. The prints led to vehicle tracks.

"It looks as though other Big Ones came and found the missing girl and carried her to their ground rollers," Emily Dickinson said. She had recovered enough to contribute to the conversation. "The new Big Ones might have found her hurt and are taking her to a medical facility. Look here; this set of tracks is from a very large man. They come to here where the girl was lying, then go back to those tracks making a deeper impression in the ground. He carried Brünnhilde."

"By himself?" Ahmed Khadra was impressed. If Rheiner was an indication of what all the Magni-Freyans were built like, it would have taken a very strong person to do that by himself. He pointed at the tracks. "Is it possible your people already found her? I don't think a lot of people short of Gus Brannhard could have carried this girl by herself. Um…no offense."

"I see your point, but I vould haff heard somet'ing if Brünnhilde had already been recofered," Rheiner said. "Dere are ferry strong pipple on many planets. A ferry vell trained Terro could be strong enough."

"Or it is somebody from another high-gee world," Cinda added. "Like Rama, or even somebody else from Magni."

That last observation disconcerted Rheiner.

"Why not make call on radio," Sarah asked. Nobody could think of a good answer. They took the question to the Big Ones.

"Radio might be down," Ahmed Khadra suggested. "Prospectors usually get their initial gear on the cheap and have a lot of problems because of it."

"Prospectors also get real lonely out in the middle of nowhere," George Lunt added. "We could be looking at a hostage situation."

"I don't think so, at least not the lonely part." Ahmed pointed at the footprints. "I would say at least one of this group is female. I won't hazard a guess as to what her function is. And the tracks suggest there are at least three vehicles. I am not saying these are a bunch of good Samaritans, but I don't think rape would be their first thought."

Rheiner nodded. "Jawohl. Efen vit' a Freyan face her build vould not encourage such activities among most men."

George shook his head. "Don't you believe it! Men with limited opportunity to blow off steam get less and less finicky as time goes by. I'll spare you any details but there are examples of it on Shesha, Thor and even Yggdrasil. This search just became a great deal more urgent."

Ahmed started back to the squad car. "I'll send out an update and maybe see if we can get more people involved."

"I vill call Bürgermeister Torseus. He vill take dis far more seriously, now."

Cinda looked at the impressions in the dirt made by the vehicle tracks. "Can't we just follow the tracks and catch up with these prospectors, or whatever they are?"

"For a ways, but there is a lot of rocky ground up ahead. The rollers won't leave much of an impression on that. Say, we need to figure out which way the tracks are leading. Little Fuzzy?"

Little Fuzzy looked at the tracks carefully then pointed west. "Go that way."

Emily was surprised. "How can you tell, Little Fuzzy?"

"See here, where ground roller stop? Tracks…um…slide, push dirt up in front. When start again tracks make dirt fly backwards, sprinkle ground."

Everybody agreed. George licked a finger and held it up. "The wind could pick up and wipe away what tracks we have. Best we get a move on."

Rheiner and Cinda went back to their aircar and the Fuzzies mounted up. Back in the squad car George Lunt and Ahmed Khadra conferred.

"Ever hear of a prospecting troop this big?"

Ahmed shook his head. "On average you have two men with one vehicle, usually a second- or third-hand aircar. Occasionally you get a trio, but never more than one vehicle unless they manage to pony up for heavy excavation equipment."

"My thinking exactly," George agreed. "And the only time I ever heard of any women out here was that, what's her name, Affanita Goncalo and the occasional husband and wife team."

Ahmed nodded. It wasn't the hard work that kept most women away from prospecting; it was the other prospectors who might try to take liberties. There was a case where somebody tried to get a little too friendly with Affanita. It did not end well for that particular gentleman.

"So what are these people doing out here? The best diggings are always west of here even if these are prospectors."

"I guess we'll have to ask them when we find them, Ahmed."

* * *

The fight wasn't as one-sided as Kealani and Cindy feared it would be. Erena used her small size to advantage avoiding most of Cutter's attacks. Still, she was showing a large bruise on the side of her face. She had been struck in other locations on her body but the injuries were not yet obvious.

Cutter was far from unmarked as well. Erena had scored some hits with her night stick. Cutter wouldn't admit it to anybody but he thought he might have a small fracture on his left ulna from the way his forearm was hurting. His opponent was small, but she fought like a demon. Deep down, he respected that.

"Cutter, that's enough," Kev yelled. "You've made your point and got your pound of flesh." Cody voiced his agreement.

"Not until one of us is down and out," Cutter grunted.

"Is that all?" Erena shifted her night stick and launched forward to jab Cutter in the chest. There was a sizzling sound and a small flash of light.

Cutter stood for a moment with a stunned expression on his face, then fell forward. Erena turned and went back to Kealani and Cindy.

"What was that," Cindy asked.

Kealani spoke up for the near breathless Erena. "Shock stick. It holds a million-volt charge backed by a five-amp battery. My mother keeps one in the house." She looked accusingly at Erena. "Why didn't you use it sooner? You could have saved yourself a lot of bruises."

"I wanted to make sure he…thought twice about…coming after us again," Erena gasped out.

"Gods, I can't believe you survived against that monster," Cindy said as she pulled out the med kit.

Erena smiled and said, "Who says I survived?" Then she passed out.

Cindy checked Erena's vital signs and decided she would be fine after a little nap.

Kealani turned her attention back to Kev and Cody. "Are we going to have any more problems with you or are we done here?"

Kev actually smiled. "Way done. When Cutter wakes up he will either agree or be out on his own."

"Cutter is really a good guy," Cody said. "He saved mine and Kev's lives a few times back in the Marines. He just isn't adapting well to civilian life."

"And he won't have a problem with Erena using the shock stick?"

Both men shook their heads. "He was the one to suggest the equalizer. And getting shocked will let him save face. Better than getting beaten down by a tiny woman…no offense!"

Kealani suppressed a smile. People underestimated her because she appeared too small to be threatening and she used that to her advantage. As did Erena. "Fine. Next time we see you following us we'll just shoot first and not bother with questions. *Comprende*?"

Kev nodded. "You got it, ma'am! Come on, Cody. Let's get sleeping beauty here into the roller."

"He'll be pissed when he wakes up, you know," Cody said. "Best to get him as far away from here as possible."

Cindy came up. "Before you go, I think you should all get some psychological counseling. Your friend shows signs of post-traumatic stress disorder. You have all been in battle? Then you might need some help. I suggest you see Dr. Mallin in Mallorysport."

"Um…yes, Ma'am," Kev said. "We will give that some serious thought."

Kealani watched as the ground roller pulled away. She wanted to believe that would be the last she saw of Cutter and crew. She doubted it. Once the roller was out of sight she went back with Cindy to Erena. The Fuzzies all gathered around: Maid Marian and Rockthrower out of concern, the other Fuzzies out of fascination.

Cindy Tezza was running the medical scanner over Erena's unconscious form. "Nothing broken. She might have a few pulled ligaments and tendons. We have some pain blockers. However, it might be better if she holds off on those until she can give us a full list of her aches. This emergency scanner isn't as accurate as the hospital models. Erena will be able to give us a better picture of her condition when she wakes."

"She should have just zapped that gorilla at the start," Kealani said. "She's lucky he didn't get a grip on her. He could have tied her in a knot."

Cindy thought for a second, then asked, "Is that what you would have done?"

Kealani thought about it and admitted she wouldn't. "I would have gone straight for his pressure points to disable him, then smacked him around a bit to teach him better manners. I'll grant Erena did way better than I would have expected. She's clearly had some serious training."

Cindy laughed. "A security guard her size would need it. I think Chief…um…Stevens? No, that's not right. Well, the top boss of CZC Security was a military man, I've heard, and takes his people's training seriously. Steefer! Chief Steefer."

Maid Marian tapped Cindy's leg. "Aunty Erena not make dead?"

"No, Maid Marian. Not make dead. Just take a nap for a while."

Maid Marian turned to the other Fuzzies and explained. Fuzzies occasionally fought among themselves so they understood that the two Big Ones fought a sort of duel.

"Will she be okay to travel?" Kealani asked. "We need to get some distance if we hope to make a new campsite and find other Fuzzies to study."

"And put some distance between us and them?" Cindy jerked her head in the direction Cutter and crew had gone. "I really don't know. I would rather have her wake up and tell us." She let out a long sigh. "Waiting around for more trouble wouldn't be any better, I guess. We can put her in the back seat and take it slow. What about our tracks?"

"I'll drive around a bit to confuse things while you pack up. Then I'll cut some branches to hang on the back. They'll drag the ground and hopefully obscure the tracks. If we are real lucky, a wind will kick up to help things a bit."

XXXVIII

Captain Trask was done. He went through all the news articles on the datastream, watched video footage from the time Little Fuzzy was first discovered up to the present, skipping over non-relevant items, sifted through every government document and even, semi-legally, rooted through the personal financials of Victor Grego, Ben Rainsford, Jack Holloway and Gus Brannhard. He stopped short of digging into Commodore Napier's accounts. One doesn't pick a fight with the military without a damned good reason.

Nothing. Even less than nothing. Nothing ever since the Fuzzy Trial. There was plenty to go after Victor Grego and the CZC for prior to that point, which was none of Supervisor Sylvinski's business, but not so much as a parking ticket afterwards. Did they issue parking tickets in Mallorysport? No matter.

Trask compiled his lack of findings into a report and transferred a copy to a data disk. The only thing even vaguely damning was Juan Takagashi's previous employment on Odin and the missing funds. Even if something did come of that it wouldn't affect the rest of the Colonial Government. It would just be a token sacrifice for Sylvinski to parade in front of his higher-ups.

Trask ejected the disk and stared at it for a few minutes. Finally, he set it aside and opened a new file on the screen. With disgust he skimmed through the Martianist case. Marshal Fane asked Trask to step aside and allow his people to handle everything. On a professional level he felt slighted. As the highest ranking FBCI agent on the planet he should have been in on everything. Privately, he suspected that the Navy was taking a part in things and wanted to keep the circle as tight as possible.

Technically, he and Marshal Fane should be working side by side on any case with a Federation jurisdiction. The Martianists bringing their activities to Zarathustra qualified. It was what used to be called "crossing state lines during a criminal enterprise." So why cut him out of the investigation? Unless the marshal and the local government might be up to something they think Trask wouldn't approve of? Possible.

From Trask's own investigations, he knew that Gus Brannhard could play fast and loose with certain rules. Ben Rainsford would likely go along with anything Gus suggested. Jack Holloway had skirted the law on more planets than Trask could name off the top of his head. But where Fuzzies were concerned they were in lockstep with the law, and then some.

So, what are they doing about the Martianists? The comscreen beeped, snapping Trask out of his thoughts. A Technicolor splash of color, then Marshal Max Fane's face crystallized into view.

"Marshal, here I was just thinking of the devil and here you are horns and all."

Max Fane chuckled at the characterization. "I hope you will promote me out of Ni-…Hell when I tell you this. You're off the bench. Come on over and join the party. My office, but come alone."

Alone.

"Why was I left out in the first place?"

Marshal Fane frowned. "Not over an unsecure line." The screen went blank.

* * *

Victor Grego's face looked back from the viewscreen as Max Fane conferred with Lieutenant (Junior Grade) Helmsworth. Finally the two men nodded and Helmsworth left.

"Mr. Grego, how sure are you of your, um, pigeon?"

"Chief Steefer did an exhaustive search along with Major Lansky," Grego said from the screen. "Just to be safe, we also targeted two more likelies. To use a fishing analogy, we'll be throwing the hook at all three."

Marshal Fane nodded. "Are you sure you can handle this without backup? Captain Trask is right here. I am sure he has ample experience with sort of thing."

Grego shook his head. "When Chief Steefer says he has it handled, it is handled, Marshal."

Marshal Fane nodded. "Good enough for me. Captain Trask?"

Buck stepped forward so he would be in camera range. "I never met this chief of security of yours but I am satisfied if both of you are. When will you put the plan into operation?"

Grego's brows went up. "I thought you knew. We already started."

* * *

The CZC commissary was the popular place for people to gather and talk shop. The Company was too large to ever completely shut down, so all shifts needed a convenient place to get breakfast, lunch, dinner or snacks twenty-four Z-hours a day. Food was fresh and human made, though there were also vending machines for those who preferred that sort of thing or were in too much of a rush to wait for a proper meal to be made. On the busiest days and times a buffet would be set up for speed and convenience.

Most often, workers would take tables with other workers from the same areas: maintenance with maintenance, janitorial with janitorial, etc., unless they had friends from different areas with the same lunch hours.

"It has to be the rocket," Jim Stiller said before attacking his hot veldbeest sandwich with gravy. Between bites he added, "There's nothing else on this planet those Martianists would want."

Carrie Wadsworth, Jerry Wayne, Maureen Potter, Jake Vance, Mike Bourne and Burt Mansfield nodded.

"Maybe we should just give it to them," Jerry groused over his pizza with riverpig sausage. "We ain't doin' anything with it."

"Why would they want the Fuzzy rocket?" Maureen asked. "What does that have to do with Martians?"

Jake rolled his eyes. "They proved that it couldn't possibly be a Fuzzy rocket, right? Well, if Fuzzies didn't build it and fly it to Zarathustra, who did? Khooghras? Sheshans? Gimlians are the closest to this world and have never developed powered flight of any kind. So who's left?"

"Martians," everybody said.

"Right. Though I wouldn't rule out some other species we haven't met yet," Jake said. "It's a big universe out there and I would be amazed if there aren't a lot more sapient races. In fact, I would bet any money that there is a species more advanced than we are somewhere out there."

"The rocket is gone," said a voice from a nearby table. "It was loaded onto a contragravity barge and taken to the outer edge of the city."

"Says who?" Mike Bourne demanded. "Something like that would have been all over the news."

"Unless it was a news blackout," Connor Dallas countered. He stood up and carried his tray over to join the other seven. "The Governor doesn't want it getting around that he caved to the Martianists. Others might try something similar. He couldn't risk more people getting killed, either. So, he loaded the ship up and mailed it to them, so to speak."

"Wait a sec," Burt Mansfield said. "I thought the Navy confiscated the thing."

Connor shook his head. "And put it where? It's a full-sized rocket ship. It's not like they could stuff it in a footlocker."

"Don't they have warehouses on Xerxes?" Carrie said. "They could store it until a transport came in big enough to haul it away."

Connor nodded. "I can see why you would think so, but storage facilities on Xerxes are all about the size of a Quonset hut. Military units that might be called away keep things small and portable. The largest units will be holding food and small equipment."

"Really?" Maureen looked dubious "What about tanks, laser canons, transports?"

"Heavy equipment is carried on the battleships and often left behind after the shooting is over with," Connor explained. "Very expensive to haul that stuff around. And Xerxes Base doesn't qualify for equipment like that, since this was essentially a baby-sitting job until the Fuzzies were discovered. I imagine they'll be getting an upgrade any time now. Especially after all this Martianist terrorism."

Everybody agreed with Connor. Then Jake said, "Wait, if they get the rocket, they'll be heading out to bother somebody else, right?"

"Unless there is something else they want," Carrie said. "Sunstones, maybe?"

Connor looked as though he gave it some thought, then shrugged. "I doubt it. Sunstones have nothing to do with Mars, which is all these fanatics care about. If it isn't connected to the 'mother planet' they just don't care. Maybe if there were other relics—"

"Oh, damn," Burt Mansfield exclaimed. "I think there are." Everybody at the table turned to him. "When the rocket was brought in there were some loose odds and ends with it. One looked like, I don't know, a plaque maybe. It hadn't been cleaned up, yet when I saw it."

Jake spoke first. "When did you see it?"

"This morning down in Science Center. It was sitting on a table with some other stuff. I think Dr. Jimenez had it pulled from the vault so Archeology could have a go at it."

"After all this time?" Maureen shook her head. "Why wait?"

"Well, the Navy did take the rocket," Carrie said. "Maybe Mr. Grego didn't want to risk losing these other items, too. They could be very valuable."

"Priceless, I would say," Jerry said. "Imagine a relic from an unknown spacefaring civilization. Even if it is from Mars, it would be valuable for its history and any scientific knowledge that could be gleaned from studying it. And to a collector—hoo-boy!"

As the discussion became more animated, nobody noticed that Connor Dallas slipped away.

* * *

Lieutenant Junior Grade Helmsworth saluted then remained at attention. With him were Captain Greibenfeld and Lt. Ybarra.

"At ease, gentlemen," Commodore Napier said. The three men relaxed. Napier gestured to the chairs and the three men took a seat. "Let's keep this casual. Lt. Helmsworth, tell me about our, ah, operative. We'll leave names out for the moment."

"Sir, the operative demobbed two years ago after Zarathustra became a Class IV planet. Honorable discharge with the usual three-year recall commitment. He was reactivated in a covert capacity shortly after he procured employment with the Charterless Zarathustra Company."

"Hmm...was that his original plan?"

"No, sir. His intent, I have been told, was to carve out some free land and start a farm. He came from a farming community on Baldur. The nine-hundred and ninety-nine year lease the CZC worked out with the governor killed that ambition, so, rather than return to Baldur, he took employment with the CZC in their hydroponics center. He has received two promotions from the CZC since that time."

Napier nodded. "Rank at time of discharge?"

"Sir, sergeant. Echo five."

"Well, if this operation pans out, let's add a stripe to that. Please continue."

"Sir, the operative reported last night that he made contact with several potential assets and, as he put it, started the ball rolling. I have kept Marshal Max Fane briefed on the operation. In person so as to avoid potential communications leaks."

"In mufti?"

"No, sir, in uniform." The Lieutenant's face reddened a bit. "I have a girlfriend who is a patrol officer. I often visit her at the police station when she is not out on patrol. I felt I would be less conspicuous in uniform as I normally see her that way."

"Hiding in plain sight," Napier said. "You may want to consider transferring to Capt. Greibenfeld's command. I think you have a knack for it. Lt. Ybarra, I would like your input."

"Yes, sir. I went over the operative's psyche profile. Less kill-happy than many of the Marine recruits I have interviewed. For the operative, joining the Space Marines was a means to see the universe. Zarathustra was the second stop on his galaxy tour and he was here to see history being made with the discovery of the Fuzzies. I would hazard that his wanderlust was satisfied and he was ready to settle down, hence his discharge and plan to farm again. However, he has proven adaptable and capable as our eyes and ears in the CZC. This was good, since we lost LTJG Ortheris after the Fuzzy trial. He is steady and without blemish on his service record."

"As good as Ortheris?"

"Sir, he doesn't have the level of access to the higher activities in the Company that Lt. Ortheris enjoyed, so I would have to say in that regards, no."

Napier nodded. "Understood. Captain?"

Captain Greibenfeld pulled out his pocket data pad. "There have been hundreds of screen calls going to and from the CZC. Twenty-seven calls in the first hour after contact, five of which were using secure settings. Thanks to the cooperation of Mr. Grego by way of his security chief, Chief Steefer, we were able to identify who had access to those screens. The first was Leslie Coombes' private line. The second was Mr. Grego's, presumably to the governor. Neither of which is our concern so we didn't pursue them.

"Of the other three, one was to a, ah, disreputable business where they charge two sols a minute. We traced the call and it was to a legitimate source. We made a note of it and forwarded the information to Chief Steefer as a courtesy'."

Napier smiled. "No point in letting a deviant get his thrills on the company deci-sol. Please continue."

"The second call was to a coworker's address. We listened in just enough to know that somebody's wife isn't entirely faithful to her vows. That call is archived for later deletion after this case is over."

"Agreed." Commodore Napier, while disgusted at the infidelity, didn't think it was the Navy's job to peep in windows for a divorce case. Let the husband hire a private eye like everybody else.

"Finally, there was the third call. This one used a scrambler in addition to a screen code obfuscation algorithm. We don't know what was said or where the call went."

"If I were a betting man I would wager that was our pigeon," Napier said. "Scramblers are pricy but not obscenely so. Anybody could get one. That algorithm, on the other hand, is very high end. Somebody has something very big to hide if they have one. That proves nothing in and of itself, of course," Napier said.

"It doesn't have to," Greibenfeld added. "It tells us that the information we wanted to get to the Martianists has most likely been delivered. We should bring in Marshal Fane and Captain Trask."

Napier turned to Helmsworth. "Feel like going to visit your lady friend, Lieutenant?"

XXXIX

It was late afternoon in Neu Freya. Janice Goodfellow was packing up her things along with a number of gifts she had received from the Magni-Freyans. She felt guilty about accepting anything from these wonderful people. However, Supervisor Sylvinski pointed out that refusal could be harmful to relations with the new colony. Jutta said that refusal of any gifts might carry the stigma of disfavor with the gods for the gift givers.

Janice sealed up the last of the tokens in a hand-crafted leather trunk on wheels, another gift, when she heard a knock on the door. It was Jutta with a young woman.

Jutta introduced the woman. "Favored one, this is Evonna. She wishes to ask a boon of you."

Janice became nervous. What if this woman wanted some sort of miracle from her? "Please, come in and take a seat." Evonna looked confused until Jutta explained that she was asked to sit down, not actually remove a chair from the room. "How may I help you, Evonna?"

The woman looked like she wanted to throw herself at the floor and prostrate herself before Janice. "Favored One, I…I ask for your benevolence in sparing the life of my…uh…mate."

Janice noticed that Evonna's accent was very slight, much like Jutta's. "Your mate? Is he ill?" What if Evonna wanted her to heal her husband? Was a favorite of the gods supposed to be able to do that?

"No, Favored One…"

"Please, Evonna, call me Janice."

"Yes, Fav…Janice. My mate is a man of Magni but not of the people."

Janice was confused. Jutta explained, "Gilfred, Evonna's mate, was one of the Overseers."

"He was not like the others, Favored One! Uh…Janice. He was kind to me and tried to make things easier for us. He brought medicine and sweetmeats to us. He didn't allow the other Masters to abuse us…at least as much as he could. He is the sire of my son Gofried. I ask that he not be executed with the others."

Executed? "I don't understand. Jutta, what is she talking about?" Jutta admitted she didn't know; as far as she knew, all the Overseers had been executed.

"Jutta, I would speak with the Favored One privately, if I may." Tears were forming in Evonna's eyes. Janice nodded and Jutta went out.

Janice patted the cushion of the settee next to her and the tearful woman sat down. "Evonna, please explain."

The woman took a moment to compose herself. "...Janice, my sister, Gertrude, works for der Bürgermeister, Johann Torseus, and she heard the Bürgermeister speak of the Overseers. They are still alive and will be brought here for punishment after Prince Morgan returns. But Gilfred never struck us, or forced us to work when injured. He helped care for us when we were sick. He wanted to help us!"

Janice listened and thought on it. "If he wanted to help you, why didn't he simply report what was going on? He could have contacted the Federation and saved you all."

"No! If he did that he would have been executed with the rest. And that only if the other Overseers didn't kill him first. There were others who tried and they all had accidents that they didn't survive. Gilfred was nearly struck by a robo-forklift. I would not allow him to take the chance."

Janice could see the predicament Evonna was in. Magni, a fully enclosed colony dedicated to mining and processing radioactive ore would be a hard place to sneak out of. It would be nearly impossible to hide, in fact. "So, he will be coming here to be tried and executed? Cannot Johann, your Bürgermeister, help you?"

Evonna broke down. "I don't know. His wife was killed in a punishment cage and Johann feels strongly that all of the Overseers must pay for what they have done. She and Herr Torseus' family were in a different section of the mines. He never met Gilfred or was helped by him. I fear his anger will force him to have all of the Overseers executed." She sobbed as she said that she wanted her son to know his father.

Janice felt for the woman. She had no idea what she could do but was determined to try. "I…will do what I can. Hopefully, the gods will help you and your mate." She hoped she said the right thing.

* * *

"Before you leave, Herr Commissar, dere are a few more of mein pipple I vould like you to meet." Johann and his Honor Guard were escorting Sylvinski, Janice with her guards and Gus through the streets of Morganstadt, the capital of Neu Freya. "Not all of die experiments done on mein pipple had the same results. I feel it necessary for you to get die full picture."

The group entered a building that looked to be a clinic of some sort. After passing several people dressed in white, they came to a lobby filled with patients.

"I vill introduce you." Johann went to a man sitting in the corner. He rose as the procession approached. He stood nearly two heads higher than Johann. "Dis ist Adalard. He has vhat ist called Marfan's Syndrome, causing his extreme height. Dis causes him great beck und joint pain. How are you doing, Adalard?"

The giant sat back down to be closer to eye level with the group. "Die lesser gravity of dis vorld helps, Herr Bürgermeister. But I am still very heavy und it aggravates die condition. I am getting massages und cortisone injections. It helps."

"Goot. I understand die CZC hospital ist making a special brace for dein beck?"

"Dey are vorking vit' a Herr Stensen on dis," Adalard said. "I am hopeful it vill help more."

"I have a cousin with the same condition," Gus said. "Do they have you on supplements for the joints?"

"Ja. Dot seems to help a bit," Adalard said.

Johann clasped forearms with the man and moved on to two men and a woman who were covered in hair. "Dis ist Carla, Fritz und Emil. Dey have a condition called hypertrichosis. It causes extreme hairiness, as you can see."

Sylvinski tried not to stare. "Are you siblings?"

"Ja," Fritz replied. "Triplets. Ve t'ink die hair vas an attempt to make us able to wit'stand die cold better. Our fat'er had die same condition as did his fat'er. Ve are here for electrolysis. It ist a long process as our, ah, pelts are ferry tough."

Gus mentioned to Sylvinski that this condition was completely unknown on Freya.

"I wish you luck and health," Sylvinski said then grasped forearms with all three.

The group moved on to a man with an obvious hunched back, then another with extra fingers and toes, then a dwarf who had to be in incredible pain with the excessive muscle growth.

"Und dis ist Claus," Johann said as they approached a man so heavily muscled the other Magni-Freyans seems like weaklings in comparison. "Die chenetic enchineering dot vas done to his family line resulted in massif muscle growt'. He can barely mofe vit' all die muscle bunching up all ofer his body. Also, obfiosly, he suffers from dvarfism. It ist a bad combination. Claus, how goes die treatments?"

"Dey inchect muscle retardant," Clause spoke through a massive lantern jaw. The muscle was so thick it was an effort just to speak. "My veight ist down two kilograms in die last mont'. Und die bone treatments seem to be vorking. I am two centimeters taller since ve started."

"Excellent! Ve vill haff you chasing die *Fräuleins* in no time!"

"Um, vell, Inga might obchect."

"Inga! She has chosen you? *Wunderbar*! She ist qvite die cetch."

"Ja," Claus said as he tried to nod. The muscles in his neck strained but could only move a little. "She likes a man vit' meat on his bones!" Claus and Johann laughed.

Gus wondered if it was the same Inga from the serving hall. She was a powerfully built woman, even by Magni-Freyan standards. She would need a sturdy man to survive her hugs, Gus mused.

After the main lobby Johann escorted Sylvinski and Gus to another section and stopped in front of a thick window. Behind the glass were a number of Magni-Freyans in gray jumpsuits.

"It vould be dancherous to take you into dis room."

Sylvinski looked through the glass. The people beyond it all seemed quiet and sedentary. "What is the problem?"

Johann sighed. "Dese pipple suffer from brain defects. Down's Syndrome, autism, brain malformations of many kinds. Ve hid dem from die Oferseers as much as possible. Vhen vun vas discoffered dey vere taken avay. Ve neffer saw dem again."

Sylvinski was horrified. Most of the Magni-Freyans, aside from the unfortunate facial features, seemed to benefit from the genetic engineering their ancestors had been subjected to. Even most in the lobby didn't appear to be too badly off as Federation medicine could help with most of their problems. But this…"My God! We have treatments for Down's and autism, now. Have you tried them?"

Johann nodded. "Ja, und in a few cases dey haff been effectif. But die enchineering has made many of us resistant to die normal treatments."

The sound of soft weeping could be heard. Sylvinski thought it came from behind the window until he saw the tears on Janice's face. "Miss Goodfellow, perhaps it would be better if you—"

"No! I…I want to give my blessing to these poor people." She turned to Johann. "That is something I can do, isn't it?"

Johann nodded. "Ja. Ve know you do not belief as ve do, but it vould mean much to dese pipple. Jutta, could you help die Favored Vun?"

"*Jawohl*, Herr Bürgermeister!"

Sylvinski became nervous. "Herr Bürgermeister, what do you expect Miss Goodfellow to do?"

Johann smiled. "You t'ink dot she is supposed to perform a miracle? Nein. My pipple hope for miracles, ve do not expect dem. It could be argued dot Herr Morgan freeing us from die mines vas our quota for die century. Die Favored Vun vill giff her blessing und ve hope die gods vill take pity on dose souls she blesses."

"So you hope that the gods will cure these people?"

"Again, *nein*." Johann took a breath. "Your pipple haff a saying; die Lord helps dose dot help demselves. Ve know dot the vays of die gods are beyond mortal understanding und dot dey can be capricious. Ve vill continue to treat dese pipple vit' medicine und t'earapy und hope dot die gods vill giff vhat help dey vill. None vill blame die Favored Vun if not'ing comes of dis. She ist merely a conduit, not a messiah."

"That is good to know. Ah, Miss Goodfellow asked me to discuss something with you before we leave for Alpha...."

XXXX

Darius dominated the sky while Xerxes was nowhere to be seen. Weaver looked about with some disappointment. He much preferred a two-moon night. Xerxes could be on the other side of the planet or hiding behind Darius. Weaver needed a calendar to be sure and didn't have one with him.

Behind him the others gathered around the roaring campfire, compliments of Brünnhilde. Weaver puffed on his cigar and quietly marveled at the sky. He chuckled when he recalled that the girl had never had a marshmallow before, let alone one roasted on a stick over an open flame. He had been to a few tin-can colonies in his time and understood not having a campfire in them, but no marshmallows seemed odd. Maybe the dietary restrictions of a heavy-gravity world made fatty or sugary treats ill advised.

Lars, who never said where he was from—everybody thought it had to be Modi—never ate sweets except for chocolate, and it was usually dark chocolate at that. Weaver shrugged it away as unimportant. He was far more concerned about getting back to civilization and the Niflheim off Zarathustra. He took one more puff, then snubbed out the cigar. It still had half its length but Weaver was running low and didn't want to use up his dwindling supply before getting to a town to resupply.

Being careful of where he stepped, Weaver started back to the camp. Halfway back he noticed some animals scampering away. A goofer, a couple zarabunnies, something else that he couldn't make out. That worried him and he ran back to camp.

"I just saw some animals running."

Brünnhilde didn't see the cause for alarm. "Don't animals always run from humans?"

Weaver shook his head. "They didn't run away from me, they ran past me."

Bo, Clem and Lars immediately stood up and grabbed their rifles.

Brünnhilde still didn't understand the significance until Lars explained it to her.

"Animals that are usually quiescent at night don't just pick up and take off for no reason," Lars said. "There has to be something around that scared them off. It's dark out, so I doubt it would be a damnthing since they would be asleep right now. A zarawolf is unlikely but not completely out of the question. Some have been seen this far south."

"Bush goblin is the most likely culprit," Clem said. "Let's hope so. A goblin wouldn't come near a fire or a crowd of people."

Bo was about to speak when he felt the ground vibrate. "Ya'll feel that? Ground quake!"

"Everybody to the rollers!" Weaver ordered. Nobody argued. In short order everybody was settled into a ground roller.

"I do not understand," Brünnhilde said. "We are out in open country with nothing to fall on us. How is being in the vehicles really safer?"

"Weaver mentioned the animals, yes?" Estefan said. "Well, more critters could run through the camp and some of them have big teeth and claws or venom or both. In the rollers we are safe. Out on the ground we could be attacked by any frightened varmint that accidently bumped into us."

"And the CZC still hasn't completely catalogued all of the flora and fauna of this world," Consuela added.

Brünnhilde nodded in understanding. Then something else struck her. "Where's Mai?"

Still in the camp was Mai, attempting to put out the fire. Brünnhilde started to get out of the ground roller only to have Estefan and Consuela pull her back. She pushed them away and tried again. Before she could get free of the vehicle Lars came bounding past her. He didn't run so much as take several leaps a step at a time. Without breaking his stride, Lars grabbed up Mai and turned back to the ground roller where he tossed the young woman into Brünnhilde's arms.

Lars started back to his ground roller when a trio of bush goblins slammed into him. One, the smallest, kept running. The other two tore at him in panicked fury. Lars tried to protect his eyes with one arm while flailing away with the other.

"*Verdammt*, let me go!" Brünnhilde screamed as she freed herself from Estefan and Consuela. There was no time to get her pistol from the backpack where she had kept it hidden and she wasn't sure she could use it effectively anyway. Instead, she jumped out of the ground roller and grabbed a goblin by the scruff of the neck.

Brünnhilde tried to throw the beast away too late. It turned in her grasp and clawed at her face and arms. Lars, now free of one attacker was able to concentrate on the one that remained. He threw a punch that caught it in the chest and sent it flying ten feet back. Noticing Brünnhilde's plight, he grabbed the other bush goblin by the back of the neck and threw it toward its mate. The goblins wasted no time in running away after their cub. Lars turned to Brünnhilde to see if she was all right.

"We need to get those scratches treated quickly," Lars said as he inspected the wounds on Brünnhilde's arms. "You're lucky they couldn't get at your eyes. Consuela, Mai, get the med kit out and clean these wounds."

"I think you should go first," Brünnhilde said as she pointed at the numerous scratches on Lars. "It looks like they got a good piece of you."

"Compare battle scars later," Consuela yelled. "Get in here before something else comes along and tries to get a piece of you both."

Brünnhilde and Lars jumped into the backseat with Mai, making it very close quarters. Mai started tending to Lars' wounds first; he looked like he had taken far more damage.

"I didn't think anything could get through that thick hide of yours, Lars," Mai said as she cleaned his wounds. "Some of these are pretty deep. There goes your rep as the invulnerable one in the camp."

"Never wanted the rep, anyway," Lars said. "A rep can get you killed when somebody decides to test it."

"I thought bush goblins were loners," Brünnhilde wondered aloud. "That was a small pack."

"That was a mated pair with a cub," Estefan said. "The couple will stay together until the cub can fend for itself, then the male will ditch the female like he owed her money. And they normally wouldn't have attacked a man as big as Lars if they weren't panicked by the ground quake. All the usual rules go out the airlock when some sort of disaster hits. You would do well to remember that," Estefan finished with a meaningful glance at Mai.

Mai finished with Lars then went over to Brünnhilde to treat her wounds. "Huh. Your goblin must have had a mani-pedi; these scratches aren't nearly as deep."

"I guess I was lucky. Lars was fighting two goblins; I only had to deal with one." Brünnhilde was concerned Mai might suspect she wasn't normal even for a heavy-worlder. "Do we need to worry about any kind of venom or toxin from the claws?"

Consuela shook her head. "Just the usual infections. The kit should have something to help with that."

Mai pulled out two tubes of antibiotic ointment from the kit. "Try not to use all of this. I don't know how much is left in the other kits."

Lars removed his tunic while Brünnhilde opened her blouse and turned away so as not to show anything as they applied the ointment. While Freyans in general did not have the same sense of modesty that Terrans possess, Brünnhilde was very aware of how her body might look to non-Magni-Freyans and exercised some modesty. Besides, Lars might not be put off by her build and she didn't want to encourage any ideas on his part. At least not yet.

"Thanks for stepping in, Hilde," Lars said as he applied the ointment. "I think I would have handled it, but you saved me a lot of damage."

Brünnhilde smiled. "Well, I couldn't just let you get clawed up. I admit I wasn't as cool about it as you were or I would have thrown the goblin away as soon as I grabbed it. It was just so fast and angry—it took me by surprise."

"Not angry, just scared witless." Lars face became serious. "Out in the bush you can't afford to lose your cool. You handled your situation with the damnthing a lot better. What was your plan with that?"

Brünnhilde thought a moment. "Well, my first thought was to just jump over him, then smack his backside hoping to panic it into charging into the ravine."

Lars' eyes went wide. "In that case, you were lucky Bo shot you. Damnthings don't panic easily and your slap, even with Magni strength, would have just made it turn around and eat you. The bullet Bo put in its backside was far more effective to that end."

"Oh." Brünnhilde thought on it for a moment. "Well, I was short on ideas at the time. If the damnthing did turn around, I would have tried to jump back over the ravine, I guess."

Lars nodded. He was about to say something when the ground roller lurched to the side.

* * *

Erena screamed as the ground shook. Her injuries, while not life threatening, were aggravated by the sudden ground quake. Cindy tried to comfort her while Kealani rooted through the supplies looking for more pain medication.

"It looks like we're out," Kealani said. "We may have to scrub the trip."

"Och. I need this for my medical degree." Cindy looked at Erena. "Well, I can always do it again. Let's call Major Lunt for a medical evac'."

"No."

Kealani and Cindy both looked at Erena.

"Compared to giving birth this is a cake walk," Erena rasped. "I'll be sore for a while, but I'll manage."

Cindy shook her head. "Nein. The scanner shows that you don't have any internal injuries, but all that bruising and those scratches are not good."

"I've…had worse. I'll be okay once the damned ground stops shaking."

Maid Marian watched the byplay between the Big Ones. "Aunty Erena need medicine?"

"Yes, but we are all out of what she needs," Kealani explained.

"Much hurt," Rockthrower asked.

"Yes. Very much."

Maid Marian and Rockthrower shared a knowing glance. "We come back," Rockthrower said. Without another word the two Fuzzies with their dog mounts ran out of the tent.

"What? *Nein!* The ground shaking will hurt their feet."

Kealani looked at the tent flap the Fuzzies had just ran through. "I am more worried about the animals going crazy out there. Ground quakes and storms can panic wildlife. They might run into something nasty that won't be thinking right."

"Don't worry about…the Fuzzies," Erena said. "They can manage a lot better out there than we Big Ones give them credit for."

Maid Marian and Rockthrower rode their dogs at a slow trot as they looked about. The tremors made the dogs nervous with the shaking and the surrounding wildlife darting every which way. A damnthing in the distance was running full out, stumbled on the uneven ground, fell, rolled, then struggled back up to resume running.

Rockthrower pointed to a plant a dozen meters away. "*Kol'maru*, there."

Maid Marian nodded and the pair made for the plant. The *kol'maru* was a short tree-like plant slightly larger than a bush with wide splaying branches low to the ground.

"Has berries," Maid Marian observed. "We take many-many."

"*Li-kou* better," Rockthrower said.

"You see *li-kou*? *Kol'maru* here. *Li-kou* not here." Maid Marian looked around. "Need *hikwu*. We find."

The ground again shook adding to Erena's pain.

"Ghu, if we even just had some aspirin or Thoran *meltok*," Kealani said as she tore through the supplies. "I wish I knew more about the local flora. I might be able to make something with the right plants."

"I would settle for some plain alcohol," Cindy said. "Some Heimdallian ale would help a lot. Won't fix the injuries but you wouldn't care as much about it."

"We'll have to resupply at the next town we come to," Kealani said, as she scrolled through the map on her data pad. "There is a village about a hundred kilometers from here. As soon as the ground settles down and the Fuzzies get back we can start for that."

Cindy shook her head. "No, we have to wait for light. We don't know what changes in the landscape the ground quake may have caused. We could fall into a sinkhole or something."

Kealani didn't like it. Erena was in bad shape though not in critical condition. For the umpteenth time she wished she had been the one to fight Cutter. Watching the fight she saw several errors in Cutter's form she could have exploited.

The Fuzzies running in broke Kealani out of her reverie. "Make medicine for Aunty Erena," Maid Marian shouted. She grabbed a bowl and dumped in the berries while Rockthrower appeared to be milking the venom from some sort of lizard. The venom and berry juice were combined then mixed with water. "Erena drink. Pain go away."

Cindy took the bowl and sniffed it. "Northern Fuzzies use something like this for a poultice. I never heard of any Fuzzy drinking it."

"Many primitive tribes do something like this for medicine," Kealani said. "Would this work on a Terro the same way as a Fuzzy?"

"I don't know," Cindy admitted. "We can all eat and drink the same things, though I wouldn't eat a land prawn—even with a gun to my head." The ground shook and Erena moaned. "I think we will have to risk it."

"Wait." Kealani dipped a finger into the bowl then put it into her mouth. "It tastes like a weird fruit punch with a bit of a zing. Oh! My tongue just went a little numb. No dizziness, though."

Cindy thought back to her medical rotation. "I think it would be safe in small doses until we know how much it will take to be effective. Here." She held out her hand and Kealani passed the bowl. Holding Erena's head up, she spooned the mixture into her mouth. "I wish we had a scanner to test this stuff with."

"I wish the ground would stop shaking."

XXXXI

"These relics were found near or maybe inside the rocket itself?"

Tars Tarkas shrugged. "Our informer didn't have access to that level of information. Only that there are some artifacts being studied at the science center."

John Carter fumed. The hypership already departed with the rocket and the suicide bombers had already been captured by the police. The rocket was the most important relic by far, but anything that could add to its credibility would certainly help the cause. The problem now was that he had hoped the Martianists, using forged identity papers, could just slip away. The plan was to break the group into five units and each take a ship back to Terra a week apart.

"Do we really need these other artifacts?" Dejah Thoris asked. "I say we leave them and get out while we can. I would rather not be executed on planet-wide newsfeed."

"The next ship spaces out tomorrow," Ulysses Paxton said. "I say we stick with the plan and start sending people home."

John Carter considered the pros and cons. The rocket should be enough to prove that Martians had made it out into space. Once that was established, it would be a short leap to conclude that Terra was actually a Martian colony that somehow lost knowledge of its otherworldly origins. Maybe a disaster or a crash landing robbed the colonists of the tools to start the colony off right. A second attempt, maybe more, resulted in the Freyan colony. Hyperspace technology or maybe a wormhole was involved.

People tended to come in three types: cynics who disbelieve everything without significant evidence, the gullible who buy into almost any story no matter how implausible, and the rational thinkers who prefer to have some evidence but are capable of taking the occasional leap of faith. Sadly, the greater part of the Martianist movement was filled with the gullible. They would need proof upon proof and even more substantiation to bring in the other two types. That meant all the evidence they could find. That also meant they would need the other relics.

"We'll start the evacuation with the members we kept in the dark about our extra-legal activities. They will use their real identity papers as they leave."

"They'll get grabbed up by the police," Tars Tarkas argued.

"Very likely they will," John Carter said lightly. "They will be veridicated and questioned and they won't know anything of value. Most of them were just here to pass out flyers and collect donations. At worst, they will have to delay their departure by a week since there is no law against believing that Mars was the birthplace of Terro-humanity."

"That makes sense," Dejah Thoris agreed. "Only a few of us really know what our mission here was about."

Tars Tarkas chuckled. "After veridicating a couple dozen members they might start to think their machine is broken. But how does that get us the relics? And if we do manage to get them, how do we get them off-world? They'll go through everybody's luggage with an electron microscope. I don't think even our sympathizers, if we have any on whatever hypership is in when we are ready to leave, would be able to smuggle the goods on board."

"We'll be taking a commercial ship, true, but there are ways to fool the scanners. As for the rest, well, the CZC will hand over the relics without argument."

Confusion was on everybody's face. Ulysses Paxton was the first to put it together. "We are back to abducting the rich boy. We, how do they say it in the old gangster movies?...we put the bag on him and, uh, jack his ride."

"There are a few decades between those expressions, but that is essentially correct," John Carter said. "Except for 'jacking his ride.' There are not enough of us to handle a complete crew complement. Even if they didn't overpower us physically, they could run gas through the air vents and we would all wake up in the brig. No, we go commercial and try to beat the scanners. Unless one of you know how to operate a hyperspace craft?"

Everybody shook their heads in the negative.

Dejah Thoris looked doubtful. "Isn't he still off-planet?"

"We have a sympathizer on the police force," John Carter explained. "He is back. He looks a bit different for some unknown reason, not that I care, but he is now in reach."

This time Tars Tarkas looked doubtful. "Okay, we grab him up, force the CZC to turn over the relics or we, uh, marbleize him, take his ship to another world, then what? We let him go, he runs straight to the cops and we never see our next birthday. And we can't just kill him since he will have his entire crew as witnesses, and we can't operate the ship without them. I doubt we could kill them all."

"Simple. We gas everybody on the ship, plant a bomb in the engine room and take a shuttle to the planet's surface," John Carter said. "The ship explodes and while everybody on the planet is distracted by that, we buy passage on a commercial flight. If we have time we can sell the shuttle to a less than reputable dealer."

Ulysses Paxton shook his head. "Too risky. We dump the shuttle and get the hell off whatever planet we light on. Not a fan of killing everybody either. Gas them, sure, let them take a nice long nap while we get gone. Blowing up the ship will just make the cause look bad."

"The target is also of Freyan descent," Tars Tarkas pointed out. "Killing him goes against everything we are trying to promote."

The others agreed. Freyans were considered almost sacred to the majority of Martianists. "Fine. Gas and go. Now let's figure out how we get our boy."

* * *

"Seriously, it is my natural hair color."

Jason Roberts eyed the bright blonde coif, then shrugged. "So why darken it all the time you were out looking for Papa Jack?"

Morgan Holloway signaled for a refill and a barmaid topped off his stein of Freyan ale. "Business reasons. While I was out looking for my sire, I was also building my financial empire. Two things worked against me: my age and appearance. Young men who seemed to appear from nowhere didn't get much respect in the circles I was traveling. Other young men could trade on their parents' reputation. I didn't even know who my father was. Being a Freyan baron didn't help, either. Freyans are still considered hick rubes away from the home planet. Then there is still that old stereotype about blondes."

"You have more fun?" Jason quipped.

"That we are somehow less intelligent. Almost every full-blooded Freyan is blond. A few go to strawberry blond. Anytime you see a dark-haired Freyan you can be sure it isn't real. This is the natural consequence of circling a star that puts out less ultraviolet light. I grew tired of the uphill battle and darkened my hair." Morgan pulled a metal comb from his pocket. "I use a photo-grade chemical in my hair. This comb emits specific light wavelengths that change the color depending on the setting. It works best on natural blondes who want to change to a darker color. It can darken or change hue, but it goes from lighter to darker, not the other way around."

"I've heard of that. Fashion models and actors use it. Hey, does your wife know?"

Morgan smiled. "I only changed the color of my scalp hair. It occurs to me that I never mentioned it to my…to Pa. I guess I should let him in on it."

"Wait, I thought Freyans didn't have any body hair."

Morgan nodded. "Very little, to be sure. If you ask a Martianist, it is because Freyans didn't mix with Neanderthals like many Terran tribes did. But I am only half-Freyan. Akira likes running her fingers through my chest hair."

"Okay, more info than I expected." Jason downed his drink and looked at Mike Hammer. "Refill, Mike?"

Mike Hammer eyed his tumbler of *hokfusinated*, non-alcoholic beer and nodded. Jason wasn't sure if Mike actually liked the taste or if he was emulating some character from the books he read. He ordered two refills.

"So, since we tracked down the source of the faux sunstones and the likely recipients, what next?"

Morgan set his stein down and leaned forward. "We don't know for certain if the Martianists took all of the stones, Jason. Or even if we recovered them all. It could be years before we get that all settled. But, I think, in a few days it won't matter."

Jason was a little surprised. "How so?"

Morgan looked around to be certain nobody was close enough to hear. "Victor intends to release the method of creating counterfeit sunstones and how to spot the fakes."

Jason digested that for a moment then nodded. "Smart. People who can't afford the real thing might still grow their own, so to speak, but anybody who can afford them wouldn't be caught dead in the street wearing a fake."

"Oh, I wouldn't be too sure on that last point. Some very wealthy people buy real diamond necklaces only to keep them home in a safe while wearing replicas in public. That could become a trend with sunstones as well. I'll mention it to Victor and see if we can't get some use out of all the counterfeits I brought back from Terra."

"Wait, aren't the fakes radioactive?"

Morgan nodded. "About twice as hot as the luminescent numbers on that antique watch you carry."

Jason pulled out his nth-great-grandfather's pocket watch and looked at the face. "So, next to nothing. Well, I hope you still put a warning label on it to keep it away from Fuzzies. I wouldn't want to take any chances with Mike here."

"Dr. Hoenveld assures me that the radioactivity is well below what could affect a Fuzzy. I was overly careful at the warehouse when Mike wanted a look."

Jason thought for a moment. "Dr. Hoenveld is going by milli-rads per karat, yes?" Morgan said yes. "Well, the diamond necklace example you gave, if you replaced the diamonds with sunstones. How many milli-rads would that put out?"

Morgan thought back to some of the more ornate and even gaudy jewelry he had seen. "Damn. I think you have a point. I'll ask Dr. Hoenveld to run some tests with larger samples. I still think it would be safe for the Fuzzies provided they didn't wear the damn things."

* * *

Outside the bar, six men gathered near the entrance. They were joined by a seventh who came out of the bar. "He's in there with another man and a Fuzzy."

"Damn. What if they come out together?" said a large redheaded man.

"Then we get all three. Remember, we want him alive. His friends, too, I guess. If he gives us any trouble, we can threaten the other man or the Fuzzy. Get the airvan ready. When they come out, we have to be ready to hit and get."

"I can't believe somebody with his kind of money would hang out in a dive like this," one with striped hair said.

The redhead snorted. "These rich types go slummin' all the time. The more money they got, the more they like seeing the have-nots struggle in their day to day lives. I think it makes them feel big."

"Maybe. Whatever, I'll feel better after we deliver this silver spoon guy and get our money. Any idea who these guys are?"

Redhead shook his head. "No clue, which is the way I like it. Can't sweat it out of me under veridication that way."

"I know, but I'll keep mum," a bald man said. "I was lucky to spot this guy, let alone recognize him with the blond hair."

"Yeah, I guess. I am going back in to keep an eye on our mark."

Before he could reach the door it opened. Morgan, Jason and Mike Hammer filed out.

"Now!"

Before the two men or Fuzzy could react, they were shot by several darts. They instantly slumped to the pavement.

"I hope we didn't overdose them," said the man wearing an old-style bush hat.

"No worries," Redhead said. "These darts were loaded with a very mild sedative. It would take more than a dozen hits to kill them. As it is they'll take a nice little nap. Now where's the damned van?"

The airvan lowered to the parking space in front of the bar and the hatch opened. Morgan, Jason and Mike were unceremoniously tossed into the rear compartment.

"Now let's get to the rendezvous, get paid, and lay low for a while."

XXXXII

"*Ja*, he vill be beck today."

Ben Rainsford suppressed a sigh. Having Sylvinski and company over on Zeta Continent gave him time to breathe. Johann Torseus was kind enough to give him a heads-up that his own personal nightmare was returning to Alpha. Ben looked at the Bürgermeister in the screen with sympathy. "I am sorry you had to put up with that, Johann."

"It vas no problem, Ben. He vas actually not so bad to deal vit'," Johann said from the comscreen. "I t'ink he ist chenuinely concerned vit' our situation und vants to help."

"Really? I was afraid he would go around telling you what you could and couldn't do. Well, I am glad he didn't make any trouble for you."

"Ehh, dere ist vun t'ing."

Uh-oh, here comes the first shoe, Ben thought. "What would that be?"

Johann explained about the Magnian slavers and how they would be brought to Zarathustra for trial and punishment. "Herr Commissar Sylvinski brought a concern from die Favored Vun. Vun of mein pipple spoke vit' her about a Magnian she vants pardoned, or at least haff die deat' penalty differed."

"Wait, Favored One?" Johann brought Ben up to speed about Janice Goodfellow. "Now why didn't Gus brief me on this? No matter. Prince Morgan privately brought me up to speed about the Magnians when he first offered to purchase Zeta. What is your concern?"

"Vell, if Prince Morgan succeeds in getting Neu Freya recognized as a principality, den ve could hold de trials here, dough I t'ink ve vould haff to empanel a chudche und chury from your community." It took Ben a moment to translate in his head that Johann meant "judge" and "jury." "I don't t'ink ve could get an impartial chury here. I am unsure vhat die churisdictional issues might be."

In other words, would a trial on Zeta be recognized as legal? Ben Rainsford asked himself. "And Sylvinski brought this to you himself?"

Johann nodded. "Ja. Die Favored Vun could haff came to me directly but, ehhh, vent t'rough chennels. She spoke vit der Commissar und he came to me."

Ben realized that Miss Goodfellow was trying to help without circumventing Sylvinski's authority. *I wonder if she would consider staying on Zarathustra*, he considered. *I could use somebody like that in my administration.* "Okay, so, what is the problem?"

"Vell, vill I haff die aut'ority to grant dis pardon if I t'ink it ist varrented? For dot matter, do I haff die aut'ority to order an execution?"

Now there was a sticky situation. On most colony planets, only the governor had the power to grant pardons. Executions were ordered by a judge during sentencing. The two notable exceptions were Thor and Freya where the local kingdoms acted on all crimes against their people. "I will have to discuss this with Prince Morgan and Gus Brannhard. However, if for some reason I can't imagine something prevents this, I will accept your recommendation should you choose to pardon anybody. I am a bit hazy on my ability to order executions."

Now Johann was confused. "Did you not order the deat's of ofer, ehhh, sixty men und vomen?"

"No, they were sentenced to death by the judge. I merely arranged the method of execution. And I could have been overruled by the legislature if they decided I had exceeded my authority. It would be a whole complicated mess." Ben was about to explain further when a thought struck him. "Say, do you know when these prisoners are supposed to come here?"

Johann shook his head. "Not exactly. Sometime after Prince Morgan gets Neu Freya recognized as a Freyan principality. Dey are currently detained on Gimli."

Ben thought it over and it made sense. Gimli was a cash-strapped colony in need of funds to restart their mining interest in the asteroids. Playing baby sitter to a bunch of felons on the Federation's deci-sol would certainly infuse some much needed revenue.

Ben leaned back in his seat. "Well, hopefully Prince Morgan will give me a heads-up before they get here. Wait a sec…where will they be detained when they get here?"

"Ve conferted a varehouse into a detention center. *Nicht so gut* as *dein* Prison House, but it vill hold efen a Magni-Freyan. Und die list of folunteers to guard dem ist fery long. Vunce dey get here, ve vill be keeping dem for as long as it takes."

* * *

Hic Farquar, Clarence Burr and Buck Trask gathered in Juan Takagashi's outer office. Captain Trask was clearly out of sorts.

"Were I not already in the building I wouldn't be here now," Trask said to Farquar. "It will be several hours before the chief prosecutor and your boss will get here from Zeta Continent. I am already busy with far more important matters, which I cannot discuss with you, elsewhere."

Farquar nodded. "I understand, Captain. Our presence here right now is more symbolic than anything else."

"Symbolic?"

"Yes. We are simply showing the Deputy Colonial Governor that we are a united front and that he will not be able to simply slip away."

Trask muttered something profane in Sheshan that he picked up from Lt. Williams. Oddly, a thought struck him: do Fuzzies curse in their own language? "Gentlemen, I do not have time for this. It serves no useful purpose beyond intimidation, and I have no legal requirement to take part in this little display of force. Besides, I have met with Deputy Takagashi and he doesn't intimidate that easily. Cool your heels here if you must, but I am going back to work."

Trask didn't exactly storm out but his departure was brisk. Farquar and Burr watched his retreating back as he went through the doorway.

"I should have expected that," Farquar said. "To him this is a nuisance case and he has much larger issues to contend with."

"Such as," Burr inquired.

"The Martianist terrorists."

Burr nodded. "Of course. The Martianists' activities cross over to several worlds, putting them squarely into Captain Trask's jurisdiction. I imagine he is headed down to see the marshal now to work out strategies for apprehending these nutcases."

Farquar started to feel for the colony. He read up on all of the shenanigans over the last three years that the locals had to deal with. The Fuzzy heist of the CZC sunstone vault, Hugo Ingermann and his attempts to disrupt things, off-worlders trying to take over the planet through extra-legal means, again with Hugo Ingermann at the root of it all, Leo Thaxter's escape from Prison House, some sort of sunstone scheme that Farquar could only dig up scraps of information on, a rocket ship discovered in northern Beta…the list seemed to go on and on. Yet, Governor Rainsford, Victor Grego and the citizens of Zarathustra managed to come out on top in each case.

"I almost feel bad about harassing Deputy Governor Takagashi," Farquar admitted.

Burr grunted. "I wouldn't worry about that too much."

Farquar looked squarely at Burr. "What do you mean?"

"Well, I haven't looked it up in the books yet," Burr said. "I didn't want to spoil the Supervisor's fun, which I would be contractually obliged to do if I became aware of anything that might interfere with his objective."

"What are you talking about?"

Burr took in a deep breath. "It is very possible that even if the Honorable Juan Takagashi has committed a crime on Baldur he is now beyond the reach of Federation law." He noted the blank look on Farquar's face. "The Statute of Limitations. It is one of those dusty old laws that we carried over from First Century A.E., America. The United States region, at least. The statute applies differently depending on the infraction. And hyperspace travel time is deducted from the clock. The point is that the statute may have expired and the Deputy Governor is a perfectly free man."

Farquar rolled his eyes and looked pained. "So this could all be for nothing?"

Burr shrugged. "Well, I haven't looked but the local laws might have a rule or two against employing known felons in government work. If he blows the veridicator interview the least that could happen is he gets dismissed from his position. At most he would be arrested and shipped back to Odin to face trial."

And Supervisor Sylvinski would return to Terra with the accomplishment he sought hoping for that promotion, Farquar thought. "Sometimes I really hate this job."

* * *

"What about the bomb threats?"

Marshal Fane relaxed in his seat behind his desk. "The Martianists made good on their word. As soon as the rocket was collected and spaced out, they transmitted the whereabouts of the suicide bombers, though in two cases that was not necessary. The Fuzzy bomb squad sniffed them out and we used anesthezine darts to take them down. Normally we would have used sono-stunners, but with Fuzzies present—" The Marshal spread his hands as if to show he was helpless in that matter.

Trask nodded understanding. By now it was known planet-wide that sono-stunners were harmful, even lethal to a Fuzzy. "And the issue with the counterfeit sunstones?"

Fane drummed his fingers on the desk for a moment. "I'm not sure. Morgan Holloway was supposed to get back to me today. We believe that the sunstones were smuggled off-planet to Terra where they were acquired by these Martianists...Ghu, I wish we had a new name for them, 'Martianist' is a bit of a mouthful...anyway, and the Martianists sold the gems on the black market to finance their little scheme here to get that rocket. If so, that is the bright spot in the affair, at least for the CZC. That means the bulk of the fakes mostly stayed on Terra and maybe Mars. They won't have to worry about the markets on the other colonized worlds. They will send out a circular, of course, to give the other planets a heads-up in case somebody tries to pawn off ersatz sunstones in the future."

"I wouldn't rule out the possibility that whoever sold the stones to the Martianists might have let a few stray on the way back to Terra," Trask pointed out. "To cover expenses and maybe pick up a few souvenirs along the way."

Marshal Fane nodded and jotted down a note on the paper pad he had on his desk. Data pads were difficult for him to work with his oversized fingers.

"Now, you were going to bring me up to speed on how we are going to get the rest of these Martianist extremists," Trask said.

Fane looked up from his note pad. "You don't think they left with the rocket?"

"Of course not," Trask replied. "You wouldn't have called me in to discuss the case if it was all over…unless this is a briefing on what to tell the folks back home."

Fane started. "Wait, you are going back to Terra?"

Trask shrugged. "My job here is done. It's time to get back home and go to work on another case. You didn't know?"

Marshal Fane sighed. "I guess I am not looped in on that. Well, I hope you can stick around long enough for this bit of drama. We let it leak that we have some additional artifacts the Martianists would be interested in."

Trask thought it over for a moment. "Okay, I get it. You figure some of the nutcases will stick around hoping to grab the artifacts. Good idea."

The Marshal smiled. "I wish I could take the credit, but it was Morgan Holloway's idea."

Trask nodded. "Are these relics real or something the CZC faked up for us?"

"Very real. In fact, Mr. Grego said that they were actually found inside of the rocket." Max Fane picked up a pack of cigarettes, extracted one and held the pack out for Trask to have one. Trask passed on the offer. "As I understand it, Commodore Napier ordered the rocket to be impounded by the Navy. My thinking is he expected some sort of idiocy, just like we've seen. The political fallout of an actual pre-human civilization spacecraft being discovered would give the Martianists more clout, something no sane person wants to see happen. It was supposed to be on its way back to Terra for investigation, study and possible destruction.

"The Martianists will claim that it is a relic of Mars and proves that they had viable space travel and, since Terrans look so much like the Martian mummies, Terra is a Martian colony."

Trask rolled his eyes. "I had to stop at Mars on the way out and took a couple tours while waiting for my ship's departure. I saw those mummies. They are anthropomorphic, yes, but much thinner than we are. Bone and muscle development designed for 0.376 gees wouldn't last twenty minutes on Terra."

"Oh, I don't know about that," Marshal Fane said. "Heavy resistance training, drugs, maybe even a special diet might allow some of the sturdier Martians to survive in Terran gravity. Just playing Devil's advocate, mind you, but isn't that how we prepared colonists for planets like Magni and Modi?"

Trask winced. He elected not to argue the difference between a Martian training to survive in over triple his native gravity versus a Terro-human getting ready for a world with only half a gravity more weight. A Marine could carry a wounded buddy on his shoulder for miles, effectively doubling his weight. Could a Martian carry three of his buddies like that?

"Okay, so the Dejah Thoris fan club will want the remaining relics. The more the merrier. What are they going to do to get them?"

Marshal Fane let out a long breath. "That is what I was supposed to discuss with Morgan Holloway, though I should think Chief Steefer would have been better qualified. Since the relics are in the CZC science lab, we need their cooperation to set any kind of decent trap for these, uh, Tharks."

Trask recalled that the Tharks were the six limbed green Martians in the John Carter of Mars series. *The Marshal has been reading the old classics*, Trask thought. "So, what is the plan? Wait for them to try to break into the CZC and snatch the relics?"

The Marshal shook his head. "I forget that you are relatively new to this planet. The CZC building is the most well-fortified structure on Zarathustra. A few years ago there was an attempted gem heist at the main building. The thieves came in through some open levels. Well, after the dust settled Chief Steefer went on the warpath and Victor Grego approved some very expensive security upgrades. The open levels were sealed off, more sensors installed, security personnel doubled, the whole megillah. The building has a polyalloy exterior with collapsium lamination. It was always intended to last pretty much forever. It will easily outlast that millennium-long lease the CZC has on most of this planet."

Trask mulled over the new information. "That sounds very impressive, but even the most well-programmed secure computer has a back door. Can we be sure the CZC building does not?"

The Marshal smiled. "Indeed it did. In one of the sub-basements. It was discovered when Gus Brannhard was abducted a while back." Marshal Fane related the details of Gus's discovery by one of the CZC employees and the subsequent rescue by then Captain Lansky and the security crew. "After all that Steefer went beyond ballistic. Security racked up a lot of overtime going over every square millimeter inside and out of the CZC building. The secret door with the connection tunnel was sealed off with a security hatch that could only be opened with a DNA sequence and retinal scan from an authorized person, but only after a security code was entered from Victor Grego's office.

Trask made a low whistle. "Okay, nobody but nobody is getting in without an invitation." He thought it over for a moment. "That means the Tharks, as you called them, will need leverage to force us to bring the relics out for them. Another round of suicide bombers, maybe?"

"I don't think so," Fane said. "After the last attempts we upped our own security. My men are everywhere with bomb-sniffing Fuzzies and dogs. We even deputized a bunch of former cops and select citizens. Henry Stensen has loaned us some very fancy detection equipment and even the Marines are involved. We can't cover everything, of course, so we went for as many priority targets as possible and the Governor is instituting a temporary curfew."

"You might consider putting out a PSA about the Martianists as an added measure. That mind control they used on those 'volunteers' could be used on the unwary." Trask glanced at the chronometer on the wall. "Exactly when was Morgan supposed to arrive?"

Marshal Fane checked the time and his face screwed up with confusion, then realization. "Oh, Ghu!"

Trask instantly understood. "Damn! There's the leverage. Holloway for the relics."

"We don't know that for sure," Marshal Fane said. "At least not yet. Morgan might just be sleeping off a long night or have aircar trouble or something."

"You don't believe that any more than I do," Trask responded.

"Let's make a few calls before hitting the panic button. I'll call Morgan's penthouse here in the city and his castle on Beta. Even if he isn't there, somebody on his house staff might know something."

"Okay, Marshal. I'll contact Mr. Grego and then his father…I am not looking forward to that last call," Trask admitted. The Marshal offered to make the call himself but Trask refused. "I might have a few questions for him."

XXXXIII

Lars struggled to push the ground roller away to no avail. The last tremor caused a crack in the earth which in turn put the ground roller into a depression. Lars fell partly out the window and was pinned at his waist between the roller and the ground. Even the strongest human couldn't push four tons of machinery up from the crevasse. Only the uneven ground saved him from being cut in half. As it was, he had no way to crawl out from under the tilted transport unless something took some of the pressure off of him.

"*Mein Gott!* Lars, are you injured?" Brünnhilde crawled out of the opposite window and ran around the vehicle. "Everybody out! We have to get the weight off of him."

Lars grunted as the roller shifted. The difference in weight was almost imperceptible. "I think most of the weight is held up by the ground around me. I am far from comfortable, but I don't think anything is broken. I can still feel my legs, so my spine must be okay."

Brünnhilde breathed a silent prayer of thanks to the gods of her people as she looked over the situation. On instinct she tried to lift the roller off of Lars to no effect. She thought back to her life before she was taken out of the mines to work as a seamstress with her mother. Accidents were not common but they did occur.

"We need to get a cable and hook and have one of the other ground rollers pull this *verdammt* thing off of him." Brünnhilde looked about hoping to see one of the other rollers. It was impossible to see through the dust kicked up by the earthquake. "*Scheisse!* We need a pry bar. The bigger the better."

Estefan carefully scrambled to the back end of the roller. "We have a tanker's bar for resetting slipped tracks." He produced a heavy bar easily two meters long and several centimeters thick in most of its length.

"That won't work," Lars said through gritted teeth. "The ground at the edge of this damned ditch is too crumbly. You'll just dig into the dirt when you apply pressure. You'll need something stronger to use as a fulcrum. Rock won't get it done, either."

Everybody looked about the ground and at the back of the roller. Consuela found an entrenching tool and brought it over to Brünnhilde. "Think this will work?"

"It might. We need to get some ropes on the other side. I'll work the pry bar while everybody else pulls on the opposite side."

Estefan was not convinced. "Beg pardon, *chika*, but even Lars wouldn't be heavy enough to get any real leverage on that bar. We need an extension. Consuela, get the pipe from the back. Be careful." The pipe, an extension of the pry bar, added another meter and a half. "You will still need more weight."

Brünnhilde thought a moment, then asked Consuela to get her backpack. Nobody else was light enough to go in and out of the roller without increasing the pressure on Lars.

The Magni-Freyan girl unceremoniously dumped everything out of her pack and started filling it with rocks. Estefan caught on instantly and stopped her. "We have something much heavier, if you can manage it. Consuela, help me get into the tool kit."

After considerable grunting and cursing the pair returned with a roller track. It took both of them to carry it. Lars nodded in understanding and immediately regretted it as pain shot down from his neck to his legs.

"Polysteel with micro-collapsium lamination," Estefan huffed. "Heavy as all Niflheim."

"Is that the only one?" Brünnhilde asked. Consuela said there were about a dozen. "Okay, I'll get the rest. We need to move fast in case the ground shakes again."

It took a few trips for Brünnhilde to get the rest of the replacement roller tracks. The entrenching tool was first used to dig a small depression in the ground at the edge of the crevasse near Lars, then put in place as a fulcrum. Next, she jammed the pry bar into place, and then hung her backpack at the end and filled it as much as she dared with the tracks. Even for her genetically augmented muscles it was hard work.

Estefan whispered to Consuela that he expected Brünnhilde to put the pack on her back. He had to admit her way of doing it was much smarter.

"Everything we can get out of the roller has to be taken out. The less weight the better. Mai, you will be pulling down on the pry bar."

Mai was shocked. "Me? I barely weigh anything!"

Brünnhilde pointed at the backpack hanging from the end of the pry bar extension. "That will be doing at least ninety percent of the work. You just get as far back on the bar as you can and pull down. It wouldn't hurt to put some rocks in your pockets."

"Um. Okay. What are you doing? I thought you would be on the bar."

Brünnhilde pointed at the ropes the others were tying to the upper frame of the ground roller. "I'll be pulling on a rope with the others. I think my added strength there will be of greater benefit than pulling down on the pry bar."

"Ladies, please, less talk and more getting busy," Lars grunted. "My legs are starting to tingle."

"Right." Brünnhilde looked over everything moved to the far side of the roller and grabbed a rope. "Consuela, I think you better stay with Lars and help him slide out when we get the weight off of him. If his legs are going numb he might not be able to use them to move." Consuela nodded and rushed to Lars' side.

"Everybody ready?" Brünnhilde was assured they were. "Okay. On *drei*! Um, I mean on three! One…two…THREE!"

* * *

The ground roller hit a bump and Erena drew in a sharp breath. Cindy noticed and felt Erena's forehead. "Is it bad?"

"Not as bad as before," Erena admitted. "Whatever it was the Fuzzies dosed me with more than just the edge off. We should bottle that stuff. I'll need to stop and do some stretches in a little while."

"According to the map on the data pad there is a town about ninety kilometers from here." Kealani said. "I'll have to change direction after we get past those rock formations. They aren't on the map so they must have been forced up from the ground during the earthquake."

"*Gut.* We can get some new supplies and refill the med kit," Cindy said as she examined some of Erena's bruises. "And maybe see a real doctor if they have one. There could be some internal bleeding that the medical scanner couldn't detect. The portable units are never as good as the standard models used in the hospital."

"We should also make sure that the, uh, magic potion the Fuzzies gave you is completely safe for us Big Ones," Kealani added. "No extra-terrestrial species biology is one hundred percent compatible with ours."

Erena smiled weakly. "What about the Freyans? We can even inter-breed with them."

Cindy shook her head. "Closer than anything else we have found, but they are the exception that proves the rule. While we can breed with them, mother and infant mortality is higher when we do. Not tragically higher, but enough to invite caution."

Erena nodded slightly. "Fair enough. I understand chocolate isn't good for Fuzzies. Not the real stuff, anyway."

Kealani nodded. "Yup. Fuzzies are like dogs that way. They also only sweat through their hands and feet. Mostly, they expel heat by exhaling it. Like most Terran mammals. Primates are the main exception to that rule." Kealani was going to add on that when she spotted something up ahead. "Cindy, do you have the field glasses handy? Take a look up ahead, will you?"

After fiddling with the settings Cindy could make out a group of people struggling to get a transport vehicle out of a crack in the earth. After she explained what she saw the three decided to see if they could help.

Erena called Maid Marian and Rockthrower up to the front and asked them to stay hidden just in case the people they wanted to help turned out to be bad Big Ones. Erena held her pistol as they approached.

Lars pushed with everything he had as Mai fought to lower the pry bar and the rest pulled from the other side on the ropes. Slowly, the ground roller inched up enough to allow Lars to get out, but he didn't feel safe relinquishing his grip. He looked about in desperation.

"Consuela, that rock over there. Try to roll it over here and wedge it under the roller," Lars grunted through gritted teeth.

The rock was easily twice her weight and she had no hope of lifting it. So, as ordered, she fought to roll it. It was more flat than round forcing her to lift and flop it over amid a great deal of some very unladylike language. Just as Consuela's strength was giving out, another set of hands joined her efforts. Many hands make lighter work, although the two women would have liked more of those hands.

Lars was sweating heavily and his arms were shaking from his exertions. The two women pushed the rock in place as quickly as they were able then they each grabbed an arm and pulled Lars out.

"*El Diablo*, Lars," Consuela gasped out. "You were heavier than that *Maldito* rock! If this *Mujer* had not helped…"

"*Mujer*?"

"Old Spanish for woman," Kealani told Lars. She turned to Consuela. "Your family must have emigrated from Venezuela on Terra. One of the few countries that still uses some Spanish."

Kealani introduced herself and Cindy, who had been helping Mai with the pry bar. "Our friend Erena is still in our roller." Lars tried to stand but his legs wouldn't cooperate. "Cindy, could you tend to him while I see what Erena is up to?"

What Erena was "up to" was backing the roller up to the stranded vehicle. Brünnhilde took hold of the winch-line and affixed it to the frame. Moments later the roller was out of the crevasse.

"Thanks for the help," Estefan said. "We didn't have anything we could attach our winch to."

"I don't think it would have helped," Erena said looking at the ground where Lars had been pinned. "Had you tried to winch it off you might have caused the roller to shift and cut…what is his name?"

"Lars."

"You might have cut Lars in half. As it is I can't believe he is sitting up and shaking his feet like that."

"It takes a lot to seriously damage Lars," Estefan said with a smile. "He's from Modi, a high-gee world. Those guys are damn near bulletproof."

"Really? Well, we should have Dr. Tezza check him out, anyway," Erena said. "She has had some medical training."

Estefan looked over Erena as she stayed in the ground roller. "If you don't mind my saying so, you look like you had a run-in with something big and mean." He looked back and forth as if to be sure nobody else was listening, then spoke in low tones: "If you are really hurting I have some Dolorzine tablets. Not strictly legal but they come in handy out in the bush."

Erena took a quick inventory of her aches and pains. Dolorzine was a prescription pain reliever. It made all of one's pain go away while giving the patient a buzz not unlike strong chuckleweed.

"Maybe you better save it for Lars," Erena said. "I have something the F…something else. I'll take some aspirin if you have any."

Estefan was out of aspirin and pretty much everything else. The best he could do was some bathtub gin leftover from before the potatoes ran out. Erena declined that as well.

Back a ways behind some boulders the Fuzzies watched and listened. The dogs growled low and had to be hushed. "Dogs not like new Big Ones," Maid Marian observed. Fuzzies were very careful to watch out for anything the Curtyses didn't like.

"Might not be all Big Ones," Rockthrower said. "Too far away to tell. Wait for Aunty Cindy an' Aunty Erena to say is hokay to come out."

Maid Marian gripped her bow. "We watch. If Big Ones make trouble, we make more trouble for them."

XXXXIIII

"Ve should go down und collect die Fuzzies *und die hunde*."

Cinda said no. "With the ground shaking like that, it would be too dangerous to land there."

"Ve can hofer a foot ofer die ground," Rheiner argued. "Dey could hop up into die hatch."

Cinda shook her head. "Ground shaking like that is very unpredictable. Rock could burst up from underneath. I don't like leaving them down there but it is just too dangerous to go down. They could be thrown under the aircar by the ground movement."

Rheiner quietly fumed. He wanted to collect the Fuzzies before they got hurt. Cinda, however, was a post-grad in geology and knew what she was talking about.

Cinda fiddled with a handheld device. "According to my seismograph the quake is starting to settle down. We can collect the Fuzzies then."

Little Fuzzy, Emily Dickinson, James Hutton and Sarah Balfour waited for the ground to stop shaking. Their dogs were nervous and upset but remained with their masters. They were too well trained to go running off at the first sign of danger.

In the distance they saw several animals running and stumbling. None were trying to eat the stragglers. The flight response was fully engaged, superseding all else.

"Why Mummy Cinda not come down for us?" Sarah wondered aloud.

"Ground shake," Little Fuzzy pointed out. "Not good to put aircar down on. Might hurt aircar."

Emily Dickinson was happy the aircar wasn't coming down to get her. The ground quake didn't frighten her nearly as much as the idea of getting back into the flying machine. "There are no trees to fall on us here. Nor are there any hills for rocks to come down from. We are safe here as long as the ground does not open up."

At the suggestion that the ground could open up and swallow them Sarah and James became frightened. Little Fuzzy had to calm them down. Emily mentally chided herself for her choice of words.

James Hutton thought about the situation. "Mummy Cinda say ground move on top when big things called tek-tonn-ick plates move way-way down underground."

Sarah also recalled Mummy Cinda talking about geology. The tectonic plates moved when there was pressure under them. Hot rock that moved like water could come up between the plates and burst above ground. Sarah decided not to mention this as it would frighten the others. She knelt down and touched the ground to see if it was hot. It seemed normal to her, but the thick calloused bottoms of her feet were not as sensitive as her hands.

Rheiner brought the aircar down near the Fuzzies. Cinda was against it, but agreed it might be better to take the chance and collect the Fuzzies rather than risk their injury in another quake.

Emily Dickenson was still shaking. The moving ground reminded her of the ground roller crash she had been in with her Mummy. Little Fuzzy saw this and tried to comfort her. He tried to think of something to take her mind off of the accident that robbed her of her native language. Then it hit him.

"Trail gone!" Little Fuzzy exclaimed. The ground movement, dirt tossed up into the air, animal tracks and smells: all served to obscure the faint trail of the lost Magni-Freyan girl. Even the heavy tread of the ground rollers were gone. He relayed the information to Rheiner with his radio. Rheiner and Cinda hadn't gotten out of the aircar, yet.

"Den ve should all get beck in die aircar und go die direction ve vere going," Rheiner said.

Little Fuzzy noticed that Emily Dickinson cringed at the idea of getting back into the aircar. Cinda also noted the reaction and said, "There could be aftershocks from the quake. It would be better for everybody if we were well above it when it hits."

Emily Dickinson shook even more. To her it was like being caught between two damnthings. "I would much rather stay on the ground. I am sure the dogs would rather not be cooped up after such a traumatic experience as well."

Rheiner knew nothing of dogs before coming to Zarathustra. As far as he knew there were none on Magni. Certainly not in the mines. He looked to Cinda. "Vould it be safe for dem to continue on die ground?"

Cinda shook her head. "Not as safe as it would be in the air with us. Aftershocks can be as devastating as the initial quake, though that is not usually the case. I also have no way of knowing how quickly the aftershocks will come without a lot of very large and pricey equipment. It could be a few minutes or several hours. Days, even."

Little Fuzzy, still holding the shaken Emily, said, "We stay on ground. Go direction of tracks. You follow, watch from above. Use little box to see if more ground shake come. Then come get us in aircar."

Cinda shook her head. "My seismograph is too small and low power to tell me if a quake is coming. Only when it gets here."

"Not need box to know ground shakes," Little Fuzzy said. "We stay on ground, move fast as we can. You follow."

Without another word Little Fuzzy and Emily Dickinson mounted their dogs and took off. Sarah Balfour and James Hutton looked torn.

After a long sigh, Cinda told her Fuzzies they could follow Little Fuzzy if they wanted to. They did. Rheiner looked puzzled.

"You allowed dem to go?"

"They're adults," Cinda said. "We tend to think of them as children and even treat them as such, but really they are adults capable of making decisions of their own. I won't pretend otherwise no matter how much I would like to."

Rheiner shrugged and restarted the aircar. "Vell, if der ist anodder qvake, I am flying down to collect dem. Dot ist *mein* adult choice."

* * *

Jack swore luridly in every language he could remember as he turned off the comscreen. Betty, surprised that Jack would talk like that with her in the adjoining office, came in to see what was wrong. It caught

Piet Dumont's attention as well and he had been down the hall. Both marched into Jack's office to see what the Niflheim was going on.

"Captain Trask and Marshal Fane think Morgan may have been abducted and there was a ground quake out in east Beta where Little Fuzzy and Emily Dickinson joined the search for that missing girl." Jack put on his hat then took it off then put it on again. He looked like a man who didn't know whether to shoot or drop ammo.

"You want to help both but can't be in two places at the same time," Betty guessed. "Piet, what do you think?"

"Go look for Little Fuzzy," Piet said without hesitation.

Jack locked eyes on Piet. "Explain."

Piet took a breath and let it out. "Have you ever been on a manhunt?"

"Yes. I did bounty work off and on after I left Mars."

Of course he did, Piet thought, at one time or another Jack has done damn near everything as long as it didn't trap him in an office… until now. "Okay, bad example. Have you ever worked with the police in an investigation?" Jack admitted that he hadn't in any official capacity. "Well, right now the richest man on Zarathustra, at least I think he is, is missing. Victor Grego, Chief Steefer, Marshal Fane, Police Chief Carr and Captain Trask are going to go at this hammer and tongs. Everybody and his kid sister will be on this one. Niflheim, they'll be tripping all over each other as it is. You will only get in the way."

"In the way—"

"Yes. I was a cop for a lot of years before I got cashiered. The worst thing you can do is get in the way and ask a lot of questions. Leave this one to the trained professionals. Little Fuzzy, on the other hand, is out in the middle of nowhere, possibly scared out of his furry little head. He's going to need his pappy a whole lot more than a grown-ass man in his thirties. Have you spoken with Major Lunt?"

Jack shook his head. "He's outside of radio range."

"Damn. I wish the CZC would get off their asses and get some more communication relays set up. Okay, then you and Betty go ahead and fly out to the last known coordinates and see if you can raise Little Fuzzy on the radio from there. I'll hold down the fort and keep Miss Alexander entertained in the meanwhile. I still have some Poictesme melon brandy. Maybe I can entice her into joining me for a drink after she rifles the files some more. There is nothing you can do for Morgan and maybe plenty you can do for Little Fuzzy."

Jack still wavered. Piet lowered his voice and said, "Look, if Morgan was abducted, not killed outright, then somebody wants to keep him alive. That means he is being held for ransom or something...do we have any idea who took him?"

"The Martianists, if anyone. Victor managed to let it leak about the remaining relics they found with that rocket. He hasn't said much about it, but I imagine they plan to use those artifacts as bait."

Piet smiled wide. "Well, then, in that case he is safer than the CZC gem vault if the Martianists took him. Those maniacs treasure nothing more than that Mars stuff. They'll take real good care of Morgan and swap him out for the goods. Stay out of it and let the real cops handle it. I wouldn't put it past Max Fane to have some clever trap set. Now go see if Little Fuzzy needs rescuing."

That settled it. Jack put on his gun belt. "If I find Little Fuzzy and Emily Dickinson fast enough, maybe I can still get back in time to annoy Marshal Fane."

Betty grabbed her handbag and strapped on her own gun. She also grabbed a spare radio. "Maybe we can get Major Lunt if we get close enough. He can help when we get in range to ask him."

Jack nodded. "Piet, you're in charge. Give Miss Alexander anything she wants."

"You got it, Commissioner," Piet said. "I hope she likes the brandy."

* * *

It was dark and cramped with the strong odor of sweat. Mike Hammer was the first to regain consciousness. He noted first that his hands were tied, then that Jason Roberts and Morgan Holloway were with him and handcuffed. Handcuffs had yet to be made in Fuzzy sizes.

Among the many and varied things Mike Hammer had learned from Jason Roberts was how to pick locks, including the old style variety that used keys instead of cards with magnetic strips. Handcuffs had not changed significantly since First Century. Better, stronger metal, different hinging and longer or shorter chains, depending on the need, but basically they were very much the same in function and purpose. That included the locking mechanism.

First, Mike needed to get out of his bindings. He noticed that whoever tied his arms didn't do it as tight as he should have. Fuzzy hands, while they looked very much like Big Ones' hands, were still slightly different. Extending all of the digits out then collapsing them together, Mike was able to slip out of the bindings. A Terro-human would have had to dislocate his thumb to accomplish the same maneuver.

He checked Jason Roberts, his pappy, first. He was breathing normally, as was Morgan. Next, Mike Hammer inspected the confines of his prison. It was just long enough for a Big One to lie down in without touching sides with his head or feet. The width was the same. It was high enough up that a Big One could sit without bumping his head. Mike Hammer was able to walk around without hunching over. Dim light streamed in through the cracks between the boards.

There was nothing else in the crate, as Mike assumed the enclosure to be, to use too escape. His backpack had been taken, along with Pappy Jason's trench coat. They did miss what Mike Hammer had hidden in his fur, but that wouldn't help him at the moment. All he could do was wait for Pappy Jason and Mister Morgan to awaken.

After a while Jason Roberts stirred. "Ahhh. Did somebody get the registration number of the airbus that hit me?"

"Not airbus, Boss," Mike said. "Bad Big Ones." He counted on his fingers then said, "Seven of them. Shoot needle things into us." Mike held up a small dart. "I hit by one."

Jason struggled to sit up. Mike helped. "Handcuffs? Mike, roll up my left sleeve. Good. That's far enough. Give me a second." Jason concentrated. A small compartment opened in the forearm of his artificial limb. Inside were a number of small lock picks and keys. "Try the silver key. It was designed to be a skeleton key for handcuffs back on Terra." Mike tried it without any results. "Okay, the locals use a different brand. We'll have to do this the hard way."

Mike looked at Jason's left arm. "Art'fishul arm very strong. Can't break han'cuff?"

Jason smiled. "I could if both my arms were artificial. As it is I could tear my other hand off if I tried. Sorry, Mike, but you will have to use the lock picks."

Mike Hammer didn't mind. In fact he liked using the picks. Fuzzies excelled at manual manipulation. A minute later Jason's hands were free and Mike started on Morgan's cuffs.

Jason looked himself over and noticed some pinholes in his prosthetic limb. *That must be why I woke up while Morgan is still sawing logs, he thought, I caught some of the dosed darts on my mechanical arm.*

While he waited for Morgan to regain consciousness, he inspected his confines. "Looks like you got it right, Mike. This is a shipping crate of some kind. Cheap one at that given the cracks between the boards. Good thing, too, or we might have suffocated. Hmm…the wood isn't as strong as the better quality crates."

Mike Hammer nodded. "You could punch through with art'fishul arm."

Jason gave it some thought. "I probably could. Unfortunately it would make a lot of noise and bring the bad Big Ones in here. And Mr. Morgan is still sleeping off whatever it was they dosed us with. Too bad I couldn't install a listening device in the arm. Only so much room to fit things in."

"Mike Hammer can hear good-good, Boss. Nobody close by outside of crate. Noise like contragrav'ty."

That brought Jason up short. Contragravity in operation meant they were in a craft of some kind going who-knows-where. Aircars and such were equipped with sound baffles to keep the whine of the contragravity engine from driving the pilot crazy. Apparently a Fuzzy could still hear the engine even through the baffles. A side effect of the contragravity was inertial dampening. That removed all sense of motion except at very high acceleration and deceleration. That was what kept passengers from going splat during mach-plus maneuvers.

"Okay, we are in an aircraft of some sort, possibly a large one since you can't hear any Big Ones nearby. No way of knowing how long—"

"Check watch," Mike Hammer interrupted.

Jason couldn't help feeling pride in his Fuzzy and annoyance at himself. He forgot about his pocket watch. Fortunately nobody took that when they relieved him of his treasured trench coat and pistol. "Mike, you just earned a raise. Umm…looks like we've been out about six hours if I am remembering the time we left the bar correctly. Depending on the speed of this thing we could be as far as Beta Continent—even Gamma Continent."

"Why bad Big Ones kidnap us?"

"Good question. I don't think they were after me or you. Mr. Morgan, on the other hand, has more money than Ghu. Ransom would be my first guess. The kidnappers could get a billion sols for his hide. You and I are just collateral damage. That means we're expendable."

Mike Hammer didn't ask what the big words meant. He read enough books to already know. "That not good," he said.

Morgan began to stir. After a few minutes he sat up holding his head. "Ghaa! My head is killing me. I haven't had a hangover like this since that drinking contest I was in shortly after I first came to this planet. Are you two okay?" Jason and Mike admitted they didn't have any lingering effects from the drugs. "Ugh. They must be interacting with the alcohol I drank."

"Or you just got a bigger dose than me and Mike." Jason quickly filled Morgan in on all they knew and suspected.

"You might be right about the motive, but I doubt it," Morgan said. "I think it is the Martianists using me as leverage to get the remaining relics."

"Ah. Yes, that makes sense," Jason agreed. "Now, what do we do to throw a spanner in their works?"

"I'm open to suggestions."

"Pretend sick," Mike Hammer said. "Ask for help. Man come, we jump him."

Jason stifled a laugh. Mike must have read that old trick in one of his books. "Won't work. We're up in the air, outnumbered seven to three and I don't think they'll care if one of us gets sick. As long as Mr. Morgan is breathing they won't care about anything else. You and me they'll just shoot."

"I shoot them." Mike Hammer pulled out the modified .38 Special he had under his fur. "Bad Big Ones take backpack an' choppo-diggo. Not find pistol."

"We are still outnumbered, Mike," Morgan said. "No reason to think they won't all have guns as well. We will have to wait for the right moment." Morgan frisked himself. He still had his wallet with all of its contents and his watch, but nothing else. "I don't suppose either of you has a deck of cards?"

* * *

"They took two people that were with him?" John Carter of the Martianist movement could barely control himself. "What the hell for? If they used the tranq-darts they wouldn't have been able to cause any trouble!"

"Witnesses," Tars Tarkas said. "We used local hired muscle that has to live here long after we have gone. I don't think we paid them enough to start over on a new world."

John Carter grudgingly conceded the point. It didn't really matter. They were well and truly out of the way and the extra bodies might mean even more leverage. "Fine. Let's make our demands. Who do we talk to? The Governor or the CZC CEO? I should have given that more thought in advance."

"The Governor," Dejah Thoris said. "He will have influence on Victor Grego. Two birds, one stone. And he is very pro-Fuzzy. Be sure to mention we have one along with some civilian. Did they get his name?"

Tars Tarkas shook his head. "They were not planned targets so nobody bothered to find out. Still, a voter is a voter and I never met the politician yet who would let a voter die, even if they supported the opposition. We were lucky we had a man at the spaceport spotting Morgan Holloway coming through. He may have suspected somebody was after him, hence the change to his appearance. We still might not have spotted him if not for the facial recognition—"

"Very well," John Carter interrupted. "Open the secure channel to the governor's office.

* * *

"The CZC has a strict policy against paying ransom," Ben Rainsford said to the screen. "And while it has never come up before, I think the Colonial Government will be adopting the same policy very soon."

It was impossible to read the face of the speaker on the comscreen as he was wearing a stylized mask. For additional anonymity the speaker used a modulator that caused his voice to constantly change its register up and down at random moments between soprano and bass.

"Governor, I happen to know that Mr. Morgan Holloway is the son of a close friend of yours and a very important stockholder and officer in the CZC," the voice said. "If we were asking for an exorbitant amount of money I have no doubt that you would do everything in your power to avoid paying while trying to find Mr. Holloway. But we are not interested in money. We only want the remaining artifacts. These are relatively useless items to you and hardly worth a man's life in the greater scheme of things. I very much doubt you are prepared to sacrifice this very important individual over a few relics. I will give you some time to consider it. We will call back later, after you have had time to consider it. I am sure you will need to speak with Misters Grego and Holloway senior. Oh, and for a little added incentive, their location is rigged with thermite charges. Refusing our demands could make things very loud and noisy. Good day."

Before Ben could respond the connection was severed.

"Damn! Did you get a trace?"

Marshal Fane spoke into a radiophone then shook his head. "They used some kind of obfuscation equipment. We traced the signal to Gamma, then Beta, Zeta and Delta continents. Pretty fancy stuff."

Ben sighed. "Then we are stuck with Plan A. I'll try to draw it out enough that they'll think I am stalling. Whose plan was this anyways?"

"Yours, Governor," Marshal Fane replied. "It's a decent plan. We just have to hope it survives contact with the enemy. If it helps, I believe he or she was bluffing about the thermite charges. Cataclysmite is the preferred explosive on Zarathustra,"

Ben didn't get the military reference. "They might have brought it with them. We just have to hope that Morgan isn't too uncomfortable wherever they have him. Any idea who the civilian and the Fuzzy are?"

Marshal Fane shook his head. "It had to be somebody he was familiar with, a drinking buddy or something. Maybe that guy who was his second for the duel. We'll check the records and see who that was, then we'll dispatch a patrol car to see if he has gone missing."

Ben nodded. "I better call Jack, then Victor, and let them know what's up. Jack is going to be a bit difficult with this."

XXXXIV

"I must say you are the luckiest man I have ever met."

Cindy Tezza examined the line of bruises that ran across Lars' midsection. Even considering that most of the weight from the ground roller was supported by the uneven earth, a man from Heimdall would have been killed almost instantly from the pressure. Despite the difference in body thickness at the impact point it, was unlikely a lesser developed human would have survived.

"Are your legs still numb?"

Lars shook his head. "No, they are still a bit tingly, though. I think I could get up and walk around, now."

"*Nein*!" Cindy said almost shouting. "We do not know if there is any internal damage. You could have a crack on the vertebra or organ damage. That was a lot of weight and you might have crushed your spleen or kidneys. This portable scanner isn't as good as the kind used in hospitals. Adrenaline could be masking the pain. We should wait a couple hours before trying anything more strenuous than wiggling your toes. Best that you not eat or drink anything before then, either."

Lars felt a bit peckish in the way large organisms are always hungry, but he didn't think he would starve in the next couple of hours so he just nodded. "You're the doctor."

Brünnhilde, who had been waiting to see if Lars would survive, noticed Cindy's use of the German negative. "Doctor Tezza, could I speak with you for a moment?"

Cindy stood up from the kneeling position she had been in while examining the prone Lars and walked over to Brünnhilde. "You were one of the people pulling on the cable, yes? Do you have any muscle pain?"

"No, I am fine. I noticed you used some German a moment ago and you have a slight accent. Is German your first language?"

"Yes, it is. We all speak German on Heimdall, though we also learn Lingua Terra and one or two non-Terro languages."

Brünnhilde switched to German. *"Kannst du mich in die nächste Stadt oder Siedlung bringen? Ich muss mich von diesen Leuten entfernen und die Polizei kontaktieren. Diese Leute sind Fuzzy-Sklavenhändler. Ich habe sie reden hören, als sie dachten, ich sei bewusstlos."*

"Mein Gott! Ja, du kannst mit uns kommen. Wir haben Platz dazu und müssen unsere Vorräte trotzdem auffüllen. Ich denke, es gibt ein Dorf weniger als 100 Kilometer von hier entfernt. Bist du sicher, dass sie nicht wissen, dass du sie belauscht hast?"

"Ich denke, wenn sie wüssten, dass ich jetzt tot sein würde."

"Wie bist du zu diesen Leuten gekommen?"

"Das kann warten. Wir müssen uns von diesen Leuten entfernen und so schnell wie möglich die Polizei kontaktieren."

"Wir können nicht gehen, bis wir wissen, dass es Lars gut gehen wird. Sonst wird es verdächtig sein. Ein paar Stunden und wir können auf dem Weg sein. Sage ihnen, dass ich angeboten habe, disch mitzunehmen, damit du deine Ihre Familie aus der nächsten Stadt kontaktieren können. Und um einen Arzt zu haben, schau sich Ihren Kopf an. Ich werde Kealani und Erena alles erklären, wenn wir einen Moment alleine haben."

"Oh vielen Dank! Ich war so nervös, dass ich mich selbst verraten würde. Vielleicht könnte Mai mit uns kommen."

"Nein. Du gerade nicht, ob ein williges Mitglied dieses Sklavenhändlersgruppe war oder nicht. Sobald wir die Polizei kontaktieren und sie diese Bande verhaften, können sie herausfinden, wer unschuldig oder schuldig ist."

The two women returned to the gathering; Cindy to check with Lars again and Brünnhilde to gather her things.

A short distance from where Cindy and Brünnhilde had been speaking, Estefan came around from behind a large boulder zipping up his trousers. He watched the two women as they walked away.

* * *

Weaver took in everything as the other two ground rollers backtracked to find the missing transport. He was surprised to see another ground roller. As he got closer he spotted two women he didn't know in the group. Very few women went out into the wilds of Beta without a man or two along. He had heard of one sunstone miner who was female and worked alone, but she was the exception by far.

"Bo, Clem, you see those two women?"

"Hard to miss at this range," Bo said. "Easy on the eyes…at least from here. Distance can hide a lot of ugly, if you know what I mean."

"They could be datastream models for all I care," Weaver growled. "I want to know who they are and what they're doing with our people."

"I don't see any badges," Clem said. "ZNPF cops use aircars for patrols. That is a ground roller. Better model than what we have, but way too slow to be any kind of law enforcement vehicle."

"It isn't a miner's transport, either," Bo added. "Miners, unlike us, like aircraft with servos for lifting on the front."

"Actually, they work up to that when they start to make serious sols," Clem said. "Most start out in rollers like what we are using. However, that vehicle is too new, hence expensive, for mining. Anybody who could afford that could afford a proper aircar with the servos."

Weaver nodded. "Okay. Not cops and not miners. What else is there? Those girls ain't out here just sight-seeing."

"Surveyors is a possibility," Clem said after some thought. "This area is well away from the Rez and the CZC might plan on some new project out here."

"Or they could be scientists of some kind," Bo said. He wasn't going to be out-guessed by Clem. "Botanists, xenobiologists, anthropologists. All kinds of 'ologists' could be running around out here."

Weaver nodded again. "Okay, let's go find out. Be ready in case there's trouble."

The two ground rollers pulled up and stopped a few meters away from the unfamiliar vehicle. That was when Weaver spotted a third unfamiliar face: a dark-skinned woman in the driver's seat. He started to approach when the woman got out of the roller. She moved stiffly, as one who had been sitting for a long time might do. Weaver immediately spotted the CZC uniform and security badge.

There's nothing to worry about until there's something to worry about, Weaver reminded himself. "Hello. I'm Eric Weaver. Is there something we can help you with?"

"Not at all," Erena said. "At least, not now. We just stopped to help pull that roller out of the ditch. One of the people I am with is a doctor and she checked out a man who was pinned between the roller and the ground."

"Somebody was pinned? Do you know who?"

Erena shook her head. "I didn't get close enough to catch any names. I could tell that it was a short man who is beyond muscular." She glanced over in the direction of the rest of the people. "That's him sitting on the ground rubbing his legs."

Weaver looked in the indicated direction and saw that it was Lars, though the description had already ruled out the rest of the crew. "Thank you for your assistance. These are all my people. We got separated during the quake and I came back to see what happened to our missing ground roller. I will check on them, now."

"I'll walk with you," Erena said. "I need to stretch my legs and get the kinks out."

Lars was attempting to stand, unsuccessfully, when Weaver and Erena walked over to meet the rest of the group. Weaver walked over to Lars while Erena went to see Kealani.

"How are you doing, Lars?"

Lars grunted something, then looked up at Weaver. "My legs feel like they're asleep. I can feel my toes when I wiggle them and I can move the legs. I just can't get on them, yet."

"Maybe you just need some help getting started," Weaver suggested. He called Bo and Clem over. "Help Lars up and support him while he tries to get his legs working proper."

Bo looked worried. "You sure that's a good idea?"

"Sure. He just needs to get his circulation going," Weaver said. "He can't do that planted on his arse."

Amid a number of grunts and curses, the two men got the injured Lars up, then—with a massive arm over each man's shoulders—they supported him as he tried to move his legs.

"There you go. You'll be back to dancing in no time."

Lars chuckled. "Great. I could never dance before."

Weaver went over to the ground roller to inspect the damage. Some models came with micro-collapsium lamination that made them virtually indestructible. This unit, a much cheaper used model, lacked that protection. Side panels and the front fender were dented and scratched. Weaver didn't care about that. The plan was to sell or abandon the ground rollers when they reached Betatown. Afterwards they would take a transport to Mallorysport and take the first ship going off-planet. As long as the roller could make the trip, that was fine with Weaver. As he inspected the rear tracks Estefan walked up to him.

"Boss, we have a problem."

Weaver turned his attention to Estefan. "What kind of a problem?"

"Well, you remember that I told you how I spent two years on Heimdall?" Weaver didn't recall that but told Estefan to continue. "Well, they don't take well to off-worlders who don't at least try to learn the local language. And you can't even own property there unless you are at least half-Germanic. They do a DNA test and everything to verify. I fell a bit short on that."

Weaver was starting to lose patience. "How does this relate to that problem you said we have?"

"I picked up enough German to hold my own as long as it wasn't too involved or technical," Estefan explained.

"So you're a polyglot. How is this problematic?"

"I overheard a conversation between Hilde and that doctor lady," Estefan continued. "I won't say I understood the whole thing but I caught enough to know that we are blown. Hilde knows what we were doing out here and she told Dr. Tezza."

Weaver's eyes went wide. "Are you sure?"

"I caught the word for 'slaver' and that isn't the sort of thing that comes up in casual conversation," Estefan explained. "I don't want to see anybody hurt, especially Hilde, but I want a bullet in my head a whole lot less."

"Damnit, I was hoping to avoid anything like this," Weaver said angrily. "If I could be sure we would be able to just leave them stranded and get away clean I would go for it. Unfortunately, we are getting closer to the Rez and the ZNPF patrols will increase. Tying them up would be worse than just shooting them. Something nasty could find them and have a banquet. Killing them outright would be kinder to them and safer for us."

"I would rather not kill them," Estefan said. "We all got to know Hilde pretty well. She's a nice kid."

Weaver snorted. "That nice kid can bend a crowbar like a rubber hose. All right, let's get Bo, Clem and Lars in on this and see what they think."

"What about the rest?"

"We'll inform them later. We can't have everybody gathered around for a secret discussion, now, can we?" Weaver looked over at Bo and Clem helping Lars to walk. "We have to keep it small so we don't panic our guests."

Cindy spotted Erena and waved her over. Erena was still feeling stiff and achy. Walking seemed to help a bit. She flexed her arms hoping to loosen them up as well.

"We have a problem," Kealani said. Cindy related what Brünnhilde had told her. "We can't leave that poor girl with these animals."

"She is gathering up her things, now," Cindy said. "We'll divert our route to the nearest town—"

"Damnthing Hollows," Kealani added.

"…and contact the ZNPF from there," Cindy finished.

Erena was momentarily confused. "Why not just call them now?"

"We're out of range," Kealani said. "I already tried on my hand-held. If we knew the combination I could reach the town. Too bad nobody uses living operators anymore; I could have just hit '0.'"

"We wouldn't want to be in the middle of a fire fight between this gang and the ZNPF," Cindy added. She was about to say more when she spotted Rockthrower and Maid Marian running over to them. "You were supposed to stay in hiding."

Both Fuzzies pointed at something behind the three women. They turned and saw Weaver with his men, minus Lars, coming at them. Their guns and rifles were out and they looked like they meant business.

Without thinking Erena drew her pistol while cursing herself for leaving the rifles in the ground roller. Cindy, at least, had her rifle, which she quickly moved into a ready position and set the selector switch from semi-automatic to full auto. Kealani pulled her blade and took up a martial stance. Maid Marian readied her bow while Rockthrower held her boomerang.

"Ladies, you have no chance against us if we start slinging lead at each other," Weaver said as he swept an arm around indicating his crew. "We understand that you are on to our little secret. Most of us don't want to kill you. We just want to keep you out of the way until we can get off-planet. But, if you make this difficult, we can just have it out now and be done with it. Oh, and in case you get any ideas, I was in favor of just killing you. I won't hesitate if it comes to that."

"What guarantee do we have that you won't just kill us anyway?" Kealani demanded. "If we have it out, as you say, we could take some of you with us. I am thinking we could at the very least kill you and maybe a few more before we go down."

Weaver nodded. "There is that. Consider this, we could have just played like we didn't know what you know and took you by surprise. Bo, here, can shoot the whiskers off a goofer at three-hundred meters. We could have let you ride out, then just shoot all of you from a nice comfortable distance."

Kealani considered that. "Okay. And if we just surrender, what do you plan to do with us?"

Weaver bobbed his head. "To be honest, we haven't worked that out, yet. All I can promise is that shooting you will be the last resort. My hand to Ghu."

"We won't take any of your stuff or harm the Fuzzies if you cooperate," Clem added. "We plan on traveling light, anyway."

Weaver glared at Clem for a second then nodded. "We don't want to hurt you or rob you. We just want to make sure you don't get chatty with the constabulary before we clear the ionosphere."

Kealani fumed. She knew if she was a bit closer she could change the odds. As it was, there was nothing any of them could do. "Cindy, Erena, what do you think?"

"They have more bodies and more guns," Erena said. "We have no cover to duck behind, even if we could get to it."

"He swore to Ghu not to kill us," Cindy added.

"Except as a last resort," Kealani reminded her.

"I don't see where we have an option," Erena said.

"We not fight?" Maid Marian asked.

"No, Maid Marian," Kealani said. "We not fight."

The women started to place their weapons on the ground when something bowled into Weaver's crowd from behind. Two men went flying in different directions as a third was launched into another man.

Kealani immediately went into action. She ran forward and sent a flying kick into Weaver's chest, knocking him down as he struggled to breathe. Next, she thrust the blade at the man called Clem. The blade struck something hard beneath his shirt and was turned. Kealani recovered quickly and struck Clem in the temple with the blade handle.

Erena and Cindy were much slower to join the fray. Neither dared to shoot for fear of hitting Kealani. Cindy used her rifle as a cudgel. Erena, slowed by her injuries, still tried to give better than she got. In back of the crowd, Brünnhilde continued to toss men about like rag dolls. The Fuzzies stood away from the fight as they would only get stepped on. Instead they watched and waited for the opportunity to assist with arrow and boomerang.

A shot rang out and everybody froze in place. Consuela leveled her shotgun at Kealani, whom she determined was the greatest threat. "Ladies and gentlemen, playtime is over. Girls on the right, boys on the left. You, too, Hilde."

Kealani said something blasphemous in old Tagalog as she backed away. Cindy and Erena backed up with her. The Fuzzies were nowhere in sight.

Weaver, still struggling for breath, staggered over to Kealani. "Nice… try. You saw…an opportunity and…seized it. I …respect that. The plan still holds. We won't kill…you unless…there is no…other choice."

With the men aiming rifles at the four women, Consuela quickly frisked them and took anything that could be used as a weapon or radio. Their properties, save for a set of handcuffs, were placed in an Army style foot locker and sealed with a padlock.

"Like I said; we have no interest in robbing you." Weaver took the cuffs and placed them on Brünnhilde, locking her hands behind her back. "I hate to do this, Hilde. I was getting to really like you like a kid sister."

"I am just as happy not to join your family," Brünnhilde said through gritted teeth.

Weaver smiled, then backed away. "Set up a tent and we'll put them in it after we finish tying them up. We might as well have something to eat while we hash this out."

Kealani, Cindy and Erena were quickly tied with the fibroid ropes. They all sat with Brünnhilde on the ground while the tent was being put up.

"Where did Rockthrower and Maid Marian go?" Erena asked.

"They jumped onto the dogs and made for the tree line when that woman…"

"Consuela," Brünnhilde said.

"…when Consuela fired that shotgun," Kealani finished. "At least they will be safe."

"Why bother with the tent?" Cindy mused. The others took a moment to consider.

"Look where they are setting it up," Erena said.

Everybody watched as the tent was set up over their ground roller. Cindy caught on. "They'll hide us and our vehicle in case a ZNPF patrol flies over. Four people tied up would invite investigation. The roller has CZC markings on it which might also rate a visit from *die Polizei*…um, the police. Three vehicles and a tent would just look like a campsite."

Erena nodded. "And if they decide we can't be left alive, they can kill us in the tent so the more squeamish members of their party won't see it." She let out a long sigh. "It doesn't look good for us."

Brünnhilde, who had been trying to keep her composure, began to weep. "This is all my fault. I should have waited before telling you what I learned. Eventually they would have dropped me off at some town and then I could have called the police."

"I wouldn't count on that," Kealani said. "Sooner or later the paranoia would get the better of them and they would have shot you anyway. Whoever heard you talking to Cindy must have known some German. But even if he didn't, speaking in a different language always invites negative conjecture."

"I would have used Sosti if I could be sure any of you understood it," Brünnhilde said.

"Same problem as the German," Erena said. "Um…what is Sosti?"

"The spoken language of Freya," Kealani said.

"So what do we do now?" Cindy said.

"Try to get out of these ropes." Erena struggled with her binding without effect. "Uhk. Too bad they didn't put you in ropes, Hilde. You could probably snap them."

Brünnhilde laughed out loud. "Those are fibroid ropes. The same kind we used in the mines on Magni. Nobody but nobody can snap out of those." She lowered her voice. "I have a much better chance of breaking out of these cuffs, but I'll need to work on them for a bit. As long as these aren't polysteel…?"

"Plain steel with an aluminum coating to prevent rust," Erena explained. "Strong enough to hold even a large weight-lifter. Not everything needs to be polysteel with micro collapsium lamination. Far less expensive, too."

"Do you really think you can break those?" Kealani asked. She had difficulty believing anybody could, even a heavy-worlder. "Won't you break your wrist?"

Brünnhilde smiled. "My bones are very sturdy. This won't do my skin any favors, though." She started straining to pull the chain apart. "I was right. This is going to hurt."

XXXXV

Little Fuzzy called a halt. He got down off his Curtys and checked the ground. It was too rocky to see any tread tracks. Instead, he found something else. He put a finger into a tiny spot of black liquid, then sniffed it.

"Is oil like Pappy Jack use in groun' rollers," Little Fuzzy declared.

"Does it appear to be fresh, Little Fuzzy?" Emily Dickinson asked. Little Fuzzy said it was. "We should spread out and look for another drop. That will tell us the direction they are going."

The Fuzzies all dismounted and looked about close to the ground. Sarah Balfour spotted another drop. Terro-human eyes might have missed the oil drops. Fuzzies had much better eyesight and lived much closer to the ground.

"They are still proceeding west," Emily declared. "In an almost straight line. I think we may be catching up with them."

"Good-good," Little Fuzzy said. He was about to remount, then noticed his Curtys panting. All of the dogs were panting. "Dogs need water and rest." From his backpack he pulled out a collapsible bowl and his canteen. He then poured the last of his water into the bowl. The Curtys lapped it up in no time flat. The other Fuzzies followed suit.

"When dogs done drink we walk. Let dogs rest. If we find water we make full canteen."

Everybody agreed. Emily worried that the delay might be bad for the lost girl. Little Fuzzy shook his head.

"Girl with other Big Ones. Should be hokay."

* * *

Cinda looked worried as she cut off the radio. "Who uses petroleum-based oil as a lubricant these days?"

"Pipple who buy old ground transport," Rheiner said. "Is *gut* dot dey do, or Little Fuzzy vould not have picked up die trail again. He said he is out of *Wasser*? Ve can giff him some of ours, *ja*?"

Cinda consulted the topographical map. "There is a narrow river up ahead about ten kilometers. We can all refill our water supplies there. Those ground rollers will have to either find a narrow crossing or drive next to it. This map doesn't indicate how deep the river is. If I was driving cross country, I wouldn't risk getting the vehicle stuck or outright waterlogged. Hmm…the river bows up after a while, so crossing isn't really necessary."

"If dey are looking for a town, following der rifer is best. Settlements always do best near a source of *Wasser*."

Cinda agreed. "If it looks like that's what they're doing, we can bring everybody back aboard and make better time."

"Sounds *gut* to me."

* * *

"Jack, at this speed you could fly right over the Fuzzies and not see them."

"I wouldn't be able to see any Fuzzies from up this high anyway," Jack said. "I know the direction they went and I estimated the speed of the Curtyses as they make their way back. When I get close to where I estimate they'll be, I'll slow down and get closer to the ground. I doubt I could spot the Fuzzies but Major Lunt mentioned that they met up with that Rheiner and Cinda couple. Their aircar I will definitely be able to see."

Betty looked at Jack with some confusion. "If Little Fuzzy and Emily Dickinson are with Rheiner and Cinda, wouldn't they most likely be up in the air?"

Jack shook his head. "A Fuzzy can't follow tracks from the air any better than I can. And I can't at all. Any tracker who knows his craft will want to be on the ground where he can see, hear and smell everything around him. There might be a clue no bigger than a cigarette butt. No way to spot that up here."

That made sense to Betty and she admitted it. "So, you figure if the Fuzzies are in trouble, this Rheiner will either be on the ground helping them out or in the air making for the hospital or whatever."

"Or just slowly pacing the Fuzzies as they followed the trail," Jack said. "They would need to be up pretty high to keep the whine of the contragravity engines from distracting the Fuzzies. The dogs, too, for that matter." Jack thought for a moment. "Another possibility occurred to me: the aircar could have been on the ground during the quake. It could have been damaged and now they are all afoot…or in some sort of trouble."

"Like what?"

Jack didn't answer at first. "I don't want to get myself all bothered with that. If there is a problem, we'll deal with it when we get there."

Betty looked out over the vast horizon. "Then stop driving like an old lady and give it the gas!"

Jack glanced at the speed gauge and smiled. He was already crowding the limit.

* * *

"I need to hit the can, Boss."

Jason Roberts understood and explained it to Morgan who didn't comprehend the idiom. "Now that you mention it, I need to hit the head as well."

"That makes it unanimous," Morgan grunted. "What kind of kidnapping is this, anyway? You would think they would want to take a photo of me as proof of life or something."

Jason laughed. "They only do that in the movies. Too easy to fake it up with modern computers. They could analyze the photo image and catch the fakery, but it would take a while."

"All right, then. They have no impetus to let us out of this crate. As I would rather not make a mess of these fine Freyan pants, what say we blow this soda stand?"

"Pop shop," Mike Hammer corrected. "You punch now, Boss?"

"I punch, Mike." Jason examined the wood of the crate. He had no doubt his cybernetic arm could get the job done; he just wanted to do as little damage to the artificial skin as possible. New dermal layering could be done with a spray can, but that still costs an arm and a leg, in his case almost literally. Then he remembered he was on the clock for Morgan and could bill it as "expenses."

"Here goes nothing." Instead of punching the wall of the crate, which would have been awkward to manage from his sitting position, Jason put all of his strength into twisting and sent his elbow into the wood slats at his left. His artificial arm easily went through the wood. He repeated the action until he made a passage that was wide enough for them to crawl through.

Jason poked his head out first. "Oh, they left my trench coat in here." He crawled out of the crate, then collected his prized overcoat and checked the pockets. His gun was not there. Jason turned his attention to the small room he was now in. "It looks like we are in the back of a cargo van. Nobody around. They must have left everybody but the driver and maybe the shotgun rider behind.

"Good," Morgan said. "I like those odds a lot better." He got to his feet and went to the panel that he figured separated them from the forward cab. The access was locked. "Do you think that arm of yours could break through this?"

Jason examined the panel critically. "Maybe. But I would need some pretty expensive repairs afterwards. My warranty doesn't cover reckless abuse of the equipment."

"You get us through this and I'll pay for you to get a whole new body if you want."

Jason knew Morgan was good for it. Still… "We would lose the element of surprise. I couldn't punch through in one hit no matter how hard I tried. And all that pounding will get the attention of whoever is on the other side."

Morgan nodded. He didn't like it but he understood Jason's point. "Okay, so what do we do?"

Jason looked about and spotted Mike using the one amenity. "Well, first I intend to use the mini-privy, after Mike, and then we will let him pick the lock."

Morgan recalled how quickly the Fuzzy got the cuffs off of him. "Think he can do it?"

"Well, he never tried this particular kind of lock, but the basics are all the same." Jason looked back and saw that Mike had finished his business. "Hey, is there any lower posterior sanitation tissue left?"

* * *

The police station was buzzing with activity. Chief Carr developed a new appreciation for Piet Dumont, who had held his position not so very long ago. Then again, things went a lot more smoothly when the planet was owned outright by the Charterless Zarathustra Company. There was the occasional murder, of course, and shylocking, prostitution and robbery back then as there was now. But kidnapping, slavery, terrorist attacks? All new.

On Carr's desk was the report of a contragravity cargo van missing, presumed stolen. The last time anybody stole a vehicle of any kind was when the planet's classification changed from Class III uninhabited to Class IV inhabited, courtesy of the Fuzzies. People were grabbing any aircar or lorry they could get their hands on to go and carve out a piece of land for themselves. Victor Grego filed charges and the aircars were recovered and the thieves jailed, mostly for a three- to five-year bit.

Now, after three years, another lost vehicle complaint. Chief Carr passed the complaint on to Officers Gilbert and Sullivan. He couldn't help smiling when he thought of those two. They both joined the Force at the same time and, hearing the names, Chief Dumont partnered them up. Whatever Carr thought about Piet Dumont as a police chief, he admired the man's sense of humor.

"It doesn't have a tracker on it like CZC vehicles, so you'll have to do some grunt work finding it," Carr explained.

"I can't help wondering why somebody took it," Sullivan said. "I know it's a multipurpose model, but it is way obsolete."

Gilbert looked over the report. "It would be a poor choice for a joy ride. Back when the teenagers would swipe an aircar for giggles, they would go for sleeker models used by the CZC. Grego installing trackers on them put an end to that right quick."

"It can double as a bus with the stow and go seating under the floor," Carr pointed out.

Gilbert shook his head. "We have mass transit. A stolen bus would stand out if somebody wanted to freelance as a cabbie."

"Why are vehicles usually stolen?" Sullivan said rhetorically. He held up a hand and counted off on his fingers. "One, joyriding, which we already ruled out. Two, chop shops, which never really took hold on Zarathustra. Polysteel makes it very difficult to damage, so no need for new parts. Three, you need a ride that can't be traced back to you for a different criminal enterprise. Four—"

"Wait, back that up," Gilbert interrupted. "There was another criminal action about, um," Gilbert rifled through his notepad. He preferred the old style paper. "Three hours after the cargo van was taken."

"Morgan Holloway's abduction," Sullivan and Carr said simultaneously. Carr continued, "It could be a coincidence, which I don't believe, but that may have been the getaway vehicle."

"How would the Martianists know to get this particular transport?" Sullivan asked. "They must know about the trackers in the CZC vehicles."

"Local muscle," Gilbert said. "They farmed out the job to local hoods that would be up on all the latest information about this world."

"I'm putting out an APB for that cargo van with a caution not to approach without lots of backup." Chief Carr turned on his comscreen and issued the orders. "A good show of force will keep the thieves from getting too brave."

"We should send patrols to Junktown and Mortgageville," Sullivan said. "Those are the most likely hidey-holes for something that big."

Carr nodded. "Good point."

"C'mon, Gil," Sullivan grabbed Gilbert's arm. "Let's get out there and see if we can find this thing before some rookie gets lucky and steals our collar."

XXXXVI

Gus Brannhard had just sat down and gotten comfortable when his door buzzed. He knew who it was so he tapped the button that allowed the door to slide silently into the wall.

"Ned, good to see you," Gus said as he stood up to shake Ned's hand. "So, what calamity faces us now?"

"Those Khooghras from Terra know you are back and are waiting outside Deputy Governor Juan Takagashi's office," Ned said as he sat in one of the fur draped chairs. "They have been chomping at the bit the entire time you were over on Zeta. Since Mr. Takagashi selected you to represent him, we can't put it off any longer."

Gus chuckled. "Supervisor Sylvinski should have considered that before taking his trip to Neu Freya. As an officer of Ben's Cabinet, it fell to me to escort him over. I'll bet he didn't see that one coming."

"Was it really your responsibility?"

Gus shook his head. "Nah. Ben could have selected a janitor if he wanted to. I asked him and he was good with sending me. Inconveniencing Sylvinski's headhunters was just an added bonus." Gus stood up and Ned followed his example. "Well, let's go get it done."

As they left the office, Ned spoke low and asked if Gus thought Juan Takagashi was guilty of anything. Gus shrugged. "No point speculating. We'll know in a few minutes."

They took the lift up to the floor where both Governor and Deputy Governor had their offices. As expected, Farquar and Burr were sitting in the outer office.

Farquar was first out of his seat. "Mr. Brannhard, Mr. Foster, thank you for coming so quickly. We are just waiting for Captain Trask to join us."

"Oh?" Gus feigned that he wasn't aware of that wrinkle. "Why?"

Burr spoke up. "If there has been a crime committed here, it has crossed planetary orbits. As such it is in the FBCI's jurisdiction."

Both Gus and Ned knew all this. Gus just wanted Burr to think he wasn't as knowledgeable as he should be. Sometimes it paid to be underestimated.

"Captain Trask is with the Marshal right now," Ned said. "He might not be able to break away just yet."

As if on cue, Trask entered the room. "My apologies, gentlemen. There is another case that I am involved in, so let's try to make this quick."

The secretary, who had been speaking softly to a comscreen with a headset on, told the group that the Deputy Governor would see them now. The door to the office retracted into the wall and they all went in. Everybody immediately noticed the polyencephalographic veridicator in the corner.

"I took the liberty of having it brought up so as not to disturb anybody else with this mess," Takagashi said. "And to keep the news services out of it. I do not want it to appear that high officials can be veridicated at the drop of a hat."

"We will need to test the machine to be sure it hasn't been tampered with," Trask said. He turned to face Farquar and Burr. "It will have to be one of you two if we want to be certain it is accurate."

"Why us?" Burr blurted out.

"Because we need a test subject that can't be compromised," Trask explained. "Everybody else here are friends and coworkers. Besides, we can't put Deputy Governor Takagashi's lawyer in the hot seat."

Burr recalled a regulation that prevented council from being veridicated unless they were directly involved in a crime. "That leaves me out as well."

Farquar shrugged. "I'll do it. Just don't get too personal with the questions."

"Fair enough," Gus said. "Captain, would you like to do the honors?"

Trask attached the electrodes and lowered the skull cap on Farquhar's cranium then activated the equipment.

"We'll try to make this as painless as possible, Mr. Farquar," Trask said.

Under his breath, Gus said, "Oh, you could make him squirm a little."

If Trask heard that he didn't show it. "We'll start with your full name."

"Hickabbible Thelonious Farquar." The globe stayed blue.

"This time tell a lie."

"I am a bat-winged Gimlian shaman who turns into a Thoran during a full moon." Red.

Gus privately gave Farquar points for his imagination.

"Have you ever kissed a Khooghra?"

"Hell, no!" Blue.

Gus and Ned suppressed a chuckle.

"If Juan Takagashi is found guilty of any crimes, will you and your boss get a promotion?"

"Don't answer that!" Burr said excitedly. "This goes well beyond the scope of a test question."

"Clarence, relax," Farquar told the attorney. "I don't mind answering that. In order for me to get promoted, Supervisor Sylvinski will have to be promoted. He told me long ago that I was his choice to replace him. However, I have no way of knowing if catching anybody on this planet with their hand in the cookie jar will have any effect at all on promotions. My sole interest is doing the job and doing it well. Period."

The globe stayed blue throughout the entire statement. Gus was impressed. Farquar wasn't expecting any brownie points on this mission. He wished he could get Sylvinski in the chair and ask him the same question.

Trask turned to everybody in the room. "I am satisfied if you are." Gus, Ned and Burr all nodded. "Okay, Deputy Governor. If you please."

Trask removed the electrodes and skull cap from Farquar, wiped them down with an alcohol wipe and placed them on Takagashi. To his credit, the deputy governor didn't appear to be the least bit nervous.

"Please state your name for the record."

"Juan Guillermo Secondus Akito Kisho Takagashi." Blue.

Trask shook his head. "I'm glad I don't have to sign your name. Okay, did you serve under Colonial Governor Ross Martin on Odin for a period of five Terran years?"

"Yes." Blue.

"Was Ross Martin ever charged with a crime?"

"Yes." Blue.

"What was he charged with?"

"For accepting bribes, kickbacks and giving government contracts to his friends."

Blue.

"Were you ever investigated for those same crimes?"

"Yes. I was found to be innocent of all charges." Blue.

"Did you ever have direct knowledge of Ross Martin's malfeasance in office?"

"Not at first. I didn't know anything for sure until shortly before he was charged." The globe wavered between a deep purple and blue.

"It appears that you are holding something back. Would you care to elaborate?"

"It has nothing to do with this line of questioning and I would prefer that it not become public knowledge," Takagashi said. The globe stayed an unwavering blue.

Burr said accusingly, "Deputy Governor, our warrant specifically states that you must answer all questions relating to your time on Odin, barring details from your personal life while there."

"I am afraid he is correct," Gus said.

Takagashi sighed then said, "I heard rumors about the governor's cronyism. I dismissed them, at first, as the usual mudslinging every politician is subjected to. But the rumors got out of hand so I started a private investigation. It was I who alerted the authorities of Martin's illegal activities." The globe remained blue.

"Why wouldn't you want that to get out?" Ned asked. "It seems to me you are something of a hero for bringing down a crooked governor."

"Yes, one with a bull's-eye on his back," Takagashi said. "Martin had some very powerful friends. Some of them in organized crime. If my involvement in bringing Martin down became public knowledge I could wind up having a very sudden and lethal accident. That is one of the reasons I left Odin."

"If anybody in this room spreads this story, I will personally have them charged with reckless endangerment," Gus said in a stern voice.

Burr protested. "You can't do that. The news services dig up information like that all the time and put it on the six o'clock report."

"Oh, I absolutely can," Gus rumbled. "Maybe I can or can't make it stick, but I guarantee the blabbermouth in question will go bankrupt fighting the charges. Ten will get you twenty that the veridicator will back up that I believe it."

"Don't let him take your money, Mr. Burr," Ned said. "Gus Brannhard never made an idle threat in his life."

Burr just shrugged. "I have no intention of repeating anything I hear in here save for what bears directly on this case. Captain Trask, can we go for the main question?"

Trask turned his attention back to Juan Takagashi. "Alright, this one is for the jackpot. Were you aware of a substantial amount of money vanishing from the Odin governmental treasury?"

"Not until recently." Blue.

"Too vague," Burr objected. "He might consider ten years ago as 'recent.'"

Trask had to agree. This was one of the few tricks people could use to fool a prosecutor when on the stand. Nothing could fool the veridicator, but the questions needed to be very precise.

"Just ask him flat out," Burr demanded.

Trask cleared his throat. "Deputy Governor did you or anyone under your direction remove or hide any amount of money from the Odin treasury?"

"Very well. No, I did not at any time take any money from the treasury save for what was on my paycheck." Blue. "Now, unless there is something else I am charged with I would like to get back to my duties."

Burr conceded defeat and Farquar thanked everybody for their time before leaving. Trask made his excuses and left for the marshal's office. Ned shook the deputy governor's hand then left. Only Gus remained behind.

Takagashi returned to his desk and shuffled a few papers. "Was there something else, Gus?"

Gus took a seat and looked the deputy governor squarely in the eye.

"While I am pleased that we can put this matter to bed, it strikes me that you may have actually fooled everybody in the room."

"Oh?" Takagashi put a surprised look on his face. "How so?"

Gus leaned forward and kept his voice low. "There is another trick that can fool the interrogator while having the veridicator bear him out."

"And what would that be?" Takagashi seemed very interested.

"You told us that the only money you ever took from the treasury was your paycheck."

"Yes?"

Gus smiled. "If I were going to rob the treasury, it strikes me that the easiest way to do so is to jigger the finance computer into moving a decimal point back one or two spaces. The funds would be multiplied by a factor of ten or more and would go straight into the recipient's bank. It would take a subpoena to get the bank records of those deposits. Not likely to happen while the governor is being impeached and all attention is on him. But even if it is discovered simply claim it must be a glitch in the finance computers. Give the money back, no harm, and no foul. Of course, he would avoid detection a lot longer if he made the computer put the decimal point back where it belonged after the transfer was complete.

"Then, after the governor is convicted and doing time on Odin's moon, a clever embezzler could skip planet and set up a practice on another world, and live very comfortably. At least, until a bench warrant was issued for all suspects in the missing funds. Then that person would have to close up shop and move to another world; preferably one where ship to shore data transfer hasn't come into use, yet. Then, if the warrant ever caught up with that person and he was put in the chair, he could say the only treasury funds he ever received were in his paycheck, and the veridicator would back him up."

Gus shifted in his seat, then added, "Of course, by the time anybody caught up with the embezzler the Statute of Limitations may have run out, in which case he could just thumb his nose at the police. Had I been asking the questions, I would have phrased it differently."

Takagashi let out a long, low whistle. "Sounds to me like a very clever criminal, though not as smart as you, it would appear. Okay, do you want to put me back in chair and see if you are right?"

Gus smiled again. "No."

Confusion colored the Deputy Governor's face. "No?"

"You and Ben are the government around here. As the Chief Colonial Prosecuting Attorney you are both my clients and I am subject to the rules of client confidentiality. But as a lawyer yourself, one who worked in a governor's office, you would already know that."

"Hmm…then I guess you should put me back in the chair and verify your suspicions," Takagashi said. "No point agonizing over it."

"No point," Gus replied. "I won't lose any sleep over it either way. If you are innocent, it doesn't matter. If you actually did liberate those funds and I verified it, it still wouldn't matter. I can't tell anybody. Not even Ben. Not even if he fired you. Again, you already know that. Of course, it would be a different story if you did something like that here."

Juan set down the papers he had been shuffling and leaned forward a little. "Well, you could at least settle it in your own mind."

"Oh, I am settled, either way," Gus said. "If you did it, then you are a very sharp person and Ben needs somebody like that to rely on. Politics are a bitch and he is still new to the whole thing. And being caught with your hand in the cookie jar, as Farquar put it, would reflect badly on Ben. We don't need a scandal like that in a brand new government. Especially with Sylvinski's crew around to muck things up even more."

"Hmm. Well, let's hope I am that sharp anyway."

"There is one thing I can do," Gus said as he stood up and went to the door. "I can borrow a couple of the CZC's computer geniuses, or even that Frank Farmer who is working for Sylvinski, and have them give our finance computers a solid once-over. Afterwards we can set up an early warning system that would watch for that kind of activity. I am referring to the hypothetical embezzlement, of course. And the one thing I cannot and will not keep silent about is any malfeasance or misfeasance in office that I discover. What happened on Odin can stay on Odin, but anything that happens here will have my undivided attention. Thank you for your time, sir."

Juan Takagashi shook his head and smiled as he watched Gus leave.

XXXXVII

"...place the artifacts in the aircar when the hatch opens. It will be remotely operated so there will be no chance of arresting anybody to interrogate. There will be bug detection equipment installed inside. It will not take off if any transmitters are detected. We want the relics but will take no chances. If you try anything cute, we will execute either the man or the Fuzzy that were picked up with Mr. Holloway. Do not underestimate our resolve in this. After we receive the artifacts, we will send you a message letting you know how to find Mr. Holloway and his companions. You will not hear from us again until the transaction has been completed to our satisfaction."

The image of the garish mask faded to black and Marshal Fane set the comscreen to quiescent mode. With him were Governor Ben Rainsford, Captain Trask, Police Chief Carr and, most recently, Gus Brannhard.

"As you can see, aside from the mask, they used a voice distorter and some kind of blank background," the Marshal explained.

"The mask looked familiar," Rainsford said.

"They copied the design from that old 'Martian Chronicles' mini-series from, oh, six hundred years ago," Trask explained. "I've been to Mars and they have tourist traps loaded with that kind of stuff."

"Did anybody see anything in the background that might help us locate these mutts?" Marshal Fane asked. "It just looked like a blank wall to me."

"I would bet that background panel was military grade fibroid," Trask said. "It would act like a combination infra-red blocker and Faraday Cage."

"Faraday Cage?" Gus said.

"It blocks signals from computers and comscreens," Carr said. "If these maniacs are someplace they shouldn't be, this would keep us from spotting them with Eye-Are scanners or electromagnetic fields, such as what comes off computers and comscreens. The military uses it as part of their camouflage."

"They could be in the building next door and we wouldn't be able to detect them," Marshal Fane added. "These people are not amateurs. Or, at least, one of them isn't."

"What about the power grid?" Carr pointed at the map on his wall. "If they are someplace like Mortgageville or Junktown where power usage is low to non-existent, they should register a spike on the grid."

"Assuming they are not using a military power generator," Marshal Fane countered. "Those things have baffles to keep the enemy from finding encampments. We can still look into it, but I am not sanguine about our chances of catching them that way."

"So what are we going to do?" Rainsford asked. "I asked Victor Grego to track the movement of the artifacts with satellite surveillance. Unfortunately, if that remote aircar goes undercover, like in a dense forest, he can't guarantee that the satellites won't lose it."

"Don't worry about that, Governor," Fane said. "We have some help with that."

Before the Marshal could elaborate, an officer entered the room with a plate of sandwiches and a fresh pot of coffee. "Who asked for the veldbeest and who gets the riverpig ham?"

"Just set it on the conference table, Marci. Thank you." Fane turned back to the others. "Dig in. I am sending Officer's Gilbert and Sullivan—"

"Seriously?" Trask said.

The Marshal chuckled. "I know, right? Blame Piet Dumont for pairing them up. But they are good officers. As I was saying, the 'Opera Boys' will deliver the package. No surprise the Martianists picked the park. No surveillance cameras set up there and lots of trees. That dense canopy like Governor Rainsford mentioned. Normally we would use a spy-eye to follow the aircar. Unfortunately, it would be pretty easy to spot once they got out of the park, assuming they don't have counter-surveillance gear. At this point I wouldn't doubt that they do. These clowns are nuts but not stupid."

"We had some Martianists come through Sydney a few years back," Trask said. "I was assigned to attend their seminars to make sure it wasn't some kind of pyramid scheme or beachfront property on Mars scam. The speaker was passionate without being manic about it. He went on about the similarities in DNA between Terro-humans, Freyans and Martians. Did you know that Freyan DNA is even closer to Martian DNA than our own?"

"For the love of Ghu, don't go down that rabbit hole," Rainsford said. "I heard enough of that from Ruth van Riebeek. Please, just get to your point."

"Apologies, Governor. My point is that they are not all crackpots."

Rainsford snorted. "I'll admit, the similarity in DNA between the three races can't be explained away as convergent evolution. I'll even allow for the possibility that some Martians made it to Terra. But all the way to Freya? No. Can't buy it. And being able to breed with Neanderthals? No. Definitely not buying it."

"Ah, as fascinating as this is, shouldn't we be concentrating on the case before us?" Chief Carr interrupted.

"Actually, there isn't anything else we can do until we make the drop," Marshal Fane said. "I'll put all the patrol cars on high alert with instructions to observe only, not to approach."

Chief Carr nodded and left after snagging a couple sandwiches. Once back in his office, he called in his detectives.

"We have reason to believe that these terrorists are using military grade fibroid weave. That stuff doesn't just grow on trees."

"Ah, actually Chief, the base components are harvested from—"

"Okay, Fritz, I'll amend that statement; it doesn't just grow on trees on this planet," Carr said with some exasperation. "W,e need to pull the ships' manifests for the last month or so to see if it was brought in and who with. Fritz, thank you for volunteering. It could also have been bought here in the city. Clint, you check all the stores and outlets that carry stuff like that. Army surplus, tent and camping supply stores, that sort of thing."

"On it, Chief."

"Matt, check with the military…"

"You think these skells went all the way to Xerxes and raided the supplies?"

Chief Carr rolled his eyes. "Of course not. Anybody who tried would be so much space dust. Commodore Napier doesn't like uninvited guests dropping by. There is, however, that new Navy base just outside of Mallorysport." Matt Kolinsky winced at the reminder and mentally kicked himself. "Any other places you boys can think of?"

"Black market," Wayne Blake supplied. "Anything that hasn't been locked in a collapsium-plated vault finds its way there sooner or later."

Carr already knew that. He just wanted to see if his men were running on all cylinders. "Good idea, Wayne. Why don't you cover that angle, unless somebody here already has an in with the BM crowd?"

"I have a CI who can help with that," Simon Steppenwolf said. "I can work with Wayne on this."

"Excellent. The rest of you team up with whomever you think you can assist on their assignments. And we're under the gun, guys. I would have liked to start all of you on this a lot sooner but we didn't know about the fibroid weave until about ten minutes ago. We need to break this fast if we want to get the hostage back. Make that plural: hostages. Use whatever resources we have and draft any beat cop you need. The CZC cops found Brannhard last year. I don't want them beating us to Morgan Holloway, too."

The detectives started to file out when Matt Kolinsky had a thought. "Transportation," he said.

"Come again?"

"Chief, if these guys are moving around a lot of military grade fibroid, they ain't gonna hump it around on their backs. They'll need a cargo van: bought, rented or stolen."

Carr blinked. "Damn! Good call, Matt. You just won the point you lost back again with interest. You think they stole it?"

Matt thought it over. "No. Vehicle theft on Alpha is so rare as to be unique. As such, it gloms too much attention. Renting would leave a bigger paper trail than just buying a lorry outright. Secondhand sales would be a lot harder to trace than from a dealership though they might not have considered that. We'll have to scan the datastream for any used vehicles up for sale in the last month and track down the sellers."

"Very good. You follow up on that and, um, Chan, you take the

Navy base. Anybody else with a flash of insight?"

"Where did they get a remote-controlled contragravity vehicle?"

That one brought Carr up short. "Good question, Sheila. You run that down if you can. They might have just bought an aircar and did some after-market work on it."

Sheila Witherspoon nodded. "In which case the mod-kit had to be bought here as it would be specific to the make and model of the aircar. I can't imagine they could even guess what would be available on a fairly new colony planet. That might be the place for me to start."

"Excellent thinking," Chief car said. "Run with it. Anybody else? No? Then let's get to it."

* * *

As Brünnhilde strained to break her cuffs, Cindy and Kealani scooted themselves into a back-to-back position hoping to undo each other's bindings…without success.

"In the old flatties it always looked easier to untie somebody like this," Kealani commented.

Erena watched then sighed. "We don't have a script that says we break free and turn the situation around." She looked closer at the ropes. "Forget it. These knots were tied by somebody who really knows what they're doing. We need a sharp knife. Broken glass won't get through fibroid rope—not that we have any of that, either."

"We have to do something," Cindy said, as she fought rising panic. She didn't have the background and training Erena and Kealani did. "I'm afraid they'll just decide to shoot us."

There was a noise behind Erena. She turned her head as much as she was able and spotted two Fuzzies coming in under the tent wall. It was Maid Marian and Rockthrower.

"Am I glad to see you two!" Erena barely remembered to whisper. Are your chopper-diggers sharp?"

"Yes, Aunty Erena," Maid Marian responded.

"Great! See if you can cut these ropes," Erena said. "Try not to cut me while you are at it."

The Fuzzies went at it with gusto. Maid Marian worked on Erena's ropes while Rockthrower went for Cindy's bindings. Kealani watched as Maid Marian sawed at the fibroid cords.

"It isn't going well," Kealani said. "Either the blade isn't sharp enough or Maid Marian isn't strong enough."

Brünnhilde watched the Fuzzies try to saw through the ropes with very little success. Ignoring the pain of the cuffs digging into her wrists, she used all of her strength in a last ditch effort to break free.

* * *

Everybody sat around the campfire discussing what to do with the four women in the tent. Weaver listened patiently hoping somebody would come up with an idea that allowed them to leave the prisoners behind without killing them. Not that Weaver was opposed to killing anybody. He had been ready to kill all of the Fuzzies they had captured instead of gassing them and slipping away. Killing was easy. Getting away with it afterwards tended to be more of a problem.

"We can disable their ground roller and radio and leave them here," Clem suggested. "It would take a long time for them to walk back."

Bo shook his head. "No good. They could start a fire and get the attention of the ZNPF during a patrol."

"Leave them tied up inside of their roller," Estefan said. "A parked transport wouldn't be cause for alarm. The squad cars would fly over it a few times before settling down to investigate."

"Too risky," Consuela said. "A ZNPF cop might want to just pay a friendly visit for no other reason than they are bored or want to cadge a cup of coffee."

Weaver decided it was time to speak up. "We don't know how far we are from Betatown. And even if we did, we don't know the condition of the terrain after that ground quake. We still haven't been hit by the aftershock, yet. Look, I don't take any pleasure in this, but I see no way out other than to bury them."

"I'll stay."

Weaver turned his head to the direction of the voice. It was Lars.

"Lars, staying behind is as good as getting a bullet in the head," Weaver said.

Lars nodded. “I understand. But my legs aren’t coming back the way they should. Still all tingly. I can barely walk as it is. You can’t be saddled with a gimp. You need to move and move fast. I’ll stay here and take one for the team. Besides, I think Hilde is sweet on me. She might help me to get away later.”

“’Might’ is a pretty small word to hang your hopes on…

“I’ll stay, too.” This time it was Mai. “I didn’t know what I was getting into when I came out with you. I might get some…um…”

“Consideration,” supplied Lars.

“Yeah, that.” Mai stood up. “And Lars wouldn’t be able to manage on his own with his legs all wobbly. I’ll risk it if it means we don’t have to kill anybody, especially Hilde. She’s even younger than I am.”

Everybody started speaking at once. Consuela was against leaving Mai behind. Estefan backed her up. Bo and Clem thought it was a good idea. The rest argued among themselves until Weaver let out an ear-splitting whistle.

“I don’t like leaving anybody behind, but Lars is right about needing to move fast. I still don’t want to leave him behind with his legs all stove up. However, if Mai is here to tend to him, then I think it is a reasonable plan. If his legs improve, he might be able to still get away. As for Mai, all she did was cook for us. Out here in the ass-crack of nowhere, the cops can hardly blame her for not running away from us. I think she’ll get probation at the most. So, are we all agreed?”

There was some grumbling but all agreed. “Good. It’s settled. Clem, Bo, come with me.” Weaver led the two men well away from the rest. “All right, here is what I want you to do. Tonight while everybody is asleep, go into the tent and slit everybody’s throat. All four of them.”

Clem was shocked. “But we all agreed to….”

“I am not leaving Lars behind,” Weaver said. “He is worth twice his weight in damnthings, stove up legs or no. Once we get to another planet we can take him to a doctor who can get him all patched up. Guys like Lars are few and far between on any planet, and I don’t want to lose him.”

“What about Mai,” Bo asked.

“We can drop her off in Mallorysport, or maybe even in Betatown.”

Weaver thought for a moment. "Bo, do you still have those sunstones?"

Bo patted a pocket. "Right here, Weaver."

"Fine. We'll leave most of our paper money with Mai to get resettled with. We can cash out those stones on the next planet we land on."

"Why not sell them here?" Clem asked.

Weaver resisted the temptation to smack the other man. "Because they will be about three times more valuable on another world."

"Hey, the rest of the group isn't going to like our killing those gals," Bo said. "Not after voting to leave them alive."

"No, I don't imagine they will." Weaver thought it over. "Ah! In my trail bag I have some bush goblin claws. After you kill them use the claws to scratch up the bodies real good. We can explain that the fibroid weave of the tent kept us from hearing what was going on."

"What about those two Fuzzies that ran off during the donnybrook?"

Weaver looked at Clem. "Damn! They took off in all of the hullabaloo. Did they have those dogs with them?"

"I didn't see any dogs, but I wasn't lookin' for them either," Clem admitted.

Weaver swore. "That changes everything. Go kill the women now. The rest of us are going to pack up and get. Leave the tent behind. We would have to dump it anyway. I'll smooth it over with the rest."

Now Bo was confused. "Why the rush?"

Weaver backhanded Bo before answering. "Because those Fuzzies most likely went looking for help. ZNPF help! And we don't have the time to try to track them down to stop them. Moreover, they probably know exactly where they are going and we don't. For all we know, the ZNPF could be headed this way even as we speak. Now get going, both of you. I want to be anywhere else but here when a patrol comes looking for us."

Bo and Clem ran to the tent while Weaver rousted the rest of the group. A minute later Bo and Clem came running back. "That was fast."

"Not fast enough," Bo said. "They're gone." He held up the severed ropes and the mangled hand-cuff chain.

The sharp chill of fear washed over Weaver. "Everybody listen up!

We are completely blown. If it ain't packed and we can live without it, leave it behind. We bug out in five minutes. Anybody not in a roller by then gets left behind. Now MOVE!"

XXXXVIII

Jack slowed the aircar and looked down at the ground. "We have to land," he said with annoyance.

"Is something wrong?" Betty said.

"Fool that I am, I left the Rez with only half a tank," Jack grunted. "We have to land so I can pull the reserve cans out of the boot and top off."

"Oh. Well, luckily we have those reserves."

Jack shook his head. "Luck had nothing to do with it. I made it policy for all vehicles to carry reserves. I got stranded once, oh, twenty odd years ago because the aircar I was in ran out of fuel and swore I would never get caught short again."

The aircar landed and Jack quickly got out and started putting the reserves into the tank. "I wish to Ghu that Juan Jimenez's people would work out the kinks in installing the Abbot Lift and Drive into smaller vehicles. Then everything would run on the atomic batteries which last damn near forever. Hmm. This might leave us short for the return trip. We'll hit the next village and top everything off, then get going again."

Jack tossed the empty cans back in the trunk, then jumped back in and took his seat swearing under his breath the whole way. Betty tried to comfort him.

"Jack, you told me many times that there is nothing to worry about until there is something to worry about."

"I should have known that my words would come back to bite me," Jack said. "Little Fuzzy disappeared on me three times, Betty. The first time was a day or two after we discovered each other. I was upset the first time but we hadn't completely bonded, yet. I figured he had something he needed to do and respected it. Fortunately, what he needed to do was go collect his family and bring them to my homestead. I went from one Fuzzy to six overnight. Then along came Cinderella and Goldilocks." Pain crossed his brow as he recalled what had happened to Goldilocks a short time later.

"Then my Fuzzies, the whole family, except for Baby Fuzzy, were taken away from me and put in cages at the CZC Science Center. They escaped easily, then vanished from the face of the planet. Literally, as it turned out. I started drinking pretty heavily around that time. When they were returned to me by the Navy, I was so happy I totally forgot I was in court at the time."

Betty nodded. She had heard about much of this before.

"Then Little Fuzzy got himself lost out at Yellowsand. I don't mind admitting I was a wreck. It was pure luck I was able to rescue him from that forest fire he and those wild Fuzzies accidently started. I just don't know if I could survive something like that again."

"Jack, you are the strongest man I know," Betty said. "And right now we don't know if Little Fuzzy and Emily Dickinson are even in any danger at all. How many times have you told people not to treat Fuzzies like babies because they survived umpteen-thousand years without us Big Ones to hold their hand? Right now you need to remind yourself of that."

Jack smiled. "Betty, my love, you are absolutely right. You know, Pat would have said the exact same thing to me. Only she would have smacked me on the back of the head, first."

Betty folded her arms over her chest. "Next time I'll do just that."

* * *

"Make aircar go down, Unka Rheiner," Little Fuzzy yelled excitedly.

Since the tracks vanished they had been following the river. Cinda suggested that the Fuzzies and dogs rest a while in the aircar. Emily Dickinson nearly fainted but went along. She sat in the back with her eyes tightly shut and her hands over her ears. Little Fuzzy was torn between watching for tracks, which was difficult from the air, and comforting Emily. Sarah Balfour and James Hutton took over trying to make Emily feel safe.

Rheiner took the aircar down to ten feet before he saw what Little Fuzzy was so excited about. "T'ree sets of tracks. You haff fery gute eyes, *mein Herr*."

"Need to look closer," Little Fuzzy insisted.

Rheiner landed and the Fuzzies all jumped out with the dogs. Emily Dickinson was the first one to hit the ground.

"What are they looking for," Cinda asked.

"I t'ink dey look for die oil drops," Rheiner guessed.

They watched the Fuzzies go back and forth between the tracks in the dirt until one of them, Sarah Balfour, pointed at something on the ground. The rest joined her, looked down then nodded, a habit they had picked up from their Big Ones. They waited a moment for the dogs to attend to some overdue business before returning to the aircar.

"We stay on ground," Little Fuzzy declared. "Tracks go away from water."

Emily Dickinson breathed a sigh of relief. She was only too happy to stay out of the aircar.

"Hokay," Little Fuzzy yelled. "We go!"

* * *

Brünnhilde rubbed her wrists where the cuffs had dug into her flesh. Once she broke out of the restraints, she took over using the chopper-digger blade to sever the ropes. It would have taken longer than any of them liked to simply untie them. Once Erena's hands were free, she pulled a spare key out of a pocket and unlocked what was left of the cuffs. Now, behind a newly created rock formation kicked up by the quake, they hid and watched the camp.

The Fuzzies were instructed to mount their dogs and get to the nearest ZNPF station or any human village and tell somebody what had happened. The Fuzzies wanted to stay and fight the bad Big Ones. It took some doing but finally the Fuzzies were convinced it was for the best.

"What do we do now?" Brünnhilde said aloud. She was immediately shushed.

"One of those people might have hailed from a planet with a thin atmosphere," Kealani explained half in a whisper. "They practically have super-hearing in a denser atmosphere."

"I thought they would have come looking for us," Cindy said. "Instead they are packing up to leave."

"They took the keys to the ground roller," Erena said. "They'll figure that we'll be stranded until help comes. Without the keys we are locked out of the roller and have no protection from the wildlife. They tossed all of the gear they took from us into the roller as well. What they don't know is I have a spare set of keys where we can get at them."

"Do you carry spare keys for everything?" Cindy asked.

"Damn straight. I got myself locked out of my house one time during a storm. By the time my husband got home with the kids I had a nasty cold and walking pneumonia. It took three days to shake that off even with the antivirals the doc gave me. As soon as I was able to leave the house, I got duplicates of all my keys and set them up in hidey holes in case of just such an emergency."

"I think I'll do that when I get home," Kealani said. "So, as Brünnhilde said, 'what do we do now?'"

"Why didn't we just take the ground roller and drive away?" Cindy asked.

"Because they have three ground rollers to our one and might have overtaken us," Erena explained. "Okay, we need to plan our next move."

"We wait for them to leave, then get our ground roller and go straight to the police," Cindy said.

"That won't work," Erena said. "Remember how I was the last one up behind these rocks? That is because I pulled all the fuses out of their ground rollers. They won't be going anywhere. I was hoping we could just drive away with them stranded but they found out we were gone too fast."

"That was gutsy," Kealani said. "But won't they just pile into our roller and make tracks?"

Erena winced. "Damn. I should have thought of that."

"There are too many of them for one ground roller," Cindy said. "Even if they toss all of our equipment out."

"I wouldn't put it past that Weaver guy to shoot the extra personnel and take off with whoever is left." Kealani looked over the grounds. "You know, we might be able to take the lot of them down."

"What?" Cindy and Erena said in harmony.

Kealani put some effort into sounding more confident than she actually was. "Sure. Most of those clowns can barely throw a punch. I sized them up pretty well when we had that dustup earlier. And the only one down there I would be the least bit concerned about is laid up."

"You mean Lars," Brünnhilde said. "Yes, Lars was the only one who might be stronger than me down there. I was never trained to fight like you, Kealani, but I know how to throw a punch. I was cautioned to be careful of the people on this planet when we first came here."

"Cautioned? Of what?"

Brünnhilde smiled. "Father said that the people of this world were somewhat, um, fragile, Cindy."

Kealani looked over Brünnhilde's powerful physique. "Let me see you throw a punch." Brünnhilde complied. "Okay, when you do that you need to twist at the hips, keep your wrist straight and let your shoulder do most of the work. Also, concentrate on striking your target with these two knuckles." Kealani tapped the index and middle finger knuckles. "These are the hardest and less likely to break if you hit something too hard."

Brünnhilde tried again.

"Yes, that will be much more effective," Kealani said. "How well can you take a punch?"

Brünnhilde shrugged. "I don't know. Nobody ever punched me."

"With her strength she might kill somebody like that," Erena said.

Kealani did not look happy when she said, "We are outnumbered by armed assailants who I believe will not hesitate to kill any and all of us." She turned back to Brünnhilde. "You might have to kill people with your bare hands today. Do you think you'll be able to do that if you have to?"

Brünnhilde thought it over carefully. She had never even been in a fight until she attacked the men who were threatening these three women. She could never bring herself to hurt Mai. Weaver she felt she would have less trouble with. "I really don't know."

Erena interrupted. "We may have to find out soon. A few of them are coming this way."

"*Scheiße*," Cindy said. "They are all spreading out."

"I guess they want their fuses back," Kealani said. "We can't defend this position. We need to get to those trees. Fast!"

Eugene, Rick and Eva walked boldly up to the rock formation. The three of them felt they had little enough to fear from the escapees since they had no weapons.

"Maybe they went into the tree line," Rick suggested. "I'm not a fan of going in there."

"Neither am I," agreed Eugene. "But I am even less of a fan of being stuck out here waiting for the ZNPF to come haul us away. You know how that will end." His left hand formed the shape of a gun and he pointed it at his temple. "Bang."

"Eugene, take point," Eva commanded. "Rick, cover my six. And that doesn't mean stare at it."

"You got it, Sarge," Rick said. Everybody called Eva "Sarge" as she was the only one with actual military training.

"Six feet apart," Eva ordered. "Remember, they could be behind each tree we come to."

The trio proceeded into the forest. Rick twisted back and forth every time he passed a tree. In his mind's eye he saw them all waiting with a branch or rock ready to dash his brains out.

From behind, Eva watched to see if somebody circled a tree when Eugene approached it. Nobody spoke. When the canopy of leaves cut off the sunlight, even "Sarge" was ready to turn around. Darkness was the friend of the enemy in this instance.

Just as she was ready to order them to turn around, Eva heard a noise behind her. She twisted around to see nothing. Rick was gone.

"We have to retreat," Eva said. There was no reply. She looked back and Eugene had vanished. She tried to look in every direction at once. She considered sending a spray of bullets all around but was afraid she would hit her own men. She started back out of the tree line when something tripped her. She tried to look up when something hit the back of her head, then all went dark.

Brünnhilde dropped down from the tree branch she had been perched on. Under one arm was the unconscious Rick. She felt giddy. It had been so easy for her to just reach down and grab the man, then pull him up before he could scream a warning to the others. The thick leaves hid her from view so thoroughly she might as well have been invisible. From her vantage point she saw Kealani punch the point man in the throat, then pull him behind the tree where she had been waiting. Cindy, who had been hiding under the fallen leaves, tripped the woman while Erena struck her from behind.

"Is everybody still breathing," Kealani asked.

"I am, and so is, um, Rick," Brünnhilde said. "He hit his head on a branch when I lifted him. He is having a nice nap, now."

"Sarge here is still breathing," Erena said.

"That makes it a hat trick," Kealani declared. "Tear up their shirts to tie them up with."

After considerable grunting and cursing Cindy and Erena admitted they couldn't tear the fabric. Neither could Kealani, who cursed softly in Tagalog about everything on this planet being made so durable. The only sharp object they had, they had left with the Fuzzies and none of the prisoners had a blade with them. Kealani looked at the prisoners and shook her head wondering what kind of idiot went out in the field without a good blade. Brünnhilde strained a bit, then the shirts came apart in her hands.

Kealani played lookout while the rest tied up the prisoners. "Don't forget to gag them," she said. "We don't want them to ruin the surprise."

"And now we have weapons," Erena added lifting the rifle she took from Eugene. "We can continue attacking them with stealth but it is nice to have some equalizers if we need them."

XXXXIL

Jared Washington rummaged around in the janitor's closet. Most janitorial work was handled by maintenance robots with built-in floor buffers, vacuum attachments and even built-in squeegees. Fortunately, there were still positions on the janitorial staff best handled by humans.

Victor Grego could have easily ordered refinements in the maintenance-bots, but he recognized the need to keep as many people employed as possible. Jared had previously owned a small business in what was now known as Mortgageville. Like most of the businesses there, his shop had failed to bring in enough customers, forcing him to close down. Jared would have ended up in Junktown had he not lucked into the job as the chief sanitation engineer for the CZC.

Jared's duties were primarily supervisory. He would double-check the robots' work. If something failed to go right, he would fill out a report and the robot in question would be serviced. Areas that needed attention that the bulky robot could not get at fell to Jared, as did the areas with fragile or sensitive items. The animal cages in Science Center were also attended by human custodians; something about the robots made the domestic and native animals uneasy and restless.

On this particular day Jared Washington was supposed to be relaxing at home or attending to personal business. Instead, he came into work. He failed to respond to the greetings of his coworkers, which was completely out of character. Clancy Slade, who still worked as a Company police officer, noticed the unusual behavior and called it in to Chief Steefer.

"If it was anybody else I wouldn't think twice about it," Clancy said through the comscreen. "For Mr. Washington to be so rude, well, that's just not how he is. He even volunteers at the Soup Kitchen now and then."

"One second, Clancy," Chief Steefer replied. As he tapped on the keyboard he wondered for the *nth* time why Clancy didn't give notice and work at the restaurant he owned full time. Since Clancy was one of his best men, he wasn't about to risk losing him by giving him any ideas. "I am pulling up his jacket...here it is. Previously owned a repair shop in Mortgageville. Always on-time, gets along with others...hey! He's supposed to have the day off. I love this place almost as much as Victor Grego, but I still take time out to decompress. Follow him. Hopefully it is nothing."

The Chief thought for a moment. "Take a Fuzzy with you in case he is carrying Cataclysmite. He might be one of those brainwashed Martianist zombies. I'll have backup on standby. Remember Rule Nine."

Rule Nine, like most of the 'Rules,' was written by Chief Steefer. It stated simply: "In the event of any suspect activity where the cause and purpose are unknown, assume the worst case scenario and act accordingly."

In this instance, that meant to treat Jared Washington as a possible Martianist infiltrator.

"On it, Chief." Clancy cut the connection and spotted a Fuzzy heading for an exit. As luck would have it, he recognized the hirsute native. "Zorro! Can you come with me? I might have a bad Big One about to start trouble."

"Hokay, Unka Clancy."

* * *

Jared pulled items from various shelves in the janitor's closet: ammonia, bleach, distilled water, rubbing alcohol, aerosol sprays—the works. Once the cart was loaded, he left the store room and moved to the lifts.

Clancy only had a moment to decide what to do: jump in the lift and continue to follow or call Chief Steefer to have men at the ready on every level. Jared seemed oblivious to everything else, so Clancy and Zorro jumped in. Jared took no notice.

Confusion screwed up Zorro's face. He was told they were following a bad Big One. All of the Fuzzies that came and went through the CZC knew Unka Jared as a good Big One. Always friendly and he often had little treats for the Fuzzies that came through the Company during his shift. Sometimes he even let the Fuzzies ride on the hard made-things, the robots, while they did their work.

Zorro looked up at Unka Clancy, who only put a finger to his mouth, Big Ones did that when it was bad to talk or make noise. The Fuzzy turned his attention to Unka Jared. The man simply started at the lift doors in front of him and said nothing.

There was something wrong with the way Unka Jared smelled. Zorro had been around Big Ones long enough to recognize most of the cleaning chemicals on the cart, especially the ammonia and bleach. The odor coming from Unka Jared was none of those. Zorro tugged on Clancy's pant leg.

"Unka Jared not smell right," Zorro whispered to the crouching Clancy. "Not know what smell is. Is new thing."

Clancy took in a large breath through his nose. All he could smell was the chemicals on the cart. He knew that Fuzzies had noses almost as good as a dog's, so he didn't doubt Zorro in the least. Did Zorro know what thermite or Cataclysmite smelled like? Clancy hoped so and realized he should have asked earlier. Jared appeared to be oblivious to the whispered conversation taking place behind him.

The lift doors retracted into the walls and the trio filed out. Clancy took note that they were now on Level 5. It was here that most of the building's internal services and maintenance were handled. Jared headed to the air quality section.

Company House had very few windows that opened and allowed fresh air in. These were on the penthouse levels. The rest of the building was very nearly hermetically sealed. This was to prevent gas attacks, attempted suicides and invasive insects. It also prevented burglars and thrill seekers from coming in. That had been a problem before the "Fuzzy Sunstone Heist," causing Chief Steefer to go on the warpath, hence no more open access from the air. The drawback was that conditioned air had to be cycled throughout the building lest carbon dioxide built up to dangerous levels.

Clancy allowed Jared to get some distance between them so as not to be obvious they were trailing him. He watched him carefully. Jared made a beeline for one of the air intake units that pulled oxygen from outside of the building, filtered out all manner of pollutants, and then circulated "fresh" breathable atmosphere to the rest of the building.

Jared opened an access panel meant for maintenance, then grabbed a gallon jug each of bleach and chlorine. Clancy, while no kind of chemist, knew that mixing those two chemical compounds together would create a toxic gas. With Zorro at his side, he ran forward to stop Jared before he poisoned the entire building.

"Hey! Get away from there," a man in maintenance overalls yelled. He started racing forward to see what was going on.

Jared, his jugs at the ready, just stood there holding a radio. Clancy assumed that Jared was waiting for the signal to start pouring the chemicals into the air purification system. Clancy was so intent on his quarry that he failed to notice the maintenance tech until they collided. The tech was sent off to the side and sprawled out on the floor.

Clancy had felt the impact but wasn't even slowed down. One part of his mind made a note to apologize later, after the danger had been dealt with. Zorro had altered his course to see if he could help the fallen man.

Jared remained seemingly oblivious to the entire affair; his attention was squarely on his hand-held radio and nothing else. It would take less than a Z-minute to throw all of the chemicals into the purifier, Clancy estimated. He didn't know what kind of protocols Chief Steefer had in place for something like this, if any at all. This was a poor man's gas attack by means of an inside man. Clancy doubted that anybody could have foreseen anything like this.

Jared stood calmly as Clancy ran up and snatched the radio. The larger man briefly considered crushing the device then thought better of it. Instead he sent it sliding away on the well-waxed floor. Something registered in Jared's mind. He grabbed the first two bottles of ammonia and bleach.

"Damn," Clancy said under his breath. *He must be programmed to go to a backup plan if interfered with.* With the two containers already opened Clancy didn't want to allow any of the contents to pour out, not even on the floor, where they could mix together and make the immediate area toxic. While it was better than allowing the chemicals to enter the air conditioning unit, it could cause significant injury to anybody in the immediate area. Clancy's choices were limited: he could shoot Jared, which he really didn't want to do, or he could tackle the man. Clancy took choice number two, thinking that Jared would recover from a beating much faster than if he were shot.

Zorro was unsure what he should do. Two Big Ones who were friends were fighting. Fuzzies would fight sometimes, then make friends afterward. But there was always a reason for the fight. Unka Jared was pushing a cart and he smelled funny. Zorro couldn't see why that would cause a fight. Still, if the cart was the reason, he could do something about it.

Jared was not as big as Clancy, yet he fought with nearly insane strength. Clancy couldn't help wondering if the mental conditioning Jared was subjected to might have caused a buildup and release of adrenalin. Of course, that assumed that Jared's mind had been washed, rinsed, fluffed and folded. The sheer viciousness he fought with chipped away at any doubt Clancy had.

"This is going to hurt me more than you, Jer," Clancy cried out, as he landed a solid haymaker on Jared's jaw and watched the man crumble to the floor. Then, looking around, he spotted Zorro moving the cart back to the lift. *That is one smart little Fuzzy.*

Not taking any chances, Clancy handcuffed the unconscious Jared then hoisted him up on one shoulder.

"Zorro, hold the lift." Clancy hustled over and boarded the elevator. Clancy decided to drop Jared off at Science Center before reporting back to Chief Steefer. Maybe Dr. Hoenveld would have a few ideas for helping the man. Another thought struck him as he stepped out of the lift: *what if Jared is part of a team and not working alone?*

L

John Carter, Dejah Thoris and Tars Tarkas watched the viewscreen intently. The screen showed the inside of an aircar with the hatch wide open. It was dull work watching the screen waiting for signs of activity. On another screen being monitored by Ulysses Paxton was the exterior view.

"I have some movement," Paxton exclaimed. "Two patrolmen are carrying a foot locker. Give me a second to zoom in." The image on the screen became enlarged enough that Paxton could read the name plates on their uniforms. "Oh, this has to be some sort of a put-on."

Tars Tarkas shifted his focus to the other screen. "What's wrong?" Paxton pointed to the nameplates. "Sullivan and Gilbert. So?"

Paxton looked up at the ceiling, as if begging for the aid of a deity. "I guess you are not an opera buff. Gilbert and Sullivan were very successful producers of opera back in, uh, First Century Atomic, I think. Pre or post, not sure which. They did *The Pirates of Penzance* among others."

Tars Tarkas shrugged. "Coincidence. Why would they bother to put fake nameplates on the officers, but leave their faces completely unobscured?"

"They could have pseudo-flesh masks on," Paxton said. "This might be some sort of double cross and they don't want us to be able to find these two if we go looking for revenge."

Tars Tarkas waved it off. "If we get double-crossed, I won't be looking for a couple of patrolmen; I would go after the Governor and maybe the Marshal."

"Well, whatever the scam is, they just placed that crate in the 'car,'" Paxton observed. "I'll let them take a few steps back aaand...lift-off!"

* * *

"There it goes, straight for the trees like we expected," Sullivan observed.

"Five will get you ten they'll run it through the under-city tunnel," Gilbert said.

In the early days of colonization, before contragravity vehicles were available, a tunnel was constructed that ran under the planned city. It acted as a shortcut for the transport of heavy equipment and supplies. After contragravity vehicles were introduced the tunnel system was abandoned, though never closed off. Most people forgot about them, while later immigrants didn't even know about the tunnels.

The tunnel system served as shelter for the homeless for a few years until a flood flushed them back out. Shortly afterwards Junktown was established.

"No bet," Sullivan said. "Every lowlife trying to dodge us runs for those tunnels. They don't seem to understand that two tunnels forming an intersection is not exactly a maze we can't maneuver in."

Gilbert pulled out two cigarettes and handed one to Sullivan. "They can't all be Hugo Ingermann."

"Thank Ghu for big favors. Something just occurred to me; these mutts might have another vehicle waiting inside to transfer the package to, then let the remote try to lead us on a wild-goose chase."

"It won't do them a whole lot of good." Gilbert used his radio to relay their suspicions to Marshal Fane.

"That thought didn't get past us," a voice told them. It wasn't the marshal, so it had to be a lower-ranking cop. "We set up covert units at all three exits. You two will just have to stay there and watch your end of the tunnel in case they double back."

"Roger. Gilbert out." The officer extinguished his cigarette on his boot heel. "Come on. If that aircar comes back I want to be ready follow it."

Sullivan stubbed out his cigarette as well. The two men never smoked in the squad car. "My turn to drive."

* * *

At the end of the north tunnel exit Officers Dooley and Feinberg, in mufti, watched as the aircar exited. Using the radar they were able to get the exact speed it was traveling then determine how long the vehicle had been in the tunnel.

"It took three minutes longer than it should have," Feinberg said.

Dooley nodded. "Enough time to move the package to another vehicle and then some." He picked up the radio. "Everybody watch for another aircar to exit the tunnel. We think they might be trying a shell game with the package."

"Roger."

"Let's follow the leader," Dooley said

"At a discreet distance," Feinberg added.

"We could just tag it…"

Feinberg shook his head. "Gil or Sully would have done that. Marshal Fane said no. These goofballs have bug catchers. They scanned that rocket to within a nanometer of its atomic structure. We get cute and try that now and they might retaliate by offing the rich boy."

"Ugh. I hate smart criminals," Dooley grunted. "They force me to work harder…hey, the car just landed."

"What in Niflheim? Let's check it out."

The covert squad car landed next to the suspect vehicle and the officers quickly got out too inspect it.

"The hatch isn't properly secured," Dooley noticed. "Like somebody in a hurry opened and didn't close it all the way."

Feinberg put on his sterile gloves then gently opened the hatch. It was empty.

"Yup. Shell game. Let's inform the marshal." He closed the hatch and joined Dooley in the squad car to make his report.

"Get back to the tunnel," Marshal Fane ordered. "They might have been waiting for the decoy to draw you off so they could slip out."

Dooley swore and Feinberg winced. "On it, Marshal."

A few seconds after the squad car was out of sight, the remote controlled aircar rose up and flew away.

* * *

There was a satisfying click, then the panel opened slightly. Mike Hammer put his tools back in the kit and handed it to Jason Roberts, who returned it to the secret compartment in his arm.

"Mike, did you ever consider a career as a locksmith?" Morgan asked in a whisper so as not to be heard from the cabin.

Mike Hammer looked up and said, also in a whisper, "Is it good to eat?" Then he laughed at the puzzled look on Morgan's face.

"Mike is pulling your leg, Mr. Holloway," Jason said. "He knows full well what a locksmith is."

Morgan chuckled as he entered the cabin. It was empty. "What in Regwarn is going on here?"

Jason inspected the control panel. After a few tense minutes, he explained what he found. "The radio has been disabled. Removed altogether, in fact. The controls are locked on a predetermined route controlled by the autopilot. As you can see, they also removed the steering column so even if we did get around the autopilot, we couldn't steer this craft."

Morgan thought it over. "So, we ride circles around the planet until the solid fuel gives out, then just float on contragravity until we are rescued or die from hunger and thirst."

Jason nodded. "Yeah, that's my takeaway, too. We had better see if they left the emergency rations in here."

Mike Hammer pulled a metal box out from under the co-pilot's seat. They opened it and found, to no great surprise, several tins of XT3. Mike was overjoyed; Morgan and Jason considerably less so. There was also bottled water and some protein bars.

"I hate to say it, but we should try to save the protein bars until the XT3 gets low," Jason suggested. "I wouldn't want my last meal to be that stuff."

"Agreed. I don't suppose you have a radio built into that arm of yours?"

Jason shook his head. "If I did, I would have used it already. This arm is just a standard market job with a few extras I had added in. It would take a much more expensive model for goodies like a radio to be added in. If you know how to build a radio I am willing to let you cannibalize the electronics."

Morgan sighed. "No, I was never that good with the electronic stuff. I doubt your arm has the right components, anyway. And even if it did we don't have any tools suitable for that kind of work."

Jason agreed. "In a way this is kind of funny."

"How so?"

"In those old Space Opera shows it seemed like the protagonists could build androids out of coconut shells and spare radio parts. The reality is not so pat." Jason sat down in the co-pilot's seat. "Hey, Mike, are you hungry?"

"Only a little," Mike Hammer said. "When food hard to find, Fuzzee eat little. Save for later."

"Fuzzies are smart," Jason said. "I am a bit hungry, too, but I am willing to hold off as long as I can before having any XT3."

Morgan took the pilot's seat. "Looks like we have plenty of time to think our way out of this predicament."

"Well, first we need to look around and see what our assets are," Jason said. "This model of lorry was used by smugglers on Shesha to run whiskey out to the natives. Very illegal. There should be some hidden compartments. Maybe our abductors left some useful goodies in one of them."

* * *

The two officers in front of Marshal Fane's desk waited patiently for their boss to get though his impressive vocabulary of colorful metaphors. It wasn't the two patrolmen that the marshal was mad at. It was himself.

"I can't believe I fell for it," Fane finished. Before him were officers Dooley and Feinberg. "It wasn't a shell game, it was pure misdirection. I should fire myself for not seeing through it." He took in a deep breath and let it out slowly. "Do we have any idea where the aircar went to?"

Both men shook their heads. "They might have still transferred the goods to a different vehicle after giving us the slip for insurance."

At this point, Max Fane would accept anything. "Or just slapped a sticker over the outer registration number and passed off the car as somebody else's." The Marshal grunted. "Secret compartment," he muttered under his breath. "Jack is going to shoot me when he finds out. I just might give him the gun to do it with."

"Well, the Martians—"

"Martianists," Fienberg corrected.

Dooley continued. "The Martianists have their loot, now. Shouldn't we be getting a call to tell us where Mr. Holloway is being held or something?"

Marshal Fane nodded. "Yes, but that call will not be coming here."

"No?" Dooley and Feinberg said together.

"No. Captain Trask has that honor. As the senior ranking FBCI agent, this falls squarely into his jurisdiction. I don't envy him if Jack's son isn't recovered in one piece."

* * *

The Federation Bureau of Criminal Investigation war room was not impressive at first glance. A few computer terminals, two comscreens, an oversized viewscreen, a couple chairs and tables and not much else. This was due to the low funding for such a small operation on a backwater colony world. Said funding came from the Federation's coffers and not the host planet's local treasury.

"The bugs don't seem to be working," Lt. Williams said. He tried increasing the gain with no visible effect.

"They could have put the package into a shielded container," Captain Trask said. "Like an old-time Faraday cage. We enjoy a lot of technological advancements but transmitters still can't send a signal through heavy aluminum shielding. Have Sgt. Schwarze look into any sale of aluminum. It's a long shot, I know, but an Old West highwayman was traced through a laundry ticket he left at the scene of one of his crimes. Maybe we'll be as lucky."

"Sir, incoming message on the designated channel."

Trask walked briskly across the room to the comscreen. The image resolved into the mask favored by the Martianists. "Okay, you got what you wanted. Now where are Mr. Holloway and his friends?"

"And a pleasant greeting to you as well, Captain Trask." The voice was modulated again. "We know you tried to follow our pickup vehicle. I could call that a breach of our agreement. Lucky for you we expected that and planned for it." The masked character held up an index card with some writing on it. "The hostages are on a robot-controlled lorry on a preprogrammed route. These are the coordinates the lorry will be at in thirty minutes. And just to save you some trouble, we are keeping the package in a shielded container. I have no doubt that you planted a tracking device of some kind on the artifacts and that you hope to find us that way. You will not. As we have concluded our business I do not anticipate meeting you again. Good day."

The screen went blank in a splash of color.

"Did you get those coordinates?"

"No need, sir," Agent Erica Banks said. "All incoming transmissions are recorded."

Of course they are, Trask thought. *Even a backwater colony world like Zarathustra has that kind of tech*. "Excellent. Print it out. Lieutenant Williams, we're going for a ride."

LI

Janice paced in her room trying to decide what to do. She really liked Buck Trask but was uncertain how he felt about her. He had already broken two dates because of his work. Of course, his being an FBCI captain meant that he couldn't keep to a normal schedule, especially when everything going on around him was far from normal.

She sat down on the bed wishing she had somebody to discuss it with. Dana was still on Beta Continent and she no longer had her four bodyguards as they stayed in Neu Freya. Her other co-workers were all men. Janice didn't feel comfortable with talking to a man about her love life.

The comscreen beeped. It was Supervisor Sylvinski.

"Yes, sir?"

"Miss Goodfellow, I feel that I should let you know that we will likely be leaving Zarathustra with the next Terra-bound ship," Sylvinski said without preamble or pleasantries. Then he seemed to change his demeanor. "I understand you have developed a relationship with Captain Trask. Should you elect to stay I will provide you with a voucher to cover all of your expenses as well as your wages to date."

"Um…I don't know that it will be necessary, sir. He and I have not discussed any long-term plans."

Sylvinski's image nodded on the screen. "I understand. Well, the offer is good for as long as you need. Think it over and make the right choice for you. And while I hope things work out to your satisfaction, know that if they don't your old position will be waiting for you on Terra."

"Th-thank you, sir," Janice stammered. "I don't know what to say."

"You are very welcome. I saw how you handled yourself back on Neu Freya. You didn't let things go to your head or try to take undue advantage of the situation. I respect that," Sylvinski said with sincerity. "By the way, Johann Torseus asked if you could visit one more time before leaving planet. We are pretty much wrapped up here and I can spare you should you decide to go. In fact, I am encouraging it. If you are uncomfortable being the Blessed One or whatever, I'll understand. Something like that can be a terrible burden."

"I will have to speak with Buck, first," Janice said. "I really need to get things worked out on that score."

Sylvinski actually smiled. Not the fake smile he used when dealing with people like the local government. This was a real smile with warmth in it. "Take him with you, if you can drag him away from the office for a weekend."

Now there was a good idea. "Supervisor, I think I will try to do just that."

The two said the usual good-byes, then cut off the transmission.

Janice opened a suitcase and selected a few outfits from her closet she had been given by the Magni-Freyans. She had tried to refuse their offerings, but Jutta told her that it would be a serious breach of etiquette. Something like saying the offerings were not good enough for one of her position. So Janice graciously accepted any gifts except bracelets. She had asked Jutta to dissuade people from bringing her anything too valuable.

How these people could make such beautiful clothing so quickly without even measuring me is amazing, Janice thought. It was her intention to wear only the Freyan-style clothing when she went back for a visit. She made a note to check the datastream to make sure she didn't wear the wrong combination or get it backwards or something. It would be horrible to wear something inappropriate and then later learn that the whole society had copied it.

Now, what should Buck wear?

* * *

Sylvinski sighed after he cut the connection on the comscreen. Dana Alexander had just returned from Beta with a report that nothing amiss was happening there. Aside from the Deputy Commissioner of Native Affairs plying her with Poictesme melon brandy, there was nothing going on there that was worth wasting his time over.

Frank Farmer printed something out, then took it to Sylvinski. "Sir, did you know that Chief Prosecutor Brannhard had been abducted a while back?"

Sylvinski thought about it for a moment, then nodded. "What of it? He's back in one piece and everybody involved is either dead, in jail or on the run from the law."

Frank nodded. "Do you know who covered for him while he was, ah, indisposed?"

"A Coombes, I believe. What of it? Is he some sort of criminal?"

Frank set the printed sheet down on the desk in front of Sylvinski. "Maybe. He is the lead attorney of the Charterless Zarathustra Company."

Now that was horse of a different color, Sylvinski thought. "Give me a list of every case he oversaw while working as acting chief prosecutor. I'll need to know what cases were won or lost, especially if they were tied to the CZC. Was Coombes still paid by the CZC or the Colonial Government? I want it all. Miss Alexander, I'll need you to get to the courthouse and dig through their files. There may be something that was never committed to electronic storage. Ms. Goodfellow…oh, right. Miss Alexander, take Mr. Burr with you. You may need a translator for legalese. Where did Hic…Mr. Farquar get to?"

"It was his turn to run for snacks, sir," Frank Farmer said. "Should be back in ten minutes or so."

"Fine. I can wait," Sylvinski said. "I hope he brings some more of that veldbeest jerky."

* * *

The comscreen beeped, annoying Colonial Governor Bennett Rainsford. Normally the secretary would screen the call.

"Governor Rainsford," Rainsford said as he opened the connection. He had no idea who he was looking at. "Is there something I can help you with?"

"Sir, I am Jim Short down in Records," said the face on the screen. "Somebody is going through the caseloads from when Mr. Brannhard was missing."

"Those are all public records, Mr. Short. Anybody can go through them if they feel the need." Rainsford was about to explain to the young man about the need to use the chain of command when he stopped short. "Did you say *only* the records from when Gus…Mr. Brannhard was missing?"

"Yes, sir."

"Can you trace where the information is going to?"

Jim Short looked like he wasn't certain how to answer that. "Um, well, normally no. But this is coming from the guest accommodations you arranged for the Terran commission. Everything in this building has a specific dedicated line."

And Mr. Short, along with everybody else on the planet by now, knew that the commission was here to throw stones at bee hives and see who got stung, Rainsford thought, *and he went straight to me in case it was either time-sensitive or maybe somebody in house was working for the commission.*

"Good catch, Mr. Short. Can you get me a transcript of everything being raided?"

"Yes, sir!" Jim Short said. "Would the Governor prefer hard copy or electronic transfer?"

The Governor would prefer people didn't get all formal every time he spoke with them. "Let's save a few hemp plants and use electronic. I suspect it would be faster."

"Much faster, sir. I'll send these to your secretary right awa—"

"I would rather you sent them to me directly." Rainsford interrupted, giving Jim the code that would allow him to send the information directly to his office. "Don't pass that code around or even tell anybody you have it. It changes every few days, so it doesn't have much of a shelf life anyway."

"Understood, sir. Can you take 120 speed?"

120? Oh, right, the CZC upgraded transfer tech recently. "Yes, I can. Ready when you are."

It took over a minute to get all of the data. Rainsford thanked Jim Short then broke the connection. He immediately called Gus Brannhard and explained the situation.

"Should we cut them off, Gus?" Rainsford asked nervously.

Gus said no. "If we do that it will look like we have something to hide. We should all get together, me, you, Leslie and Grego, and go through the transcripts. We both know that Leslie was the most qualified man on the planet to fill my position while I was gone."

Rainsford nodded. "What do you think Sylvinski is after?"

"I would hazard a guess and say he wants to see if Leslie put the CZC over the law and swept something under the rug," Gus said. "Then he would have to see if you were involved in any of that. We both know that wouldn't happen, but Sylvinski doesn't. I have to say he is doing his job pretty well. Something like this would warrant a good hard look on any planet. I don't have to like him, but I sure respect his dedication and thoroughness."

Rainsford relaxed a bit. "I guess nice guys make lousy inspectors."

"Maybe. I'll call Leslie, and maybe you should call Victor."

"I'll do that," Rainsford said. "I hope this turns out to be another nitpicking exercise."

LII

"I say we just shoot them and have done with it," grumbled Ramirez as he stepped over a log.

Estefan shook his head. "There are a few things wrong with your plan. First of all, we have to find them. Second, we have to get those fuses or we ain't goin' anywhere. Maybe they have the fuses on them or maybe they buried them. We can't dig up this entire area lookin' for 'em. And maybe only one of them hid the fuses without tellin' the others where. Nope. We need them alive and talkative."

Something that looked like a cross between a feathered lizard and a snake skittered across his path. Estefan barely restrained himself from shooting it.

Ramirez spit. "How talky do you think they'll be with a bullet waitin' for 'em? And once we get them, how do we keep them? Hilde snapped those handcuffs like they were made of tinsel. I would have bet even Lars couldn't do that. I'll admit that I would hate to shoot her. Seems like a nice kid—whoops!" Ramirez stepped on a land prawn and nearly lost his balance.

The 'prawn didn't appreciate being stepped on one bit and pinched Ramirez's ankle before racing away. Ramirez expressed his appreciation for the pinch with a very colorful collection of words in Lingua Terra and Spanish.

"Keep it down," Estefan cautioned. "We don't want them to know where we are."

"It's a bit late for that."

Both men spun around to face the direction of the voice. Estefan was struck in the nose with the heel of Kealani's right hand. He went down like a sack of potatoes. Ramirez lost his rifle from a quick grab and yank by Cindy. He never even knew she was there. He quickly pulled out his .38 special.

"I wouldn't do that."

Ramirez turned to face Brünnhilde. He quickly leveled the gun at her.

"I really wouldn't do that, if I were you," Brünnhilde said lightly. "One of my countrymen was shot several times with a 9mm. All it did was make him angry. You don't want to make me angry, do you? You wouldn't like me very much when I am angry."

Ramirez froze and Brünnhilde simply plucked the gun out of his hands. "Thank you. Now, I am afraid, it is past your nap time."

Ramirez didn't have time to think when the lights went out. Erena stood over him with the rifle she had taken from Sarge. She examined the butt stock of the rifle. No damage from Ramirez's head.

"I didn't know you watched old Terran viewscreen shows," Erena said.

Brünnhilde was confused. "I don't understand."

"That line about how he wouldn't like you when you're angry. Didn't you get that from the viewscreen? This skinny guy would get all big and green—"

"*Nein*. All of my viewscreen time has been filled with educational programming."

"Huh." Erena looked down at the unconscious men. "Huh."

"Was that true," Cindy asked. "What you said about your countryman?"

"Oh, yes. What I didn't mention is that he spent three weeks in hospital recovering from his injuries. Well, to be fair he had also been subjected to the vacuum of space," Brünnhilde added. "But he struck down many men before that." Everybody looked at her with wide-eyed surprise.

"I would really like to meet this countryman of yours," Kealani said.

"Are you, um…?" Cindy couldn't think of a polite way to ask if Brünnhilde was human.

"My people are all of Freyan descent, but much was done to our ancestors," Brünnhilde explained. "It would take too long to explain. Just accept that we were experimented on and made stronger."

Erena shrugged. "None of my business. Okay, that is five down.

Who is left?"

Brünnhilde thought about it. "Weaver, Bo, Clem, Consuela, Mai, Lars and Gardner. Mai doesn't like guns and is too small to worry about and Lars is laid up."

"Who do you think is the most dangerous?" Kealani asked. "For us, that is."

"Bo." Brünnhilde said without hesitation. "He could pick us off at long range." She pointed at her wound for emphasis.

Kealani thought it over. "When they notice these two and the other three are missing, they won't want to take chances. They know that we'll have to come to them to get the ground roller. Out here without it, we'll be sitting ducks. I don't think we could cover the hundred miles or so to the nearest town on foot. Assuming we could find it without our maps and gear."

"And didn't run into something big, mean and hungry," Erena added.

Cindy had only ever hunted small and medium game back home. She knew nothing of military tactics. "So, what do we do?"

"We wait," Erena said. "And hope they make a mistake. Meanwhile, let's tie these two up and put them with the others."

* * *

"They're taking too long," Weaver muttered. "We should have heard something by now, even if it was just an animal spooking them and getting shot at."

"That wouldn't happen with Sarge's group," Lars said. "She did two or three tours with the Army. She wouldn't shoot at just anything and she would keep the others under control."

"Okay, I can see that. What about Estefan and Ramirez? Neither of them did a hot second in any military."

"Estefan is good under pressure," Consuela said. She helped Lars to his feet and walked him around as she spoke. "He did a lot of hunting and knows better than to spook his prey. Random gunshots would do that."

Weaver considered it. "Ramirez isn't that cool or good at restraint.

Still, I imagine he is smart enough not to give away his position without good cause."

"Weaver, why not just let them go," Lars asked. "We are miles from anywhere and they won't get far without their ground roller."

"There is the matter of the fuses, Lars," Weaver said angrily. "How far do you think we will get without our rollers?"

Lars thought for a moment. "All we need are the fuses to the ignition and lights, right? So, we pull the fuses from their roller and distribute them among the other three. We won't have radio or air conditioning or wipers, but we can still go."

Weaver thought it over. It was a good idea. It had the added bonus of the women not being able to use their roller to get to a town and sound the alarm. "There might only be enough compatible fuses to get two of the ground rollers operational."

"So we have to squeeze in," Lars said. "Mai and Consuela can sit on my lap. Bo could sit on the roof with his rifle and goggles. It'll be snug but doable. And don't forget: each minute we waste searching for the ladies is a minute closer to a Terro settlement for the Fuzzies. And if they have those dog mounts…."

Weaver didn't need to be hit with a brick. "Nobody will be sitting in your lap until a doctor has a go at your back and legs. Fine. Bo, Clem, go round up our hunters and get them back here. Consuela, here are the keys to that CZC roller. Go grab some fuses."

"Why don't we just take that roller," Consuela asked.

Weaver's voice dripped with sarcasm. "That roller? The CZC roller with the tracking device hidden in it like every damned vehicle owned by the CZC?"

"Forget I said anything." Consuela ran to the tent with the ground roller still inside.

"I'm staying behind."

Weaver spun around to find Mai holding one of the rifles like it was a dead cat. "Ghu's gonads! Why? We can all make it out of here and get off-planet—"

"I don't want to leave Zarathustra," Mai said with surprising calm.

"I just wanted to get away from that son-of-a-Khooghra that attacked me back in Mallorysport. Maybe I'll find work in Betatown or something. I don't want to spend my life bouncing from world to world going from one bad thing to the next. If I stay with you, I'll either end up dead or mixed up in some other bad stuff. I never wanted to hurt any Fuzzies or anybody else and I don't want to go with you. This is it. I'm out."

Weaver was about to respond when he felt a hand on his shoulder. It was Lars. "If she wants out, let her go. You were going to do that anyway, right?"

Weaver began to feel cornered. He couldn't tell Lars that his original intent had been to kill the women so Lars would have no reason to stay. Mai he would have turned loose in Mallorysport, right before boarding an outgoing ship. Leaving her behind was too dangerous, she could get picked up by the ZNPF and spill all she knew.

With Lars standing right there, there wasn't anything he could do without the risk of having to shoot the Modian, which was something he really didn't want to do. As it was, Lars was against killing the women. Weaver had to give the kill order while Lars was otherwise occupied.

"I would prefer to let Mai go after we get back to Mallorysport, Lars," Weaver said, after explaining his concerns about Mai getting chatty with the constabulary.

Lars nodded. "My offer to stay with her stands. I really can't do much walking around, anyway, much less run if we have to scoot quick. Let's catch the women before something nasty eats them, bring them back, and I'll take charge of them until the rest of you make it off-planet. I'll even wait for six hours after lift-off to make sure the cops can't radio the ship for a turn around."

"Lars, I get what you want to do," Weaver said. "You were against killing the Fuzzies. Now, you're against killing the women. You just plain don't like killing."

"Unnecessary killing," Lars corrected. "I have no problem killing anyone or anything that is trying to kill me. Those women, as far as I have seen, don't have any interest in killing me or anybody else here. They found out what we were up to. Somebody said something out of school where Hilde could hear them, so she passed the word along, hoping to get some help and get away from us evil Fuzzy slavers. I respect that, even if it causes me some inconvenience."

"Inconvenience? You should have gone into politics."

Lars chuckled. "There is doing bad, and doing *bad.* Politics is a level I will never sink to. But as I was saying, there is no reason to kill the women or drag Mai anyplace she doesn't want to go. Good legs or bad, I am staying behind. If you think about it, you'll realize that I stand out in a crowd. If word of our activities gets to the cops, they could catch us all just by spotting me. But if we separate and take different ships, we improve our chances of getting away clean."

Weaver considered it and decided Lars was correct. Anybody who is five foot six inches tall and about three feet wide was going to draw attention. "Okay, you make a good point. We split up. Now, how do you avoid detection and get away?"

"Nobody here knows my real name, right? I'll just mix in with the other heavy-worlders for a while."

That brought Weaver up short. "Other heavy-worlders?"

"Oh, yeah," Lars said. "We don't all stay home and work on our muscles. We go out into the galaxy like everybody else. When we settle on a planet we tend to gravitate to other heavy-worlders and start our own little communities. Like Chinatown, Greek Town, what have you back on Old Terra before World War III. On the east side of Mallorysport there are about two or three dozen of us. We have a Gravity Bar with artificial gravity set at Magni normal. A bit on the light side for me but it's the median average. Cheaper than setting a different gee for each table, if such a thing is even possible. I'll just mix in with them and nobody will be able to spot me based on my description. I stay a couple weeks: maybe clean out a few guys playing poker, then hop on a ship headed to Gimli. You can leave me a coded note at the data-messaging center, telling me what world we can meet back up on."

Weaver nodded. "That sounds like a good plan, though it means that it could take up to a year to get the band back together."

"Objective time, maybe. Subjectively a lot less since we'll be in hyperspace where time moves at about, what, an eighth compared to space normal? We could all get back together in about two months subjective time. Oh, and whatever the next caper turns out to be, let's pick something that doesn't automatically earn us a bullet in the head if we're caught."

"I'm with you there! All right, you stay behind to guard the women. We'll leave you and Mai one of the ground rollers. The rest of us will crowd into the other two rollers. Shouldn't be too difficult without you and Mai taking up space." Weaver looked around. "They should be back by now, with or without our guests. Consuela, take Bo and Clem and see if the others got lost or injured."

* * *

"That is Clem," Brünnhilde indicated from behind the ironwood tree. "I don't think I ever saw him without Bo before."

"Old partners," Cinda said. "Sometimes two people will pair up non-sexually and form a deep bond. It happens with soldiers and policemen sometimes, usually after an exceptionally traumatic shared experience. It is unlikely he came looking for us alone. Bo should be around as well."

"We can psychoanalyze him later," Kealani whispered. "If he keeps coming this way we can take him out without gunplay. I just wish I knew where this Bo was."

A new voice interrupted the conversation. "Bo is roughly fifty feet away under cover, holding a very large rifle pointed at all three of you. The same rifle that nearly took your head off, Hilde."

Everybody turned around to see Consuela holding a pistol. "All I have to do is make a gesture and Bo will start shooting."

Erena wasn't buying it. "How do we know this isn't a bluff?"

Consuela put her left hand up and made a quick gesture. The tree behind Brünnhilde appeared to spit off some bark. The women felt the sizzle of the bullet as it passed them and struck the tree. The sound of the gunshot followed immediately.

"That was the signal to fire a warning shot," Consuela said. "From this point on, if any of you try anything, he will shoot to kill."

Brünnhilde absently touched the scar on her forehead. Kealani said something in Tagalog and dropped her rifle to the ground. The rest followed suit.

"Here is the situation, ladies," Consuela said as she gestured for the four women to back away from the guns. "If we wanted you dead, you would already be dead. Lars and Mai will stay back with all of you while the rest of us get the Niflheim off this dirtball. You will be inconvenienced but alive. Whichever one of you has the fuses now would be a good time to return them. Otherwise, we'll just pull the fuses from your ground roller and leave you stranded."

Erena let out a sigh. "I buried them inside the tent."

"Fine. By the way, did you happen to see any of the others? We don't leave until they come back." Consuela looked a Kealani and recalled how she handled herself in the free-for-all. "Are they still alive?"

"They were when we left them," Kealani said with a smile.

LIII

"These relics appear to be as genuine as the rocket," Dak Kova announced. "I would need more sophisticated equipment before I can claim one-hundred percent certainty."

"Like what?" Dejah Thoris asked.

"Well, I would like to do a radiation decay ratio test," Dak Kova admitted. "Sadly, we have no equipment for such a test."

"We can buy it," Tars Tarkas said. "We still have money enough for some equipment even if we do have to abandon it."

John Carter shook his head. "That isn't the sort of thing they carry in a five and deci-sol store. No call for it by the average private citizen."

"Quite right," Dak Kova said. "I imagine the only place on this entire planet to possess such an item would be the Science Center."

Ulysses Paxton laughed for a moment. "Could you image one of us going to the CZC and asking pretty please if we could use their doohickey to test the artifacts we extorted from them? I don't mind admitting that I don't have the stones for that."

Tars Tarkas and Dak Kova joined Paxton in laughter.

John Carter waited for the laughter to subside. "Well, we really have no other feasible option than to get these artifacts to Mars and give them the thorough going-over they deserve there."

"That brings up another issue: how do we smuggle these back to Mars?" Tars Tarkas asked. "The old false bottom in the crate gag?"

That brought everybody up short. Suggestions were floated back and forth and quickly dismissed. Ulysses Paxton came up with an idea.

"False sides and bottom," Paxton started. He was almost immediately shouted down. "No, no, no! Listen. We are going to use misdirection. What could we plant in the bottom that would be confiscated, but only get a fine, not detained?"

"Sunstones?" Tars Tarkas ventured.

John Carter shook his head. "The locals have had a lot of problems where sunstones are concerned lately. We would definitely be detained. That goes for any precious gems or metals, like gold, as well."

"Fuzzy relics," Dejah Thoris ventured. John Carter told her to go on. "Fuzzy artifacts would be an interesting conversation piece on other worlds. You can get simulacrums of those chopper thingies at any local tourist trap."

"Oh, yeah, somebody tried to sell me a *coup de poing* axe over near Junktown," Paxton added.

"Is it illegal to carry such genuine items off-world?" John Carter asked.

Paxton said no. "Not even a little bit. Fuzzies cheerfully trade their homemade stuff for a good metal blade with a long handle. But that doesn't mean we knew about that as far as customs is concerned."

"Go on," John Carter urged.

Paxton continued smugly, "We go get as many of the real thing as we can find. Buy up a few simulacra, too. We put them in the false bottom of the crate with our goods on top. The artifacts will be in a separate case in the sides. One of us carries the first case through the scanner. Pack the stuff loosely so it rattles as it goes through. The inspector will want a look inside. So we let him. He finds the Fuzzy tools and maybe gives us a lecture or laughs at us. Doesn't matter. While all the attention is on the decoy, we should be able to go through with the relics."

Tars Tarkas shook his head. "Sounds too easy."

"Of course it does. That's the point." Paxton sat down on the edge of the table holding the relics. "It is so easy, it's obvious. That's why no one believes anybody would try it. Besides, when somebody gets pulled aside for inspection, everybody rubbernecks trying to get a look; including the other inspectors."

"Who carries the decoy?" Dejah Thoris asked.

Paxton pointed at her. "You do."

"What? Why me?"

John Carter caught on. "Because an attractive woman also draws more attention. Do you still have that see-through blouse?"

"What?" Dejah Thoris blushed. "I only wear that when I go out dancing."

"Well, you can do a little dance routine for the inspectors," John Carter said flatly. "Wear a light jacket over it then remove it when you get stopped. It is perfectly legal to wear in public and it guarantees all eyes will be on you."

"How do you know it is legal?" Dejah Thoris challenged.

"Gods of Mars, am I the only one who reads the pamphlets? On this planet a woman can go bare-chested any place that a man can. Haven't you noticed the transparent tunics the younger men wear? And I noticed some see-through clothing at the spaceport when we first arrived. And let me assure you, you have no reason to be modest where your endowments are concerned."

John Carter turned his attention back to the rest of the group. "We will have to use other names when we leave. John Carter is a common enough name away from Mars but the rest of us need something a little more 'John Smith-ish' if we want to avoid detection."

"We should have thought of that before we left Mars," Tars Tarkas said accusingly.

John Carter shrugged. "The original plan didn't call for us to stick around and acquire more goodies. The hand has been dealt. We play what we have."

"I know where I can get us some forged papers," Paxton said. "I'll need a holo-photo of everybody."

"Not everybody," John Carter said. "Some of the lower echelons will leave with their Martian names." Everybody spoke at once until Carter let out a sharp whistle. "Not everybody knows what we have been up to. That is why I brought extra personnel. Those that are ignorant of any, ah, extra-legal activities can go to the spaceport, get picked up and questioned under veridication, get cleared and sent packing. More misdirection."

Everybody agreed it was a sound plan.

"Now, all of us who had beards when we arrived had best shave them off. Those of us that didn't should pick up some follicle stimulators and grow one quick. We will also color our hair. This is to defeat the facial recognition tech at the spaceport. We'll take our holo-photos afterwards."

* * *

Morgan, Jason and Mike had gone over every square millimeter of the lorry's cargo bay opening any and all panels they found. The contents were disappointing at best.

"Tools not meant for working on a control panel, a couple repair manuals, a few adult magazines, some dried pool ball fruit chips, stale, and more damned XT3," Jason Roberts summarized.

Mike took the bag of chips, sniffed the contents then, started eating them. He offered to share with no takers.

"I hate to say it, but it looks like we'll have to be rescued," Morgan said. "I am prepared to give a hefty finder's fee for whoever finds us. Provided they keep their mouths shut about it."

Jason chuckled. "Bad for the reputation to be rescued?"

Morgan nodded. "Even worse to have been captured in the first place. If word of this gets around, it could affect the stock market. I could lose billions of sols."

"Wouldn't the market bounce back?"

"It could," Morgan admitted. "Or it could not. In either case speculators could buy up stocks at depressed prices and gain some control in the companies I own a major share in."

Jason suddenly laughed. "Sorry, Mr. Holloway. I'm not laughing at you or your financial concerns. We might die up here, our bodies floating around in this tin can waiting for somebody to trip over us or, even worse, for the contragravity to lose power and send our remains down to who knows where. And here you are, concerned about how your disappearance might affect something you may not even see again."

Morgan smiled. "I guess it is a Freyan thing. We worry less about our personal safety than how it might affect those we leave behind. I have Akira and Little John to think of and how well they will get along without me."

Jason nodded. "I get it. My only family is Mike here, and he is in the same boat, literally, that I am. Mike, if I die before we are rescued and you run out of food, you have my permission to eat me."

The look of disgust that crossed the Fuzzy's face was almost comical. "Fuzzee not eat People. Big Ones are People, too."

Jason turned to Morgan. "Cannibalism is anathema to Fuzzies. No Fuzzy I ever heard of ever resorted to it, no matter how hungry they got."

"In that case," Morgan said, "whichever of us dies first gets tossed out the hatch. If we can't be useful as lunch, at least we can avoid stinking up the place."

"Do Freyans resort to, um, cannibalism?"

Morgan shrugged. "Beats me. I never heard of it happening. I can't say for certain that it couldn't. I was never hungry a day in my life. A benefit of being in the noble class. The lower…" Morgan was interrupted by a pounding on the hatch from the outside.

Jason wasted no time opening the hatch. The blast of thin air knocked him backwards. Outside was a constabulary squad car. An officer looked back at them holding a bean bag gun. The bean bags had been replaced with hard rubber loads in order to have the necessary impact on the hatch.

"All right, I want you to pull over and show me your registration, insurance and pilot's license," boomed the voice over a loudspeaker.

Morgan was taken aback while Jason, a former cop himself, laughed with relief.

"We have no way to steer or land this piece of junk," Jason yelled back.

The officer turned to talk to somebody else before speaking into the loudspeaker again. "Can you cut the propulsion system?"

Jason moved back to the cabin and used his cybernetic arm to rip the control panel open. He tore the pseudo flesh of the fingers off in the process. He looked at the wiring, then mentally kicked himself. All he needed to do was pull a couple fuses. He did so then returned to the cargo bay. The squad car was gone.

"What the…"

"When you cut the propulsion the squad car raced off," Morgan explained. "I expect they'll be back in a…there they are."

The officer returned to the open hatch of the squad car. "We are going to get on top and force you down. We'll try to stop short of hitting the ground but overlapping contragravity fields can be real tricky. I strongly advise you to strap in and brace yourselves."

Jason threw a thumbs-up at the officer. Morgan and Jason took the only two seats. "Ah, Niflheim. What do we do about Mike? I would give him my seat but the straps weren't designed for someone that small."

Morgan considered possibilities. "We need to jury rig a harness for him. Too bad we didn't find any cargo straps.'

Jason looked around and realized what he needed to do. He gathered up his treasured trench coat and tore it into straps.

Mike protested. "That your best coat, Boss!"

Jason smiled at the Fuzzy. "I can always buy a new trench coat, Mike, but there is only one Mike Hammer Fuzzy. Now sit on my lap and I'll strap you in."

Over in the squad car, Gilbert, acting as the pilot, said to his partner, "I'll bet those FBCI guys will be hacked-off that we found the hostages first."

Sullivan shrugged, then strapped himself in. He had no interest in being bounced around during the force-down maneuver. "The feebs should have used satellite telemetry like we did. Chief Carr will be thrilled. He has been wanting to one-up the feebs since they rejected him as a candidate."

LIV

Supervisor Sylvinski had the uncomfortable feeling that he was being called on the carpet. It was ridiculous, of course. If anybody called anybody on the carpet it was him. On Zarathustra he answered to nobody but his own conscience.

The secretary escorted Sylvinski into the governor's office where he was met by Ben Rainsford, Gus Brannhard, Victor Grego and Leslie Coombes. Ben indicated a chair and Sylvinski sat down.

"Supervisor, I won't waste your time with any runaround," Rainsford said. "We know you were going through the courthouse records."

"And we have a pretty good idea what you were looking for," Gus added.

"And you asked me here to clarify any misunderstandings I might get," Sylvinski responded. "Well—"

"I wish to go on record, here and now, that I recused myself from any and all cases that involved the Charterless Zarathustra Company during my brief stint as chief colonial prosecutor," Leslie Coombes interjected.

"And, he was granted a sabbatical from the CZC at that time, so as not to create any conflict of interest," Victor Grego added.

Sylvinski couldn't help smiling. "Did you all rehearse this little scene?"

"What is it that you find so amusing, Commissioner?" Rainsford demanded.

"I will explain after you have finished," Sylvinski said lightly.

The four men shared a glance with each other. Gus shrugged and spoke first.

"I was indisposed at the time of Leslie...Mr. Coombes' appointment. However, I looked over his caseload right after I returned. I didn't find a single action that I wouldn't have taken myself. In fact, he prosecuted a few cases involving former clients of mine, from when I was in private practice, that I would have had to recuse myself from."

"I went over the records as well," Rainsford said. "The win-loss ratio was about the same as when Gus…Mr. Brannhard was in charge. Mr. Coombes performed admirably with some very large shoes to fill."

"If you have any questions, I would be happy to answer them under veridication," Coombes said.

Sylvinski's eyebrows went up. "Really? I would think you would prefer to stay out of the hot seat. Especially after we put your Deputy Governor through the wringer."

"It is my understanding that Juan Takagashi came through the experience unscathed," Coombes said. "I am equally confident that I will come through vindicated."

"Oh, I have no doubt of that," Sylvinski said.

"What?" All four men said at once.

"Would you care to explain, Supervisor?" Grego asked.

"Yes, of course. As I started to say before I was interrupted, my people went through those records very thoroughly. All the court cases that Mr. Coombes oversaw were handled very well. Elegantly, even, according to Clarence Burr. In fact, we could only find one single discrepancy."

"Discrepancy?"

Sylvinski fought not to laugh. "How do you all do that in harmony? Have Barbershop Quartets made a comeback?"

Rainsford started to lose his temper. "What kind of game are you playing? What is this discrepancy?"

Sylvinski couldn't hold it in any longer. He laughed out loud. After a few moments he regained control of himself. "Gentlemen, we went through all of the records we could. Even a few I am sure were not strictly legal for us to comb through. You are within your rights to proffer charges if you so wish."

"We'll put a pin in that for now," Gus said gruffly. "Did you find something or not?"

"We did. It was the kind of tragic oversight almost every government is guilty of at some point." Everybody just stared at Sylvinski. "Gentlemen, you neglected to pay Mr. Coombes for his time and trouble."

Sylvinski laughed again. After a moment Grego joined him. "Well,

Ben, it looks like your whole cabinet will be brought down over this."

Gus joined in. "Did you remember to dock my pay for those days I was lollygagging in the CZC's sub-basement?"

Rainsford was too relieved to laugh. He just smiled and said, "I'll have the Treasury check on that."

Eventually the laughter died down and Sylvinski became more serious.

"Governor, this has to be the most sickeningly honest and straight-forward government I have ever even heard of. As Mr. Brannhard put it when we first met, I am throwing my hands up in surrender. We have already started packing and expect to be out of your hair when the next ship to Terra departs." He stood up and held out his hand. Rainsford took it.

"I won't say this has been fun," Rainsford said. "But it has been interesting."

Gus looked like he was uncertain whether or not to speak. Finally, he asked, "Supervisor, what about the colony on Zeta Continent?"

That gave the Supervisor pause. "Hmm. Quite right. If Mr. Holloway returns from wherever he is before I leave, please have him messenger a copy of the document or scroll or whatever the Freyan monarchy uses for royal decrees to my office. If we leave before he returns, just forward it to my offices on Terra. I have no interest in stirring up trouble for those folks. They have been through enough. I will need the documentation at some point, though. Otherwise, you'll get another off-worlder with a briefcase coming out to give you grief."

"Morgan is already back, Supervisor," Grego said. "He has just been, um, otherwise occupied. I will ask him to drop by your office as soon as he becomes available."

"That will be fine." Sylvinski said. "Oh, did you have a chance to speak with Bürgermeister Torseus?"

"Yes," Rainsford said. "Do you need to know how it worked out?"

Sylvinski thought it over. "No. My business with your government is done. Whatever you and Johann worked out does not involve me or my people. Well, maybe Miss Goodfellow."

Rainsford nodded. "I'll be happy to read her in since the Magni-Freyans hold her in such high regard. I'll admit that I would like to meet her as well."

"Indeed," Sylvinski said. "She will be going back to Neu Freya for a visit before we all leave. I am sure she could spare a few minutes for you."

* * *

Hugh Lennon had just sat down to his lunch when the chime from the door sounded. He almost called for the valet to get it when he remembered his staff was off that day. One of the things he had learned from his father was to always give the employees at least one day off to explore whatever planet he dragged them to so they could sample the sights and culture and cuisine.

Lennon got up, hit the plate-warmer switch and set the cover over his meal. Once assured his food would not get cold, he went to the door. One of the benefits of staying in a five-star hotel was the viewscreen next to the door that allowed him to see who had come to call. It was the man with the unusual name…Hackamore? Hufflepuff? Hickabbible Farquar! He hit the button that opened the doorway.

"Mr. Farquar! Did we have a meeting scheduled?"

Hic looked a bit uncomfortable. "No, sir. I just wanted to give you an update on the Supervisor's progress."

Lennon was momentarily confused, then recalled why he had seen the supervisor in the first place. "Ah, yes, the Fuzzies. Come in. I was just sitting down to lunch. Can I get you something? There is plenty of roast veldbeest. I prepared it myself but I assure you my culinary skills are such that you will not regret trying the fare."

"Thank you, Mr. Lennon, but I really don't have the time." Hic could smell the food and regretted he didn't have the time to try it. "But there is no reason to make you wait. I can talk while you eat."

Lennon shook his head. "I never discuss important matters while eating. I prefer to give my meal the attention it deserves. It will hold. Come with me to the terrace. The view is quite good."

Hic followed Lennon out and took a seat on the waterproof memory foam easy chair. Lennon sat across from him on a similar seat.

"So, what dire tidings are you here to present?"

Hic hesitated for a moment, then decided it would be best to just get it all out. "We questioned Juan Takagashi under veridication and came up dry."

"So he didn't bilk the treasury of Odin before leaving the planet?" Lennon shrugged. "Okay. I didn't really have a dog in that fight."

"The point is that Supervisor Sylvinski doesn't have any leverage he could apply to get you the Fuzzies you wanted," Hic explained. "He would like to know if there is something else he could assist you with."

"Really? Humph. Nothing comes to mind," Lennon said absently. "It no longer matters. I have come to the realization that by taking the Fuzzies to Magni with me I would be, essentially, putting them in a very big cage. My visit to Neu Freya reminded me what the Freyans had gone through. While I had nothing to do with that, it still turns my stomach. I have decided to start a homestead here on Zarathustra and make this my primary base of operations. This will allow me to legally adopt a Fuzzy or two without taking them away from all they know."

Hic nodded. "I am glad. I will admit that I wasn't comfortable with the idea of the supervisor working around the local laws where the Fuzzies are concerned. Neither was he, as it turns out."

"Oh? So he would have never assisted me in this anyway?"

"Only if he could do it legally, sir."

Lennon smiled. "Good. Too many government types think the rules don't apply to them. But with my new mindset on the matter, I wouldn't have taken a Fuzzy off-world even if Supervisor Sylvinski provided me with one."

Hic was relieved. Lennon had enough clout that he could have made trouble for the whole commission had he wanted to. "I might suggest that you go to Beta Continent and speak with the Commissioner of Native Affairs, there? If you still want a Fuzzy, he is the man you need to impress."

Lennon felt his blood run cold. It was an odd feeling, for him, as he had never been afraid of anything in his life before now. *Is this what fear feels like?* "I am not so sure that is a good idea. I met the Commissioner some months ago, briefly."

Hic read Lennon's face. "I take it that it didn't go well."

Lennon laughed at that. "He pointed a fairly large gun right in my face."

"Not a lot of ambiguity in that," Hic admitted. "Still, I have been doing some reading on Jack Holloway. He is the type of man who would cheerfully beard a lion in its own den. Afterwards, he wouldn't even talk about it unless somebody pointed at the furry trophy and asked how he came by it. If you want his respect, you'll need to show that you have the moxie to face him on his own ground."

Lennon chewed on it for a moment. "Mr. Farquar, I like the way you think. I'll do exactly that. The worst that can happen is he says 'no.' I have survived far worse than that. If you ever get tired of low-paying government work, swing by my offices on Terra."

Hic smiled. "Actually, I like my work. And Supervisor Sylvinski isn't the ogre he pretends to be. He recognizes ability and respects underlings who tell him the truth, not just what he would want to hear. He doesn't know it, yet, but he is in line for promotion and had tapped me for his replacement long ago. His ability to handle even the most boring task is a major plus. And he isn't afraid to get down in the dirt and roll around with the pigs if he has to."

"Which is why he took the job of coming all the way out here," Lennon added. "Good for both of you. But if your promotion doesn't pan out, come see me. I think I can make a very attractive offer for somebody with your skill set."

Hic stood up. "I'll keep it in mind. Now I have to get back. Good luck with Commissioner Holloway."

Lennon stood and offered his hand, which Hic shook. "Thanks. I wish I could say I won't need it."

LV

"We'll leave the tent, your ground roller and all of your gear," Weaver stated. "I trust you will understand, if we lock up all of your guns in the roller and leave the keys with Lars."

Brünnhilde, Cindy, Erena and Kealani just sat and glared at Weaver. None of them were tied up this time. Instead, Lars sat in a canvas field chair holding a rifle behind them. At this point, Weaver had no faith that anything he could come up with, using the limited materials at hand, would keep Brünnhilde from getting loose.

"Okay, you are all alive, you will keep your possessions," Weaver continued. "Now, all you have to do is sit tight for a few days while we get the Niflheim out of Dodge. Lars and Mai were gracious enough to volunteer to stay behind and guard all of you, so that it wouldn't be necessary to do anything unpleasant with or to you. So if you have any sense of gratitude at all, don't give them a hard time. Try anything funny and I have no doubt that Lars will take the comedy out of it quick, fast and in a hurry."

Behind Weaver the women could see two of the ground rollers pulling forward. Five people per ground roller was snug, but not uncomfortably so. Weaver pulled out two sets of keys.

"I almost forgot; here, Lars." Weaver tossed the keys underhand to the Modian. Lars easily caught both sets. "Give us at least two days to get back to Mallorysport before setting these ladies loose. You and Mai sleep in shifts. These lovely ladies are not to be trifled with; especially those two." Weaver indicated Kealani and Brünnhilde. He walked around the prisoners to shake Lars' free hand and give Mai a hug. "It isn't too late to come with us."

"No, I'll stick it out here," Mai said. "I don't think I am ready to face the whole galaxy, yet."

Weaver shrugged. "Suit yourself. Take this." He held out a wad of sol notes. "This is to help you get on your feet when you get back to civilization. Stay away from Junktown and don't let yourself get dragged into anything bad. A lot of girls your age out on their own end up on drugs, hooking or both."

Weaver turned on his heel and started for the lead roller. Taking a shotgun, he signaled to get started. The third roller was for Lars and Mai.

Nobody spoke as they watched the procession move away. It was a full ten Z-minutes before even the dust of their departure was out of sight. Mai took some water to the prisoners being careful not to get grabbed. Nobody tried.

"Okay, ladies," Lars said. "You can get up now."

They stood and turned to see Lars standing there with his rifle slung over his shoulder. He had a big smile on his face. "Now, before you all get riled up I should tell you…"

Lars' voice was drowned out by the whine of a contragravity engine overhead. Six Fuzzies on dogs came around the tent at the same time. Cindy, Erena and Kealani recognized two of them.

"Rockthrower! Maid Marian!" Cindy shouted. "You brought help!"

"Find Little Fuzzee an' Emily Dickinson an' James Hutton an' Sara Balfour," Rockthrower explained.

The aircar landed and Cinda and Rheiner joined the reunion. "Brünnhilde! Ve haff been looking for you eferyvhere."

"Who are your friends," Cinda asked. At first glance she thought that Lars might be another Magni-Freyan. Rheiner had told her that he was the first of his people with a normal Freyan face so the older Lars had to be from some other heavy gravity world.

Lars looked over Rheiner and was impressed with the younger man's muscle development. He set down his rifle and went to introduce himself when another contragravity vehicle entered the scene.

"Little Fuzzy, Emily Dickinson!" Jack called out. "Are you two okay?"

"We hokay, Pappy Jack!" Little Fuzzy called back.

Jack was so relieved it took him a moment to realize there were a few new faces in the crowd. "What is going on here? You must be this Brünnhilde everybody has been looking for."

"Yes, Mr…?"

"Holloway. You can call me Jack."

"Prince Morgan's father?" Brünnhilde went down to one knee. "My apologies for my disrespect, Herr Holloway the Greater."

"Oh, for Pete's sake," Jack said to himself. "Brünnhilde, please stand and address me as an equal. I expect no man or woman, Terran or Freyan or anything else to prostrate themselves before me."

Betty giggled. "I'll bet you would if I—"

"BETTY! None of that in front of...well, in front of anybody." Jack's face actually reddened. "Now, who are these two?"

Lars stepped forward with his hand out. Before he could speak Brünnhilde yelled at Rheiner in German to grab him. Rheiner didn't hesitate to wrap his arms around the man trapping Lars' arms at his sides. Lars was actually surprised when he couldn't break free.

"Unh. That's quite a grip you have there, Rheiner," Lars grunted out. "I think my ribs will crack, if you don't ease up a bit."

"Why are we grabbing this man, Rheiner?" Jack demanded.

Rheiner nodded toward Brünnhilde. "Ask Hilde."

Jack turned to the young Magni-Freyan. "He is part of a band of Fuzzy slavers," she said.

Jack turned back to the immobilized Lars. "Is this true? I'll verify it under veridication when we get back to the Rez so you might as well tell the truth, now."

"Yes and no," Lars grunted. "If Hercules here will let me go so I can breathe, I'll tell you everything you need to know."

Jack nodded to Rheiner. If Lars tried to pull something, there were two Magni-Freyans, Kealani and himself to deal with it.

Lars took a few deep breaths. "Rheiner, I want a six-pack, no, make that a case of whatever you been taking to get that damned strong." After a few more breaths, Lars stood up straight and said, "Corporal Lars Pederson, Mallorysport Constabulary, Undercover Division. I was sent out into the field to look for Fuzzy slavers, what, eight months ago? I allowed myself to be recruited by Abe Weaver so I could infiltrate the network. Unfortunately, I've been stuck out here beyond radio range. I couldn't call for backup and I was too outnumbered to make a pinch on my own. These slavers work in cells and nobody knows anybody else from another cell."

Mai, who had been silent thus far, walked over to Lars and punched him in the jaw. It hurt her far more than it hurt him. "I've been stuck out here with these animals all this time while you have been gathering evidence?"

"Relax, Mai. My report will show that you were not a willing participant in Weaver's cell." Lars turned his attention back to Jack. "Without any prompting from me, Mai did everything she could to keep the Fuzzies comfortable while they were held in cages."

"Where are those Fuzzies now?" Jack's tone of voice suggested the answer had better be a good one.

"Set free," Lars said. "Mai wouldn't let Weaver kill them and most of the crew backed her up. Had they tried to kill the Fuzzies, I would have started shooting people. I have been waiting for us to get to a town or encampment where I could call in the cavalry."

Lars then explained how Brünnhilde had been wounded and the circumstances of their meeting Kealani, Cindy and Erena.

"And the Fuzzy slavers? Where did they get off to?"

"You just missed them, Commissioner," Kealani said.

"They went that-a-way," Cindy said using a term she heard in an old western flattie.

"About ten or fifteen minutes ago, Commissioner," Erena added.

"They are too well-armed for us to deal with right now," Lars said. "Eight men, two women and a whole lot of bang-bang. They will try to get covert passage back to Alpha, then make for the spaceport."

Betty didn't wait to be told; she got on the comscreen and tried to raise Major Lunt. No luck. "Still out of range, Jack."

"Damn. Looks like we'll have to try to get them in Betatown," Jack said. "I could catch up to those ground rollers easily enough, but that would just let them know they are blown and they'd likely scatter."

Lars went to speak with Rheiner, while Jack turned his attention to Kealani, Erena and Cindy. "Ladies, I am afraid we will have to cut your field trip short. You will all need to come back and testify under veridication about everything you saw and heard while a guest of these slavers. You can come back out afterwards."

Kealani couldn't be sure if she could come back out. "It will be up to Supervisor Sylvinski. He might change his mind about the necessity of my being out here."

"I am sure that Dr. Mallin will approve the return trip in my case," Cindy said.

"If Dr. Tezza comes back out, I'll be open to coming with her," Erena said. "Kealani, I hope you can make it back out. I think we make a good team." Cindy agreed with Erena.

"I'll send somebody back for the ground rollers," Jack said. "You four need to come back with us."

"Jack, it will be a bit crowded with the Fuzzies and dogs along," Betty pointed out.

"Fair point. Rheiner, would you mind playing taxi for some of this mob?"

"It ist no problem, *Mein Herr*."

Little Fuzzy tugged at Jack's trouser leg. "Pappy Jack, me an' Emily Dickinson will ride back on dogs."

Jack didn't have to ask why; everybody on the Rez knew about Emily Dickinson's aversion to mechanical transports. "Okay, Little Fuzzy. Try not to take too long. There might be another ground quake."

"Commissioner, I would like to ride with Rheiner and Cinda, unless you want to question me on the way back," Lars said.

Jack was fine with it.

"Thank you. So, Rheiner, is it true you took several 9mm slugs and laughed it off?"

"I vould not say I vas laughing," Rheiner replied.

"Let me tell it, Big Guy," Cinda cut in. "It was amazing…"

* * *

Hickabbible Farquar escorted the visitor into Supervisor Sylvinski's office. There was little more than the furnishings that were part of the room left inside. Everything business-related had been sorted, organized, and, where applicable, reduced to electronic storage mediums, shredded and sent down to the M/E converters to be transformed into so many ions.

"Supervisor, a Mr. Morgan Holloway to see you," Hic said.

Sylvinski was momentarily confused, as he didn't recall any scheduled meetings. Then it struck him: the "Prince Morgan" that was off-planet. He had forgotten the younger Holloway had returned.

"Mr. Holloway, come in and have a seat," Sylvinski said. Normally he would have used his "business voice." This time he decided to keep it light and friendly. "I spent some time over in Neu Freya, as I am sure you already know. Do I address you as Prince Morgan or Your Grace…"

"Morgan will do, Supervisor."

"Well, as I expect this to be a fairly informal meeting, please feel free to call me Kim."

Morgan extracted some papers from his brief case. "I would have gotten these to you sooner, but I was tied up with other affairs."

"Yes, Captain Trask filled me in about an hour ago," Sylvinski said. "We can do this another time if you are fatigued from your recent incarceration."

Morgan waved that off. "There is a saying on Terra that is also used on Freya: don't put off until tomorrow what you can do today. I am here, you are here and the documents you require are also here. This is the official proclamation from Great King Jettorius the Fifth, ruler of blah-blah-blah. I'll spare you the other eleven different titles."

Sylvinski accepted the vellum document and looked it over. "This is in Freyan?"

"Sosti is what the language is called." Morgan extracted another document. "I personally transcribed the translation to Lingua Terra for your convenience. I'll summarize for you if you like. The prose tends to be a bit flowery compared to standard Terran business contracts."

"Please do."

"The hard and fast is that Neu Freya is now recognized by the Great King of Freya as a legitimate principality and under the sway of Freyan law. Because the principality is not on Freya proper, Neu Freya enjoys a permanent deferment where tribute is concerned."

Sylvinski held up a hand. "Allow me to read between the lines. You buffaloed the king into that deferment by agreeing to keep the origins of the Magni-Freyans secret so as not to embarrass the Crown. How am I doing?"

"Bull's-eye. In exchange the citizens of Neu Freya will not go visit the home world. I did manage to get an exception entered into the agreement for the Magni-Freyans with…pleasant faces."

"The throwbacks, I believe is the term I heard, like this Rheiner I have heard so much about," Sylvinski said. "I imagine in another three generations everybody on Neu Freya will look like him. Good exception to sneak in. So, you are, technically, Prince Morgan, yes?"

Morgan looked uncomfortable. "Only for ceremonial purposes. I do not own any of the land that the Magi-Freyans have colonized save for a small parcel of about one thousand acres. That may sound like a lot to people on Terra, but on Freya even the lowliest, um, Baron would have many times that area. As with old Terran royalty, the title is supposed to be supported by the land he owns. On Freya I possess sufficient land to support the title of Baron…that is the closest translation from Sosti I can think of. A Prince would need land enough to cover, mmm…a quarter of Australia."

"Zeta Continent is around the size of all of Australia. Wouldn't that make you a High King or whatever you call it?"

"Well, it is a bit more complicated than that," Morgan explained. "To be a king I would need to rule over a number of vassal states. And the population of those states would have to be a certain level with lower ranking nobility...it is somewhat involved. And I don't actually own all of that land. I simply represent the people in Royal Court."

"I understand you have a castle on Beta Continent. Why bother with a second one?"

"Again, for ceremonial purposes, mainly. Any Freyan noble house must have a castle for appearance sake if for no other reason. A Principality without a castle would be like a state without a capitol. I have arranged for one to be built using a floor plan based on a traditional Freyan palace."

Sylvinski was somewhat impressed. "You have gone to a lot of effort for the benefit of people you owe no allegiance to."

"If I recall my Terran history correctly, the northern provinces of the United States fought a very bloody war to free the slaves of the south. Did the Unionists owe any allegiance to the southern slaves? Besides, I am half Freyan so I see these people as my countrymen."

"You make an excellent point," Sylvinski agreed. "Well, I am satisfied that the monarchy of Neu Freya is a legitimate power on its own though still subject to Federation Law. And I hope you will let me know when that castle is completed and ready for visitors. I would like to come back and see it."

Morgan smiled. "I can certainly arrange for that."

Sylvinski nodded. "Oh, one other thing: now that Neu Freya is recognized as an independent power, more or less, you might consider appointing an ambassador to the Federation. If you don't, your people won't have a voice for a lot of matters that could affect them."

Morgan was surprised and his face showed it. "I had not considered that. I will have to discuss it with Johann Torseus. I am afraid I need to be on my way. There are a number of issues I need to attend to that have been delayed too long already." Morgan extended a hand and Sylvinski grasped his forearm in Freyan style.

"Look me up the next time you swing by Terra if you have the time," Sylvinski said.

"Indeed I shall. May your journey be short and filled with laughter."

Sylvinski watched as Morgan left. *I think he'll make a good prince*, he thought.

LVI

"We found the ground rollers five kilometers out from Betatown."

Major George Lunt asked the question knowing what the answer would be. "Were the owners with them?"

"Only if you count the three sunstone prospectors who bought them," Ahmed Khadra replied. "The miners traded some sunstones for both of them. From there these Khooghras must have hiked it to Betatown and jumped on the first transport to Mallorysport."

"Any idea what time it left?"

"Sixteen hundred," Ahmed said. "They'll have already arrived and scattered by now."

"And we don't even have so much as a photo to post." George Lunt swore under his breath. He discouraged that kind of language over an open mike. "I should have posted more men in Betatown to watch the transport station."

"It might not have helped," Ahmed said. "Lots of people take their private aircars over to Alpha as a sort of private taxi service. They could have split up and taken different transports. Without a photo ID, all we had to go by were some rough descriptions and the size of the gang. Cleaned up and split up, we really didn't have much chance of catching them that way."

Major Lunt knew that Ahmed was correct. He did have a man checking IDs at the transport station, but even the names could have all been faked. Or, the slavers could have gotten new forged IDs before boarding. No doubt they'd get fresh forgeries in Mallorysport as an added precaution. Some might still be in Betatown if they did split up, but how to spot them was beyond him.

"Too bad the eyewitnesses are all over on Alpha," George said. "We could have used them here."

"Jack understood that but he wanted them checked out and to get their story down under veridication while it was still fresh in their minds," Ahmed said. "Maybe they could have helped here, maybe not. Once they work with the graphics artist, we will have some good images to work from."

George grunted in agreement, then said, "Bringing them here was dangerous, anyway. They might have been spotted and silenced. We can still get those Khooghras at the spaceport, assuming they don't lay low for a while first. All right, let's do one more sweep, then make out our reports."

* * *

The aircar settled down in the open field near Junktown and the hatch opened wide. Three people, two men and a woman, stepped out.

"What do we owe you for the ride," Estefan asked.

"Nada. This is my regular run to hire temp workers," the man said. "Not a lot of scrubbers on Beta. People over there either have their own money or they are out prospecting hoping to make some. Nobody there wants to work picking fruit or harvesting crops. In about five minutes I'll have my pick out of a crowd that will form up here. A few more farmers will be out as well."

"Thank you for the ride, Mr. MacDonald," Consuela said.

"Don't be too surprised if we come out here for work," Estefan added. "Our last job didn't pan out."

"Well, I'll keep an eye out for yaw."

Consuela noticed the police tape surrounding an area that looked like a quick war had broken out. "What happened over there?"

MacDonald glanced in the direction indicated. "Oh, yeah, there was a suicide bombing here a while back. I lost a few good workers in that. Something to do with Mars if you can believe that."

"Mars?" Estefan and Consuela said together. Estefan decided to check the datastream when he could get to a kiosk. They made their good-byes and walked toward the city proper.

After they walked a while, Consuela smacked Estefan in the back of his head. "What did you tell him that for? We'll be leaving the planet first chance we get."

Estefan stopped and spun Consuela around to face him. "No, we are not. Maybe the cops know about us by now, maybe they don't. I choose to believe they do; safer that way."

"Okay, then. What do you think we should do?"

"First, we get cleaned up and put on new clothes. The kind favored by city folk, not these bush beater outfits that will stand out like a damnthing in a goofer parade. We get new papers afterwards. Then we go to the Soup Kitchen, have a good meal and look at the job board. We find something outside of the city where we can lay low for a while. Make a few sols and then, only then, do we try to get off-world."

Consuela was concerned and her face showed it. "Weaver wanted us to meet back up at that hotel in Mortgageville."

"And that is why we are going somewhere else," Estefan said sternly. "I don't care if he has us going in smaller groups. We would still all be in the same place at the same time; too easy for one of us to get spotted that way. The smart thing would be to leave the planet one or two at a time."

"That would take over a month...."

"I agree, and that is why it would be harder to spot us at the spaceport. The police are looking for twelve people."

"Ten," Consuela interrupted. "Lars and Mai stayed behind, remember?"

"Right. And if they were already picked up, the cops will have our general descriptions, the number of our group, and it doesn't take a Sheshan mystic to know that we'll be hot to leave the planet." Estefan stripped off his field jacket and pulled it inside out. "I was afraid something like this would happen. That is why my clothes are all reversible." He looked down at his trousers and boots. Both were of a common style and color. He decided not to bother with them. "Come on. We need to get you into something else."

"I guess, I'll need to change my hair color, too," Consuela said. "Hey, I bet I could get a different jacket right here in Junktown."

* * *

Weaver paced back and forth in his room at the abandoned hotel in Mortgageville. With him were Ramirez, Bo and Clem. Across the hall were the rest of the crew save for Estefan and Consuela.

"Where the Niflheim are they?" Weaver said for the *nth* time.

"They took a ride with that farmer," Bo said. "You thought it was a good idea to not all come back on the same transport."

Clem stubbed out his cigarette. It was the first tobacco he had had in months. "The farmer had his own schedule. Dropping off Connie and Estefan was an afterthought for him. Didn't he say he was headed to Junktown?"

Bo nodded. "Yup. There wouldn't be any taxis or rentals in that area…not that they could take a rental anyway."

"Need ID for that," Clem agreed.

"I know all of that," Weaver growled. "But they still should have made it here by now, even if they had to walk from Junktown."

"I have spoken with Estefan many times about what we would do if the operation was busted," Ramirez said. "He would avoid large groups and lay low until the heat was off, then he would try to quietly leave the planet. I think he will try to get a job away from Mallorysport."

Weaver considered the possibility. It was still risky, though possibly less risky than trying to take the first ship out. It mostly depended on whether or not the operation had been discovered and warrants were out on them.

What he worried the most about was the possibility that Estefan and Consuela had been grabbed up. They knew where the rest of the group was located so if they talked the rest were already blown.

"Time to go," Weaver declared. "We can't take the chance that they just went their own way. For all we know the cops are already circling the building." Nobody argued. Ramirez asked where they were headed. "That no-tell hotel on the edge of Junktown."

Bo wasn't sure about that. "Isn't that the first place they'll look?"

"Second," Weaver said. "After they check here. Give me that notepad." He scribbled something on it, then tore off the sheet and tore it up.

"What was that about?" Clem asked.

"If the cops come here and go through this room, they'll find the torn paper in the bin and impressions on the pad," Weaver explained. "I made a note about meeting a contact on Gamma. I made it cryptic enough to get their interest and vague enough to make them want to chase it down."

"How can you be sure they'll make it to this room?"

Weaver pointed at the floor. "See all the dust? We left footprints all the way in here. That reminds me; we'll need to get new footgear so they can't do a print comparison."

"Why not just sweep the floor on the way out?"

"And what do we do about the residual infra-red imprint? Let's just pick up and scoot." Weaver threw his backpack over his shoulder and started for the door.

Bo blocked Weaver's exit. "What if Connie and Estefan come here later?"

"What if the police show up sooner?" Weaver shot back. "We already had to leave Lars and Mai behind. Maybe they have been picked up and interrogated by now. I'm just glad I didn't tell them where we were meeting up. Estefan and Consuela know where we are and are way overdue to be here. That tells me it is time to be elsewhere. Come or stay; your choice."

Bo hesitated only a moment then allowed Weaver through. He grabbed his own gear and followed Weaver and Clem out.

LVII

The FBCI unmarked aircar settled down on the Dura-cement pad. The hatch lifted to reveal Janice Goodfellow and Captain Starbuck Trask. An armed and armored Honor Guard quickly marched onto the pad to form two ranks, facing each other for the newcomers to walk between.

Trask looked at the welcoming committee. "I take it you were expected."

Janice laughed. "I wasn't expecting this! Best we don't keep them waiting. I see Bürgermeister Torseus is coming with his retinue."

Trask looked out with some wonder. "Do we wait at the head of the ranks or do we move forward to meet them?"

"I think it best we wait here and see what Johann says."

"Johann?"

"Bürgermeister Torseus." Janice stepped forward to stand half a meter from the lead guard's men. Trask stood next to her.

"This is very impressive," Trask observed. "These guards are shorter than I expected but they all look like they could go hunting damnthings with a stick."

Janice suppressed another laugh. "I have heard that said before. It isn't as much of an exaggeration as you might think. Now be quiet. Herr Torseus is the big boss around here."

Johann Torseus came up to Janice and bowed low. Janice curtseyed while Trask tried to copy Johann. The Bürgermeister stepped forward with his right hand extended. Janice whispered to Trask to grasp the forearm. If Johann was surprised to be met with a proper Freyan greeting, he hid it well.

"Favored Vun, ve are pleased to haff you among us again, efen if only for a short time." Johann spoke plainly, not like a politician putting on a show. Trask, familiar with Terran politicians, gave him points for that. "I see you are vearing traditional Freyan dress. Ve are honored."

"Thank you, Herr Bürgermeister," Janice replied. "If my apparel is somehow incorrect, I hope one of the ladies here will help me correct it." Janice had spent several hours on the data stream studying Freyan fashion hoping to avoid any *faux pas*.

"Ach! I am not fery goot mit' dot, but mein dotter, Heidi, can be of serfice, Favored Vun. Und, bitte, call me Johann."

Janice smiled. "Only if you will call me Janice. And this is Captain Buck Trask."

"Please call me Buck, Herr Bürgermeister," Trask said. He hoped he wasn't speaking out of turn. He also hoped he didn't show surprise when he saw Johann coming. The Honor Guard's faces were obscured by their helmets. Johann was the first barefaced Magni-Freyan he had ever seen. Trask didn't find his countenance unpleasant, simply brutish in a non-threatening way.

"Und I am Johann for you, too, Buck," Johann said. "Come. It ist varm und die Honor Guard cannot stand down until ve haff gone."

"They look so regal," Janice said. She walked over to one of the guards and looked over the armor. The breastplate gleamed in the sun.

"Janice, it might not be proper etiquette to do that," Trask said.

"Not to vorry," Johann said. "But ve should be getting to der Rathaus. Der Honor Guard vill escort us dere. Come, ve haff a contra-grafity platform.

As the platform made its way to the Rathaus, Janice and Trask felt a bit like a float in a parade. It looked like every man, woman and child on Zeta Continent were out on the street. Some tossed flower petals in the street before the platform. She waved to the crowd, hoping it was the correct thing to do. She imagined that this was how the Queen of England felt back when the British Isles were still above water.

The platform stopped and lowered itself for simple access to the entryway into the Rathaus. The Honor Guard took up positions at the front, sides and rear of the procession. Once inside, everybody relaxed.

Janice caught the aroma of food cooking.

"Ve prepared a banquet in your Honor, F—Chanice," Johann said. He struggled to pronounce the "J" sound of her name and failed. "I hope it ist to your liking."

"It smells wonderful." Janice looked about the Main Chamber. Johann indicated a set of chairs around a small table. Janice and Trask took seats.

Johann sat across from his guests. "No doubt you are vundering vhy I asked you here before you leafe planet." Janice and Trask both nodded. "I vould like to ask you to take four of mein pipple vit' you."

"What?" Trask almost yelled. Janice sat silent though her eyes widened a bit.

"Bitte, allow me to explain. Or better, Jutta vill explain." Johann gestured at one of the Honor Guard and the armored individual walked over to table. "Remofe *dein* helmet, bitte."

The helmet came off and Johann indicated a chair.

"Jutta!" Janice was delighted and surprised. The armor and reflective faceplate had made it impossible to determine gender. "I was hoping I would get to see you before I go."

"You may get to see me after you go, Milady." She looked back to Johann. They had a brief exchange in German, then she turned back to Janice. "Janice, we have spent almost our entire lives working in the mines of Magni. I never even saw the sky until Prince Morgan exposed the entire operation. Since then we have seen Gimli and Zarathustra, and only in areas where we were unlikely to see any Terros. The seclusion was our choice. We knew what had been done to us and suspected what the response would be.

"Now we are free, though still isolated. Drugi was one of the first of us to go out on his own. He was fortunate that he went to the auditions and they liked him. Not everybody is so fortunate. Wulfgar also went out to see the world. At a *Gasthaus* he was accosted by six men who started mocking him for his face. Wulfgar is a bit sensitive. He fought the Terros and, of course, won the battle but then more people came out and attacked him. It became very messy. Wulfgar was badly injured by the time the police arrived. Every person there put the blame on him. *Danke Gott* these officers had a portable lie detector with them. They apologized and didn't even get angry about the handcuffs he had broken."

"Badly injured and he still broke a set of handcuffs?" Trask could not believe his ears. There was a story about a local man who had been shot multiple times, but still succeeded in escaping a Fuzzy slaver ship. Now Trask knew that man had to be a Magni-Freyan.

"His adrenaline vas ferry high at dot time," Johann supplied. Trask nodded and Jutta continued.

"That was the only violent incident that I know of," Jutta said. "Mostly we wear big hats and dark glasses and large billowy overcoats to avoid anybody noticing us and starting trouble. Now some of us want to go farther. We want to see the galaxy. Terros make up the greatest population of the Federation so I think we should see Terra."

"That is a wonderful idea," Janice said.

"Where does Janice come into this plan?" Trask asked.

Jutta took a moment to formulate her response. "Other than Prince Morgan and Cinda Dawn and the Overseers we have seen very few Terros. We also know next to nothing about your culture and laws and *mores*. We need a guide to keep us out of trouble, like what poor Wulfgar got into."

"I hope you see der point," Johann said. "Ve need to go to Terra vit' somebody ve can trust."

"How do you plan to get by? It takes money to travel, eat, find a place to stay—"

"Dot ist not a problem." Johann interrupted, gesturing to another member of the Honor Guard. The guard went to another room then returned with two chests somewhat bigger than a breadbox. The table creaked warningly as the guard set the chests down.

"Whatever you have in there is pretty heavy," Trask said.

The guard threw open the lids to reveal hundreds, if not thousands, of Freyan gold coins. Without considering potential consequences, Trask reached out to grab a coin. He felt the heft, judging it to be roughly a Troy ounce.

"Great Ghu on a goat!" Trask tossed the coin back into the chest. "Where did you get all of this? I estimate each coin is worth at least four hundred sols."

"It could be much more than that to a collector," Janice said, as she picked up two coins. "See the different faces? They are from different dynasties. I don't know what the Sosti term is for that." She looked at Johann who reddened a bit.

"I am embarrassed to admit dot I don't know eit'er. Such t'ings vere not discussed in die mines. Und Sosti was mostly spoken in private vhen ve vould teach our young." Johann made a note to increase efforts in teaching Sosti to the children.

"Well, collector rates or no, this looks like enough to cover everybody's expenses for years and years," Trask said.

"Oh, only one of the chests is for expenses," Jutta said. "One goes with the Blessed One."

Janice's eyes went wide. "What! Johann, I can't possibly accept this. Would anybody favored by the gods on Freya accept such a lavish gift? I would feel like I was abusing my…my status."

Johann held up a huge hand. "Favored Vun, ve understand und appreciate your honesty. As a Terro, you t'ink ve might be a bit, um, unsophisticated. But dis gold ist more den a tribute for you. Ve vant you to purchase a house vit' many rooms. Vhen my pipple fiset Terra, dey vill need accommodations. Dis vill allow you buy a fine home, if you are villing."

More like an entire block of fine homes! "But what if I come back to Zarathustra?"

Johann shrugged. "Den you hire people to handle such t'ings. If you vish to do dis. Ve don't vant to pressure you. If not, den die gold ist still for you."

"The Hotel Freya," Trask quipped. "Actually, that is not a bad idea. Buy an older building, renovate, get in some people with hotel experience, then let sapients of every species come in. The Magni-Freyans would stay for free, of course, but every other sophant could pay market rates."

"Vy vould mein pipple be free?" Johann asked.

Trask pointed at the chest filled with gold coins. "Because you are investors."

"It would need its own bar and restaurant," Janice added. "Where visitors could still get a taste of home."

"Exotic foods could get very pricey to import," Trask pointed out.

"You might consider setting up a farm and ranch. Most of the plants and some of the animals are available on Terra."

"Or somebody who has a ship that visits all those planets could arrange to get you the starter stock," a new voice added.

The Magni-Freyans all turned to the new voice and assumed the position of attention, then gave a short bow.

"Prince Morgan, ve are pleased you haff returned."

"And I am glad to be back, but please, none of this bowing when I walk into a room," Morgan said. "You are all free men who owe allegiance to none but yourselves. Perhaps you would introduce me to your—" Morgan went silent as he gazed upon Janice Goodfellow.

He placed his right fist over his heart and bowed much as Johann did a moment before. "Blessed One, I am honored to be in your presence."

Janice was mortified. Here was a prince, as real as any she ever heard of, bowing to *her*. "Prince Morgan, please do not bow to me. I think it makes me as uncomfortable, as it did you."

"My apologies, Blessed One," Morgan said. "Unlike my unfortunate friends here, I was raised on Freya and the traditions are strong within me. How do you wish to be addressed?"

"Janice is my name. I don't really think I need to embellish beyond that."

"And I am Morgan, something I am having a small problem getting across to my friends, here." Morgan shook forearms with Johann and Trask, then took a seat.

"I was not eavesdropping but I did hear you talking about starting a hotel with a bar and grill," Morgan said.

"We were just spitballing, really," Janice said.

"It sounds like a good idea," Morgan said. "Johann and I want to encourage people to get out and see the galaxy. I never wanted Neu Freya to become isolated and insular. The Lokians were somewhat xenophobic after they were freed from slavery. It took years and the public execution of their former masters before relations normalized again. The Magni-Freyans had it even worse. Now, too many want to hide out of shame."

"Out of shame? Out of SHAME!?" Janice realized she was starting to yell and fought to control herself. "I haven't seen a single bloody thing you should be ashamed of. Your ancestors were sold to evil men who took delight in using you for guinea pigs. They are the ones who should be ashamed."

"That isn't the problem," Jutta said. "It is this," she pointed to her own face. "We know the reputation of great beauty the natural Freyans possess."

"Nonsense," Janice said. "By that logic I should be ashamed to show my face anywhere but Freya, and then, ironically, only because of my birthmark that isn't valued so much on the world of my birth. Many Terros consider it a disfigurement. Yet, every day I get up, go out to work or shopping or something else even though I feel the eyes staring at me. Buck, here, is one of the few men I've met who wasn't bothered by it." Janice settled down after a moment. "Pr…Morgan, Johann, if you need a safe haven for your people when they visit Terra, they have it. I hope Drugi will come and perform there. I think he would be a hit."

Johann, who had been a little stunned by Janice's reaction, smiled wide. "*Ach*, yes, about dot. I vould like die party going to Terra to come join us."

Three more of the Honor Guard came over to the table where they were instructed to remove their helmets. Janice recognized one of them instantly.

"Drugi!"

"Aye, Favored One," Drugi said. "'The Gnarly Man' has turned out to be a hit. Ve…ahem, we will be going on tour to the different worlds. We will do Terra, then move out from there."

"That is wonderful," Janice said with a sincere smile. "I look forward to seeing you on stage again. And you have just made my point for me." Janice turned her attention to the rest of the room. "Drugi went out. He took a chance and it paid off for him. And none of you are ugly, just different. Great Ghu! So much drama over such a minor thing."

There was silence for a moment while Janice's words were considered, then everybody cheered. Drinks were brought in and passed around. Morgan pulled Johann off to the side.

"This Janice has to be the best Blessed One the gods ever sent to us," Morgan said. "I have known a few in my time back on Freya. They were usually well intentioned, but sadly out of their depth. Janice is a natural. Double the tribute and I'll make sure she gets the needed real estate and everything needed for the ranch."

Johann nodded and smiled. "I vanted to giff her more. She ist so humble und so vort'y I feared she vould object."

"Tell her that starting up a hostel is a very expensive venture. I'll arrange for some land in a suitable location…where does she live now?" Johann shrugged. Morgan nodded and continued. "I'll contact Supervisor Sylvinski. I think we last parted on good terms. I imagine we should send out more than just four volunteers…no, wait, the hotel needs to get up and running before then."

"Pr…Morgan, only four volunteered; actually, der vere a couple more under die age of responsibility."

"You made the right call, Johann. We had better get back to our guests and get the banquet going."

LVIII

"*The City of New Lansing* will be taking boarders at 1700 hours and spacing out at 2200 hours."

Marshal Fane nodded. "Are our people in place?

Chief Carr also nodded. "We have as many officers in plainclothes as we could find. We even brought in some of the cashiered for cause cases that were working the Junktown crime scene. We couldn't put out a general call for volunteers without alerting the John Carter Gang."

Fane snorted, thinking: *The John Carter Gang? Well, it rolls off the tongue a lot easier than Martianist extremist.* "I think we can trust Chief Steefer's boys in the CZC security branch. They get veridicated pretty often."

Carr mulled that over and decided that they should have more than sufficient men. "Okay, Marshal. So, what is the plan?"

Marshal Fane drummed his fingers on his desk. After a moment, he leaned forward in his chair. "We really don't have much of a plan. We'll have those three women who were taken hostage there behind cover acting as spotters, the Magni-Freyan girl as well. They will keep an eye on everybody that comes through. They spot somebody they know, they can tell us about it over the radio."

"Too bad we don't have any spotters for the extremists," Carr mused aloud. "It sounds to me like the John Carter Gang will have an easy time slipping through."

"Well, I'll admit that that is a possibility," the Marshal said. "However, we put some of those undetectable trackers Commodore Napier gave us on every relic. Sadly, these little green man enthusiasts might have enough sense to put the relics in baffle bags."

"Baffle bags?" Carr chewed on that for a moment. "Ah, like those ant-static covers the computer techs store some of their parts in."

Marshal Fane nodded. "If I were planning to smuggle something that size off-planet, I would use as many of those bags as I could get my hands on. That would keep our detection gear from finding them, even at close range. If any witnesses ever saw their faces, we don't know who that might be."

"Did you have anybody go out and check the supply stores where something like that could be had?"

"The second I thought of it." Fane stood up from his desk and went over to the bar. He prepared two highballs, gave one to Chief Carr, and sat back down. "Some were bought with cash, so no record of who or where. A few were bought with a Company expense account by a Joe Vergano. We ran down a few more names, all for nothing. My thinking is that if the Carter Gang bought any at all, they paid in cash."

"Or they settled for aluminum and maybe even military grade fibroid," Carr said. "It would be bulkier than the baffle bags but just as effective."

That got the Marshal's attention. "I considered the fibroid but not the aluminum. The metal detectors should catch the luggage going through scanners."

"Wait, metal detectors?"

"Sure, Ben Rainsford and Commodore Napier got together about how to improve security in Mallorysport after those suicide bombings. Rainsford wanted it on the QT so potential troublemakers wouldn't have a chance to plan around it. I gotta tell you that I never saw a governor go all out to protect the people like Rainsford. And he tries his best not to cramp any civil liberties while he is at it."

"How was it paid for?" Carr asked suspiciously.

"Everything owned by the CZC, or the CZC had a significant interest in, Grego covered out of the Company's coffers. The rest was paid for out of that ten percent administration fee from the Yellowsand operation. Why?"

"Because a dream paradise of no taxes never lasted forever. Eventually, this planet will get too big for the CZC to cover the services. When that happens, we're going to get hit and hit bad."

Marshal Fane nodded. "I think he knows that. That is why he put the fifty million sols from the sale of Zeta into a trust account. Every surplus sol at the end of the year goes to that account as well, or so I have heard. Relax, he has it all handled."

"One big catastrophe could wipe out most, if not all of that backup cash."

"Well, it's our job to keep the catastrophes as small as possible." Fane drummed his fingers on the desk again. "My concern right now is that in the confusion of trying to catch the slavers, the Carter Gang will slip away."

"Couldn't we hold the hypership long enough to go through the passengers?"

"Are you kidding me? Ship captains are very fussy about getting from Point A to Point B with minimal delays. In fact, I saw one case where the captain was arrested and put in jail for refusing to wait for something, I forget what, and that son-of-a-Khooghra ordered the first mate to go ahead and leave without him. A ship's captain will delay departure for one thing and only one thing. Maintenance. Oh, wait, there is one other thing."

"And that is?"

"The Navy. All of Federation space is in their jurisdiction. That includes the spaceports as well. If Commodore Napier says 'sit and stay,' the ship's captain will have no choice in the matter no matter how much he barks."

"Well, then," Carr said seriously. "We better make sure we catch these illegitimate sons of Mars before we nab the slavers."

Fane laughed. "It would be nice if they cooperated like that. Well, we have until tomorrow morning to get it all prepped. I just wish there was a way to keep the civilians out of the crossfire."

Carr agreed. While no action could be taken against anybody attempting to stop a crime, many a policeman's career was cut short by an unlucky bystander who took the bullet meant for the criminal.

* * *

Kealani, Erena and Cindy stayed at Cindy's apartment. Chief Carr had offered more secure accommodations closer to the spaceport. Cindy declared that she wanted to sleep in her own bed. Erena called her husband to let him know she would not be coming home just yet. She had not been discharged from her duties. Kealani found that the quarters she had been assigned were being cleaned up in preparation of the commission going back to Terra. Cindy insisted that Kealani stay with her as well.

"I have two *schlafcouches* that I think you will be comfortable on. I don't have anything in the refrigerator as I expected it to all spoil while we were away. We can order out from my comscreen…"

"Do you think that wise?" Erena asked. "We might have a price on our heads or something."

Kealani doubted it. "If they wanted us dead, we would already be dead. They had plenty of opportunity. What good would it do to kill us now? We have already given our veridicated statements which will hold up in court even if we are not around to confirm anything."

"I am not thrilled about going to the space station to identify those *Scheißköpfe*," Cindy admitted. "Chief Steefer said we will be safe, I know, but I am still a bit nervous about it."

"I think we all are," Erena said. "I'll just tell myself we had enough to worry about today then deal with what comes tomorrow."

"It is a shame Brünnhilde couldn't come with us," Kealani said. "I would have liked to ask her more questions about her culture."

"You'll get your chance tomorrow when we all go to the spaceport," Erena said. "For tonight she will be fine at Cinda Dawn's place. She will get to play with Cinda's Fuzzies, there."

Cindy sat down with a beer. "I hated returning Rockthrower to the Mental Sciences Department."

"Are you thinking about adopting her?" Erena asked.

Cindy hesitated before answering. "I would like to. Very much. I just don't think it would be fair to her with all the hours I am working."

"You don't know about the Fuzzy Nightclub?"

That caught Kealani's attention. "Fuzzy Nightclub?"

"Not really a nightclub so much as a social club," Erena explain. "It gives Fuzzies a place to be with other Fuzzies while their Big Ones are working."

"I had forgotten about that," Cindy admitted. "Okay, I'll discuss it with Dr. Mallin in the morn—oh, right, the spaceport. After we are done with that, then."

* * *

Jack paced nervously in Morgan's penthouse apartment.

"Keep that up and you'll owe Morgan a new carpet," Betty admonished him.

"It's military grade fibroid weave," Jack said absently.

Betty looked down at the carpet. She thought it was high-end Berber. "Fibroid? Really?"

"Morgan doesn't like things that wear out too easily." Jack stopped pacing and sat down at the table. "On Freya they tend to build things to last. Planned obsolescence is a concept they never have grasped."

"Well, you were giving the carpet a run for its money." Betty placed a plate with veldbeest steak, mashed potatoes and la-la beans on it. She filled another plate and sat down across from Jack. "Better eat that before it gets cold."

Jack snapped out of his reverie. "There are warming units in the table. The switch is in front of you on the table-side."

"I am less concerned about the dinner getting cold than I am about it being ignored," Betty said. She flicked the switch on her side of the table. The pressure sensitive control identified the exact location of the plate and elevated the temperature to match that of the plate's contents. It did not engage under the wine glass, which was controlled by a separate switch. "You have been in a bit of a snit ever since you got off the screen with Ben Rainsford."

Jack sat down but only picked at his dinner, then put the knife and fork down. "There is going to be a big whoop-de-do at the spaceport. At least everybody thinks there will be. We are anticipating that the Martianists will be trying to sneak away on the ship bound for Terra. Marshal Fane has started a building by building search in Mortgageville and in the buildings in and around Junktown. Not the clapboard shanties and pods, of course, unless nothing falls out of the other areas."

"Why not the clapboard areas?" Betty asked. "Lots of people go into hiding there. Well, that's what I heard."

"These people have money and are a fairly large group. In Junktown they would stand out like a damnthing at a goofer convention. And anybody who lives there would sell out the newcomers in a heartbeat. Not to mention all the attention that area got when that suicide bomber went off."

Betty nodded. "You don't defecate where you masticate."

"Exactly. One or two people could blend in well enough, but there has to be at least a dozen or more of these Khooghras running around. A group that large, even spread out, would raise some eyebrows. In Junktown, pretty much everybody knows everybody else. And the pods are issued to select individuals, like that fella that blew up."

"Okay, so Junktown is out and Mortgageville is being searched," Betty summarized. "Why the big push now? Why didn't they do this kind of search before?"

Jack considered his response. "Up until now they have been using infrared scans of Mortgageville and abandoned buildings. All that turned up was a bunch of squatters and a tea pad. They were all either relocated to Junktown or arrested for trespassing. The prevailing wisdom held that the Martianists were either spread out among the various B&Bs and hotels or even in the homes of sympathizers.

"After we received the last video, somebody noticed that the background might be fibroid weave, which would defeat infrared scans and even effectively soundproof a room if diligently and liberally used."

Betty stopped the fork headed for her plate, momentarily sparing a chunk of meat from being stabbed. "Why didn't they think of that sooner?"

Jack pointed at the carpet. "Do you have any idea how expensive fibroid is? Even Victor Grego doesn't use it for carpeting. The cheapest version of fibroid runs about twenty-five sols a square foot. Military-grade fibroid can run up to two hundred sols or more. That is a hell of a lot of money to cover the walls and ceiling of a room, let alone several rooms unless they were all huddling in one big area. That is millions of sols worth of fibroid. And it is heavy, bulky and impossible to carry around in quantity without raising questions."

Betty looked confused for a second. "Is fibroid illegal?"

"Not at all," Jack said as he reached for the gravy boat. "Neither is gunpowder. But when somebody carries around a serious quantity, people get curious as to why. They had to get it after they arrived, most likely from the black market."

"Where would the black market get fibroid from?"

Jack shrugged. "That is a good question. Maybe some was brought in by, say, the Fuzzy slavers or a back-alley deal with a less than scrupulous supply sergeant. Surpluses appear in military supply rooms all the time and supply sergeants like to wheel and deal for items they are short on, or even for supplies they shouldn't have. My bet is there was a stockpile of it from when Hugo Ingermann was running things behind the scenes in the underground. Fibroid would be very useful for the criminal element."

"What all does it do?"

"Oh, lots of things: bulletproof vests, soundproofing, infrared diffusion…it even insulates against hot and cold. And it can take a hell of a lot of abuse without wearing out. The good stuff, at least. This carpet here, if it ever gets replaced, it will be because Morgan decides he likes a different color. Anyway, now that we suspect the Martianists are using fibroid, the marshal has approved the overtime for a building by building search. That will take up a chunk of his operating budget, which is why it wasn't his go-to right at the start."

"Doesn't the CZC cover the costs," Betty asked. "The Company handles all of the planetary services, right?"

"Not any arm of law enforcement. Before this became a Class IV world the police were paid out of a Federation treasury. When the CZC lost the charter, the police became the responsibility of the local government."

Betty nodded. "I can see that. You can't have the Company paying for the police for fear of undue influence. Now, back to my original question—why are you in a snit?"

Jack sighed. "We also think some Fuzzy slavers who, somehow, managed to avoid all the dragnets, are going to be trying to make a break for it on the ship as well. Ben asked me to stay away from the spaceport."

Betty almost dropped her fork. "What? As the Commissioner of Native Affairs, this is very much your jurisdiction. Why would Ben ask you to stay out of it?"

Jack had hoped his explanation of fibroid would distract Betty. He should have known better. "Actually, it was the Marshal that asked Ben to ask me. He's concerned that the slavers would recognize me and scatter."

"Are you sure that's it?"

"Either that or he's concerned I'll start blasting away the second I spot anybody matching the descriptions of the slavers."

Betty suppressed a laugh. "It would have to be the first thing. I know you've, um, discorporated a lot of people in your time, but I never heard of you acting precipitously."

"Discorporated?" Jack chuckled, "I never heard it put that way before. However, I agree with you. I never drew on anybody without good cause to do so. And these descriptions could apply to a lot of people. I don't blame the Marshal for asking me to stay out of it. It just chafes a bit."

"Hmm...maybe we can do something about that," Betty said. "After we eat."

LIX

Of all the buildings on Zarathustra, the spaceport was one of the few not erected by the CZC. It was the sole property of Terra-Baldur-Marduk Spacelines. It was built within a year of learning the planet's true potential. Like all spaceports built in the last century, it was heavily framed and shielded with collapsium, a necessary expense for safety's sake. If a ship lost control and crashed, the resulting damage could destroy the entire city. For this reason alone spaceports were rarely located within the city limits on any world. The collapsium endo- and exo-covering would reduce the potential damage. The theory was that since both the spaceport and the spaceship were layered with the impenetrable metal, an out-of-control ship would simply bounce off of the roof. The jarring would likely kill most of the people on board the ship but that was preferable to destroying an entire city.

The two busiest days at the spaceport were always the result of a ship coming in or preparing to depart. The actual ship remained in low orbit like a small moon waiting to escape the bonds of gravity. Egg-shaped shuttles would make the trip down to the planet off-loading passengers and cargo, then return with new passengers and new goods.

During the process of the shuttles going back and forth, a two-way exchange of information raced through the ether bringing news, documents, and electronic mail as well as police reports and secure data from the Navy base on Xerxes.

Personnel were given shore leave on a rotating basis, maintaining a skeleton crew to keep the ship operational and to deal with issues that could not be addressed while the ship was in motion. Fissionable material would be brought up while depleted materials were simply placed in the matter/energy converters to further power the ship.

The spaceport was divided into sections to keep the flow of coming and going traffic manageable. Incoming passengers crowded at the customs stations to wait while strangers with badges went through their luggage looking for contraband plants or seeds or animals. Some species that were completely harmless in their natural environment could overwhelm the environment on another world. Medical scans were also required for much the same reason. German measles had killed hundreds of Freyans in the early days of intergalactic space flights. Nobody wanted to deal with an unknown pathogen from some alien world after it infected the populace.

From a vantage point in the space port, Marshal Fane and Chief Carr looked out at the coming and going people. The main focus, of course, was the people planning to leave the planet.

"Do you see any likely prospects?"

Chief Carr shook his head, then resettled the long-view spectacles he and the Marshal were wearing. "To me, most of these people could match the descriptions." Carr looked down at the computer-generated images on his data pad. It showed front and side pictures of each described person and could be reset by voice command to show each image with or without facial hair or even different-colored hair and skin. The long-view specs automatically recalibrated focus for the close-in object. "Too many of these people come close to the computer images. Facial recognition hasn't hit on anybody yet."

Marshal Fane grunted. "Centuries of technical refinement and the damn thing can still be beat. I just hope those mutts didn't get pseudo-flesh masks."

"Those things are pricey and they don't grow on trees," Carr said. "I have men stationed at every place we know that can supply pseudo-flesh: Halloween outlets, beauty parlors, spy shops and costume shops."

"Spy shops?"

"Yeah, you know, a place where you can buy belt cameras and spy pens...all kinds of silly stuff a real spy wouldn't be caught dead with."

"A fool and his money," Marshal Fane said. "Have the ladies spotted anything?"

Carr consulted with the radio. "Not yet, and they have the best vantage point for incoming foot traffic. I am not too worried about the slavers; we'll get them right enough. With all the cops in plainclothes out there, we can't miss. Assuming they come here today. It's those dammed Martianists I want to get a piece of. We don't even have a description to work from."

Fane nodded. "We aren't even sure how many of them there are—"

The radio squawked, interrupting the Marshal. "We got a live one, sir."

"Live one what?" Carr demanded. He was informed that men with names from one the Mars books were being detained at the debarking station.

"We have a Djor Kantos, a Dotar Sojat and a Phaidor Shang," said the voice from the radio. The officer admitted he didn't read any of the fiction about Mars, but the names sounded too weird to be normal.

"I think we have a winner, Marshal." Carr instructed the officer to take the three people to the command center for veridication. "We might catch a break, here."

Marshal Fane nodded. "If we can squeeze something useful out of these three mutts, maybe we'll be able to get the rest."

"You think there are more?"

"Oh, yeah," Fane said. "A copy of every cargo manifest and passenger list finds its way to my desk every time a ship comes in and before it leaves. I usually just file them for later reference. This time I pulled every manifest for the last two months. There were at least two dozen of those weird names when *The City of New Amarillo* came in and none when it spaced out. Not counting any John Carters, mind you. Now, they could spread their numbers out a bit and take separate ships over time, but I think they want to make a break for it now."

Carr changed the image on the screen to the GPS tracker app. "Still nothing on the tracker."

"I'm certain they have it covered in something that acts as a baffle," Fane said as he nodded. "Fibroid if they have the gear to cut it to size."

Carr sighed. "Remember the good old days when we only had to deal with people like Thaxter, Bowlby, LaPorte and Ingermann?"

Marshal Fane nodded. "Good times."

* * *

Weaver and company entered the spaceport, then immediately spread out into smaller units. As per Weaver's instructions, everybody was clean-shaven with their hair cut, and in clothes that blended seamlessly with that worn by city dwellers. Makeup was used to color the pale skin where beards had been, much to the annoyance of the users. Careful attention was given to make sure they were not all dressed alike as well. It would do them little good to be in a seeming uniform.

"Let's hit the bar," Bo suggested. "Better than walking around in circles." Clem agreed and Weaver went with it provided they stuck to beer.

"We have to keep our heads clear," Weaver said. "We leave that Freyan stuff alone as well."

The trio took seats in a booth and ordered through the automat at the end of the table. A few minutes later, an attractive brunette delivered the order. Weaver tipped her three sols and she went on about her business elsewhere.

"Okay, we just sit here nice and quiet until the boarding call," Weaver said.

"I'm ordering some food," Clem announced. "This might be our last chance to have some real fresh veldbeest. Carniculture is never as good."

The order was placed in the automat and they waited for their food. After a few minutes, Bo pulled out a deck of cards.

"Three-handed poker?" Weaver shook his head. "Any game with less than five people is a waste of time."

"Not poker," Bo said. "We get a game going and there are always a couple of guys who want to join in. As often as not they're sharps. They lose a couple of hands and push to raise the stakes, then they clean you out. Pass."

"Then what…"

"Lightning solitaire," Bo explained. "Four rows and the idea is to get the aces to the top." He did a quick run through showing how cards were eliminated by high cards eliminating the low cards in each suit. This time he didn't make it. A king was above the ace in the same suit leaving no way to eliminate it. Weaver watched until the food arrived.

"That looks like a good time-waster," Weaver said. "I'll pick up a couple of decks before we board."

* * *

"Did that look like Weaver, Bo and Clem to you?"

Kealani looked out at the sea of people coming and going in the spaceport terminal. "Where?"

"They walked into the bar over there," Brünnhilde pointed. "All cleaned up like they were going to meet some ladies."

"I think I know who she is talking about," Erena said. "I'll call Chief Carr."

Erena spoke softly into the radio with her ear piece in. Cindy sat with Rockthrower on her lap watching for signs of any of the others from the slaver camp. She started for a moment then relaxed. "I thought I saw Consuela. It wasn't her."

"The woman over there with the…um…animal," Kealani asked. She didn't recognize the species of animal beyond guessing that it wasn't from Terra. It looked vaguely simian.

"That is a kholf," Brünnhilde said. "I have never seen a real one. Only in images on the teaching machines Prince Morgan provided us."

Cindy looked and nodded. "Yes, we have some kholfs in the Science Center. Dr. Mallin does some intelligence tests with them. He says that if kholfs were able to avoid human interaction for a few thousand years, they could become a sapient species."

That surprised Kealani. "I would think that being around other sophants would speed up their mental development."

Cindy shook her head. "Dr. Mallin believes that sapience arises in difficult environments where the species has to constantly adapt to novel conditions. Being put in a cage and fed on a regular basis defeats that."

Kealani agreed that it made sense. "What about the kholfs in the wild?"

"What about human incursion on their habitats?" Erena countered. "Once a sapient species achieves an industrial stage, they tend to encroach on pretty much everything, as exemplified by Terra and Hetaria."

Kealani was surprised. "You took anthropology in college?"

"Nah. I just work around a bunch of eggheads all day at science center," Erena explained. "Sometimes I hear Dr. Mallin lecturing the students."

"I think we have another one," Brünnhilde said. "It looks like the woman they all called 'Sarge.' Are you sure they can't see us through this glass?"

"As long as we don't turn on the light in here, we are completely invisible to the people on the other side of the glass," Erena explained. "I'll call Chief Carr again and let him know we have another bogey."

Something caused a mild ruckus in the terminal. Cindy struggled for a better angle to see. "*Was ist das*?"

Brünnhilde watched as the source of the ruckus came into view. "That is a Freyan Honor Guard. We have that in Neu Freya. They must be protecting somebody of great importance to come all the way from Zeta." As the procession shifted direction, Brünnhilde could see Janice Goodfellow and Captain Trask. "*Mein Gott!* A Blessed One here on Zarathustra!" She wanted to run out and meet the procession. She stopped herself before leaving the room.

"What is a Blessed One," Cindy inquired. Brünnhilde quickly explained. Cindy nodded. "Acht. In the midst of those armored men with her she is certainly safe enough. They are even bigger than you, Hilde."

"I want to go out and meet her," Brünnhilde said. She fairly vibrated in anticipation. "I hope we can spot the rest of those horrible people before the ship leaves the planet."

Erena set down the radio. "Chief Carr says we can't all run out and grab the slavers until we have at least spotted most of them. Jumping the gun would allow the others to scatter and make it harder to catch them later."

"With Mai and Lars at the police station for debriefing, we have ten to go," Kealani said. "So far we have spotted four. I am guessing the Chief will put some plainclothesmen on the ones we spotted."

"Absolutely," Erena said. "He has them staying at a distance so as not to spook the marks."

"There is Ramirez," Brünnhilde announced. "I almost didn't recognize him all clean shaven."

"Ja, they all cleaned up, it seems," Cindy observed.

"Well, so did we when we got in," Erena said. "But those are new clothes they are wearing. I'll bet they burned the old ones."

"Why would they do that," Cindy asked.

"Trace evidence," Kealani suggested. "Fuzzy hairs and such. And they don't want to leave anything behind that might give them away." That made sense and Cindy said so. "We need to keep a sharp eye out. The shuttles will be starting to load in about ninety Z-minutes. The rest of Weaver's gang should be here before then."

Erena nodded. "And it will get more crowded and harder to spot them from this…say, what is this room for, anyway?"

"I think this was an old ticket booth from when the station was first constructed," Cindy said. "When the planet became a Class IV world, traffic picked up and they restructured the terminal for better flow. This one-way glass is brand new. See the molding? No sign of age."

"I'll bet this was a rush job done maybe yesterday just for us to have this vantage point," Kealani said. "Hey, is that Gardner there? With the tan bush hat."

* * *

"When we got there, it turned out to be a public comscreen," Trask was saying to Janice. "I thought Williams was going to pop a gasket. My apologies for not explaining why I was late getting to Zeta with you before. When I met the Magni-Freyans, everything else just got shoved to the back of my mind."

The group wound their way through the crowded terminal with surprising ease. Then again, Trask reflected, with four bodyguards in full armor and built like tanks, people just naturally gave them lots of room. Added to that were the S&W .500 Magnums and the 5.56 repeaters they each carried. Even a rabid Sheshan would get out of their way, Trask thought.

"They surprised me as well," Janice admitted. "Johann kind of looks like my Uncle Edgar, on my father's side. Much more heavily built, of course. Jutta, do you all have to keep us surrounded like this, or can we take a break and go sit down?"

One of the Honor Guard turned to face the Blessed One. "We can only relax in a secure location." She swept an arm about to indicate the crowded conditions. "This is not anybody's idea of secure. Drugi spotted a purse grabber shortly after we came in."

Trask glanced back at Drugi, at least he thought it was Drugi under that opaque face plate, and recalled that he had "accidentally" knocked somebody to the floor. A moment later a woman came over to the prone man. At the time he had thought it was a family member. Now he realized the woman was simply reclaiming her property.

"'Purse snatcher' is the colloquial term," Trask corrected. "But I think your point is well made. Drugi, what about the rest of your acting troupe?"

"They are also going to Terra on the next ship," Drugi replied. "We have already done Mallorysport and the larger towns. Now we are taking the show to Terra. From there we hope to book appearances on other worlds. Terra, then Mars, then whatever planet seems promising. We send out the booking requests while we do the Terra-side tour. By the time we finish, we hope to have some responses. Communication between worlds is very slow, you know."

Trask did know. "Well, I didn't have the chance to see the play so maybe I'll catch it Terra side."

"Oh, I would love to go see it again!" Janice said. "You must tell me when the show starts up."

"It will be my honor, Favored One."

"We should all go over to the diner while we wait," Trask suggested. He didn't want to mention that there could be trouble if the Martianists were caught while trying to leave the planet. He would have tried to convince Janice to take a later ship but there was no guarantee that the extremists wouldn't take that ship instead. All he could do was try to keep Janice and the Honor Guard out of harm's way. "Drugi, will you and the rest be able to sit and eat with us?"

"In shifts," Jutta said. "Two at a time."

That made sense. "Well, we don't want to stand around out here for the next hour and a half. You go on ahead, Janice. I need to make a call."

The procession went to the diner while Trask moved to a quiet spot off to the side then pulled out his radio. "Marshal? Chief? Can I get an update?"

Chief Carr's voice issued forth from the earpiece that Trask wore. It wouldn't be smart to let others listen in on both sides of the conversation. "We've spotted about half a dozen of the slavers so far. As for the Carter Gang, we have no way of knowing. Right now we are looking at anybody with a large trunk who might be smuggling the relics. That is really all we have to go on right now. We did grab up three likelies but they came up clean on the veridicator and we had to cut them loose."

"Understood. I'll try to keep the Magni-Freyans and Janice out of the line of fire if it comes to that," Trask said. "Any chance we can just gas the whole terminal and sort through the unconscious people?"

"Too large an area to cover, not to mention the likelihood of getting sued if somebody has an allergic reaction," Carr explained. "We'll have to do this the hard way and hope people will have sense enough to dodge for cover if any shooting starts."

"Gotcha. Well, let's hope this doesn't turn into a bloodbath. Trask out."

* * *

John Carter of Mars Colony, armed with his shiny new forged identity papers, escorted Dejah Thoris through the increasingly crowded terminal. Not for the first time he marveled that the spaceport of a back-water planet with a little over a million colonists could be so busy. *It must be because this was the turnaround point for the spaceline*, she decided. *And, no doubt, many of the tourists wanted to get a look at the most recent addition to the sapient races: the Fuzzies.*

Dejah Thoris pulled the wheeled trunk with the decoys behind her while trying very hard not to look suspicious, which to a trained observer looked suspicious in and of itself. John Carter, pulling a similar wheeled trunk, urged her to relax.

"Look, if you keep on looking so stiff somebody is going to wonder why," Carter said as quietly as he could in the noisy terminal. "Rubberneck a bit. Look around and take it all in."

"Easy for you," Dejah replied. "You aren't putting yourself on display just to distract the customs agents."

"Say that a little louder," Carter snarled. "I don't think the customs officials heard you. And, by the way, I have the real contraband, remember?"

Dejah forced herself to calm down. She knew Carter was correct. What made her nervous was the importance of what they carried: proof that the ancient Martians had spaceflight capability. It was absolutely vital that she get it back to Mars and have it authenticated. She privately admitted to herself that the rocket, already headed back to Mars, should be more than enough evidence to back up their claims that Mars colonized Terra, then lost all knowledge of their origins, but more proof was better than not enough.

"The customs line is still pretty long," Carter observed. "It might be best to wait until about ten minutes before boarding time. The customs officers should be pretty bored by then and will have to hustle to get all of the late arrivals through. That means they'll be sloppy."

Dejah nodded in agreement. Back before Carter joined the Martianist cause, he was a smuggler by trade. Unfortunately, the contacts he had built up over the years were not available on Zarathustra. While there was little doubt that some sort of smuggling occurred, Carter didn't know who to talk to in order to arrange a covert shipment of goods. Smugglers were distrustful by nature and Carter didn't have the time it would take to establish himself as a safe risk. He couldn't even cash in on his reputation since smart smugglers worked very hard to avoid building up any kind of notoriety.

"There's a diner over there," Carter pointed. "We can sit and relax until it's time to go."

The diner was full of people though there were still plenty of open tables. Carter wanted to get one near the back so the trunks would not be in the way of foot traffic. Unfortunately, there was some sort of special delegation with armored guards at the back.

An idea struck Carter. "See those people in security armor? Go ahead and look; everybody else is sneaking glances at them. There must be somebody very important back there to warrant that kind of security."

"I suppose so," Dejah said. She couldn't help marveling at the build on the armored men. *Heavy-worlders?* She wondered. "Something like that will draw a lot of attention. We should stay well away from them when we go through customs."

"Wrong," Carter declared. "We will follow them as close as we can through customs."

"What?" Dejah was confused. She thought the idea was to be as covert as possible. "Why? Every eye in the terminal will be on them."

"Exactly! Every eye, including the customs agents," Carter said with some excitement in his voice. "They'll be distracted by the nice men in shiny armor. We could almost march a darnthing…"

"Damnthing," Dejah corrected.

"Really? Huh. Well, then we could almost march a damnthing past them and they would hardly bat an eye," Carter said. "We couldn't ask for a better distraction. When we get to the customs station, keep looking over at the armored guards. That will subconsciously encourage the agents to do the same. People are just natural voyeurs when something unusual comes along."

"Which is why you had me wear my see-through blouse," Dejah said accusingly. Privately she considered the possibility that Carter just wanted a free show.

"Forget about that," Carter said. "Keep your coat on unless the agent gets too curious about the trunks. The men in shiny suits should keep him distracted. Your blouse would just distract him from the distraction. We'll keep that in reserve."

LX

Supervisor Kim Trahn Sylvinski entered the spaceport terminal accompanied by Hickabbible Farquar, Frank Farmer, Dana Alexander, Clarence Burr and a group of porters hauling their luggage. Sylvinski decided to splurge a bit and spare his personnel the trouble.

Looking out at the growing crowd, the Supervisor shook his head in disbelief. "This is almost as bad as the spaceport in Sydney," he declared. "Where are all these people coming from? How many people are even on this planet?"

"One point two five million according to the last census," Farquar said. "With a three percent margin for error."

Sylvinski spun around and looked at Farquar. "That did it. How do you always have the answer to damn near everything?"

Farquar looked a bit sheepish. "Remember I told you I have a twin brother? We were conjoined at the head. In fact, we shared the same hippocampus. Because of the location of the joining, the doctors couldn't correct it in utero like other cases. When we were separated I lost the hippocampus to my brother. The doctors grew me a new one and added some cybernetics to make sure it worked correctly. Growing replacement parts for the brain is still iffy, unlike the rest of the body. My ear, for example, was grown after the surgery. Anyway, the cybernetics enhanced my memory and even gave me a special advantage."

Farquar pulled back his hair to reveal a tiny hole behind the ear. "I can jack into a computer and transfer any information I like directly into my brain. It was a big plus in school when I was younger. I absorbed virtually all my classes directly from my data pad. Unfortunately, I was never allowed to compete in spelling bees and such. It wasn't fair to the normal children to compete with a cyborg."

Sylvinski was stunned. "So when I told you we were coming to Zarathustra…?"

"I jacked into my computer and uploaded everything on space

flight, hyperspace, astronomy, astrophysics and planet classifications as well as everything I could find on Zarathustra and colony law."

Sylvinski was impressed. "You can hold that much information in your head?"

"Yes. I used to have to dump the surplus information before I received a few upgrades. Now I could almost fit the complete Library of the Federation in my head. However, I just absorb whatever I think I will need for any project in which I am involved."

"Great Ghu! You should have been promoted over me with that in your head," Sylvinski said seriously.

Farquar shook his head. "Knowledge is useful, certainly, but so is experience. I can't jack in thirty years of practice. And there is a great deal not covered in the data-pad info. Interoffice politics, for example. You have to live it to use it. Working for you has been quite the education for me."

Sylvinski tried to decide whether he was being buttered up or not. He decided not. Farquar had always played straight with him and had even helped him dodge a few pitfalls along the way.

"I appreciate your candor," Sylvinski said. "I hope this wasn't too personal a subject for you." The commissioner raised his voice to address the rest of his party. "Everybody, let us adjourn to the bar. First round is on me."

"Sir?"

"Yes?"

"You do know that your status in the Federation government qualifies you for early boarding, right," Farquar asked.

"Oh, I know. I also think people in the government too often abuse their status. Besides, I would rather enjoy the open air for what little time is left before boarding. Now, to the bar! I heard of this drink called a Three Planets."

* * *

"Oh, Great Ghu on a goat," Marshal Fane swore as he looked out the two-way glass. "That commission bunch is going back to Terra today?"

Chief Carr swore even more blasphemously. "That's all we need: one of the commission's people getting caught in the crossfire if things go sideways."

"This is starting to look like the big finish of an action movie," Marshal Fane said. "Any moment now, Darla Cross will come running into the arms of her hero all weepy and in need of protection."

"Oh, I saw that one, *Rendezvous on Rama*. Shot on location. Darla Cross and Roland Radcliff, I think." Carr shook his head as if to clear the cobwebs out. "What do we do about the commission?"

Marshal Fane watched as they entered the bar. "Damn. They're in the bar with three of the suspects. Nothing we can do without tipping the suspects off."

"The...Freyan delegation is in the diner with Captain Trask. We could call him on his radio and ask him to find a pretext to get the Supervisor and party out of there."

Marshal Fane shook his head. "Too risky. The problem may sort itself out. No reason to think they will all come out of the bar at the same time. We can pinch the suspects as they walk out."

"Better to grab them out of the queue. They will all be in the same line and easier to round up." Carr continued his surveillance. Another face popped out at him. "Hey, isn't that John Morgan down there? In the khakis wearing a hat like Jack's."

"Can't be." The Marshal looked where Chief Carr was pointing. "Sure looks like him. Last I heard he was over on Zeta. Maybe he is here to check on something in his yacht."

"Can't be," Carr said. "I checked this morning. Only shuttles are docked except for one other yacht belonging to a..." Carr consulted his data pad, "...a Hugh Lennon from Magni. I believe Morgan took his yacht to Zeta."

Marshal Fane marveled at the extravagance of using a hyperspace-capable ship to tool around a planet. "Rich boys and their toys. If his yacht isn't here, then I can't think of any reason for Mr. Morgan...correction, Mr. Holloway, Jr. to be here. Must be a look-alike. Besides, didn't he change his hair to blonde? That coif is about as dark as it gets."

"He could have changed it back," Carr mused. "He might be here to see those Magni-Freyans off with that woman." Even Carr didn't quite believe that.

"Unless he is a Martianist or a slaver, I don't care if he is Ghu made flesh," The Marshal said. "Let's concentrate on the matter at hand."

* * *

"That's everybody except for Estefan and Consuela," Brünnhilde announced.

Kealani checked her new watch, fresh from the spaceport gift shop, with Z-time settings. "It's getting real close to boarding time. I don't think they are coming, at least not for this ship."

"I'll radio Chief Carr," Erena said.

"We should stay here out of the way while the police do their work," Cindy suggested. She noticed that Kealani looked ready to go out and join the fun.

"Of course," Kealani agreed. "But if it looks like any of them try to get away, I'll be out there like a shot." As they were situated near the main entrance/exit, anybody trying to escape would have to run past their booth.

"The Marshal has been doing this for a while, now," Erena said. "I doubt anybody will get past his men." She looked up at the spaceport observation deck. "He certainly has a good enough vantage point."

* * *

Janice and company approached the customs station and got in line. Jutta seemed to take exception to this.

"The Blessed One should not have to wait in the queue like a serf," Jutta complained.

"Jutta, remember that to Terros I am no different from anybody else. And I would not want to abuse my position, even if Terros recognized me as somebody special." Janice thought for a moment. "You know, when we get to Terra nobody will think me different from anybody else. You need to understand that so you don't get into any trouble while you are there. Besides, you won't be guarding me all of the time. There is no need. I expect you to get out and see the sights, meet new people and try new things. Drugi will mostly be out performing with his troupe, or at least I hope he will. I want all of you to enjoy your time on Terra."

Jutta wanted to argue but the Blessed One was the Blessed One and her wishes should be obeyed. She could also see the wisdom in Janice's words.

The line was long and the customs agents looked a bit harried. People lined up behind her. One woman had a large trunk on wheels as did the man behind her. Janice wondered why they didn't check their luggage earlier as she and Trask had done. She entertained the possibility that Trask had pulled some strings to allow her to check her things. It wouldn't do to have four heavy chests loaded with Freyan gold come through the customs for all to see and possibly make trouble later.

Trask rejoined her in line, ignoring the grumbling from those in the queue behind him. He was tempted to flash his badge. That would have been counter-productive as the slavers might see it and try to leave the terminal.

"Janice, do you mind if I speak to your guards for a moment?"

Janice glanced back. "I think they will only talk to you two at a time."

That made sense. "Okay, I'll speak with Jutta and Drugi." The two Magni-Freyans stepped out of line with Trask to a slightly less crowded location. Trask wasted no time getting down to cases. "There might be some trouble. How protective are these suits you are wearing?"

Jutta responded first. "These are fibroid weave suits with wafer-thin polysteel and micro-collapsium lamination plates. They would be too heavy for anybody not coming from a heavy gravity world, I think. For us it almost feels like normal gravity."

Trask thought it through. Fibroid, in military grade, was bullet-resistant by itself. Polysteel was strong and light. With the micro-collapsium lamination it would be a lot heavier. Typically, micro collapsium was one centimeter to two and a half centimeters thick aluminum compressed down to a nanometer thickness. It would stop any bullet short of depleted plutonium. Impact and weight were the main problems for a Terro human. The Magni-Freyans were made of much sterner stuff. The weight didn't bother them at all. Impact where the metal was absent might be a problem.

"All right, you guys are as bulletproof as you can get short of wearing powered armor," Trask said. "I know I don't have to tell you this, but if any shooting starts get Janice to any cover you can find. I am hoping there won't be any."

"Have no fear, Captain," Drugi said. "With us here the Blessed One will be the safest person on Zarathustra."

That was good enough for Trask. "I have another question; some of you call Janice the Blessed One while others call her the Favored One. Why is that?"

Jutta nodded. "It is the approximation of the meaning in Sosti. On Freya the same word describes both. So, in German and Lingua Terra the translation is just a matter of choice."

Trask made a mental note to learn some Sosti when he had some time. They rejoined the line, again ignoring grumbles from the back. Trask checked his watch then looked over the queue. If things were going to heat up, it would be very soon. Trask unsnapped the holster flap on his pistol in case he needed to draw his weapon quickly. Noticing this action, the Honor Guard did the same.

* * *

"I can't believe our luck," John Carter whispered to Dejah Thoris. "We are right behind the couple with the bodyguards. That makes up for the rest falling into line right behind us."

Carter's original orders were for everybody to spread out in the queue. That way, if one or two got pinched, the others might still get through undetected. Everybody gathered together made it too easy to catch everyone simultaneously. Unfortunately, by the time they all filed out, most of the boarders had already gone through customs. Carter hoped all the attention would be on the bodyguards with the odd armor.

"If the guards move out of sight before you get to the customs agent, take off your jacket," Carter said to Dejah Thoris.

Dejah was less than thrilled with putting herself on display as a distraction and said as much. "I don't mind putting on a bit of a peep show when I go out clubbing, but this just feels wrong."

Carter nodded in understanding. "Look, if I thought my wearing that blouse would get us through, I'd swap with you in a heartbeat. Sadly, I would create the wrong kind of distraction. Just remember, this is for The Cause."

While far from placated, Dejah Thoris knew this was not the time and place for an argument. Instead, she loosened her jacket so it would come off quickly, if it became necessary.

* * *

Weaver was not happy. Everybody came together in the lineup. He looked all around as if taking in the sights one last time. In fact he was looking for Estefan and Consuela. Not seeing a sign of them, he hoped they had just gone off on their own to lay low. The alternative was that they had been grabbed up by the police. If that were the case they were all blown but good. Weaver decided he would much rather be killed while trying to escape than go through the humiliation of a very public trial and execution.

Looking down the line, he saw a man behind his people whose very appearance screamed "bureaucrat." Terran-style business suit, super-glossy shoes, briefcase, bored expression combined with a quiet arrogance, as if it had been chiseled into place: the whole shebang. If things got hairy, he would be the one to grab as a hostage.

Weaver suspected the woman with the bodyguards might be far more valuable, but with those armored guards she would be far more dangerous to try to grab. The guards were short yet appeared to be powerfully built. No doubt the armor was bulletproof. Weaver studied the four armored men, at least he thought they were men; they could be anything under all that armor. Making a grab for the couple the armored men were guarding would be about as smart as hunting a damnthing with a toothpick. They were all built like Lars, only a couple inches taller. Maybe they were from the same planet as Hilde? Weaver had no intention of finding out. He recalled how easily Brünnhilde threw his men around back on Beta. These guys looked like they could even toss around Hilde!

Everybody in the terminal was looking at the bodyguards. Weaver appreciated that. The more people looking at them, the less attention on him and his group. Weaver turned his attention back to the customs station. The agents were moving quickly through the baggage while stealing glances at the four armor-clad figures. Perfect.

"Weaver?"

Weaver turned to the sound of the voice, prepared to rip whoever said his name aloud a new one. It wasn't one of his people.

"Hey, Weave," a short man in bush gear repeated. "Remember me? We came in on the same ship."

Weaver spotted the man. He struggled to recall the gentleman's name. He had engaged the man in card games on the ship that brought them both to Zarathustra. George? Jim? Jackson?

"Jarrod Honeycrest from Baldur colony," the man introduced himself. "Fancy heading out on the same ship. Hey, maybe you'll give me a chance to win some of my money back, eh?"

* * *

"Look at that," Marshal Fane said. "They're all lined up together like a cadet review. There were supposed to be ten of them. I count eight unless I missed something."

"No, that is all Brünnhilde fingered," Chief Carr said. "She said they cleaned up real good: shave, haircut, new clothes—wait! There is somebody else talking to the one called Weaver. One of the missing mutts?"

Marshal Fane consulted his data pad. "He doesn't match any of the descriptions. That Weaver character looks like he's getting nervous."

"Damn. I was hoping we could take these guys one at a time after customs sent them through." Carr picked up his radio. "Everybody move in slowly. Try to act natural but get as close as you can before identifying yourselves. We don't want this to turn into a shoot-out if we can possibly avoid it."

Marshal Fane looked over the situation critically. "Trask's group and some tourists are right in front of them in the line. Give Trask a heads-up."

* * *

Erena pointed out the undercover policemen moving into position. "I guess the Marshal decided to get Weaver and the rest and try to get

Estefan and Consuela some other way."

"If they were coming, they would be here by now," Kealani said. "A last second arrival would draw too much attention."

"Who is that man talking to Weaver?" Cindy asked. "Is that a *polizei* or another slaver?"

"I never saw him with the group," Brünnhilde said. "Maybe a slaver from somewhere else? A contact?"

That started a discussion about other slaver cells that might still be active on Zarathustra. Rockthrower, unable to keep up with the discussion, hopped off of Cindy's lap and left the booth. She wanted a better look at the bad Big Ones.

* * *

Weaver tried to politely extract himself from the one-sided conversation with Jarrod Honeycrest when something caught his eye. It was a Fuzzy. Realization struck Weaver like a bolt from the blue. Jarrod was supposed to keep him distracted while one of the Fuzzies he let go back on Beta came out to identify him. It also explained where Estefan and Consuela were; they were in police custody, getting squeezed for every drop of information they had. No doubt under veridication. Cops would be dressed in mufti so they could sneak up on them.

That was when Weaver pulled his gun.

LXI

John Carter first heard the shot, then saw men and women with guns in hand racing toward the queue. One of them yelled for everybody to freeze and that they were surrounded. Carter added two plus two and came up five.

"We've been made," Carter yelled as he drew his pistol. "We'll have to force our way through and try to take control of the ship's bridge."

Carter knew his chances of pulling off a hijack were slim. His chances of coming out of the spaceport free and alive were a lot slimmer. His people all pulled their weapons and started firing at anybody who also had a gun in hand, including the others in the queue with them. Dejah Thoris didn't have a gun as per Carter's orders.

"Sorry, Dejah, but we need to make it look like you are another victim."

Dejah Thoris was about to ask what he meant when the lights went out to be replaced by stars, then nothing.

* * *

"What in Niflheim just happened down there?" Marshal Fane demanded of nobody in particular.

Chief Carr didn't catch the rhetorical nature of the question and attempted an answer. "The one identified as Weaver just pulled out his pistol and shot the man who was talking to him. Then the rest of them pulled their guns. That bunch ahead of them in line also started shooting. More slavers that we didn't know about?"

Marshal Fane watched the movements of the players for a moment. "Slavers my Aunt Fanny. Those guys are shooting at everybody, including Weaver's gang. I'll bet platinum to peanuts that those other men are the Martianists we were watching for. Warn Trask and the rest to arrest everybody. We'll sort them out afterwards."

* * *

With the first shot fired, the Honor Guard sprang into action. The two closest to Janice Goodfellow quickly hustled her to the customs station, over the counter and down on the floor. Janice noticed a black smudge on the otherwise immaculate armor of one of her guards and realized a bullet must have struck there. Whichever guard it was, Janice couldn't tell as the armor all looked alike and nobody had a nameplate. The guard either didn't notice or didn't care that he or she had been shot.

Trask didn't have the chance to answer his radio. One of the people in the rapidly scattering queue had a gun aimed right at him. He drew his own pistol knowing it wouldn't be fast enough. The other man fired. Trask was surprised he wasn't dead. Even more surprising was that one of the guards had stepped between him and the shooter. The bullet hit something that wasn't metal. Trask shot past his living barrier and dropped the shooter.

"Are you okay?" Trask asked the guard.

"I think I will have a nasty bruise," Drugi said. "This, ehh, fiberoid? Prevented more serious harm."

"Good. Try not to shoot anybody wearing the blue trousers or shirts. They're on our side."

"*Jawohl, mein Herr.*" Drugi drew his .500 Magnum and moved toward the people not wearing any blue. He plowed into a man who would later be identified as Tars Tarkas. Rather than shoot, Drugi backhanded the man and sent him flying several feet away to land, unconscious, on the floor.

Trask spotted Weaver taking aim at Drugi and put three rounds in his chest.

* * *

As soon as the shooting started, Rockthrower quickly went back into the booth. She leapt back up on Cindy's lap and hugged her while shaking badly. Cindy tried to comfort the frightened Fuzzy while Brünnhilde raced out of the booth, gun in hand. Cindy heard her say something about "The Blessed One" as she ran past.

"She knows not to shoot anybody wearing blue, right?" Erena asked nobody in particular.

"I hope so," Kealani said. "That .500 she's carrying is a take-no-prisoners kind of weapon. I'll go and back her up."

Cindy watched Kealani run out and turned to Erena. "Should we go out and help?"

Erena shook her head. "You are a doctor, not a cop. And I am still sluggish from that beating I took over in Beta. We'll help more by staying out of the way. Kealani has had some security training from her father's business. She can take care of herself just fine, I'm sure. I am more worried about Brünnhilde. She doesn't have any armor like her friends."

* * *

When the shooting started most of the non-combatants ran for cover. A few of the hardier souls drew their own weapons waiting for a chance to help…as soon as they knew who was fighting whom. As civilians, none of them knew what the police undercover color of the day was and hesitated joining the fight for fear of shooting the wrong people.

One dark-haired man showed no such hesitation. Standing behind a support column he carefully took aim at one man who was in the process of pointing his gun at Captain Trask. Three trigger pulls put three rounds in the center of the man's chest. Trask remained blissfully unaware of his close call and concentrated on bringing down another shooter.

By this time people had scattered in every direction seeking cover. A few attempted to run past the customs station only to be struck by a very large gauntleted fist.

Running from cover to cover, the dark-haired man took aim and fired whenever a target presented itself. Had anybody been free to notice, they would have been impressed by the man's steady hand and remarkable accuracy. He was about to fire again when something charged through his field of vision. It was a girl with incredible muscle mass.

Now what is that fool kid doing? the dark-haired man thought. *She'll get killed running around like that.*

* * *

Brünnhilde wasn't thinking straight as she ran through the terminal. Only the luck that the gods give to fools and small children kept her from getting her head blown off. She narrowly avoided catching a bullet to her leg as she raced to the customs station. Just as she made it to the counter, an armored figure rose up from behind it and pointed a very large gun at her. She recognized the model as an old style S&W .500 Magnum. It was the same weapon of choice used by almost all of the Magni-Freyans, including her father.

"Don't shoot," Brünnhilde said loudly. She had to yell over the sounds of gunfire. "I want to help protect the Blessed One."

The gun was raised to a neutral position and she was invited to join them behind the counter. "You are lucky I recognized you, Brünni."

Brünni? Only one person ever called her that. "Klaus? Is that you under that faceplate?"

"*Ja.* I am part of the Honor Guard escorting the Blessed One to Terra," Klaus explained.

"You two know each other?"

Brünnhilde turned to find herself face-to-face with the Blessed One. "Oh, uh…um. Yes, Milady. Klaus is like a, um, step-brother."

"My parents were killed in a mining accident and Brünhilde's family took me in," Klaus explained. He turned back to Brünnhilde, "Did you call Mother and Father and let them know that you are safe?"

Brünnhilde stifled a laugh. "Safe is kind of relative at the moment. But, yes, John Morgan Holloway the Greater let me call them from his comscreen at his office. Rheiner was there, also."

"I wish Rheiner was here right now," Klaus said. He risked poking his head up for a look at the action then raised his pistol and took a few shots of his own. "He is much better with a gun than I am."

Janice noticed that Klaus and Brünnhilde carried the same model of hand gun. "Does everybody in Neu Freya use those monster guns?"

"Pretty much, Bl…Janice," Klaus said. "Our hands are very big so most models of gun are difficult for us to handle. These .500s require very little modification to allow us to use them effectively. And the kickback doesn't bother us at all. We do have to be very certain of our targets, though. These seven hundred grain bullets could go through five people with one shot."

Brünhilde's eyes went wild at the familiarity Klaus showed the Blessed One. Janice noticed her expression and explained that she requested being addressed in that manner. "And I would like you to do the same."

"Yes, Mi…Janice." Brünnhilde chanced a quick look and ducked as a bullet whizzed past her head. She had quite enough of her head being used as a target. "I hope Kealani, Erena and Cindy are staying safe. And Rockthrower, too."

* * *

When the shooting started, Supervisor Sylvinski reacted purely on instinct. He turned and ran away from the gunfire as any rational person would do. In the process he scooped up Dana Alexander and shielded her with his body until they reached some cover. Close on his heels came the rest of his entourage save for Clarence Burr. Sylvinski looked back and saw Burr on the floor with a shoulder wound.

"We have to get Clarence out of there before he gets killed," Sylvinski said. "It'll take two of us to carry him back. Who's with me?"

Hickabbible Farquar put a restraining hand on the Supervisor's shoulder. "You've done your part. Frank, care to give me a hand?"

To his credit, Frank Farmer didn't hesitate. Both men dashed out, grabbed up the unconscious attorney and raced back. They almost made it unscathed. Behind the cover of a pretzel vendor booth, they gently set Burr on the floor. Dana ripped off his jacket and made a field dressing to slow the bleeding.

"Good job, Frank," Farquar said.

Frank shrugged. "I've played those bang-bang shoot 'em up computer games a million times. This is the first time I did it for real."

"I'm putting you both in for a commendation," Sylvinski said. "You both surprised me wi…Frank, you're bleeding!"

Frank looked down and saw blood spreading down his pant leg from his thigh. "Damn. I didn't even notice it. Now it hurts like hell."

"Niflheim," Sylvinski corrected. "Never mind that. Let's cut that pant leg off and get you patched up. Dana?"

"On it."

"Good. By any chance does anybody have a gun?" Nobody spoke. Sylvinski sighed. "I guess all we can do is wait it out, then. Dana, how does that leg look?"

"I only have basic first aid training but it looks like the bullet missed the femoral artery and the femur. It went clean through." Dana examined the bandage she wrapped around the thigh. "He isn't gushing blood so I don't think we need to put on a tourniquet unless it gets worse. Frank, lay down so we can elevate that leg. We don't want you going into shock so I have to loosen your clothes and keep you warm."

"I wish Kealani was here," Farquar said. "Lucky for her, she has to stay and testify in court about what happened to her out on Beta."

Sylvinski chuckled without meaning to. "She may be here a good while longer. We still need her report of the effect of Terro-humans on the Fuzzies. That means going back out into the field and the Fuzzy Reservation to do developmental studies and such. I arranged with the Navy to handle her wages."

"I didn't know that," Farquar complained.

Sylvinski shrugged. "You were busy with the Deputy Governor."

"So, Kealani shouldn't be here in the spaceport terminal?"

"I can't imagine why she would."

Farquar pointed at something moving on the other side of the terminal. "It looks like she found a reason to be here."

Sylvinski looked, then pulled back when a bullet ricocheted near him. He thought for a moment before it came to him. "She's here to finger the Fuzzy slavers, if they try to leave planet. I should have thought of that. Hic, make a note to get her hazard pay."

"What is she doing running around with a gun out there," Dana demanded.

"We'll ask her after we get out of this alive," Sylvinski said. He wouldn't entertain the possibility that they wouldn't survive. As he saw it, he was the captain of this crew and he needed to keep morale high. He pulled a few sols out of his wallet and reached up to set them on the counter. The pretzel vendor was gone, no doubt running for his life. Sylvinski grabbed the pretzels that were in reach without having to stand up. "Anybody hungry?"

Nobody answered. Instead, they looked past the Supervisor at something behind him. Sylvinski turned to see the barrel of a gun pointed right at him.

"I don't suppose you would be interested in a pretzel?" Sylvinski asked showing surprising calm. "The salted ones are particularly good."

The gun wielder, bleeding from wounds in his shoulder and left arm, was not amused. "I need a shield to get out of here. You're elected."

Sylvinski shook his head. "I am afraid that will not be possible, sir. I have a ship to board—"

"Enough with the wisecracks, smart-ass," the gunman barked. "Either you get up and come with me or I start shooting your friends."

Sylvinski seemed to space out, staring out into seemingly nothing, then regained himself and shook his head. "I am afraid that isn't going to work out for you. I suggest you hand me your gun and surrender peacefully."

"Like Niflheim I will!" The gunman raised his weapon to aim it at Hic Farquar. There was a shot, and then the gunman fell to the floor. Another man came up from behind.

"Is everybody all right?"

"We are now, sir." Sylvinski studied the newcomer. "By any chance are you Morgan Holloway's brother?"

The man looked confused. "What makes you think that?"

"You look like a much younger version of Commissioner Holloway whom I met when I first arrived. I was informed that he had a half-Freyan son who was very active with the Neu Freyans. They speak very highly of him. I also met Prince Morgan and you are definitely not him, though you look almost like his twin."

"No, but thanks for the compliment," the man said. "I suggest one of you take the dead man's gun. You may need it."

After a brief discussion it was determined that only one of them had any real experience with firearms. Dana Alexander accepted the gun, inspected it and nodded with satisfaction.

"A bit larger than my Kimber back home but I'll manage," Dana said.

"Excellent." The man turned back to Supervisor Sylvinski. "You were very cool for a man in your position."

Sylvinski shrugged. "I'll be honest; I almost passed out. But I am responsible for these people. My father always said 'If you can't dazzle them with brilliance, baffle them with bullshit,' pardon my Sheshan. When I saw you coming up from behind, I figured either we were saved or dead. Very happy it was the former."

"I have to get back out there. Stay safe." The man turned and carefully moved away from the pretzel cart. He didn't say anything, but the Supervisor managed to impress him.

* * *

Hugh Lennon had just left his private yacht with the intention of getting a hot meal in the city when all Niflheim broke loose. People started shooting in every direction. Normal survival instincts kicked in and the Magnian merchant ran through the nearest door. Literally. Some small part of his brain registered the fact that he would have to make good on the door he had just destroyed. The rest of his mind was busy processing his surroundings and taking inventory of his body parts.

No holes or leaks, Lennon thought with some relief, then cursed himself for not bringing his sidearm with him. On Magni nobody bothered to go armed. It was even rare for two Magnians to get into a fistfight. Guns weren't as dependable against rock hard bone and sinew and fights between two Magnians usually meant a prolonged stay in the hospital for everybody involved in the altercation. Nobody fought for fun as a result.

He took in his surroundings then swore. He was in the Men's Room. There was nothing that he could fashion into an acceptable weapon there. Lennon took a moment to smile at the situation. It could be worse; he could have just as easily found himself in the women's privy. Still, it galled Lennon to just sit on the sidelines and do nothing.

Carefully, he poked his head out just enough to see what was happening. There was a man shooting at seemingly everything near the demolished doorway. Was this a white hat or a black hat? Then he saw the man taking aim at a running figure that looked like John Morgan Holloway.

Before Lennon even knew what he was doing, he stepped out and backhanded the gunman, sending the hapless man into the wall, then down on the floor. He glanced at the fallen pistol the now unconscious shooter had dropped and considered making use of it. Then he realized it was far too small for his oversized hands to grip and use effectively. In fact, his thick index finger wouldn't even be able to get inside the trigger guard.

Logic won out. Lennon tossed the weapon into a trash bin, then ran for the nearest exit hoping that nobody would waste any bullets on him. Once outside he ran to a public comscreen and contacted the police.

His civic duty done, Lennon decided that since he couldn't do anything else, he might as well get that meal. He knew by the time he could find a weapons shop, purchase a suitable weapon and come back to join the action, the police would likely have everything under control. In fact, he might even be a hindrance. All he could do is hope he didn't knock out the wrong man and let a criminal get away.

* * *

Kealani fired off three shots as she dove for cover. She had intended to catch up with Brünnhilde and provide cover for her. What she hadn't expected was how fast the Magni-Freyan girl could run. Actually, it was like she launched herself with each step, spanning several feet between each foot fall. Brünnhilde made it to the customs desk before Kealani covered ten feet.

Now what do I do? Kealani wondered. From her vantage point, she could see the shooters, those that were still alive, anyway. Some of the people on the floor wore the blue shirts or trousers that told her they were the police officers in mufti. There was very little blood that she could see by the bodies. She hoped that meant they were wearing bullet-resistant clothing.

Kealani was about to make a try to get back to the booth when a large man in khakis raced toward the exit. Subconsciously she realized that the man was not wearing any blue, was not one of the Fuzzy slavers that she knew, and the man had a gun out suggesting he was one of the active shooters.

On the conscious level Kealani figured if the man was just trying not to get shot he shouldn't be waving a gun around. She moved from her point of cover and blocked the man's path. Whatever the running man may have thought about the small figure barring his exit, it certainly wasn't that the woman was any kind of threat. He tried to push past her like a running back with the football. What happened was that as soon as he came near Kealani, his feet went out from under him and his head struck the floor. Hard.

Kealani debated pulling the man to safety. His size relative to hers made that problematical. Adding in the possibility of catching a bullet in the process made her decide to let unconscious men lie.

There were fewer people still exchanging gunfire. None of the slavers were visible, or at least not vertical. She decided to risk it and ran toward the customs station where Brünnhilde had been headed. As she approached she spotted a woman lying on the floor next to a large wheeled trunk. She didn't appear to have been shot.

Kealani moved the trunk so as to use it for cover while she checked the woman. No visible wounds and she had a strong pulse. Ether knocked unconscious or fainted, Kealani concluded. The woman's coat was open and Kealani noticed the translucent blouse. *A bit showy for a spaceport*, she thought.

The gunfire abruptly ceased. Kealani risked a peek over the trunk. Before she could see anything, she was abruptly grabbed from behind and lifted into the air. She tried to twist out of the grasp of whoever held her but failed to break the grip.

"Kealani! What are you doing over here?"

It was Brünnhilde pulling her to cover behind the customs counter. "You about scared me out of ten years growth, Hilde! And I can't spare any of it."

"Kealani, are you okay?"

She turned to see Janice Goodfellow. "Janice, what are you doing here? And who are these action figures?" Kealani referred to the two figures in armor with opaque face plates.

"These are my Honor Guard. Two of them, anyway." Janice indicated one then the other. "This is Klaus and that is Wolfram. Jutta and Drugi are out there with Captain Trask."

"Klaus is my brother," Brünnhilde added. "Sort of."

Kealani realized that the two men weren't wearing padding; they really were that muscular. "They are from your colony." It was a statement, not a question. She did have some questions but decided it could wait. "The shooting has stopped. We should see who won."

"We did," a new voice said. "Brünnhilde, right? Then you must be Kealani. Pleased to meet you both. Can one of you come help me identify some of the bodies?"

Kealani and Brünnhilde went with Trask.

"That one is Weaver," Brünnhilde pointed at a prone body. "He was the boss. Or at least he acted like he was."

"That woman there is the one they called 'Sarge,'" Kealani added. The two women identified eight of the bodies' altogether. "The rest are unfamiliar to us."

Trask nodded knowingly. "We think these are the Martianists that have been giving us so much trouble of late. They all have fresh forged identity papers. Pretty good ones, though I have seen better."

Kealani pointed toward the entrance at the unconscious man. "He might be one of them, too."

Trask asked two officers to collect the man. "Medics are on their way. We'll sort through this lot after we've taken care of the dead and wounded. Drugi, do you need medical attention?"

"No need, *Herr Hauptmann*. I have had worse injuries in the mines."

Trask didn't know what *Hauptmann* meant. Brünnhilde explained it was German for captain. "Hmm. I like the sound of that."

"There is an unconscious woman behind that trunk," Kealani pointed out. "She might be one of those Martianists."

Trask saw the trunks and bells went off in his head. He went over to the trunks. The woman appeared to still be unconscious.

No warrant, Trask told himself. He opened the first trunk anyway. Clothes, a few souvenirs; the usual tourist fare. Trask felt the bottom and sides and found what he expected to find, then inspected the other trunk.

"Hey, we need a medic over here," Trask called out. He quickly closed the trunks. By the time a medic responded, the woman was sitting up rubbing her head. "Miss, are you alright?"

Dejah Thoris stood up on shaky legs. "What happened?"

"Ah, we had a little trouble. Nothing for you to worry about." Trask pointed at one of the bodies. "This man was in line behind you. Were you together?"

Thoughts raced through Dejah's mind, mostly of the "admit to nothing" variety. "No. I don't know him. Was he some kind of criminal?"

Trask nodded. "Yes, we think he was. You should let a medic look you over."

Dejah Thoris fought to keep her near-panic down. "No! I mean, I can't. I have to get on the ship."

"You can take the next one, ma'am," Trask said. "You might have a concussion."

"No, I…I'm fine. I can't afford to miss the ship. People are expecting me…back home."

"Well, I can't force you to stay if you don't want any help," Trask said. He showed her his badge. "Can I get your name?"

"D…Dorothy Thompson. Here are my papers." Nervously, she handed over her forged documents.

Trask looked over the documents, then returned them to the woman. "Everything appears to be in order, ma'am. Enjoy the trip."

Surprised that her papers passed muster so easily, she quickly collected a trunk and went to the customs station. The agents were gone and in their place stood two armored men and a woman with a very large birthmark.

Janice looked over at Trask who made a subtle gesture to send the woman on her way. "Customs is suspended for the moment, Ms. Thompson. Just go on ahead."

Dejah wasted no time doing exactly that. Trask watched the woman move down the hall with Carter's trunk instead of the one she had been pulling around.

When the woman was no longer in sight, Janice turned to Trask. "What was that all about?"

"Have you ever gone fishing?" Trask asked. Janice admitted she had never been. "Well, sometimes you use a little fish as bait to catch a bigger fish. And she is swimming away right now. But we have her on a short line. In fact, you and I are supposed to be getting on that ship as well, you know."

"Won't we have to stay and testify?"

"No need." Trask pointed to an opaque globe on the wall, then at several more all about the terminal. "Everything was caught on surveillance. Marshal Fane and Chief Carr are also witnesses up on the observation deck. In fact, we have too many witnesses. That can muddy things up quite a bit. Besides, I have to tail Miss Thompson. I'll explain more later. No telling who might listen in."

LXIII

The aftermath of the shootout left the spaceport in a state of chaos. Injured bystanders, police and suspects were treated by emergency medical technicians as quickly as they could. Passengers who hadn't made it on board grumbled about the lack of security and word of legal action was discussed by several of them. The passengers who had made it safely aboard were escorted back off of the shuttle.

By order of Commodore Napier, the spaceship was delayed indefinitely. The ship's captain tried to fight the order to no avail. Everything concerning space travel, including the spaceport, fell under Federation Naval jurisdiction, a law enacted in the early days of space travel to smooth out such legalities as jurisdiction for warrants and search and seizure orders. Beyond the bounds of a planet's gravity, save for the spaceports, the Navy was the law.

Captain Trask was surprised that Napier would go so far as to hold the passenger liner. The Commodore, not having a sense of legal niceties, wanted the ship held until every person involved in the gunplay was veridicated. Trask shielded Dorothy Thompson from being interrogated, stating that she was unconscious at the time of the incident. Trask also spoke with Supervisor Sylvinski to assure him the delay would be brief.

"That isn't a problem for me, Captain," Sylvinski said lightly. "I won't mind a day or two to go out and see some of the local color. I was far too focused on work to see any of the sights. Oh, you should speak with the gentleman who shot that…person over there." The Supervisor indicated the corpse near the pretzel cart.

"I intend to speak with everybody," Trask said. "What was the name of the man that did the shooting?"

"I'm sorry, but he didn't give me his name," Sylvinski said. "He looked a great deal like Jack Holloway, whom I met in the governor's office, only much younger."

Trask recalled that Chief Carr had told him somebody looking like

Morgan Holloway was seen just prior to all Niflheim busting loose. That makes no sense, he thought; I left Prince Morgan on Zeta yesterday.

Trask looked about and spotted a man who matched the description. He was assisting an officer. "Excuse me, Commissioner."

"Don't let up pressure until the medics have a go at him, Officer Sullivan," the man was saying. "That is a sucking chest wound. They can fix that up at the hospital and he won't even have a scar to impress the ladies with; but only if he is alive when he gets there."

"No worries, sir," Officer Sullivan said. "Gil has been my partner since I landed on this rock. I have no interest in breaking in a replacement. Besides, his wife will kill me if he doesn't come home for dinner."

Trask looked over the situation. Sullivan had opened his partner's shirt and applied a piece of plastic, possibly from a cigarette pack, to create an airtight seal over the wound. Airtight, that is, as long as there was pressure on it. "I have seen wounds like this before. I am afraid he'll have to miss dinner with the missus. I think breakfast is doable."

Reassured, Sullivan nodded and maintained the pressure. A medic arrived a few minutes later. "Hear that, Gil? You'll have to suffer through Gail's undercooked eggs and overcooked home-fries in the morning."

"Any…chance I...could stay…at hospital…until lunch?" Officer Gilbert quipped.

The medic, a former Corpsman, shook his head. "We don't like malingerers taking up needed bed space. Okay, move your hand." The medic glanced at Gilbert's nameplate. "Okay, Officer Gilbert, I need you to hold your breath for a moment while I make a proper dressing."

The medic quickly and skillfully removed the plastic and replaced it with a pseudo-skin patch that automatically adhered to the wound while also disinfecting it. Gilbert breathed better though there was still some difficulty.

"No talking, laughing, screaming or chasing nurses until we do a proper reconstruction of the lung and surrounding tissue." He looked up at Sullivan. "That was smart thinking using the plastic to create a temporary seal."

"Not my idea." Sullivan jerked a thumb at the as yet nameless man.

"He told me to do it."

"That kind of field dressing goes all the way back to First Century," the man said. "An old friend used one like that on me years ago."

"Sir," Trask interrupted, "could I speak with you?"

The man stood up from his kneeling position. "Sure thing, Buck."

Trask looked at the man's face critically. More than a few people called him Buck, at his insistence, but only after he introduced himself. The familiarity and resemblance to Morgan Holloway told Trask who he was dealing with. "Jack? Is that you under that Makeup?"

Jack Holloway sighed. "I guess I'm busted."

Trask put it together quickly. "You came here to get the slavers but couldn't risk being recognized as the Commissioner of Native Affairs."

"Got it in one," Jack said. "Marshal Fane asked me to stay out of this for that reason."

"And I am guessing Betty had a hand in this."

Jack nodded. "She used a cream to iron out the wrinkles and dyed my hair." He brushed a hand over where his mustache had been shaved off. "Hated to lose the 'stache. Betty said she had some follicle stimulator ointment to grow it back quickly."

Trask marveled at the difference. "You really do look like your son this way. Ah, well, enough of that. I need to get your statement on the events here."

"I expected as much. Officer Gilbert is in good hands. I'll talk with you later, Sully."

"Thank you for the assistance, Commissioner," Sullivan said.

"Call me Jack. There's too damned many commissioners running around right now." Jack followed Trask off to the side away from prying eyes and open ears.

"Jack, how many of these people did you, personally, shoot."

Jack was confused. "Don't you want this under veridication?"

"I don't want it at all," Trask said. "How many?"

"Three that I know for sure," Jack said. "They were near the front of the line with you and that woman…that must be the Janice Goodfellow Gus told me about. With the 'Mark of the Gods' that large and prominent,

I am surprised the Magni-Freyans didn't build her a temple on the spot. Sorry, my mind wondered for a second. I saw you and Janice up near the man you put three slugs into. When the others drew their guns, I figured you could use an assist. I dropped the two closest to you. When it turned into Dodge City on a Saturday night, I fired at anybody that looked like they might fire in your direction. It was lucky that I saw a few cops I knew blasting away at the others. I didn't know about the color of the day."

"Hmm. Hopefully, you didn't kill any of the slavers," Trask said.

Jack couldn't believe what he was hearing. "I was hoping I did."

"No doubt. And since your feelings about Fuzzies and those who abuse them are well known on this planet, an argument could be made that you were after revenge. While the ones here in the spaceport are all dead, there are still two unaccounted for. They could hire a lawyer to make a lot of trouble for you, and in turn, the local government. You being in disguise makes it look like you intended to do it on the sly."

Jack didn't care and said so. "I'll take my chances."

"No," Trask said. "You'll take your ass out of here and back to the Rez. Get your normal appearance back as quick as you can. I believe I'm the only one here who made you, besides Officer Sullivan, so the mystery man that helped the police can just stay that—a mystery. I'll have a word with Officer Sullivan about the merits of discretion."

Jack wasn't comfortable with that. "Gil and Sully put it together after you came over and started talking to me. But they'll stay mum if you ask nicely. Captain Trask, for good or ill I stand by my actions. If it comes back to bite me, I'll bite it back. Since you are so concerned about it, I will leave. However, if anybody asks me directly about this, I won't gloss it over."

"Fair enough," Trask said. "And I will do the same."

* * *

"Twenty confirmed dead, most with forged identity papers." Chief Frank Carr stated for the audience. The "audience" consisted of Marshal Fane, Commodore Napier, Gus Brannhard, Captain Trask and, as a courtesy, Supervisor Sylvinski. Ben Rainsford would have liked to attend. Gus talked him out of it as he might have a chilling effect on the exchange of information.

Supervisor Sylvinski allowed himself to be veridicated to remove any doubt that he was not a part of the Martianist cause. They were all seated around the large table Marshal Fane kept in his spacious office.

"That sounds like the good news," Marshal Max Fane said seriously. "Now give us the bad."

Chief Carr nodded. "Sixteen critically injured, twenty-seven with relatively minor wounds. As yet no sign of dead civilians or police, though that could change with the critically injured. Officer Gilbert is expected to make a full recovery and be back to work next week. Patrolman Westlake is on the critically wounded list with a nick to the heart and a damaged liver. The CZC is fast-tracking replacement organs for both. For now, he is on full life support."

"I can attest to the quality of the liver," Gus said. He was something of an expert since getting his own liver replaced.

"Wasn't he wearing his fibroid vest under his shirt?" Marshal Fane demanded.

"No, sir. He was off duty seeing a visiting relative off at the spaceport," Carr explained. "When the shooting started he pulled his sidearm and joined in. It was by sheer luck that he was wearing the color of the day or he might have gotten worse."

"I am holding *The City of New Lansing* until this is cleared up," Commodore Napier said. "I hope we can get the interrogations done and send them on their way soon. Did any of the Martianists survive?"

"Several," Captain Trask responded. "Many of the Martianists were veridicated and found to have no knowledge of the extra-legal affairs of the extremists. They were already on board the shuttle when the battle erupted in the terminal. One, who has been identified as, get this, Tars Tarkis, was taken alive thanks to that man dressed like a silver Oscar."

"And our special interest person?" Marshal Fane asked. Chief Carr looked vacantly back. "I think we can trust everybody in here with this information."

Carr glanced at Sylvinski then shrugged. "Dorothy Thompson a.k.a.

Dejah Thoris is alive and well and anxious to be on her way with the counterfeit artifacts. We compared her likeness to the security surveillance images for every ship that came in prior to all the trouble the John Carter Gang started up." There were a few chuckles in the room. "Her registered name on *The City of New Amarillo* was Dejah Thoris. Pretty sloppy, really."

"I imagine they had originally planned to take the super-freighter with the rocket back to Mars," Gus Brannhard said. "Only the hopes of grabbing the additional relics kept them here. That would explain the forged identity papers being so new. They were done locally. What knocked her out? Or did she just faint?"

"Jason Cartwright a.k.a. John Carter smacked her with his pistol," Carr said. "I imagine he figured that if she was unconscious, she wouldn't be connected to the rest of them."

Gus nodded. It made sense. "They really wanted to get that ersatz relic back to Mars."

"We believe you are correct, Mr. Brannhard," Carr said. "What they don't know is that we have some very special impossible-to-detect tracking devices on those phony relics. Captain Trask?"

Trask took Carr's place at the head of the table. "I will be returning to Terra on the same ship as Miss Thoris. No doubt she will de-ship on Mars, so I will track her there and enlist the aid of the local FBCI chapter. I expect by the end of the year the extremist arm of the Martianist cause will be either wiped out or in prison. They will be discredited at the minimum. Commodore Napier?"

Napier took Trask's place. "The ersatz rocket the Martianists took is also bugged with undetectable tracking devices. The Navy will continue to track the movements of the rocket. Most importantly, the CZC made the most perfect replica of the real rocket imaginable. With one major detail that will prove it to be a fake and deal a blow to the Martianist cause that they may never recover from. I admit that I do not understand the science involved. Something similar to a carbon-14 test for metal. The test will prove that the rocket is less than ten years old. I would wager they will be laughed out of the galaxy." Everybody in the room clapped at that. "Chief Carr?"

Commodore Napier returned to his seat while Chief Carr returned to his place at the head of the table. "On the issue of the Fuzzy slavers," Carr continued, "of the twelve now known to have been operating in western Beta, eight died in the gunfight at the spaceport. One is an officer who had been on an extended undercover assignment."

Supervisor Sylvinski interrupted. "This undercover officer: why didn't he contact his superiors once he saw the crimes being committed? I understand he was out there for several months."

"An excellent question," Carr said. "In fact, I asked Corporal Lars Pederson the same question: he said our man was out of communications range and couldn't devise a pretext to go to a town to make contact without raising suspicion. Additionally, he wanted to protect Mai, last name unknown, from the attentions of certain other members of the slaver cell. The girl, Mai, is a runaway who claims to have shot her foster father when he tried to take some liberties with her. I have some investigators working on her story. In the meanwhile, Corporal Pederson is her acting foster father."

"I don't mean to keep interrupting," Sylvinski said, "but isn't that a conflict of interest?"

Gus raised an eyebrow. "Ordinarily, it might be. However, I have no intention of putting her on the stand so we have no concerns about her testimony being influenced. All but two of her associates are dead anyway. Corporal Pederson is the only person Mai feels safe around. If something does come out to cause a problem, it will be my backside getting bitten."

"That accounts for ten of the twelve," Trask pointed out. "What of the other two?"

Carr nodded. "The suspects known as Estefan and Consuela—we don't know if those are their real names—are currently in the wind. It is our belief that they intend to lay low, perhaps have cosmetic surgery to alter their appearance. then will try to slip off the planet on a hyperspace ship. I hate to admit it, but I am unsure how we could prevent this. Currently we are passing around the computer generated images we have, thanks to Brünnhilde Autullis, hoping to get lucky. Every confidential informant in Mallorysport is getting squeezed for any possible information. So far, nothing."

"I spoke with Gov. Rainsford and he has agreed to waive the death penalty for these two if they will come forward and surrender and give up any of their associates we may be unaware of," Gus said from his chair. "We want this slaver organization completely and irrevocably destroyed…if it hasn't been already."

"We can get the word out through our snitches," Chief Carr said. "One final curiosity. On the surveillance video we spotted a hulking man who…well, better to show you."

Carr inserted a disk the size of a deci-sol into a slot on the larger comscreen on the wall. Everybody recognized the spaceport terminal and the gunplay taking place at the time. On the vid one of the shooters, a Martianist, was backing up to the men's restroom. Where there should have been a door stood a hulking man of below average height. The hulk looked about and saw the gunman backing up toward him. When the gunman was in reach, the hulk delivered a backhand blow that sent the Martianist several feet away into a wall and left him unconscious on the floor. At that point, the hulk must have decided that discretion was the better part of valor and ran out of the terminal.

"We don't know who this man is, and he certainly committed no crime, but we still need to interview him," Carr said.

"I know this man," Sylvinski said. All eyes turned to him. "That is Mr. Hugh Lennon of Magni Colony, a wealthy businessman who desperately wants to adopt a few Fuzzies."

LXIV

"…I would rather not discuss the nature of my business with Mr. Lennon," Supervisor Sylvinski said on the comscreen. "I just wanted to let you know that he is very interested in adopting some Fuzzies and that I believe he would make a good surrogate parent. I won't ask you to violate any of the established rules on his behalf. Only that you give him an interview." Sylvinski looked a bit sheepish, as he added, "I know I didn't make a very good impression when we first met and I hope you will not hold that against Mr. Lennon."

Jack smiled at that last statement. "Supervisor Sylvinski, I…heard about what you did back at the spaceport when all Niflheim was breaking loose. I saw the footage where you scooped up Miss Alexander and carried her to cover. By the way, I think she could have outrun you if you gave her the chance. I'll grant you came across as a three-dimensional bastard when we first met, but I realize that was just you doing your job. There have been occasions when it was necessary for me to behave just as badly and maybe even worse. However, anybody who puts their own life second to protect his people is aces with me. You have my respect and I don't give that easily.

"Now, about Mr. Lennon," Jack continued. "He and I had a similarly rocky start. I actually pulled a gun on him up close and personal. I also saw the footage where he incapacitated one of the gunmen at the spaceport. I don't hold it against him, when he ran out of there, as he was unarmed and a rather sizeable target. I'll give him his interview. Should I mention to him that you helped to arrange it?"

Sylvinski actually looked scandalized. "Oh, Niflheim, no! I can't have him thinking I am his personal fixer."

Jack actually laughed out loud at that. "Your secret is safe with me, Supervisor."

"Thank you, Commissioner. Say, you look a lot like the young man who saved my backside at the spaceport. Any relation?"

Since Trask asked him to get out of the spaceport to avoid certain difficulties, Jack had washed the temporary dye out of his hair and used some follicle stimulators on his mustache, bringing it half-way back. The wrinkle cream had to wear off on its own. "You could say that we are very close."

"I thought so," Sylvinski said. "When I first saw him I thought it was Morgan, your son. You know, if you dyed your hair and shaved that mustache you would almost be a dead ringer for him."

"So I have heard," Jack said. "I hate to cut this short but I have to get back to work."

"I know how it is. Thank you for your time and tell your…brother?… he has my gratitude." The screen went black and Jack stared at his own dark reflection.

Betty entered and saw Jack staring at the blank screen. "Looking for something?"

"My lost youth, maybe." Jack spun around and looked up at Betty. "Do you think I should get some cosmetic rejuvenation treatments?"

Now what brought this on? Betty wondered. "Why would you go through something like that? Are you growing vain on me?"

"No, no, I just realized how we must look to people when we go out in public. I look like your grandfather—"

"Father, maybe," Betty interrupted. "You're a bit younger than Dad. Since when do you care what people think when they see you?"

"Actually, I was concerned about you. You, being seen with an old man, an old man who has a fantastically wealthy son…"

"And you think people see me and figure I am a vamp after your son's money?" Betty tried to decide whether to be insulted or amused. Amusement won out. "So, you think all of a sudden shaving a few years off of your face would stop tongues from wagging? Wrong. They would think you were some old fool chasing his lost youth with a trophy girlfriend and some makeup."

Jack smiled at that. "Trophy girlfriend? Is that really a thing?"

"If not, it should be. I am interested in you, Jack Holloway. The real you, not some plastic idealized version of you. I want that mustache to grow all the way back, along with the lines on your face. If people want to talk, let them talk about how lucky we are to be together."

Jack was silent for a moment. Betty had just knocked down the one obstacle to something he had wanted to do for some time. He stood up and went to his desk and pulled a small box out of a drawer, then came back around to stand in front of Betty.

"I have been debating if and how I should do this," Jack said. "I have been concerned about what people might think of you with an old geezer like me. And what you thought of us when we went out. Not anymore. I really should do this in a very expensive restaurant with some mood lighting and candles, but I just can't put it off anymore." Jack got down on one knee, opened the box to reveal a ring with a very large sunstone blazing from the heat of his hands and said, "Betty Kanazawa, would you do this old fool the honor of marrying him?"

Betty was speechless. This very scene had played out in her head hundreds of times, only she always saw herself as the one on bended knee. Tears trickled down her cheek as she said, "Yes, you old fool! Quickly before you change your mind! Now get up here and kiss me!"

* * *

"They were going to just leave without even saying *auf wiedersehn*?"

Kealani tried to settle Brünnhilde down. The Magni-Freyan girl didn't like the idea of the Commission going back to Terra without as much as a farewell to her friend. Kealani understood that could happen when she signed on. The field work took her well beyond communications range, making it impossible for Supervisor Sylvinski to contact her.

Kealani, Brünnhilde and Cindy were back at Cindy Tezza's apartment until they were all interviewed under veridication. Erena went home to see her family and to rest up after her experiences on Beta. Brünnhilde was waiting for her parents to come collect her.

"I have made *maultaschen* for dinner." Cindy looked at Brünnhilde trying to come up with a delicate way of saying she made plenty in case the Magni-Freyan girl required more. "Mmm…Hilde, does your… unique biochemistry require more nutrition?"

"If you are asking will I eat a lot, then yes," Brünnhilde said. "Our bodies were designed to be very efficient, but we still require a lot of food. That was one thing the scientists who altered my people couldn't get around. You don't have to worry about hurting my feelings about my size. Besides, I am thinner than most of my friends."

Cindy couldn't decide if Brünnhilde was joking or not. Her reverie was interrupted by the comscreen. She opened the channel to see a handsome blond man looking back at her. Brünnhilde saw who was on the screen and became excited.

"PRINCE MORGAN!"

Morgan could see the excited girl in the background. He nodded at her, then directed his attention to Cindy. "Greetings, Miss Tezza. I am looking for the woman known as Kealani Matedne and was told she could be reached at this connection."

"I go by Ancheta professionally," Kealani corrected. The three women crowded around the comscreen. "How may I help you, Miste… Your Grace?"

"Morgan will do, ladies," Morgan said. "Brünnhilde, your parents are very upset with you, but my father is grateful for your help with those Fuzzy slavers. I had the aircar you borrowed transported to Betatown where it is being repaired at my expense by way of a thank you for your help. Hopefully, that will mollify your family. Miss Ancheta…"

"Kealani will do…Morgan."

"…Kealani, you and your friends are invited to my father's engagement party."

Kealani was confused. "Me? I only met him once. Oh, make that twice."

"That meeting impressed him," Morgan assured her. "He would consider it an honor to have the daughter of Phillip Matedne in attendance. It will be held at my castle on Beta. Miss Tezza—"

"Cindy, Herr Morgan."

"…Cindy, you may bring Rockthrower. There will be other Fuzzies there for her to socialize with. By the way, if you decide to adopt Rockthrower, my father says he will fast track the paperwork. Have you already selected an adoption name for her?"

"Thrud Thorsdottir. *Danke*, Herr Morgan!"

"*Bitte*," Morgan replied. "If any of you has a paramour you would like to bring that will be fine. Brünnhilde, have you explained about the Magni-Freyans to your friends?"

Brünnhilde felt a bit shaken. "Not everything, Your Gr…Morgan."

"Well, it might be better if you do," Morgan said. "Johann and Heidi will be there as will your parents. Rheiner, also. I managed to talk Supervisor Sylvinski and his team into taking the next ship to Terra, so Miss Goodfellow and her colleagues will be in attendance as well."

Brünnhilde's eyes went wide as she whispered, "The Blessed One."

"The party is tomorrow evening. The CZC will manage transport for those who don't have private vehicles." Morgan glanced up to something off screen. "Time for me to go. Good day, ladies, and I hope to see you there tomorrow." The screen went blank.

Brünnhilde couldn't contain her excitement. "Do you think Lars would go with me?"

Cindy and Kealani looked at each other, then at Brünnhilde.

"Lars has to be in his late twenties to early thirties, even if you account for the extra wear and tear heavy gravity does to the skin," Kealani said. "Maybe twice your age."

Brünnhilde waved that off. "On Freya it is common for a woman of fifteen to marry a much older man. He would work to build his fortune before taking on the added responsibility of a wife and children. Some men don't marry until they are in their forties or not at all."

"Wait…a Freyan year is something like seven Terran months, *ja*," Cindy asked.

"We Magni-Freyans were taught to use the Terran system for months and years. On Freya I would be in my mid-twenties," Brünnhilde explained.

"Well, Lars is from Modi," Kealani pointed out. "He would have a very different view of dating somebody your age. The Federation frowns on that sort of thing though I know of a few planets that wouldn't bat an eye. And Lars is a cop."

"A cop?" The word was unfamiliar to the young Magni-Freyan.

"*Polizei*," Cindy explained.

"Oh, well, I am not asking him to marry me, just come as my escort," Brünnhilde said. She would have liked to pursue a more intimate relationship but Erena had spoken with her about the rules of this world before going home.

"Wait," Kealani said, hand up in a stop position. "You were raised on Magni, right? As were your parents and your grandparents going back over two hundred years. How do you know so much about a planet you never saw?"

"We handed down as much as we could through oral tradition," Brünnhilde explained. "That is also why I can speak Sosti. And Prince Morgan added everything about Freyan life and culture to the teaching machines. He feels that it is part of our birthright."

"Prince Morgan sounds a little too good to be true," Cindy opined.

"Well, he is married and has a son and fought a duel with his father…"

"Wait, what?" Kealani couldn't believe what she was hearing. A duel with Jack Holloway? "Details, Hilde. I want to hear everything."

"Oh, I think the video is still on the datastream," Brünnhilde said. "I believe it is very popular."

Kealani and Cindy nearly knocked heads together in their rush to activate the viewscreen.

* * *

"Where did you get the sunstones to pay for this?"

Estefan examined his new face in the mirror critically. The jaw was a bit more lanternish than before. His eyes were given a slight Asian character. The cheekbones were a bit higher as well. The lips were thinner as was the nose. He paid extra for the scar removal to make the work less obvious.

"Remember those sunstones Bo had? Only three of them were real," Estefan smirked. "The rest were those fakes that were making the rounds last year. I lifted the real ones."

"How could you tell the difference?"

"The fakes glowed without any body heat to draw from," Estefan said with a bit of superiority. "Bo probably never laid them out on the ground to see the difference."

Consuela shook her head with disbelief. "How did you even get that little bag away from him?"

"Oh, please," Estefan said while rolling his eyes. "I was a pickpocket long before I hooked up with Weaver's gang. Anyway, what do you think of the new face?"

"The jaw doesn't fit with the rest of the changes," Consuela said. "The top half of your face looks like what you would expect of a male model while the jaw looks like it belongs on a professional boxer. Widen the nose and add what would look like a healed break at the bridge and it will match up better."

Estefan again looked in the mirror and decided Consuela had a point. He would also pick up some Thoran steroids on the black market to help him quickly bulk up. "How do you like your own face, Connie?"

Consuela washed the red dye out of her hair, then darkened it to raven black. Her face was slightly thinner and her normal olive complexion lighter. "I can live with it. That's the point, right? I don't really care what I look like as long as I keep breathing."

Consuela flopped down on the bed of the cheap hotel room they were hiding in. They took the room after their surgery so as to not raise suspicion. "So, what next?"

"Well, after I fix this nose we go get some jobs."

"What?" Consuela had difficulty believing what she heard. "If I wanted to be a wage slave I would have never hooked up with Weaver."

"A living, breathing wage slave is a lot better than a dead sl—" Estefan cut himself off. The walls might have ears. "Have you decided on your new name yet? We'll need that for the ID docs. I am going with Esteban Rodriguez."

"Esteban? That is practically the same as Estefan."

Estefan nodded. "That's the idea. I used to work with an Esteban and every time one of our names were called we both reacted. I'll adapt easily to it. And what cop would ever think that I would take such an obvious name?"

Consuela thought it over and decided Estefan/Esteban had a point. "I'll go with Condoleezza. I can still use Connie as my nick. Now what kind of jobs will we be looking for?"

"Whatever is on the board at the Soup Kitchen."

Consuela was about to object, then thought better of it. Forged documents would not stand up to a serious background check. Jobs posted on a board at a local eatery would mostly be of the day-laborer variety but nobody would look too closely at their papers, if at all. It was too risky to do any extra-legal work.

"Fine. I just hope it won't be anything too demanding," Consuela said. "How long before we blow this pop stand?"

"I figure three months," Estefan replied. "Unless some big whoop-de-do happens that draws everybody's attention. That or there is a sudden mass migration to leave this rock. Then we could mix in with the crowd."

"We have new faces!" Consuela screamed. "Nobody will know us from Adam and Eve! Why wait?"

Estefan sighed. "Police have portable veridicators, especially the spaceport cops that are under military jurisdiction. They also have DNA testing kits. And we didn't change our height and weight. We should gain or lose a few pounds. Cops know all about cosmetic surgery. Hugo Ingermann got the whole package: height, weight, face and hair, and he still got busted and executed on DNA evidence."

Who the Niflheim was Hugo Ingermann? "How did you get so well informed all of a sudden?"

"I have been playing catch up with the news on the datastream since we got back. What did you think I was doing on the computer all this time?"

"I was afraid to guess," Consuela said half in jest. "How could they get our DNA for comparison, anyway? We sprayed down all of the equipment before we got rid of it on Beta."

"Don't know and don't want to find out the hard way. Better we establish ourselves in these identities for a few months, save up some money for the ride out of here and just generally keep our heads down. Capeesh?"

LXV

Hugh Lennon set down his rented aircar and paused before getting out. All around him he saw Fuzzies busy in various activities. A sizeable contingent stopped whatever they were doing and came over to see who the new Big One was. Lennon feared he would step on one as he opened the hatch, but the Fuzzies all stepped back a respectful distance, allowing him plenty of room.

This was the first time he had seen a Fuzzy up close. At least a real Fuzzy: Lennon had acquired a number of Fuzzybots for study and to let children on Magni play with. All of the Fuzzies he had seen to date had been via viewscreen images and still photos.

"You come to see Pappy Jack?" one of the Fuzzies inquired. Lennon was surprised. He had expected all the Fuzzies to have high-pitched voices like young children; this Fuzzy's voice bordered on a low tenor.

"If you mean Commissioner Jack Holloway, then, yes, I am. Could you tell me which of these buildings, ah, Pappy Jack would be in?"

The Fuzzy pointed to the administration building and, after gently patting the Fuzzy's head, Hugh Lennon trod off in the indicated direction. Inside the building, a pretty, raven-haired woman was briefly startled, then directed him to Jack's office. Lennon took in her appearance and the sizeable sunstone she wore on one finger. Women on Magni tended to be shorter and more robust due to the high gravity.

"Excuse me, miss, I am Hugh Lennon of Magni Colony. If the Commissioner isn't too busy, I would like to see him."

"I will inform Commissioner Holloway that you are here," the woman said as she moved to the door of Jack's office. "Commissioner, a Hugh Lennon of Magni Colony is here to see you. Can you fit him in?"

"Magni Colony? Sure, Betty. Show him in."

Lennon entered, saw Jack and took the indicated seat in front of Jack's desk. He opened a box with cigarettes in it and offered one to Lennon, who politely refused.

"Very few heavy-worlders smoke, Commissioner," Lennon explained. "We need our lungs clear and operating at maximum capacity to keep our bodies properly oxygenated. Our muscles have to work much harder than yours just to get out of bed."

Jack closed the box and set it aside. He had been to a few heavy worlds and understood. "So, Mr. Lennon, we meet again."

Hugh Lennon started in his chair. "You remember me?"

"I remember the face of every man and woman I've ever pointed a gun at." Jack let his gaze go up and down Lennon's physique. "Especially the ones who look like a section of brick wall gone walkabout."

Lennon sighed. "Yes, I imagine you would, at least in my case. If it helps, I would like to apologize for my behavior that day at the adoption center…."

Jack waved that off. "No need. I can understand wanting a Fuzzy and you, believe it or not, were not the most difficult person we have had to deal with since the Fuzzies were first discovered. Now, about taking a Fuzzy off-planet—"

"Never mind about that," Lennon interrupted. "Taking them off-world is no longer any kind of priority. I want nothing to do with causing them any kind of harm."

Jack set down his pipe. "Really? Why the change of heart? At the adoption center you were prepared to walk over anybody standing in your way to get a Fuzzy."

Lennon's shoulders sank as he slumped a bit in his seat. "You know about the Magni-Freyans and what was done to them, of course. If nothing else, I am sure your son would have filled you in. While I had nothing to do with that travesty, I have come to realize that taking Fuzzies to Magni and putting them into what amounts to a giant petting zoo is no better than what was done to the Freyans. I am disgusted with myself for ever considering it."

Lennon went up a few notches in Jack's opinion. "So, you don't want to start a private Fuzzy colony on Magni?"

"I never did. I just wanted to take a few with me and give them a good life. But I spend a lot of time off-world and wouldn't be able to bring them with me. That would not be fair to them even if they liked the enclosure I am building. It is even going to be equipped to generate Zarathustran gravity."

Jack nodded. "I am glad you see it that way. I wouldn't worry too much about the gravity. Are you familiar with the cube-square law?"

Lennon thought back to his university days and recalled that an animal twice as big would be three times as heavy and would need to be equally stronger to function. "Yes, though I don't see how that applies here."

"A Fuzzy the size of a Terran man would be about three times stronger than even you. Fuzzies are way stronger than a critter that size should be. A Fuzzy with a ten-pound backpack can still carry another Fuzzy a surprising distance. They would adapt to your world's gravity faster than any human you ever saw. And you could take them out to see the universe with you."

Lennon shook his head. "As much as I would love the company, I can't stomach the idea of sterilizing them. I have children of my own though I rarely see them. They all went with my three ex-wives." Lennon lowered his voice and spoke solemnly, "Don't get so involved with your work that you end up ignoring the people who should be most important in your life, like that pretty little assistant of yours. Don't be surprised; two of my ex's were my personal assistants and I saw that boulder on her finger."

Jack smiled wide. "No chance of that happening. Betty wouldn't let me even if I tried, and I have no interest in trying. And, technically, she is on loan from the CZC to help organize our files. But back to the Fuzzies: there is a group of Fuzzies who have expressed an interest in getting out and seeing the universe. While the new colony laws prohibit anybody from *taking* Fuzzies off-world, it can't prohibit Fuzzies from *leaving* if they want to."

Confusion covered Lennon's face. "That is a fine distinction. Last I checked Fuzzies weren't up to astrophysics and spaceflight. Besides, don't the Fuzzies know that they could be prevented from ever having offspring if they leave this planet?"

"It has been made abundantly clear to them," Jack said. "There are a number of Fuzzies who are not concerned about that."

Lennon shook his head in disbelief. "What? How could they not be?"

"Because they are already sterile." Jack explained about the Fuzzies who had been abducted and taken to Terra and other planets. Every test they were given came up with the same result: permanent infertility. "No more harm can come to them, so Governor Rainsford is willing to sign a waiver for you to take them off Zarathustra. Provided you bring them back for a visit every so often, and any Fuzzy that wants to come back and stay is allowed to do so."

"Wait…you knew I was coming and why?"

"I make it a point to be aware of anything that could affect my Fuzzies. And you don't strike me as the kind of person who gives up easily."

The smile on Lennon's face was so wide that it looked painful. "It was my intention to build a compound here and make Zarathustra my second home! You see, I am brokering a deal with the Magni-Freyans for wood carvings and furniture. I intend to export them all over the Federation. The skill and detail of their work will make them famous. And I will personally transport it from Zarathustra to Odin where I have a distribution center. I expect the *shranks* alone will make a big splash on Thor and Heimdall." A suspicion crossed Lennon's mind. "You seem to be pushing for these Fuzzies to get out in the galaxy. Why is that?"

Jack took a puff of his pipe then leaned back. "One thing I learned from my time roaming around the universe is that travel broadens the mind. Most Fuzzies are stuck here if they want to have children, and I never met a Fuzzy yet who didn't want to have kids. But Fuzzies incapable of breeding may as well go wherever they like, and some want to see more worlds. I approve because I want those traveling Fuzzies to come back and tell the others what they have seen and learned. One day we will lick this radiation problem and Fuzzies are going to get out into the galaxy and, hopefully, live and work with us side by side. I would like for them to first learn about what's out there from the people best equipped to explain it to them—other Fuzzies."

Lennon digested that and nodded. "You know, my own father had much the same idea with me. He immigrated to Magni from Modi for his health and bought into the Charted Magni Cooperative. I choose to believe he knew nothing about the Freyans' plight. Whenever he had business off-world, he was always sure to take me along. I got a real education about life on different worlds. I will admit my privileged upbringing may have made me a bit arrogant, but I have nothing but respect for the people who keep this universe going. My father even had me take several menial jobs on and off Magni so I would learn to appreciate the so called underclass." Lennon sighed. "Too many years in the boardroom made me forget a lot of that. Those folks over in Neu Freya helped to remind me."

Jack nodded. "I suppose we all need a mild attitude adjustment now and then. I've received a few doozies in my time. Now, let's see if any of the Fuzzies like you."

Lennon's eyebrows went up. "No background check?"

Jack laughed. "That was done the day after we met at the adoption center. The real test will be whether or not the Fuzzies accept you. They are very good judges of character. One thing, though, if I find out you mistreated my Fuzzies in any way, shape or form I will find out about it. Then I will get the biggest damned gun I can find and personally shoot you in the head."

Lennon smiled at the threat. "Commissioner, I would expect no less."

* * *

Everybody who was anybody was there, including some nobody expected to see. Akira and Little John with Thor Folkvar, and Akira's parents from Terra had come in on the *Adonitia* several days ahead of what was expected. Little John wasn't much bigger than when he left due to the time dilation effect.

Johann Torseus and Heidi stood with a number of other Magni-Freyans. The Autullises, Brünnhilde's family, stood with Lars a little off to the side. Lars looked distinctly uncomfortable.

"*Vater*, this isn't Freya and Lars isn't Freyan," Brünnhilde tried to explain to them. "On this planet it would be a crime for Lars to do anything like that."

"But he rescued you from dose *Schweinhunde*," Gunther Autullis insisted. "By tradition he can claim you as his bride."

"Herr Autullis," Lars broke in, "Hilde is very correct about the law in this instance. However, if she is still free and interested in three years we can revisit this discussion. I am still a relatively young man and am not seeking a bride right now."

"Wie alt bist du?"

Lars looked to Brünnhilde. She explained that her father asked his age. "Oh! I am twenty-six Terran years of age. Modi's gravity tends to age the skin a bit faster than low-gravity planets. I guess I would be in my mid-to-late-thirties on Freya…."

"Ach! You haff plenty of time, *mein Freund*," Gunther said slapping Lars' back. Lars nearly fell over from the strength of the friendly gesture. He made a mental note not to annoy anybody from Neu Freya. "Brünnhilde ist a comely voman und vill become more so in die next few years."

"*Vater*!" Brünnhilde protested.

Hugh Lennon stood off to the side holding a Freyan ale that one of the wait staff had brought him. He considered joining Johann's circle, then decided against it; the Bürgermeister was speaking with Prince Morgan. Lennon had no idea what proper etiquette was in a situation like that, although he suspected it wasn't cricket to interrupt a monarch. Besides, Morgan Holloway was the majority stockholder in the Chartered Magni Cooperative; it wouldn't pay to antagonize a fellow board member.

Instead, Lennon stood away from the different circles of conversation until a powerfully built young man in the company of a redheaded woman came to him.

"Herr Lennon?"

"Yes?" It took a moment, then he remembered who the young man was. "Rheiner!" Lennon had been present when Rheiner gave his testimony after the slaving operation was discovered. All of the board members had to be veridicated as well. It went very badly for many of them.

He grasped Rheiner's forearm in the traditional Freyan style of "shaking hands." "Great Ghu, boy! You have done some growing since last I saw you. How have you been since getting away from Magni?"

"*Sehr gut,* Herr Lennon." Rheiner turned to Cinda. "Herr Lennon vas vun of die stockholders at der Chartered Magni Cooperative dot fought for reparations for mein pipple...people."

"Very pleased to meet you, Mr. Lennon." Cinda held out her hand and Lennon gently kissed it. "I can see you are quite the charmer."

"Call me Hugh, please. I don't know how I wrangled an invite to this shindig but I am glad that I did."

"Prince Morgan invited you, H...Hugh," Rheiner said. "Bürgermeister Torseus mentioned your visit to Neu Freya und der Prince vas pleased dot you had come. He vanted a chence to speak vit' you before you leafe planet."

Lennon looked surprised. "Really? Well, I will be happy to speak with him as well. Ah, how should I address him?"

"Die same as you vould in a board meeting," Rheiner said. "Avay from Freya und Neu Freya, Prince Morgan does not stand on ceremony."

Lennon nodded in understanding. Calling himself a prince away from those places would mark him as eccentric at best.

Most of the wait staff was less than experienced in working a party. Morgan did not maintain a large staff in a castle he didn't spend a great deal of time in. During the week he was usually in Mallorysport where he kept the penthouse apartment. Unlike his previous parties, he wanted non-Magni-Freyans to work in the service positions. The kitchen staff remained unchanged. Morgan wasn't worried about what people thought of the denizens of Neu Freya. It was his ascension to the position of "Prince of the Realm" that disturbed him. Morgan didn't want a lot of bowing and scraping around him, especially at a social occasion with non-Freyans.

Among the wait staff were people who applied at the Soup Kitchen from the job board. The part of the concierge was held by Parsec Paul. While normally in a fog, he came around to demonstrate uncanny competence at organizing and instructing the others. Jason Roberts thought it was because those skills were stored in another part of the brain.

"You two," Paul pointed at a man and woman, "Go get some trays of hors d'oeuvres from the kitchen. The buffet won't be set up for another hour."

The pair did as ordered and went to the kitchen. There they saw the chef going back and forth supervising everybody and occasionally taking a taste of the food. All perfectly normal. What wasn't normal was the chef and most of the kitchen workers.

"What…what are those things," the woman asked her companion in a low voice.

"Beats the Niflheim out of me. Maybe a new race got discovered while we were out of reach of civilization." The man looked around and listened as the chef chided one of the cooks. "They are speaking German."

Cold chills went down the woman's spine. "Like Hilde."

"Yup. Maybe these are more people from Magni," the man thought aloud. "Their faces could be a mutation caused by radiation. I feel bad for Hilde if this is what she was surrounded by."

"Estef…Esteban, what if we're recognized?"

"Connie, our own mothers wouldn't know us with these faces," Estefan/Esteban said. "Let's just grab the trays, work the party, get paid and get the Niflheim out of here."

Consuela/Condoleezza took the tray and started making the rounds. She spotted Brünnhilde across the room and went the other way. New face or not, she had the same voice. She came upon Commodore Napier, Marshal Fane, Governor Rainsford and somebody she couldn't identify. The rest at one time or another had been on a viewscreen broadcast or had their photo appear in the datastream.

"I appreciate you letting us handle the situation at the spaceport, Commodore," Marshal Fane was saying. "It was technically your jurisdiction."

"If those extremists had made it into space we would have been all over it," Commodore Napier said. "Thanks to that ship we confiscated from the slavers, we have the capability to follow them into hyperspace. Most of my men not on other details were up there in that ship waiting in case things went sour. Besides, I had a couple of squads already on board *The City of New Lansing.*" He took a drink before continuing. "I think I should have had some on that shuttle. They could have backed you up."

"Oh, I think Captain Trask here had it all under control," Rainsford said momentarily putting a hand on Trask's shoulder. "I admit we didn't expect the extremists and the slavers to be there all at once."

"The slavers moved faster than we thought they could," Trask admitted. He spotted the hors d'oeuvres and snagged a couple. "Say, these are good. What's in them?"

Consuela felt the blood drain from her face. Here she was standing next to the three most powerful officials in law enforcement on the planet plus the colonial governor. "Ah…um…I am afraid you would have to ask the chef about that. We mere mortals are not privy to his recipes."

"I see," Trask said as he grabbed a couple more. "I might be better off not knowing."

The rest helped themselves to the contents of the tray and Consuela moved on. It was all she could do not to run. Next she came upon Native Affairs Commissioner Jack Holloway and a man that had to be his son. The resemblance was striking. *Didn't Holloway have more wrinkles?* With them were two women.

"Of course you'll have to undergo the tests of worthiness before the nuptials," the younger Holloway was saying.

"What? Wait, what? What kind of tests?" Betty couldn't believe what she had heard. Akira just nodded at her.

"Oh, yes," Morgan said. "Since you are not of noble blood, we have to make sure you are fit to become a mother that will produce strong offspring. The first test is to pull a plow over, um, half a Terran acre, I think. Units of measurement can be tricky between the two cultures. Then you would have to clean the castle."

"Pull a plow? Why? I never heard of any queen or noble woman doing anything like that. Is somebody going to put a pea under my mattress?" Betty turned to Jack. "Did you know about this?"

"No, but I had to jump through a few hoops to marry Morgan's mother, and you better believe that her brother didn't cut me any slack at all…oh, maybe I shouldn't mention her."

"What else? Hunt down a damnthing with a spear and turn it into supper?" Betty started to get angry. Jack thought it looked cute on her as long as he wasn't the focus of her ire.

"Oukry, actually," Morgan supplied. "We don't have damnthings on Freya, and you would be allowed to use a bow."

Betty sputtered for a moment. "If you think for one second…that I am falling for this, then you must have the IQ of a Khooghra!"

Betty started laughing. Morgan turned to Akira. "I think she's on to us."

"That's for not bringing me in on the joke when Jack said we couldn't get married," Akira laughed. "What gave it away?"

It took Betty a moment to stop laughing. "I should have caught on with the plow gag. I got suspicious with the castle cleaning but the oukry hunt was just too much. None of those skills would have anything to do with running a castle and I don't expect Jack to build one."

"Actually, I offered to take care of that as a wedding gift," Morgan said. "Father said no."

"I like the place I am in right now," Jack said. "I built most of it with my own two hands. Should the need arise I'll add to it as necessary."

Betty gently poked Jack in the ribs with an elbow. "You mean, like, if I become pregnant?"

"Certainly," Jack said. "I know most men my age don't want the burden of raising a family from scratch, but I missed all of Morgan's life. I wouldn't mind being around for all the crying and skinned knees with a second child."

"You better add diaper changing to that list, buddy," Betty said as she playfully punched Jack in the arm.

Morgan looked like he wanted to say something about that but he refrained. Now was not the time and place.

"Hors d'oeuvres?"

Everybody turned to Consuela and took something from the tray. Jack's eyes went wide.

"*Guintu*! Gods, I haven't had one of these since...since I was on Freya!"

"Don't fill up on those," Betty cautioned. "We still have the buffet."

Jack ignored Betty's warning and took another. "Mmm...just like I remember."

"I have to speak with Johann and Mr. Lennon," Morgan said. "I'll be back shortly."

Consuela moved on to the next group.

Victor Grego chatted with Gerd and Ruth van Riebeek along with Dr. Mallin. Dr. Mallin seemed to be trying to talk Grego into something.

"Dr. Tezza did bring back some useful data even though her field work was cut short by circumstances," Dr. Mallin went on. "However, I think we have been overlooking a valuable opportunity."

"Such as," Gerd inquired.

"The Magni-Freyans," Mallin said excitedly. "An entire society created by people who were the result of significant genetic manipulation! Not to mention that they were used for slave labor. I have seen footage of Neu Freya. These people are doing fantastic work building a new society. The cooperative effort alone speaks volumes!"

"It sounds like you are leading up to something," Ruth said. She had a good idea where Dr. Mallin was headed.

"We need to do a field study of the new Magni-Freyan culture as it develops." Mallin started to go into all the benefits to the psycho-sciences as well as preparing for any problems that might arise of their own. "We need to get some people over there sooner rather than later."

Grego took it all in, then nodded. "And who were you thinking of sending?"

"Dr. Tezza," Mallin announced. "She needs the field study to complete her residency requirement and she speaks fluent German, which would facilitate easier communication. And...she has already become friends with a few of the residents there."

"I agree except for one thing; I really wanted to get those field studies on the wild Fuzzies done," Grego said. "Since the day Fuzzies were discovered…make that after the court case that cemented their status as sapient beings, we have been so busy going from emergency to emergency we never got around to doing any field observations. We think we understand Fuzzies based on the ones on the Rez and those that were adopted. We don't. I want to know what made them tick before we came along and upset the applecart."

"There is somebody else interested in studying the Fuzzies," Ruth cut in. "Kealani Ancheta. She is a postgrad in anthropology, which carries some mandatory psychology courses. She could report to Gerd and me since we'll be working on Beta anyway."

"I took the liberty of checking her academic record when I first heard about her going out in the field," Gerd added. "Solid 3.98 GPA, survival training, martial arts…I say we should put her on the payroll."

Grego listened as he absently reached for a cigarette. He reminded himself that there was no smoking in Morgan's castle due to the presence of the Magni-Freyans. It took a lot of lung power to keep those massive muscles supplied with enough oxygen. Tobacco smoke could impair that process. Grego thought of it as Kryptonite to the Magni-Freyan supermen.

Grego pulled his thoughts back to the issue at hand. "Gerd, you are a division chief. Hire or fire as you like. I don't get involved until the division suffers for some reason." He finally noticed the woman with the tray. "Oh, have you tried these? Some sort of delicacy from Freya. I don't know what is in them but they are very good."

The tray now empty, Consuela returned to the kitchen for a fresh one. This time the tray was loaded with more familiar fare: cocktail weenies, mini-pigs in blankets, Swedish meatballs with toothpicks, deviled eggs and more.

She didn't see Brünnhilde around so she worked the other side of the room. The first group she encountered had a familiar face.

"I heard about the deal you worked out with Johann to distribute furniture and wood carvings," Morgan said to Hugh Lennon. He looked accusingly at the Bürgermeister. "I seem to recall making the same offer."

"My apologies, Your Gr...Herr Morgan," Johann looked truly apologetic even to someone otherwise unfamiliar with his facial construction. "You had done so much for us und ve t'aught dot you vere making die offer out of charity. Ve did not t'ink our vood vorking vas dot gute until Herr Lennon came to us und vas also impressed."

Now Lennon looked surprised. "How could you doubt it? The work I saw could stand up proudly even in a showcase with Thoran carvings. Freyans...the unmodified ones...do excellent work as well, but the pieces I saw in Neu Freya outshine it all. Mr. Holloway, perhaps we could work out a deal. You have distribution centers on planets that I never ventured to."

"I am sure we can, but that isn't what I wanted to discuss," Morgan said. "And call me Morgan. This is a social occasion, not a board meeting. It is that enclosure you are building on Magni that I am interested in."

Lennon looked confused. "The one I was building for the Fuzzies? Humph. I suspect in a few years it will be known as 'Lennon's Folly' since I won't be placing any Fuzzies there."

Morgan shook his head. "Actually, I was thinking it could be expanded to a series of bio-domes on Magni. The Magni Cooperative has always been a mining colony. As such very little was done to make the planet more comfortable for the people living there."

Johann nodded. "Dot is true."

Johann would know, thought Lennon with some sadness.

"The way I see it, a series of those bio-domes could vastly improve living conditions for the people that stay there," Morgan continued. "What's more, we could export the design to planets like Fenris, Imhotep and Yggdrasil..."

"Yggdrasil?" Lennon thought it over. "Of course! A self-contained bio-dome where Earth crops could be grown and processed without the local bacteria destroying the flavor. It would have to be almost hermetically sealed...."

Morgan nodded. "Soil brought in...fortunately the main export is guano for the land reclamation projects on Terra."

"Maybe even add an amusement park in a couple of them...."

Consuela listened for a moment, then moved on. She made a mental note to see if there was a way to invest in those projects if she and Estefan could get up some capital...assuming they could put their money into such a venture without being found out.

She was so deep in her musings, that Consuela didn't notice that the next group she came to was the last one she wanted to see. Brünnhilde, Kealani, Cindy and Erena were chatting among themselves along with Lars and two people she didn't know. A woman Consuela didn't recognize was talking.

"...I stood there and watched it," the redhead said. "Rheiner stood against the wall while the medic pulled the bullets out him. He didn't even complain about the pain."

"I would have liked to have seen that," Lars said clearly impressed. "I took a .38 to the ribs, once. It came at just the right angle for my rib bones to turn it but it hurt like all Niflheim."

"I confess die experience vas not pleasant," the other man said. If anything, he was even more powerfully built than Lars, which Consuela had difficulty believing despite the evidence before her eyes. "Die bullets vere lodged in my torso muscles und vie had no anest'etic to dull die pain."

"That didn't stop you from bowling three men over when we escaped," added the redhead.

"*Mein Gott*, Rheiner!" Cindy exclaimed. "Do you have scars or did you have them erased?"

"Die chenetic vork done on my ancestors make die scars go avay after a time," Rheiner said with a hint of disgust. "It may sound stranche to you but Freyans take pride in der scars."

"They think of it as sort of a trophy of their accomplishments," Cinda explained. "Unfortunately for Rheiner's, people very few scars are permanent."

Brünnhilde was nodding. "I have heard that people from Terra have their scars removed. Even the Mark of the Gods. Oh! The Blessed One!"

Janice along with Dana came over to the gathering. Janice wore an elegant white gown accessorized with Freyan lace. "Brünnhilde, I didn't get the chance to thank you at the spaceport. You took a very big chance running across the terminal like that. You, too, Miss Ancheta."

Consuela moved on. Nobody seemed interested in eating anything and she was afraid something would give her away like her voice or even body language. The woman called Kealani was a martial artist. She might recognize something in the way Consuela moved.

A small gong rang out three times. That meant the buffet would be coming out shortly. Consuela returned to the kitchen as fast as decorum would allow.

* * *

The ballroom of the castle was much like its Terran counterparts in Germany and England before they were destroyed in the Great Wars. The only significant exception would be the added technology common to Seventh Century A.E. civilization, hidden light sources that illuminated the entire hall which were set in the medium range save for the directed radiance that covered the unusually wide podium at the far end.

John Morgan Holloway the Lesser, Prince of Neu Freya, if in name only, stood on the podium as people filtered in. Everybody found their place setting then stood by their tables. Most of the attendees were unfamiliar with the protocol in this instance. Did one sit while the Lord and Master of the castle stood?

Morgan noticed the confusion and asked everybody to take a seat. "This is not any kind of official royal function so I think we can dispense with the normal protocols that most of you might find strange and unfamiliar.

"As you know, we are here to celebrate the engagement of my father, John Morgan Holloway the Greater, better known as Jack to most of you," Jack came onto the podium from stage left and stood at his son's side, "to Miss Betty Kanazawa." Betty came onto the podium from stage right and stood at Morgan's other side.

"Before I can give my blessing, I must ask if anybody here finds reason to object to this union. On Freya we get this little detail out of the way before the wedding. It saves a lot of bloodshed we have found. Brides really hate having the wedding interrupted in that manner."

Most people laughed and some clapped. "So, does anybody here see any reason why my father and his chosen bride should not be wed?" Silence. "Excellent. Then I give my consent, as if I could stop them," more laughter, "and to make sure they get a good start, I ask Janice Goodfellow, the Favored One, to come up and grant her blessing on this union."

Janice had been warned of this and Heidi Torseus had explained the ritual to her. She approached the podium with her Honor Guard. At the podium, rather than walk around to the steps, two of the guards gently lifted her up to stand before Morgan. Morgan stepped back so Jack and Betty could move closer together.

"John Morgan Holloway the Greater and Betty Kanazawa, I give my blessings and well-wishes to your union and wish you many fine strong sons and beautiful daughters. May Junatia, goddess of fertility and fidelity bless your house and lands, and may Aretyr, god of war and defense protect your lands and family."

Janice placed a red and black ribbon around first Jack's wrist, then Betty's. "May your journey through life be filled with love and laughter."

Janice stepped back and was received by the two guards who lifted her down from the podium. They walked back to their table, one that was in a place of honor, and took their seats.

Morgan stepped forward. "Ladies and gentleman, please enjoy the feast we have prepared. Afterwards the Mallorysport Players will entertain you with a play called 'The Gnarly Man.'"

Unlike buffets served on Terra and Terran planets, carts loaded up with the offered fare moved through the tables where people could take what they wished.

"One thing I like about Freyan ceremonies," Jack was saying, "is that they tend to be brief and to the point. At least until the wedding itself."

Morgan shook his head. "Apparently you never had to stand through a coronation. I think the speakers at those things are chosen for their lung capacity and willingness to test it with long-winded speeches. I appreciate your allowing me to use Freyan custom to announce your engagement."

"I only wish that I had thought to throw a similar shindig when you and Akira got engaged."

"I thought it would be more involved," Betty admitted. "This was surprisingly brief."

Morgan smiled. "Well, if you allow me to arrange the wedding, you'll get all the pomp and ceremony you can stand."

"I'm game," Jack said. "Ah, here comes Akira with Little John."

* * *

The party was over and the most of the guests had left. Remaining, aside from Morgan, Jack, Betty and Akira, were Victor Grego, Commodore Napier, Captain Trask, Ben Rainsford and Gus Brannhard.

"Wonderful party, Mr. Holloway," Trask said. "I wish I could be here for the wedding. As it is, I had to send Lt. Williams in my place to follow Dejah Thoris. I'll have to switch places with him on Odin where incoming and outgoing ships overlap, the ones coming from Terra and the ones going back."

"Call me Morgan, please. What will happen to Miss Thoris after she delivers her package?"

Commodore Napier spoke up. "After the Martianists are well and truly discredited—thanks to the fancy replicas of rocket and relics—the Navy will move in and bust the lot of them. We'll have the story all over the data steam and on every news cycle for weeks afterwards. That should discourage new members from joining while the old members are put through the wringer. Humph. I use that expression a lot, yet have no idea what a wringer is."

"Something unpleasant to go through, no doubt," Gus said. He drained his glass and held it up for a robot to refill. "I almost wish I could be there to prosecute them. Sadly, Terra may not be safe for me, still. Besides, I wouldn't want to leave Natty and Alan. Did you know they were looking for mates over on the Rez? I may have to put an addition on my cabin before long."

"Only a few of the, what did Frank Carr call them...The John Carter Gang who were involved in criminal activity survived," Napier explained. "You can prosecute them right here on Zarathustra. The rest we had to let go. They were just dupes and pawns."

"I am a bit annoyed that two of the slaver cell got away," Ben said. He downed his highball and declined a refill.

"I'm with you, Ben," Jack said. "However, the two that got away are less of a concern than the possibility that there are still other cells out in the bush."

"What!" If Rainsford's glass had been full it would have spilled all over the floor.

"Damn," Trask said. "If that is true, my job here isn't done. I'll have to send a message for Lt. Williams and let him know he'll be getting an all-expense-paid trip to Terra on the FBCI's centisol."

Victor Grego had stayed silent. Now he had something to add. "I can get some satellites to focus on eastern Beta. I'll also light a fire under some asses to get those communications relays set up out there."

"Don't forget about Gamma, Delta and Epsilon continents," Jack said. "Beta has the Fuzzies but there are also the ZNPF patrols. A separate cell could have been set up on other continents to store the Fuzzies until they could be picked up. They could be sitting out there now wondering what happened to the ship that was supposed to collect them. Beta isn't the only continent with spotty communications. Curse me for a fool for not thinking of this sooner."

"More fires under more asses," Grego said. "It will take a while to get more satellites up, though."

"I'll release some from base stores," Napier said. "We keep recon-satellites for skirmishes. Not as fancy as the civilian models, but they get real good images in UV, IR, and enhanced."

"I think it is time we armed the Fuzzies so they can defend themselves better," Gus opined. "Wolves go after sheep because they can't defend themselves. But they give mountain lions a wide berth."

Trask was surprised. "You mean give guns to Fuzzies?"

"Why not? I did."

Everybody turned to see Jason Roberts walking in with Mike Hammer. "Sorry I missed the party, Mr. Morgan. The arm was on the fritz and I had to get some emergency repairs."

"Too bad," Morgan said. "You missed a good party. Come by the

CZC next week and I'll set you up with a top-of-the-line model." Morgan turned to Trask. "Mike here can operate an aircar, pick locks, read and carries a modified .38."

"In fact he is a better pilot than I am," Roberts added.

"Got that right, Boss," Mike Hammer added.

Trask was impressed and said so. "It works for me. When do we start?"

* * *

The ride back on the chartered bus to Mallorysport was tense for Estefan and Consuela. They couldn't help imagining that somebody would see through their cosmetic surgeries and turn them in. Estefan tried to console the woman. He spoke in Spanish in case somebody was listening.

"Look," Estefan whispered, "not even Brünnhilde recognized you. I was more worried about Lars. He had been around us for months. I can't believe we had a cop with us that whole time."

"Gods, when I saw him I nearly dropped my tray," Consuela moaned. "His testimony alone would win us a bullet each."

"It's over now. We won't take any more jobs in east Beta. I am getting some gear together to go prospecting. A few months out there away from civilization will give us a chance to be forgotten. They might think we already skipped planet."

Consuela looked up at Estefan. "And we have nothing to do with Fuzzies. Promise me that!"

"You got it, Connie. If any wander into our camp we'll just give them some XT3 and send them packing."

* * *

Little Fuzzy found Emily Dickinson sitting by herself on the drawbridge to the castle. The drawbridge was functional though hardly necessary. It was Morgan's tendency to emulate the pre-Federation designs of Freyan castles. And it was a good conversation piece.

"Emily Dickinson," Little Fuzzy said softly.

"You may call me Emily, Little Fuzzy." Emily responded. "Hu—Big Ones often have three names but only use one of them among themselves."

Little Fuzzy thought that over. Pappy Jack was called Commissioner Holloway by some Big Ones, Jack by Aunty Betty, and he heard Unka Morgan call him John Morgan Holloway the Greater. How did Big Ones keep up with all those names? Of course his own name had been something else before Pappy Jack gave him a new one.

"Hokay, Emily. Why you look sad? Is happy day! Pappy Jack is taking a mate. Aunty Betty will be Mummy Betty. Is good thing."

Emily sighed, an action she had learned from her own mummy before she died. "Big Ones do not mate the same way the People do. They have a ceremony, exchange rings…round metal things they wear on their fingers…and pledge that they will always be together."

Little Fuzzy studied on that. The People took mates without making a fuss the way Big Ones did. He remembered Unka Morgan's ceremony, something the Big Ones called a wedding. There was much happiness and soon afterwards Aunty Akira had a little Big One. Little Fuzzy recalled his own mates of the past. They had stayed together for a time, and then they would go separate ways. One had gone with three others when the tribe had split up, another made dead, and one stayed with Little Fuzzy for a time, and then went to another member of the tribe. It was the way of the People.

"Big Ones mate once and stay with that mate?" Little Fuzzy had never thought about it before.

"Well, sometimes the mated pair do not get along after a few yea— many moons have passed," Emily tried to explain. "Then they have a thing called a divorce and are free to mate with other Big Ones. Or one of them dies…makes dead…the Big One has to find a new mate, or just be alone."

Little Fuzzy's head started to hurt from trying so hard to keep track with all the new concepts. "Pappy Gerd an' Mummy top-of-the-line model are mates, and they made two new Big Ones that are still very small. Is good thing. So why sad?"

Emily struggled to explain it in terms a Fuzzy could more easily grasp. She could understand some concepts better than other Fuzzies because of the way her Mummy had taught her. But the accident that killed her Mummy also damaged the part of her brain where the Fuzzy language was while leaving the Lingua Terra she had learned intact. It made communication with her own kind somewhat awkward. "When Big Ones mate, get married, they can become…um…they might not remember to play with Fuzzies."

Little Fuzzy sat down next to Emily. She had given him much to think about. Pappy Jack was often too busy to play now because he was the Wise One for all Fuzzies. That was a big job. Little Fuzzy remembered when he was the Wise One for his tribe, before he brought them to the Wonderful Place. The Wise One always had to think and make sure everybody was safe and had good to eat things.

"No," Little Fuzzy said. "With new mate Pappy Jack has help. He has more time to be with Fuzzies. Pappy Gerd was helper to Pappy Jack, and then Unka Piet became the helper when Pappy Gerd went to be the Wise One of new Science place. Now have Aunty Betty for more help. Is good thing."

Emily looked down. "I hope that is so, Little Fuzzy. I lost my Mummy in the accident that erased my understanding of the People's language. I do not want to lose Pappy Jack as well."

Little Fuzzy shook his head. "Not lose Pappy Jack. Get Mummy Betty. Is good thing. You see."

In the back of his mind Little Fuzzy wondered if he said a not-so thing. In many moons he had learned much from Pappy Jack. He learned to make bow and arrow, shoot guns, smarter ways to hunt. He felt he was a much wiser Fuzzy, now. But what Emily said made him wonder. Could mating…getting married…take Pappy Jack away from them? There were still so many things the People needed to learn about the Big Ones.

The End

AFTERWORD

What you are holding may or may not be my final Fuzzy novel. I won't say I am done with Fuzzies once and for all, since I have no idea where the muse will take me in the future. However, at this point in time, I have written more words on Fuzzies than any other author living or dead. In fact, this may even be the single largest book on Fuzzies ever written. Not sure; I would have to get a word count on William Tuning's *Fuzzy Bones*." It is time to try my hand at something else.

Eleven years ago I was working on *Fuzzy Ergo Sum* as fan fiction. I hadn't even considered that it might see actual publication. John F. Carr saw something there that I had not. This isn't to say it was ready to go straight away. In fact, at John's direction, I had to trash the first eighty pages and rework a couple of characters. In the process, I learned something about myself: I took revenge on the characters for making me rewrite them! How dare they? I won't go into all the changes, save to say they got a whole lot darker and, hopefully, made the book a lot more interesting.

It has taken almost two years to complete *Fuzzy Logic*. Partly due to my own health issues. In fact as I write this I am on an IV drip. I know some people will be disappointed, but it looks like I will survive. Most of me, anyway.

A few people have taken a dim view of my treatment of the Fuzzies, that they are not as childlike as Piper wrote them. Well, speaking from experience, children have this annoying habit of growing up. The Fuzzies have been exposed to a whole new world of what is possible and given an education from the Big Ones. Sometimes not in the right way, as evidenced by the Jin-f'ke and how they learned to deal with bad Big Ones. I admit, I went with the David and Goliath trope there. But I never made a Fuzzy do anything that I thought H. Beam Piper would have objected to—I hope.

Believe it or not, I am a little sad to be moving on. However, I believe I need to stretch myself and work out of my comfort zone in order to become a better writer. So, if I come back to Zarathustra, it will be with a wider experience and a refreshed voice. "This is good thing," as Little Fuzzy would say.

I would like to say something about *Fuzzy Conundrum*. The character of Patricia Lorain Holloway was based whole cloth on my own Aunt Pat. I didn't have the character say or do anything that Aunt Patsy (she hated that name) wouldn't have said or done herself had she been in that position. She passed away before I wrote that book but everybody in the family agreed that I nailed it for her character and that she would have been tickled pink had she lived to read it.

There are a few other ideas I would like to get into print for the Fuzzies, but I really need to take a break. Even Piper himself got a little sick of the Fuzzies by the third book. Not the Fuzzies' fault, of course. Piper wanted to move on and was buffaloed into doing sequels. However, by that time, he had a much larger body of work than I ever expect to achieve.

So, here it is, maybe or maybe not my last Fuzzy book. You might even say I am a bit fuzzy on that. Muses are fickle things that take you where they want to go and not always where you want to be taken. I won't say what I am turning my attention to as I might not get it done or published. I have a stack of stuff like that. Many authors do, I think. Whatever happens, I will continue to write and, hopefully, you will get to read it.

I hope you enjoy this (maybe) final installment. Feel free to look me up on Facebook or Twitter and tell me what you think. Be it positive or negative I like to hear your opinions. I do not shy away from harsh criticism, as I believe it is sometimes necessary to make oneself a better writer.

Thank you all for your patronage.

Wolfgang S. Diehr

www.ingramcontent.com/pod-product-compliance
Lightning Source LLC
Chambersburg PA
CBHW070834020826
48982CB00019B/1102/J

* 9 7 8 0 9 3 7 9 1 2 8 1 2 *